Just before Christmas, Mr Goelette was delighted to see that Thomas Chance was again in his store.

"This may astound you," Chance told him, "in light of all the nonsense they are writing about my romances in the newspapers these days, but I've decided to be married. And my fiancée seems to want my pearl."

"If there *were* another pearl," Mr Goelette said, "that is, another pearl *almost* like the Pearl of Macao, it would almost certainly be in private hands, probably in a collector's vault. It might take several times the price you paid to coax it out."

"One million dollars!" Chance said then. "That's ten times the price. Don't go over one million dollars and try to get it as cheaply as you can. I have great trust in you, sir, and I expect that we shall be doing business for a long time to come. I shall appreciate the best you can do."

"I can only try," Mr Goelette replied.

"Just think of her face when she sees it," Chance said with obvious excitement.

And Mr Goelette decided that Chance must be very much in love. And very, very rich.

Line of Chance

THOMAS CAPLAN

ARROW BOOKS

Arrow Books Limited
17–21 Conway Street, London W1P 5HL

An imprint of the Hutchinson Publishing Group

London Melbourne Sydney Auckland
Johannesburg and agencies
throughout the world

First published in Great Britain by Severn House 1981
Arrow edition 1982

Made and printed in Great Britain
by The Anchor Press Ltd
Tiptree, Essex

ISBN 0 09 927290 3

BOOK
I

THE GAME

(1867–1869)

For

My Mother

and

My Father

God Bless

Home is where one starts from. As we grow older
The world becomes stranger, the pattern more complicated
Of dead and living. Not the intense moment
Isolated, with no before and after,
But a lifetime burning in every moment
And not the lifetime of one man only
But of old stones that cannot be deciphered.

—T. S. Eliot
East Coker

CHAPTER

1

In the high spring of 1867 Thomas Chance arrived in New York City from Baltimore. He was an extraordinarily handsome young man of twenty-seven, and there was a roguish air about him, an air of adventure and a look of breeding; some thought too much breeding.

He had never before visited New York and yet, as he stepped from his train onto the long steam-clouded platform of the New York Central Station, he presented a figure which had been perfectly outfitted according to the particular standards of the city's upper class. His coat, having been cut from a single piece of the finest charcoal cheviot, hung elegantly on his tall and slender figure, evidence of half a dozen fittings. His trousers, of like material and tailoring, were creaseless and but a shade lighter, breaking over all but the toes of the richly polished waxed-calf boots he had ordered from London. He wore a waistcoat, a fine white cotton shirt with a roll-front linen collar, a sedately checkered teck scarf, and a new silk hat.

Auburn-haired and beardless, at a height of just over six feet, with an athlete's body, a weather-tanned face, and eyes containing all the greens of a forest, his beauty was both boyish and arresting. He had barely alighted from the Pullman when he began to draw a subtle attention from those he passed. Their quiet glances—ripe with admiration, approval, envy, or desire—fell on him with all the steadiness of light itself. And though he had known others like them all his life, and long ago learned to mask his reaction, he could not subdue the little fire of satisfaction they produced in his spirit. So he shot a faint smile back at those whose eyes had caught him—nearly a wink; and his step, which had magic in it, seemed to promise something as he moved out toward the city, past the huge bronze statue of Commodore Vanderbilt.

He walked along the platform, past the Cockney porters in their pastel jackets, past the long-skirted women and diffident men whose baggage they carried, into the station itself and, once there, through the tubular, dank, and ghostly corridors until, at the end, he came into Thirtieth Street and the funneling New York twilight.

He had arranged a hansom cab in waiting, and as he looked on and about in every direction, porters placed his several bags into the hold behind the passenger seat. When they had finished he paid each man and thanked him. Then, almost impatiently, he mounted the coach.

"Fifth Avenue Hotel," he ordered, leaning forward to the driver, his diction as precise and melodic as an actor's. "Fifth Avenue and Twenty-third Street, please. In Madison Square."

"Right, sir. Right you are," came the effusive reply. The driver was a burly man—to appearances English—whose facial skin was chapped and broken from the weather. All ten of his knuckles had swollen to gigantic size. And he seemed unusually jolly as he added: "Eno's Folly, it is."

"I beg your pardon?"

"Fifth Avenue Hotel, you said. Eno's Folly! That's what they call it. After Eno, the fella what built it."

"I know nothing about Mr. Eno," Chance answered. "I am not from New York."

"I wouldn't know a bloody thing about him either, and I am." The driver laughed. "Except that's what they call it. But to be truthful for a moment, sir, it's meant to be the best hotel in town. Exclusive, if you understand. All the ones I take from there is ladies and gentlemen. Very few exceptions. You can always tell."

"Always?" Chance asked.

"Oh, always—yet it's funny too, sir. Since I would anyday have taken you as a New Yorker, if you weren't with all those bags I mean and going to an hotel. I'd've said you were a Wall Street man."

It was April and the moist grass along the roadbeds shot a strong, sexual fragrance into the dusk. Something about Manhattan caused him to pause and tremble at this first sight, as if its reality might somehow endanger a dream he had nursed. For always, in his soul, there had been a city like this that now sprung up around him. And always, from those original and bright-hued dreams of adolescence, he had known that fate would bring him to it.

A few minutes lapsed as the coach trundled along the grooved Belgian blocks of the streets and Tom studied the city. The cool night air swirled around him and he drew up the small violet-colored blanket which lay next to him. His eye had traveled barely a mile, but his heart was quickened by what it saw, certain that, beneath this rock of Manhattan, one would quickly come upon the axis of the earth.

The Englishman said: "I drive with a light rein, sir. Ordinarily. But I can tighten her up at a moment's notice if you should be watching the clock."

"N'a'tall," Chance answered, huddled in the folds of wool, fighting shivers. "But tell me one thing, if you will. Where are the theaters from here? I know they're on Broadway, and along Twentieth Street. But where is that?"

"All but straight ahead of us," the driver responded, not turning at all, fixing his eyes on the road so that his words floated back to his passenger on the steady wind. "And some of them is lower down. Which one are you looking for?"

"The Rheesbeck Theatre," Thomas Chance said. "Have you heard of it?"

"It's in that neighborhood," the driver responded. "Shall I take you by it?"

Chance thought for a moment. All about him the work of the city seemed to have come to a halt. Stores were dark now, shadows long, traffic furious. Young men in groups of four or five walked briskly away from their jobs in the long squat buildings. Some of them laughed. To Thomas Chance they all seemed quick-stepped and expectant.

"No," he told the driver. "Not now. I'd much prefer to settle in my rooms first."

And so they moved on as the traffic swirled about them: one-horse open carts with loose wheels, driven by farmers; hundreds of bland, black carriages; hansom cabs like their own, some more elaborate; fine coaches drawn by matched pairs with exquisite traces. Chance watched these vehicles carefully and silently, making a mental record which matched each to the sort of person it conveyed.

Between Ninth Avenue and Broadway they took a short-cut along Twenty-fourth Street. Twenty-fourth was one of those dark thoroughfares fronted entirely by stables, and the driver gave his horse a little whip, brought him up to a full trot as they passed through the putrid smells of hay and dung. "It ain't beautiful," the driver said as they came out into the light expanse of Broadway. "But then beauty's hardly everything. And here we are, on your right. This is your hotel. A good ten minutes ahead of the traffic, too. I could tell you were a bit chilled."

"Thank you."

"Now, around the next corner, don't let me forget to tell you, you'll see the home of Nathan, the famous banker that was murdered, you may remember. And also the Eden Musée, where they have wax figures of all the most sensational crimes—and horrors. I wouldn't pass that by, if I were you, if I hadn't been there."

"Famous crimes," Chance repeated distantly. "Well, thank

you very much." He smiled as he slid up to the hotel's classical portico.

His bags were unloaded by a high-hatted doorman, who handed them in turn to an apprenticing teenage footman, who placed them, one by one, on a low wooden trolley with creaky bearings. The hotel was a large, light stucco affair on a broad corner. It was six stories high and now, beneath their individual awnings, the windows of most of its rooms were ajar.

Chance settled with the driver of the hansom cab, tipping the man with a small gold coin before dismissing him. The footman began to wheel the bags through the columned portico into the lobby, moving two or so paces behind Chance. Then Chance stopped and, rather than proceed directly inside, began to walk along Fifth Avenue, staring into the several hotel shops which fronted there. The florist, the tobacconist, and, oddly, the custom coach maker had still not closed their doors for the night. A ladies' dress shop had. Chance admired a magnificent carriage in the window of the coach maker, noticed a small easel-backed sign which read: "Rentals May Be Arranged With The Management."

A director of the hotel, whose razor-scraped neck showed red and prickly at the line of his stiff collar, met Chance on the carpet outside the front entrance and escorted him from there. Except for the bagginess of his pants, the man was formally attired and he wore a pince-nez. In a small advertisement in the *Times* of London a few years before, the hotel had described itself to prospective guests as *de luxe*; and *de luxe* was now the natural term to come to Chance's mind. Waxed mahogany and painted paneling, forest-green ferns—the small lobby was bathed in rose light and whispers. It was, Chance thought, quintessentially Victorian—and emblematically rich. A dozen or so uniformed boys stood at attention or hurried about the lobby, in and out of the restaurant, up and down the staircase. They had the bright, cherubic faces of English schoolboys, and therefore reminded Chance of *David Copperfield,* a novel he had followed in serial form as a boy. Also, they paid him great attention.

Even before his arrival—in fact, from the moment his reservation had been entered—rumors about him mysteriously had begun to circulate among the hotel staff: He had made a fortune growing tobacco. No, stealing tobacco. Or was it raising cotton? He had been a war hero. No, a deserter! His family were old, aristocratic Marylanders. He had no family. He had killed a man. These were the same rumors which had inexplicably surfaced in theatrical circles a few months before and quietly spread from there. And about only one point was there general agreement: Thomas Chance indeed possessed a formidable fortune.

"Where did he get it?" one desk clerk, a junior, asked another as Chance moved toward them across the lobby.

"I don't know for sure." Low voices now, fixed smiles. "They say he got it trading as a sutler in the war."

"Sutler? What in hell's a sutler?"

"You don't know what a sutler is? You're not so bright as I thought. . . . A sutler's a man who sells to armies. Confederate armies. Yankee armies. All this money people have these days! Half of it came out of the war. They say he's bought enormous tracts of land, too. All over! In the Carolinas, I heard, and all through the Maryland and Virginia tidewater . . ."

At this moment, Chance and the hotel director came within earshot of the registration desk and the clerks, with a little too much coughing, terminated their conversation. Chance signed the hotel book, giving an address on Mt. Vernon Place, Baltimore. Above his signature, he noted those of two senators and a middle-rank European king.

"Have you an envelope and paper?" Chance eventually asked the younger clerk.

"Of course, sir," the man answered nervously, producing them at once.

Chance placed them on the ebony surface of the desk, wrote out a short note which no one dared try to read, then folded the sheet and slid it into its envelope, which he addressed in a small script. "Would you be so kind," he asked the same clerk, "to see that this is delivered to Miss Frances Alexander at the Rheesbeck Theatre?"

"At once."

"She is a member of the cast."

"Of course, sir. Very good, sir."

"Thank you." Chance flashed the clerk a wide, abundant smile.

"A nice sort, wouldn't you say?" asked the senior clerk after Chance had left.

"But *very*," replied his assistant.

"That's what I've found. Those that really have it always are."

Chance's bags had long ago disappeared from the lobby when he and the director set off for his suite. The director filled him with information about the hotel's past and Chance listened carefully, even as he admired the tailoring of several men and the figures of several women who passed them. The air was full with the scent of perfume: pleasantly so, thought Chance.

"Of course, the Prince of Wales was here seven years ago," the director said, "and it amused him quite a lot."

"What did?" asked Chance, for his mind had been absent for a few seconds.

"Our elevator. It was the first passenger elevator in New York, you know. Designed by Mr. Otis. Well, not really the first. There was one in Haughevout's store on Broadway a month or two before this one was installed, but they tell me that was converted from freight use."

"Really?"

"I hope you won't think me indiscreet when I tell you that His Royal Highness would ride it for minutes on end, for the sheer pleasure of it."

"Not at all," Chance said as they entered the magic box and ascended.

"Of course, one night, in the company of Mr. Bennett—Mr. J. G. Bennett of the *Herald*—he did not ride at all, but had a 'night on the town' as they say. Precisely where, I'm sure I don't know."

Chance had engaged a suite containing large and small sitting rooms, two bedrooms, and two baths. The price, unmentioned in his conversation now, had been quoted by letter at twenty-two dollars per day, a sum which, having once struck Chance as exorbitant, appeared more than fair on inspection. White on white. Cream on cream, carpeted and slipcovered softly for the season. The rooms possessed a fragile quiet even as the night wind rippled the edges of doilies and fluttered the loose fringe borders of the curtains. From a table the scent of freesia drifted into the air, and from the bath the soft bouquet of lemon soap.

"This is one of our very finest apartments," the director told Thomas Chance. "A floor above, but otherwise identical to the one the Prince himself occupied." He moved about the room as he spoke, waving curtains aside with his hand, raising and replacing objects, checking details. "Any service you require, simply ring us." He pointed to a group of braided cords which hung from a nearly invisible hole in the parlor wallpaper.

"Excellent," said Chance.

"I take it that you are traveling alone and not expecting any of your personal staff to join you."

Chance bridled a bit at this remark, but concealed his annoyance. "No servants," he said. "I've left them all in Baltimore."

"No need anyway," the director said. "Now, if there's anything we can do to make—"

"There is one thing," Chance interrupted. "I should like to engage a coach."

"Certainly."

"There is one in the window of the equipage maker. A deep blue one."

"I know it well. It takes a pair, I believe."

"Can it be let?"

"With driver, of course?"

"Naturally. And if not, I'd like to know the price being asked to buy it."

The director started for a moment. "Oh," he said. "I'm sure that will not be necessary. I'm almost certain it's for hire."

"Then I've learned something," Chance replied, "haven't I? I've learned that the Fifth Avenue Hotel receives a commission on the rental of coaches, but none on the sale. Otherwise, you, as a director, would be more anxious for me to buy than to rent."

The director looked at Chance for a long moment, but the first smile was Chance's. "If I don't hear from you in the next quarter hour," he continued, "I shall assume that I may meet my coach in front of this building at nine o'clock this evening."

"I shall do my best, Mr. Chance. For how long, may I ask, would you like to engage it?"

"As with this suite," Chance said. "Indefinitely."

CHAPTER

2

HIS SEVERAL TRUNKS WERE SET OUT IN FRONT OF A LONG walnut wardrobe in the grander bedroom, but Thomas Chance ignored them for the moment. Heavy blinds closed against the New York night, and too many gas lights burning, Chance undressed and ordered a bath. He felt strong, hard; looked tan from the early springtime sun.

He took his long bath in a cool, dark room with a single candle going, its white flame multiplied a hundred times by the beveled mirrors before which it flickered. Then, flushed by the warmth of the tub and worn by his journey, he staggered into his bedroom, where sleep, like a thief, suddenly threw him across the vast goosedown mattress. He slept, without dreaming, for the best part of an hour, waking only from the tingling friction of the breeze across his skin, a sensation that made him think at once of women, that made him want them, fiercely. There was a smile beginning in his eyes as he stood, unpacked his evening clothes, and dressed.

At nine o'clock his coach, the most splendid one in sight, was waiting at the curb before the portico. The lights of moon and streetlamp danced across it; its doors and body seemed to have been fired with hard enamel. The driver, a long-legged, elegant black man, sat quietly erect, his gloved hand loose in his lap as he waited. Beneath his tobaccoed breath, he was humming, but the sound could barely be heard from the sidewalk.

Chance asked to be taken directly to the Rheesbeck which, the black man assured him, was located on Broadway, not far from Thirteenth Street and directly beside the famous Wallack's Theatre.

An alley—more of a cobblestone path—ran between the two buildings, and when Chance left his coach, he shocked his driver by shunning the main entrance in favor of this narrow cul-de-sac and the stage door, which opened on it. Alleys at this time in New York were quite safe for public use, and this particular one was full of flowers. Following the custom in London, flower girls circulated in the theatrical district, offering corsages and small bouquets to the hopeful escorts of ripe young women; and the largest wholesaler of these had long ago established the claim of his baskets to this well-situated space.

So Chance made his way among the bunches of carnations, pom-poms, tulips, and roses, among the spreads of lavender orchids toward the heavy, handleless door at the back of the Rheesbeck. A short, buxom flower girl followed him with her eyes; but he ignored her. His own eyes studied the ground instead, and he stooped to see it closely. What he found was a long, thin, but solid slice of wood—a two-by-four slat broken off from a box—which he picked up at once and began to use as a pry. Little by little, and with a fortunate silence, the door yielded on its cylinder, and soon he could see that it led directly into the wings of the stage.

Two clusters of girls stood in his view: one tall and tightly formed, rigid-backed and clearly anxious as they awaited their cue; the other plainly relaxed, despite the quiet that the house rules imposed upon them. Two girls from the latter group, in the process of changing costume, had removed all of the clothing above their waists. But the girl for whom Chance searched could not be seen.

Maintaining only the narrowest crack in the door, he stood in the alley, waiting for the music to die and the cast to exit. But then a draft caught and startled one of the girls and he was forced to step away. To the flower girl who watched him, Chance seemed no more than another light-headed young gentleman, overprivileged, up to no good.

The buxom girl adjusted her dress and drew up her breasts into melon shapes beneath the tight, ruffled cloth as he came back into view. She kept her eyes on Chance, displayed no embarrassment. And he watched her now too, found her pretty in a coarse way. Neither of them spoke. The girl wanted to, but was afraid owing to the quite obvious difference in their class. Chance wanted to, but was afraid owing to . . . circumstances. But he stared at her until she smiled. She was beginning to feel like Cinderella—and indeed might have been (at least for one night in the Fifth Avenue Hotel)—had not the stage door flown fully open at that moment.

"Tom!" came a voice then; and after it, a young actress. She was a slender, dark-haired young woman, angel-skinned, with wide brown eyes more moist and huge than even he could hold in memory.

"Frances!" Chance exclaimed. They hugged, kissed quickly. He raised her off the ground. So contagious was their pleasure that the flower girl, watching, felt an involuntary twitching of her own tongue.

"Why in heaven's name are you standing out here in this dreary place?" Frances exclaimed. "Why didn't you come in and see the show? We were wonderful tonight!" She laughed as she talked. And even in the distant artificial light he could detect that dew of innocence that had kept her looking seventeen at twenty-seven.

The sound of applause was spilling out through the open door. "I've got to make curtain call." She promised him, "I'll change and meet you in the foyer."

"You got my note?" Chance called as she ran on ahead of him into the footlights.

"Yes," she responded breathlessly. "I wish you'd seen the show."

The flower girl endured all this in silence. Chance, after a moment, regarded her and shrugged. Then, without warning, he approached her; and, seeing for the first time how truly handsome he was, she straightened up a little, smiled, waited for him to speak.

"How do you do?" he asked her, pausing before going on. "I wonder if you would be kind enough to sell me one of your lovely orchids."

Choking a bit, she told him, "They're thirty-five cents each."

And he reached into the slanted pocket of his coat at once, withdrew a five-dollar gold piece, and pressed it into her hand. He took the orchid stem in his fist then, and fled quickly, silently into the theater before she had time to make him change, or understand.

"Mister, mister," she cried at last—but he was far away, inside the Rheesbeck, waiting for Frances.

There were four for dinner at the center table of Delmonico's, on Beaver and William Streets. Frances, even more beautiful without stage makeup, sat between Chance and a round-chested bald man named Murdoch, who not only owned the Rheesbeck outright, but was impresario of a dozen other New York entertainments. Murdoch was twice Chance's age, but his date, an immensely tall singer called Veronica, looked scarcely grown-up.

They ate a large, mock-French meal: poached fillet of sole with a white burgundy, clear turtle soup, grilled pheasant with a bottle of claret, some salad, a Sacher torte for dessert. The large room was full of late-evening diners.

"Well, Mr. Chance," said Murdoch at one point. "Frances has told us a great deal about you." He raised his glass. "Welcome to New York!"

Veronica took a long swallow of wine, giggled. "Frances has told *everyone* a great deal about you," she added.

Frances blushed.

"Chance," said Murdoch then. "That wouldn't be a Dutch name, would it?"

"Pure English," Chance replied.

"So is Murdoch," the impresario continued. "But I'll tell you one thing. It's the Dutch that run New York. England may be the mother to the rest of the country, but it's Mother Holland here."

"Mother Holland," Veronica repeated nonsensically. "That's silly."

"What exactly do you mean, sir?" Chance asked, looking intently at Mr. Murdoch now.

"The Astors," Murdoch said. "The Schuylers. The Stuyvesants. All those whose surnames begin with 'van.' When I want to buy a building, or a piece of property where I can put up a theater, they're the ones I have to go to. Because it all belongs to them. They bought it from the Indians, so to speak."

"That's very interesting," Chance said. For the moment, the men were content to leave the women out of the conversation.

"Your business is land, Mr. Chance, isn't it?" Murdoch inquired politely.

Chance looked shocked. "Excuse me?"

"I'm sorry," Mr. Murdoch went on. "But I understood that you are in land."

"Only in part," Chance said, resuming his attack on the sole.

"Only in part?"

"Tell him, Tom," Frances spoke up, apparently half-drunk with wine. "Tell him all the kinds of businesses you're in."

Chance looked embarrassed. His silence and sly smile encouraged the rumor and mystery about him. Finally he said, "My business is money, sir. It's as simple as that."

Murdoch laughed heartily, brought the napkin to his lips. "Never let that embarrass you, Mr. Chance. This city is a temple to money. It talks here. Prays here. And it answers prayers, louder and better than anywhere else on earth. And I, for one, never hold money against a man. In fact, I've always found it rather an attractive quality."

The girls laughed as Murdoch continued.

"*My* business is theater, Mr. Chance. And that takes money. So, being that I have been around as long as anyone, I know, personally, a fair number of the richest gentlemen in town. New York's a nicer place when you have a group of friends like that. If you understand what I mean."

"I'm afraid I've just come to town," Chance said.

"Nonsense," Murdoch said. "What are friends for? To do each other favors. Right?"

If nothing else, Chance thought, Murdoch was direct. Chance took a long drink and nodded.

"One of my shows opens next week at the Italian Opera House and I'm giving a ball afterward," Murdoch said. "Everyone will be there. Why don't you and Frances come?"

Chance thought back over the day that was now behind him, the long, jolting train ride through the gray mid-Atlantic farmlands. New York was splendid in comparison. In a way, he felt as though he were already in heaven. And yet he knew his plan had just begun. "We would love to," he said as he smiled at Frances.

And he knew that, sooner or later, Murdoch would ask him to invest in a play.

Frances Alexander was eye-catching. Chance looked dashing in his English dancing clothes. They did an almost professional waltz together. Because they danced so well, because a reputation had preceded Chance into the room, because they were new flowers in an old garden, they became the hit of Murdoch's party, met everyone there.

"So you've come to New York," said one middle-aged lady, a little tipsy, as Chance two-stepped her about the floor. "Why? Looking for love?"

"Always," Chance smiled. "And for investments."

The woman's husband was a celebrated Wall Street banker —they were sitting at a table of bankers—and the remark was repeated all the way around the table.

Chance gave a dinner of his own a few nights later in the beamy restaurant of the Astor House. There he entertained a number of prominent businessmen who had been attracted by the stories about him. And there he had, as was becoming his trademark, a beautiful woman on his arm—a different one this time.

Over the next weeks, as gossip about him multiplied, he lunched with Joseph Seligman, the banker, with August Belmont, the Rothschild connection, and with J. P. Morgan, who was still employed at Drexel and Company at Broad and Wall; he discussed separate ventures with each man, in private and in confidence.

With food, drink, and entertainment, and sometimes even with cash, he bribed the social editors of three newspapers to record his goings and comings. And so successful was he that, in one week alone, his name appeared on twelve occasions in the *Herald* and on four in the *Times*.

He spent lavishly. Most of the better stores were still downtown, about half of them below Canal Street and the rest along Broadway to Fourteenth and from there over to Union Square. Chance loved to walk past them, impulsively stopping to buy a variety of items. He bought woolen scarves at A. T. Stewart's new marble palace, silk foulards and gloves at Arnold Constable, daring negligees and other risqué bonbons for his lady friends at Lord and Taylor, glassware and gold trinkets for Frances at Charles Tiffany's. His presents to Frances, in fact, became increasingly grand as the days of his stay lengthened. The northern economy was booming in the aftermath of war and Thomas Chance, who seemed to be scouting some mysterious opportunity, became widely sought after by those who had something to sell.

CHAPTER

3

One afternoon, he entered Goelette and Company on lower Fifth Avenue. Goelette and Company were then among the most celebrated jewelers in the world, having, for thirty years, served the most distinguished clientele in America. It was a fine, proud store, in the Louis XIV style, staffed with a liveried doorman, several gray-uniformed young boys who served as pages, and a sales staff of apparent gentlemen attired in morning coats and striped trousers. He was greeted by a punctilious man who appeared to be the floor manager.

The man was tall, proper, with gray hair combed back; but to Chance, he smelled too strongly of cologne, seemed a trifle too urbane. He introduced himself as Percy Thistle.

"I've been thinking of acquiring a gem," Chance told him as they stood on a plush Persian rug in the middle of the salon, surrounded by desk-high, glass-topped vitrines filled with simple and fabulous jewels.

"Of course," Mr. Thistle replied mechanically. "Will it be for yourself or for a lady?" He was plainly distracted by something.

"It will be for myself," Chance said, then began to make his way about the store, studying the inventory on view. "Strictly for myself!" Chance did not look up as he spoke. The floor manager was following him now, attempting to point out the virtues of stones upon which his client had bestowed only summary glances. But it was no use.

"Strictly for myself," Chance repeated, moving even faster. "For pleasure—and as an investment, of course; and another thing: *not* a diamond. I don't want anything that sparkles like a diamond. What I have in mind should, shall we say, 'blend in.' " He raised his eyes, met Mr. Thistle's. "I was, in fact, thinking of a pearl."

It was the age of pearls. Queen Victoria wore pearls.

The floor manager recovered himself and moved briskly now, leading Chance to a low pearwood case. He stopped behind it. "Would you care to have a seat?" he asked.

Chance looked on curiously as the man, one by one, brought out a series of mediocre gems, placed them on a dark velvet pad, and allowed his customer to touch and to scrutinize them under a magnifying glass.

But the quality of the pearls disgusted Chance. He shifted in his seat, constantly about to rise. "None of these is satisfactory," he said finally.

"You understand, sir, that anything finer will be considerably more expensive," the floor manager answered.

"That's safe to assume," Chance told him. "I was not aware of having mentioned any price, much less any limit."

"What do you think of this one, sir?" the man asked then, holding a much better pearl between his thumb and forefinger. He seemed, in odd seconds, to be looking over Chance's shoulder, and Chance noticed that the man's fingernails were lined and yellowed.

"It's an improvement," Chance said after considering it quickly. "But not enough of one."

So Mr. Thistle reached into his case again and withdrew the most expensive gem it contained. It was a perfectly round, rose-colored Oriental priced at twenty-five thousand dollars. His face wore a connoisseur's smile as he appraised it. But Chance studied the pearl only a few seconds before rejecting it.

"Who is he?" Chance asked suddenly.

"Excuse me, sir?" The floor manager was startled.

"The man you've been looking at." Chance pointed to a hinged silver mirror which sat on the case directly to his right. It had obviously been put out so that ladies might study themselves in prospective necklaces and earrings, but Chance had used it to see behind him to the back of the store, where two men stood talking beside an office door.

"The shorter man is Mr. Goelette, sir, our proprietor, don't you know."

"And the taller?"

". . . is Mr. Peter Cooper." This was clearly the man who had drawn Thistle's attention. And Thistle began to whisper as he added, "The richest and most distinguished citizen of New York. He gave Cooper Union and—"

"I thought I recognized him," Chance interjected then. He could feel something in his blood begin to race.

"I'm not surprised, sir. His picture has been in the newspapers any number of times. And his portrait hangs in the Cooper Union itself."

"*Not* from the newspaper," Chance said dismissively. "From a dinner I attended. But, let's see, whose dinner was that? Where in hell did I meet Peter Cooper?"

The floor manager seemed at last to have been suitably impressed. Still, Chance disliked the almost female cadence of the man's gossip.

There was a long pause now. In the background, Chance could hear Mr. Goelette's voice resonate through the hushed room as he escorted Cooper to the door.

"Perhaps you might like to consult directly with Mr. Goelette," the floor manager suggested to Chance immediately Peter Cooper had made his exit. "He has a large private stock in his vaults and might be able to turn up something that would gain your approval."

"Yes," Chance agreed, with only a brief flutter of hesitation in his voice. "A very good idea."

With Cooper gone from the room and the aura of his wealth and celebrity no longer swirling about, a pronounced relaxation came upon Goelette and Company.

"If I might have your name, sir," the floor manager asked, already on his way back to his employer's office.

"Chance. Thomas Chance."

Thistle, more than a little awed by those green and inscrutable eyes, lost a moment as he composed himself. "Thank you so much," he said at last. But it was impossible for Chance to be certain if the floor manager recognized his name.

Thomas Chance met Goelette in the latter's outer office, a plain but fastidiously neat room in which two women worked at large desks with quill pens. Both women wore their hair in buns. Both were matronly. Two Semitic-looking men, one a Persian, the other a Jew, sat across from them in a waiting area. The men were gem merchants traveling together. Each had a small leather valise next to his chair.

Goelette himself was a compact man, freshly barbered and carefully tailored. He had a slate-gray beard. Behind it, his black eyes were calm, although the left, owing to a degeneration of its muscle, occasionally wandered out to the side of his skull. "A pearl. . . . A pearl," he repeated thoughtfully to himself, steepling his hands. "Do come inside!"

As they walked, Chance was quiet. And Goelette, in passing, smiled kindly at the Jewish salesman. "Tomorrow might be better," he suggested, in a voice filled with promise. And so the two men nodded and got up to leave.

Chance and Goelette then came into a truly magnificent room, small, but high-ceilinged; one wall of it was set with two Fragonard panels. There was a massive Louis XV ormolu-mounted tulipwood desk, twin chairs before a fireplace, and a large window with its heavy drapes tied back. An even north light filled the entire room. A sheer white pleated curtain ran only high enough to block the vision of those who passed on the street outside. And there were carved gold door handles in the shape of cherubs.

Goelette sat at his desk, Chance across from him. "Let me show you something interesting," the jeweler said. "It's not a pearl, but if you have a minute, you might enjoy it." Deliberately or not, he had kept a healthy trace of his original Gallic accent alive in his voice.

"Certainly," Chance replied.

Goelette slid a drawer open, removed a small paper, unfolded it, and placed a huge ruby on his blotter. "Cushion shape. The color of pigeon's blood," he said. "The very finest there is."

Chance stood silently, moved closer to the desk, reached for the ruby. "May I?" he asked.

"Of course."

Chance picked it up, held it to the light, moved his head about to check its every facet. Goelette watched him, finding in him just that fine degree of awkwardness he had suspected. "Do you know gems, Mr. Chance?" he asked.

"What? Oh, some," Chance replied as he replaced the ruby on the blotter.

"Lovely, don't you think?" Goelette inquired. But without waiting for an answer, he went on, "I acquired it nineteen years ago, in France. During the riots of 1848, to be exact." As he spoke, he wiped the ruby with a soft chamois cloth, almost caressing it. Then, with the same cloth, he placed the stone on the back side of his outstretched left hand, setting it into the small crevice between two fingers. It was the most professional of gestures, exaggerated now for Chance's benefit. He stared at it, moving his hand only slightly as he spoke. "Louis Philippe was tumbling from the throne, you may remember. I was in Paris on a buying trip. All of a sudden, revolution broke out. The barricades went up, everything was madness. People had only one thought. They wanted to flee. But they didn't always have the money they required. A few did have gems, however, and they sold them wherever they could. Prices fell to a fraction of what they had been. Or are now. But it was their lives they were buying, so they were happy with anything. I made many wonderful purchases."

"Were there any pearls among them?" Chance asked.

Goelette, ignoring Tom for a moment, continued to watch the play of light in the ruby. "But the fact that it might be a good, portable investment is only a small part of a truly great gem's romance, you know, Mr. Chance. Gems are like people—each one an individual, no two alike. And the really magnificent ones are just like magnificent people. They are never forgotten. They blaze a path through history." He traced his free hand through the air. "Take, for example, the large pearl you saw outside. It's an outstanding gem by any measure, with quite a story behind it."

Thomas Chance removed his gold watch from his pocket and pointedly read it. "Mr. Goelette," he said, "I have been told by those who are said to know that you are the foremost expert on gems in this country. That is why I have come to your shop. I would not be honest if I did not tell you that it is not the first shop I have visited. And, sir, if you'll pardon a mere amateur for saying this, I suspect there are probably a hundred pearls of the same quality in this city at this very minute. And I suspect you know that even better than I."

The jeweler looked at Chance carefully, stalled, examined his client, trying to measure the breadth of his knowledge. He was accustomed to rich young men with good, if predictably upper-class taste. Yet, almost invariably, he had found that they possessed very little real knowledge of gems. Chance was somehow different. He had not known how to hold a ruby, but, instinctively, he seemed to have a keener eye for quality, a more relentless determination to own it. "What is it you want?" Goelette asked.

"The best," said Chance.

"I have one pearl."

"Shall we have a look?"

"I must tell you I am reluctant to sell it." For Goelette, who had a patrician love of the jewelry in his store, this was true. But it was skillful bargaining as well, and he smiled to himself.

"As you wish," Chance said again, on the point of departing.

"Reluctant to sell. Not reluctant to show," Goelette said. He walked over to a small iron safe, took out a silk box, and presented it to Chance. "The awesome Pearl of Macao," he announced as he lifted the lid. He might, in the same tone, have announced the arrival of a king.

Thomas Chance studied the huge white pearl, one of the best known of Goelette and Company's treasures. Its natural lustrous covering drew the purest silvery tones out of the iridescent daylight. He handled it, held it against his tie as if it were already set into a stickpin.

"The Queen of Gems," laughed Goelette. "Supreme among the treasures of Neptune's domain. You won't find anything like this in Mr. Tiffany's shop, Mr. Chance. Or anywhere else, for that matter. The Pearl of Macao is absolutely induplicable. It was stolen from the crown of a Nepalese princess."

Chance continued to examine it. "You call its texture its skin, isn't that correct? And its color its orient?"

"Exactly."

"I'm sorry it's not for sale," Tom said.

"Yes."

"Let me ask you, simply for the purposes of discussion, if it were to be for sale, what would be its price?"

"I truly couldn't say."

"Come now, sir. You must have some idea of what you'd take for it. Forgive me if I am wrong, but I was under the impression that you are in business to sell. That this is a commercial establishment, not a museum."

"Indeed we are, Mr. Chance. But how does one price such an object as this pearl? There is no regular market. All one can do is guess. In reality, it's priceless, but you ask for a figure. I don't know, I should say not less than one hundred thousand dollars. After all, we cannot replace it."

"Then it's sold," declared Thomas Chance flatly. "If you want it to be."

Goelette, being used to long hours of bargaining, was taken aback. "Yes," he said, nearly choking. "That will be agreeable, Mr. Chance." He grinned broadly, extended his hand, and his eye, as shocked as the rest of him, traveled as far to the left as it could before he was able to bring it back into focus.

"I wonder," asked Chance, "if you might permit me to take it . . . today."

But Goelette hesitated. "It really ought to be mounted," he said. "You will notice that it has been half drilled already."

"It will be enough for me just to have it in a box," Chance replied, "until I can decide exactly *how* to mount it. I wonder if you would be kind enough to bill me."

Mr. Goelette seemed nervous, for it was afternoon; all of the banks were closed, and he had no way of checking Chance's credit. "Of course, we are aware of your considerable reputation," he began, "and I am sure there is something that can be done, but ordinarily—"

Chance smiled reassuringly and interrupted him at once. "No offense at all," he said. "It was just an impulse. I haven't any need of it tonight. I shall pick it up in the morning and settle with you then."

It was a long, anxious night for the jeweler, but Chance did arrive in the morning, about half an hour after Goelette and Company opened. Mr. Thistle, looking rested, ushered him into Mr. Goelette's private office, where the pearl sat in a purple satin box on the desk.

"Good morning," Chance said. "It's a beautiful morning. A beautiful city. I trust everything is ready."

His good humor was infectious. Goelette laughed. "Oh," he exclaimed. "To be your age again! It's right here on the desk."

"In one of your best boxes, I see."

"We're going to miss it."

Chance said nothing. He placed his briefcase gently on a chair, opened it, and removed a stack of one hundred new one-thousand-dollar bills. Mr. Goelette stiffened his expression, tried to conceal his shock. He had expected a bank draft, had gone so far as to make a telegraphic arrangement with his banker whereby the validity of Chance's personal check could be discreetly determined in a matter of minutes. For a moment, there was a formidable silence.

Chance closed the small purple box and placed it in his breast pocket. "I cannot express my appreciation, Mr. Goelette, for bringing this pearl to my attention. I shall not forget your kindness. Nor Goelette and Company."

"We are always at your service." Goelette was grinning now and he bowed slightly.

"Unfortunately, I don't know when I shall be in New York again. I go back to Maryland day after tomorrow, then South on business."

"Write us at any time," Goelette assured him, "and we shall be glad to serve you."

CHAPTER

4

DURING THE NEXT EIGHT MONTHS, CHANCE DID WRITE, ORDERing a variety of gifts: scarf pins, bracelets, a small diamond ring, a gentleman's watch. And his bills, between $500.00 and $1,000.00 each month, were always paid at once. He even returned the pearl via messenger and had Mr. Goelette mount it on a stickpin for his tie.

Then, just before Christmas, Mr. Goelette was delighted to see that Thomas Chance was again in his store.

"This may astound you," Chance told him, "in light of all the nonsense they are writing about my romances in the newspapers these days, but I've decided to be married."

"How wonderful!" Mr. Goelette could not help himself from moving—it was an instinct, all but automatic—toward a low case containing trays of diamond rings.

"I want to swear you to secrecy."

"Absolute secrecy, Mr. Chance."

"Good. Now, I want to give her something—you understand—something I *know* she will like."

"There *is* one diamond I know of—"

"I gave her my mother's ring," Chance answered peremptorily. He looked at Mr. Goelette intently and smiled.

Mr. Goelette seemed unsure, both of himself and of Chance's intention.

"I wouldn't have had the foggiest idea what that would have been," Chance continued, "—what she would really have liked—before the other night. You see, my fiancée is also from the South, from Virginia, and, to be frank, she has been spoiled by some of the Southern ways."

"A great many Southern belles have made their way to New York," Goelette said in a neutral tone. He felt no rancor toward the former Confederate enemy.

"Yes," said Chance. "Perhaps one day we might as well. At any rate, I suppose we spoil our women down there. They get used to having what they want—when they want it."

Goelette laughed.

"And Alexandra seems to want my pearl."

"The Pearl of Macao?"

"The one and only."

"It would not be a problem if you should want us to design something suitable," Mr. Goelette advised him. We could set it very nicely for you in any number of ways. Perhaps as a pendant on a chain of diamonds or—consider this—as the centerpiece in a tiara."

"I am afraid it *is* a problem Mr. Goelette," Chance explained, "if only because she has her heart set on earrings."

Goelette laughed again. His beard tickled him. His eye fluttered in its socket. "Another Pearl of Macao!" he exclaimed. "I'm afraid there is only one."

Chance declared, "*I'm* afraid she is adamant. Come now! There must be a second pearl *almost* like it—somewhere."

"I wouldn't know where."

"It wouldn't be a question of money," Chance said. "And Alexandra would be forever grateful."

Chance so perceptibly shivered with joy whenever he mentioned her name as to conjure in Mr. Goelette an image of this spoiled young girl whom he had never met. He had a vision of her going through life, of her adoring husband indulging her every whim, often enough at Goelette and Company. And this vision showed on his face and at the edges of his mercantile smile.

Chance was pleading with him. "Nor would it be a question of time," he said. "We could wait into the spring, for we are not to be married until June."

"If there *were* another pearl," Mr. Goelette said, "that is, another pearl *almost* like the Pearl of Macao, it would almost certainly be in private hands, probably in a collector's vault. It might take several times the price you paid to coax it out."

"One million dollars!" Chance said then. "That's ten times the price. Don't go over one million dollars and try to get it as cheaply as you can. I have great trust in you, sir, and I expect that we shall be doing business for a long time to come. I shall appreciate the best you can do."

"I can only try," Mr. Goelette replied.

"Just think of her face when she sees it," Chance said with obvious excitement.

And Mr. Goelette decided that Chance must be very much in love. And very, very rich.

Mr. Goelette immediately advised his European sources that he was seeking an important pearl, but, until March, he heard nothing in response. One or two pearls, obviously unacceptable, arrived for his inspection and had to be returned, but there was no word of anything that might fulfill his requirements. Then, on the tenth of March, a letter arrived from a pearl merchant in Paris, informing Mr. Goelette that a pearl "very much like the Macao might be available" from the estate of a Belgian collector. The pearl merchant, named Klaustein, was an old connection of Goelette and Company and a man of indisputable knowledge. He affirmed that the pearl was "as nearly a twin to the Macao—in size, in color, in luster—as any I could imagine"; Goelette experienced a spasm of delight as he read. The Frenchman cautioned only that the Belgian heirs were not in need of funds and that the principal heir, acting for the group, would probably demand a large price. Goelette immediately telegraphed France that he would be willing to pay as much as $150,000. The first successful trans-Atlantic cable had been laid less than two years before between Valentia, Ireland, and Heart's Content, Newfoundland, and the child in Goelette relished each occasion to use it. But his offer was rejected by reverse wire almost at once.

Klaustein wired: "The heirs in no mood to bargain, will accept $500,000, payable immediately. Above $500,000, twenty percent commission due me."

Goelette thought over the offer and accepted it, pending, naturally, his inspection of the pearl.

But this proved no obstacle at all, for the new pearl was at least as fine as it had been represented to be. At once, Goelette dispatched a letter to Chance, to which he received a quick reply saying that Chance would be in New York on other business during the first week of April and would come by to see the pearl as early in his trip as he could.

"It's a miracle," Goelette told him when they met. "A twin to the Macao, if ever there were such a thing."

"I'm putting my faith in you," Chance told him.

"As a pair they will be priceless."

"Really?" Chance seemed cool.

Goelette wondered if he had changed his mind. Had he lost his fiancée?

The jeweler went on nervously. "Independently the pearls were and are expensive. And I know that I used the word 'priceless' about the first pearl, but, you must remember, Mr. Chance, that there was a price after all." He began to smile, to laugh, then caught himself. "As a pair, there would not be," he said seriously. "They would be beyond value. Only their possessor would be able to set one."

Chance looked at the pearl, stared into the drilled hole that ran halfway through it, and studied it under a magnifying glass.

"It's not quite a twin," he said. "But you are right, Mr. Goelette, it's very nearly so."

"Yes, yes," Goelette replied anxiously. "A true miracle of nature!"

"The growth lines are a little different," Chance pressed. "Look inside the hole! In the Macao they are somewhat more pronounced and the hole is also wider."

"I would have to study them together," Goelette said. "But even if you are right, such a slight variation would be unimportant—like a broken fingernail on one of identical twins." He worried for a moment over the lack of grace in his simile, then continued. "To the naked eye, they are a perfect pair. In a way, I confess, I never thought would be possible."

"Yes," Chance agreed at last. "They do seem to be. I'll tell you what I would like to do, Mr. Goelette. Let me take the new pearl with me to Baltimore."

"Of course."

"Let me look at it beside the Macao, show them to Alexandra, and if—"

Goelette was relieved to hear her name, to sense Chance's acceptance of the gem, yet something in his temperament made him hesitate. Then Chance, in anticipation, said, "Naturally, I will take responsibility for it. And I won't keep you waiting too long."

"If it were my own," Mr. Goelette said, "you would be welcome to all the time in the world, but I will have to give my associates some word rather soon."

"Oh, of course I'll take it," Chance said. "I'd be a damned fool not to, even at, what did we say, seven hundred fifty thousand dollars."

"Eight hundred thousand dollars."

"Even at eight hundred thousand dollars. It's Monday. Give me four days. If you don't hear from me by Friday, I'll send you a draft."

Goelette was overjoyed. He thrust his hand forward. Chance shook it. Goelette placed the pearl in a second scarlet box which, like the first, Chance slipped into his breast pocket.

Then Chance went onto the street, which was filled with

the scent of spring. He continued past the roses blooming in their public beds and the unlit gas lamps, until he found a vacant hansom cab, which carried him to the harbor at the foot of South Street. There he boarded a sailing ship that was bound that night for Bermuda. It was a cargo clipper, long in its bowsprit, but he had managed to book two staterooms ordinarily kept for its owner.

Frances Alexander was already inside when he got there. He looked at her intently for a moment, then suddenly his face broke into a wide grin.

"It's back," he said. "The Pearl of Macao. I bought it once, sold it once, and now I'm buying it again: Except this time"—he kissed the pearl—"I'm not going to pay for it."

CHAPTER

5

Frances smiled. "To tell the truth," she said, "I'm just so glad—so very glad—that the whole thing's over. Missing you the way I did, and—"

"And all those other women?" Tom teased.

"Yes. That a little bit, I suppose. But keeping an act going for a year . . . it drains something from one—some vital fluid. And you'll have to admit, I gave a bravura performance."

"Bravura," Tom agreed.

"Still, I'm only happy that it's over."

"Yes," Chance said flatly.

"And you must be too," Frances said. "I would think you'd be even happier than I. After all, it's been your plot from beginning to end. I was just a small part of it."

"Not small at all. An essential part. I couldn't have done it without you."

Frances looked away for an instant, gave a little sigh. "Don't pay any attention," she said finally. "I'm being sentimental again. Before this, I'd never done anything . . . criminal, and sometimes it bothers me. A little, not for long. After all, who knows what's right and wrong in this world. Who's to say that it is perfectly right and moral to shoot your own brother in the name of the Union or the Confederacy, but that cheating someone who would probably just as soon cheat you as look you in the eye is a sin? Who's to say that?"

"No one," Tom answered calmly.

"Of course, I'm just repeating your own argument, so why should you disagree?"

"There's no doubt about it," Chance replied. "You *are* the most exquisite woman I've ever seen." He was wearing a little boy's grin.

"I've known you too long for that," Frances said.

"You taught me everything I know." Chance smiled. "But come here anyway. Come lie here with me."

"You know I will," she purred. "You don't have to flatter me into loving you. I do. That's the basis of everything else."

"I know," Tom whispered.

"And it always has been."

"Quiet now," Tom said as he drew her toward him across the bunk and began to remove her clothing.

"The theater," she said softly. "That's all I ever gave you—and that was a long time ago."

"When we were children," Tom said, cupping her breasts in his hands now, sliding his palms lightly across her large nipples.

Frances shivered. "You were never a child," she told him.

"Hush," Tom said. He ran his palms along her sides, along her thighs. He kissed her fiercely. Frances bit the bottom of his lip. Then she grabbed him. He was a furnace of nervous passion. She undressed him quickly, tugged at him, caressed his russet hair, his smooth, hard chest. He straddled her legs with his knees. Afterward, in the damp and briny air, they lay still for an hour, thinking back and ahead, dreaming.

And Chance was still smiling later, as he lay atop her. "You know," he said, propping himself on one arm but staring directly at her, certain that she could feel him inside her again, "One of these days this man you're with is going to be so rich and so famous and so powerful there won't be anyone in this country who doesn't know him." It was a paroxysm of happiness through which he spoke; but he was right.

* * *

In Bermuda, they took a cottage in the hills near St. George's. The owner of the cargo ship had found it for them and they enjoyed the privacy, the wild, tropical foliage, the orchids which seemed to grow everywhere. But they had been there only a week when Frances began to talk about New York again. At first, it was little more than reminiscence, but Chance sensed that, gradually, she was coming to be concerned for what her absence might be costing her career.

"I don't understand what we are waiting for," she told him eventually.

"I told you," he replied gently. "One letter."

"But you didn't tell me what was going to be in it."

"Good news."

"Why do we need any more good news?" she asked. "You've already made all the money we could ever spend."

He laughed. "Let's start at the beginning," he said.

They were walking on the coral-rock hills above Horseshoe Bay. Below them, the long, pink-sanded beach spread out, crescent-shaped, among the great stones. There was a strong wind and the whitecaps lapped at the shore; the water filled and emptied from the reefy caverns. The ocean here was emerald green, wild and yet warm-looking, inviting. It was, thought Frances, like a landscape from paradise. She stopped, looked carefully at Chance, fell slowly to the ground, and lay back on the high soft grass, watching only the spring clouds pass in the sky. "Yes," she said. "Let's start at the beginning."

Her beauty distracted Tom. But he kept his composure, sat down beside her. "We're the same," he began. "Don't make a riddle out of something you would understand immediately if you only looked inside yourself."

"You've stolen a pearl that is worth one hundred thousand dollars. That's enough money to live on for the rest of our lives, Tom—and *live on it* is precisely what *I* would do. So we are not the same. We must not be the same at all!"

"One hundred thousand dollars?"

"Yes."

"It's nothing."

"Then you *are* crazy."

"No, Frances. That's the one thing I'm not."

"Well, it can't be normal, for heaven's sake, to want as much as you seem to."

"Wheels have been set in motion," Tom said obliquely. "We have no choice now. We have to wait until the plan has run its course." He was picking grass, tearing bunches of the ripe onion-like stalks from the hill, pulling at it unconsciously.

Frances persisted. "I agreed to help you with your scheme, Tom, even though, at first, I really didn't know what it was you were doing. I loved you, so I guess that was natural enough. And then when you told me you wanted to come up to New York to seem like something you're not—"

"—Wasn't."

". . . I spread the stories you asked me to—about your land and war money, all of that. And they got around New York very well. And then, all of a sudden, you told me you were going to use this reputation you'd built—that I had built up for you—to commit a theft." Frances knew what would follow. She braced herself visibly.

"*You* did not seem to mind," Tom said.

"But we have enough now. We could go back."

"On the stage? Don't be a fool. I've committed a crime, Frances. And you've helped me. Abetted a thief, darling, because, you're right, that's what I am in New York. If we went back now you'd be painted by the brush."

"Are you saying that we're here forever? You can't be saying that." There was momentary panic in her voice that welled into her eyes. "Because if that is what you're saying, it would mean I'd never act again; it would mean. . . . Oh, what in hell have you done, Tom? When will this letter of yours come?"

"I don't know. I wish I could tell you, but I don't know." He touched her compassionately.

She leaned back, took a long, deep breath, gathered up the thoughts floating inside her. "You're like a man who's imprisoned by mirrors," she said ultimately. "Of course, I've always known you had that in you, but now I think it may be all you are. You see only yourself wherever you turn. Nobody else."

Tom's eyes closed for an instant. "Don't say anything more," he said. "Don't say anything more that we will regret."

Frances stared at him.

"When I was a boy," he told her softly, "I made a promise. It was on Christmas Eve—that terrible one. And I remember when I made it I vowed to myself that I would never break it. If I broke every other promise, I knew I would never break that one."

"Was it a promise you made to your mother?"

"I made it to God."

"That you'd never be poor?"

"That I'd never be *ordinary*."

"So you became . . . what you've become. Is that what you're telling me?"

"All of life is a confidence game." Tom smiled. "People want to be taken in one way or another. But I haven't *become* anything yet. Certainly not a swindler!"

"I truly don't understand," she said.

"Come on," Tom said. "When all of this is over you'll have better parts than you've ever dreamed of. And a different life! And you'll look back on this beach and this ocean and these rocks and wonder why you ever wanted to leave."

Her tears were drying now. "You confuse me so," she said, a small laugh struggling to rise from the bottom of her voice.

For beneath his touch and those unflinching eyes she was suddenly frightened at the idea of losing him, suddenly certain she would never love anyone else.

"Confuse you?" Tom said. "You've known me far too many years for me to do that."

"But you're a step ahead. You've always been."

"And you have always trusted me."

Both faces were blank with uncertainty.

"You said we were going to start at the beginning," Frances told him.

Tom glanced up. A white gull traced a wide parabola in the sky above the shoreline. "The beginning," Tom repeated. "That would be the original hundred thousand dollars. The money I used to pay Goelette the first time. Didn't you ever wonder where it came from?"

"You said you'd made it in the war."

"But you didn't believe that?"

"No."

"You thought I had stolen it."

Frances shrugged.

"Didn't you?" Chance pressed.

"I suppose."

"Well, I didn't steal it. Not a penny. I may not have been a wealthy sutler, but I was a corporal in the Army of the Potomac. At least until the twenty-sixth of June, 1862. That was the battle of Mechanicsville."

"Go on, Tom."

"I had to rush across a whole valley of enemy fire to reach one cannon to defend the few of us that were left. The most awful, goddamned thing I've ever had to do: mortar like hail. Worse. And then it turned out that two of the ones that I saved were on McClellan's staff and, for that, on their recommendations, the general himself gave me a battlefield commission."

"Then you became a captain." Frances understood that

this simple recounting of his story would appeal to his considerable vanity.

"A little while after that. First for McClellan himself. Then Halleck. And that's when I came into contact with the sutlers. They followed the Union armies, selling clothing, tobacco, and alcohol to the troops, and I was in a position to direct considerable business to some of them. Mostly to a fellow I knew from Baltimore. I'm sure you've heard me talk of him before."

"I've heard you talk about a lot of those people from Baltimore, but it's been a long time. I never knew anything about your 'directing' them business."

"For a percentage, of course. By the time Lee met Grant at Appomattox, my accumulated percentages were almost one hundred thirty-five thousand dollars."

This came as quite a piece of news to Frances, and her mind swirled. "So you did buy the pearl with your own money! And that was how you paid for everything else."

"In the beginning."

"I knew you had bought the other things so that Goelette would trust you."

"Most of them, if I remember, I gave to you." He moved to lie against her now.

Frances kissed him, then smiled. "And even though I knew you had made up the story about your fiancée wanting the second pearl, it worried me a little. I have to confess that."

"I knew it would. I had a bet with myself," he teased her. "But that worked perfectly, because what it did, you see, was to create a demand. It made Goelette believe that I would be willing to pay a much higher price than anyone had ever heard of for such a pearl."

"All you had to do was make sure the original pearl found its way back to him."

"Exactly. So I went to Belgium and left it with a dealer there—"

"*You went* to Belgium? You never told me that."

"No. I'm sorry. You thought I was in Baltimore. But if you had slipped even once . . ." He kissed her again, a quick brush of the tongue. "I told the Belgian that privacy meant everything to me, that I wanted five hundred thousand dollars for it—not a penny less—but that I would demand that my American identity be kept a secret. I suggested some story about a Belgian estate to him. And—what did he have to lose? The world of great gems is small. I knew it would get from him to the Frenchman who deals with Goelette. And I knew Goelette would buy it to offer me. And I would get it back."

Frances sighed. She felt much better now. "I'm surprised Mr. Goelette didn't recognize it," she said.

"Oh, no," Tom said. "That's the point. He saw it through his greed. He saw what he wanted to see. People always do that. It's one of the few things in life that can be relied on."

"You've got the pearl from Goelette and five hundred thousand dollars from the Belgian," Frances gasped. "Four hundred thousand dollars if you deduct what you paid for it originally. So the whole thing *is over*."

"Over?" Tom repeated in an astonished voice. "That was just the beginning." He reached down, held her, fixed her with his gaze.

Frances's nails dug into him. "Make love to me," she begged.

Tom stared. She worried him, . . . delighted him. Women, he told himself, would never understand.

CHAPTER

6

In the meantime, Mr. Goelette increasingly had begun to realize that he had been the victim of a swindle. Payment had been demanded by the French pearl merchant and Goelette, unable to locate Thomas Chance, had stalled as long as he dared before borrowing the money. Then, precisely four weeks to the day after Chance had left the store with the Pearl of Macao, he took out the needed loan, placing his company as collateral, and posted his check to Europe. He did this even before he consulted the police, for he knew it was an obligation he owed in any case, and he hoped that his developing fears were misplaced. He worried that he was now fooling himself, losing valuable time in which Chance might be tracked down. And, against this possibility, he worried that he had become too much of a cynic: that Chance was merely in love and reckless with time, but certainly not a criminal. Goelette, when in the latter frame of mind, had grown afraid of losing his sale by precipitously calling in the police. And so he waited.

Ninety days passed. August was nearly over. Chance and Frances Alexander continued their life in Bermuda. Frances's anxiety had been put to rest by Tom's much-reiterated assurance that he would soon be in a position to do more for her career than she might imagine and by the fact that she had begun to grow fond of her domestic life.

In the meantime, Mr. Goelette's bank debt had become due and he was unable to meet it.

"It's a *terr*-ible world," he told the icy Thistle. *"Il est emmerdant."*

But the floor manager did not alter so much as the arch of a brow. "Only if you take it seriously," he said.

The police had begun to search for Chance only recently, but he had left no trace in New York and communications with other cities were poor. "Besides," the police inspector (who owed his job to Tammany Hall) reminded Goelette, "no one knows which city to check."

"Or if he is even in a city," Goelette replied sarcastically.

"That's right. We can't be expected to work miracles."

"As you said," Goelette told him curtly. "You have more important cases."

"For intents and purposes, he is merely late with his payment," the inspector said. "We have men out there who are guilty of murder."

"All the same," Goelette asked, "what good does it do me?"

Goelette was in danger of losing his business. He was fifty-one. His father had founded Goelette and Company and the thought of losing it frightened him.

"C'est très simple," he told one potential source of capital after another. "I need six hundred thousand dollars."

"You were overextended then," they all answered.

"In anticipation of a further boom. But it has not materialized."

"Nor for us," they all said. "We're sorry."

He was rejected everywhere, and it began to seem that he might have to liquidate the firm in order to realize the money he needed. His bank, with decreasing subtlety, was beginning to pressure him for just such an action. But, for as long as he could, he delayed. He thought of his days as a child in his father's shop, of his years as an apprentice and salesman. He even thought briefly of suicide, but it was not in his character.

At about this time, when outside pressure and his internal

depression had grown most severe, he received a short note from the representative of a syndicate interested in acquiring Goelette and Company. "Sir," it read, "I write on behalf of certain interests desirous of discussing the possibility of merging themselves with your firm, or of acquiring you outright. Would you meet me for lunch, at your convenience, at the Breevort. C. C. Chamberlain."

Ordinarily, Goelette would have refused even to discuss this matter; but the idea of selling the firm intact had begun to seem preferable to liquidation. "Tell him," Goelette instructed his secretary, "to meet me here. An hour before lunch, day after tomorrow. We can go by carriage to the Breevort if he wishes. But I want to see him in my own light first."

Goelette, as a jeweler, was accustomed to probing beneath the surface of an article before pronouncing it genuine. And so he was not fooled by Chamberlain's elaborate manners or by his vaguely Continental dress. He saw in the man's features, in their natural width and the set which life had imposed upon them, a disturbing hardness; heard, in the man's vowels, an echo of something plebian.

"Let me make it clear that I speak for a group of traders who have built their fortunes in shipping and are, that is, *would be,* intent on maintaining the fine reputation of Goelette and Company."

"I am glad to hear that."

"And, if I may venture a guess, relieved?"

"Yes."

"Very capital then," Chamberlain said. "While I am here, why don't we take a few minutes and have a little look around?"

"A *little look*?" Goelette smiled. "There will be time enough for that. You had in mind the Breevort?"

"The Breevort. Or anywhere else—"

"The Breevort is fine," the jeweler said.

"Very capital then."

Over a lunch of grilled lobster, Chamberlain said, "My people value your name as importers of the highest quality silver and gold. And gems, of course."

"And often enough," added Goelette, "as exporters too."

"When you travel all over the world, you ultimately come to the realization that the only thing of permanent value is beauty. We want to be in the business of beautiful things. It is as simple as that."

"As simple as that?"

"Have no fear," the stranger said.

"It is a very great decision. I have a staff: men in my workshop, men in my showroom, ladies in my office . . ."

"Accept my assurances, sir. By selling to us—or merging—"

"Merging is out of the question," Goelette interrupted. "Once I am no longer *proprietaire*, my daughter and I return to France."

"As you wish. But accept my assurances, sir, that your personnel shall be continued."

"That is very important to me. I'm sure you understand. It is essential, in fact."

Chamberlain grinned broadly, but Goelette saw that there was no sympathy in his eyes. "Now, as to money, we would be prepared to offer you seven hundred fifty thousand dollars."

"Pardon me," Goelette said, remembering, wistfully, when he had asked more than that price for a single pearl. "I thought the customary procedure was to ask the seller to suggest a price."

"Those are my instructions. I rather thought you would consider it quite a generous offer."

"Generous? Yes. I imagine it is." Chamberlain's posturing struck him as fulsome, but he could not afford to jeopardize the arrangement being offered.

"I shall need your answer, though."

"Not today."

"Within forty-eight hours."

Goelette hesitated. "Within forty-eight hours," he repeated at last.

They signed the agreement over amontillado sherry in Mr. Goelette's office two days later. Chamberlain presented Goelette with a draft on the Tenth National Bank for the full amount. In a tone more politic than genuine, he once again asked the jeweler to remain at his desk, but the Frenchman could not bring himself to accept the role of employee, no matter how magnanimous his superiors might be. He felt he had been brought to ruin by a swindle and by the ineptitude of the New York Police in not having protected or rescued him from it. He therefore wanted to leave New York—for, in a curious way, he no longer felt safe there. "No, I'm going to France," he muttered. "And once I'm there, I'm going to retire. *En Provence*. With the people I know. *Only* with them."

Mr. Chamberlain and the other members of the syndicate left Goelette in his office and walked toward Tammany Hall. There, before the ridiculous facade of arched windows, Chamberlain removed two sealed envelopes from his coat pocket. He delivered the one with special markings to a pockmarked man who sat reading a newspaper in the lobby. The man was a well-known stooge of Boss Tweed's organization. The second envelope, already addressed and stamped, Chamberlain placed in the postal box at the corner.

The letter arrived in Bermuda in ten days and when Chance claimed it at the Post Office in St. George's he began to laugh wildly, ecstatically.

Chance and Frances sailed on the next ship to New York. There were no staterooms on the ship, but two crew berths isolated in the bow were available and, since there would be no more luxurious accommodations leaving Bermuda for a month, the couple took them. The owner of the ship, a former supplier of Civil War profiteers and Chance's friend, also owned the more elaborate ship on which Chance and his mistress had made passage from New York. His name was C. C. Chamberlain. He was the same Chamberlain who, as a sutler, had engaged Tom's services, the same Chamberlain who had negotiated the purchase of Goelette and Company.

There were storms the second day out of Bermuda. At first, these involved no more than heavy swells and steady drizzle; but it seemed, eventually, that they were passing into the eye of the hurricane.

At night, the boat pounded the sea, and loose objects, fallen from their normal places, rattled on the floorboards or floated in the bilge. The cantilever holding the main table in the galley broke under the strain. Chance sat at the edge of the cot on which Frances lay, awake again. He braced his foot against the support post of the opposite bed, trying to hold her in. Frances was quiet, but frightened. In a still moment he leaned over to kiss her. She put his right hand to rest against her. He leaned his face against her breasts, drawing back her nightgown. Then the boat rose on a giant wave and Frances grew sick with terror. Suddenly, the bunk tore from the side wall of the ship; she slid hard against the wall and was thrown back with the sea. Bilge water lashed her. She became chilled.

Frances took a fever that night. The cabin stunk with vomit, blood, all the maliferous odors of sickness save medicine. One of the crew, an older Irishman, who had a habit of reading medical books during his long watches, attended her. She was sick for three days and, by the time she recovered, the weather was mild again.

They arrived in New York early on a Monday morning. Tom was physically and emotionally drawn. He and Frances were living on nervous energy to which, in his case, was added the narcotic of his business venture, the reason for their trip. He took Frances to a sterile-looking women's hospital that had been recommended by the physician at the Fifth Avenue Hotel, but the doctors there pronounced her well at once, in need only of rest, and so they returned together to their suite.

The azaleas were in bloom along the perimeter of Madison Square, but Chance barely saw them. His feelings, so intense and extreme in the week past, so primal at one moment, so hopeful the next, all seemed exhausted, far away from him now. He could not touch them, nor summon them; he felt disoriented on what had promised to be the day of his greatest triumph. He mounted the bed and, for twenty minutes, sank into a dreamless nap.

Chamberlain and another man met him in the hotel dining room for lunch.

"From your letter I take it everything went very well," Chance said.

"It did," Chamberlain told him.

"I am now president of Goelette and Company, is that correct?"

"It was your money that bought it," Chamberlain said matter-of-factly.

The other man was silent. Chance addressed him. "Will you notify the police that Goelette and Company no longer wishes to prefer any charge against Thomas Chance?"

The other man smiled, looked up from his consommé. "We've already taken care of that with Tweed's people," he said.

"I know," Chance said, "but I'd like to do it officially."

"One thing puzzles me," Chamberlain said then. "You could have bought the whole enterprise for six hundred thousand dollars. I'm sure of that. Why did you pay him seven hundred fifty thousand dollars?"

"Don't worry, Chamberlain," Chance replied intently. "You'll get back your money at the agreed-upon time—and with extravagant interest. I didn't want to bankrupt him, you know. Goelette seemed rather a nice fellow actually. I may be a tough businessman, sir, but I'm not a thief."

BOOK II

THE PRACTICE

(1853–1867)

CHAPTER 7

ADAM CHANCE, AWAKING FROM HALF AN HOUR'S NAP AT SEVEN o'clock on a summer evening, took a great morning-like belch and looked around the small, dark parlor for his son. "Where is he?" he called in the same throaty voice he used in his work as a longshoreman on the Baltimore docks.

"Tom?" his wife said.

"Who else?"

"He's gone out long ago."

"I might have known," replied Adam Chance. There was considerable disgust in his voice.

The Chances made their home in a tiny house in the back reaches of Federal Hill, in South Baltimore, and, at that moment, their only son, Tom, was no more than a few cobblestone blocks away, looking out from the hill's other slope at the municipal harbor. Schooners of all sorts were moored there and a few were moving, throwing long shadows against the orange and rippled light of sunset. It was a tranquil and magnificent sight. But Tom, age thirteen, and his friend, fourteen-year-old Peter Parton, were not concerned with the view. They had lived beside it all their lives, regarded it as commonplace, and, hiding now in a warren beneath the gray-painted slats of Peter's father's porch, they had much more serious matters on their minds.

"I've heard that before," Tom Chance said ultimately. "Lots of times, in fact. But I don't believe a word of it."

"Suit yourself," Peter said calmly.

"What makes you so sure it's true?" Tom asked.

"Come on," Peter said. "Let's get out of here. I'm wasting my time."

Tom Chance stayed fast. "Have *you* ever done it?" he demanded.

"Yes," came Peter's quick reply.

But Tom fixed Peter with his eyes. "No, you haven't," he challenged.

"Well, I *will,*" Peter shot back. "*I* want to, at least. And at least *I'll* know how."

They were playing a game of bluff and it was Peter's turn. He pretended to be on the point of quitting a conversation which, in truth, both boys felt compelled to continue. So Tom yielded and lay back lazily against an old, propped two-by-four. "All right," he said slowly. "It's late at night. There's no one around. One of us is walking along the street with Mary Wardman. And suddenly we look at her. And this thought of yours comes to us. What do we do? We can't ask her very well. We can't say, oh, darling, dear Mary, would you mind undoing your skirts and taking down your panties because I want to put my hickey in you." Tom puckered his lips and smacked them as a gesture against the ridiculousness of such an idea.

"She'd probably knock us one," he continued. "And, anyway, who'd want to do it? It makes me sick to think about! What would you do if you did put it there, Peter? Seems like it would get to bore you after a while, don't you think?" He smiled complacently.

Peter Parton was growing excited. "Look, Tom," he said. "You know that word ol' Hoss Hudson's always using?" Tom nodded. "That's what it means. Don't be a bloody fool. And it doesn't happen like you said. It happens between married people."

"How?"

Peter hesitated. "I'm not sure. But you have to be married to do it."

"I don't see why," Tom declared.

"Well, some women do it for money," Peter elaborated, "so they say."

"Then what makes babies?" Tom demanded, half scornfully. "Tell me that?"

"You're only thirteen, aren't you?" Peter teased. "Maybe I shouldn't."

"I'll be fourteen come February," Tom said.

Peter studied him from head to foot. "Pull down your pants," Peter demanded.

"You're crazy."

"All right, forget it."

After a few minutes' hesitation, Tom said, "I'll do it if you do."

Both boys gave in then and were relieved. They unbuttoned quietly and lay with their trousers bundled at their ankles.

"Jeez," exclaimed Peter. "You've got a long one."

Tom looked at himself and at Peter. "Is that good or bad?" he asked anxiously.

"Think of some girl you really like," Peter told him then. "Just be very quiet. Don't say anything at all."

Tom did as he was told. The damp night air slid across his exposed skin and he trembled in it, thought of only himself, and then of Mary Wardman. She was dressed, pert, the prettiest girl he knew, the only one with both a good face and breasts; and then, in his mind, she was naked—from the waist up at first, then altogether. How delicious, he thought, for he had never seen a girl naked.

Peter looked at him. "That's how it happens," he said at last. "You don't have to do anything."

Tom agreed soundlessly; studied his new sensation; did not answer.

"Do you still think it would bore you?" Peter asked smartly.

"Go on," pressed Tom. "I've felt like this before, but there's more, isn't there?"

Peter hesitated. "Yes," he admitted finally. "Of course, it's meant to be much better with a girl than by yourself . . . but I'll show you . . ."

Baltimore was a maritime capital and took its life from its port. It had grown up at the head of the long, leaf-shaped Chesapeake, which was the largest natural estuary in the world; and its harbor snuggled among the city's wide swells and was constantly trafficked with trading ships. Federal Hill made a point out from the west end of the harbor basin, green-sloped, walled in stone at its base, with a Romanesque church atop it and rows of proud houses lining its summit, displaying a kind of brick and mortar solidity that those who lived in its nether reaches could not hope to know. For there the houses, like the Chances' and the Partons', were poor, cramped, wooden, even misangled upon their foundations.

But going north from them, even a little way along the path of Tom Chance's dreams, the whole city unfolded. Here were the offices of Alexander Brown and half the banking houses of the American South, the grain, cotton, and tobacco exchanges, in small brick and show-windowed buildings, no more than a block's walk from tidal water. And here were the Baltimore Museum of Fine Arts, breathing a steady and gentlemanly hush into the commercial streets, and the restaurants where businessmen lunched, and the unaffordable stores with their privileged quiet, their rich bouquets so different from the sawdust smells of shops where working people bought.

Tom, a few fingers of pomade slicking down his long, chestnut hair, was used to walking the streets of this quarter when he had something on his mind. And now, in the aftermath of his initiations, feeling momentarily embarrassed that he had had to learn from Peter something which he felt he should have had an instinctual hold upon all along, he was especially pensive, excited, and shy.

"Look at that," Peter said finally, directing Tom to a tailor's window in which a disembodied morning coat and trousers hung on display. "I say, you'd look mighty swell in that, Tom."

"I'd outgrow it in no time," Tom replied immediately.

"Right," said Peter. "I guess we all would."

"How tall are you, Peter?" Tom asked then.

"Five feet, eight inches," Peter replied.

"I'm an inch behind you."

"Don't worry about it," Peter answered. "You're a year younger too. You know, I'd like to be six feet."

"I probably will," Tom said. "My father's more than that."

"He's a big man all right."

"Peter," Tom said suddenly, in a new, more supplicant, tone of voice.

"What?"

But before he could utter the two simple words "thank you," something caught him in his throat, an old inhibition, and he said only "nothing" and began to pick up his gait.

Tom revered Peter Parton, considered him his best friend, the only person he could talk to and learn from without fear. He did not approve of himself for being brusque with Peter now, but, somehow, his mood had passed beyond his control and he guessed that Peter knew it.

Despite the difference in their ages, which might have been crucial at their time in life, they had been companions since Tom was six; and into most of life's adventures, Peter had blazed the trail which Tom followed. Peter was thicker of feature than Tom, less athletic and clever, but he had a year's advantage and, quite self-consciously, had employed it to cement their friendship. Even in his limited way, he had always understood that Tom was probably designed for some heightened destiny, the fulfillment of some larger internal promise than most people contained, and, almost completely without envy, he had sought to attach himself to Tom's star, perhaps to glow in the wake of its trajectory.

In one sense, Peter had not required an unusual degree of perception, for Tom Chance was indisputably the most handsome boy in South Baltimore. All their mothers said so, had always said so; and all their contemporaries agreed. It was no secret that Tom's extraordinary popularity among his classmates had been founded upon the rock of his boyishly beautiful looks, nor that he had maintained it with very little effort. And Peter, as much as anyone, felt a strong pull toward him, even a disturbing attraction at times.

He watched Tom now as he moved through the diminishing dark, so absorbed in private thought that a gray landau, which had jumped the curbstone and nearly careened into him, provoked no reflex. It was a fine, lemony, mid-Atlantic night, with a wisp of salt in the air, and Peter Parton could feel, if not explain, the poignance of it. But Tom was silent.

"Whoo-oo," Peter said. "That was close. The driver must've tucked a few under his belt."

"I'll bet," Tom replied automatically, but that was all.

Peter appraised his friend. Thirteen years old. Almost fourteen. Growing a few inches each year. Graceful. Coming, more and more each day, into the full bloom of his looks; a boy still, innocent, but something worldly in the face, in the eyes. The eyes were as green as spring fir, Peter remembered, although he could not see them now in the half light. He watched Tom, walked at the same brisk clip he did in order to keep beside him, but his mind wandered back to the warren beneath his father's porch, to the events an hour or two ago: He saw his friend naked alongside him, seeming more than a year younger than he was, smooth-skinned and inexperienced, with fresh, globe-shaped muscles just beginning to form at his shoulders, and that long penis, half again as long as his own, rising, rising. . . . The thought excited him, disgusted him. Instinctively, he wanted to be again in that warren, to go there again, now, to repeat the immediate past. And yet, as powerfully as it impelled, it also sickened him, seemed the most unnatural of passions, a symptom of something dread within him.

A couple passed them, middle-aged, arm in arm. Then two more carriages, and a booted courier on what looked to be a quarter horse. Tom ignored them. He was concentrating now on Mary Wardman, inventing a situation in his mind, and he wished Peter would leave him alone to imagine his conquest. He felt grateful, resentful, confused.

But Peter continued to follow him. "Look," Peter said. "I don't know what's the matter with you. But I'm sorry I ever said anything about it if you're going to . . ."

"How many times can you do it?" Tom interrupted.

"How should I know?"

"More than once?"

"Well, I can answer that at least. A lot more than once."

"Are you sure? How do you know?"

"Take it from me," Peter said.

"If you swear."

"I swear, but this is stupid, Tom."

"On your . . . on your mother's grave," Tom continued solemnly.

"Yes," agreed Peter, a bit shaken by the reference and anxious to change the subject now.

"I'll be glad when I'm older," Tom said, after a pause.

"Who won't be?" Peter asked.

"I'm goin' to get me a beautiful wife. And a bundle of money. It won't be bad at all. Maybe I'll be a banker like the fellas work in some of these buildings around here."

"I thought you wanted to be an actor."

"I did. I may."

"And before that, you wanted to own your own ship."

"So what?"

"You're amazin'," Peter said. "I can't figure you out at all."

"So what?" Tom said again.

"Maybe you'll marry Mary Wardman," Peter said.

"No," said Tom. "Well, to tell you the truth, I think I might like to try this other business out on her one day. But I don't think I'd care to marry her. You see, Peter, I mean to be a rich man before I'm too old, and, somehow, I can't see Mary Wardman as a rich man's wife. Know what I mean?"

"It'd be fun to poke her, though. Can't deny that," Peter fancied.

"Could be," Tom said. "But I got plenty of time for that."

Successively, since they had begun to discuss such matters, Tom had wanted to be a seaman, soldier, merchant, jeweler, burglar, banker, tailor, farmer, preacher, and actor–whatever he had seen, heard, or read of last had enticed and held his mind until the next dream had come along to replace it. And this grand fickleness perplexed the more practical Peter, who had wanted only to walk his father's footsteps along the wharves, and to marry.

"You know, Tom," Peter said. "I've been thinkin' that I might like to try and become a doctor, except for it takes more money than I reckon I'll have."

The dusk swirled about them now, as they had walked a circle and were close again to the water. The stink of horse dung rose from gutters and alleys and traveled the night wind through the streets of the summer-warmed city. "Listen to me," Tom cautioned Peter. "You don't care two hoots about bein' a doctor. What you wanna be is rich! That's what you wanna be." He delivered these words with an inescapable force, for they sprang from the well of his psyche, from that central part of him which preferred being envied to being liked.

"I might just want to be a doctor," Peter shot back. "That's every bit as good a thing to be."

Tom stopped dead at a corner. Mary Wardman had drained from his mind. His penis had gone flaccid again. His thoughts were far away, not in the present, not even in the near future, but at some distant time when he could imagine his dreams had been fulfilled. He reached down beside the curb where tall grass grew between paving stones and, with a quick tug, uprooted a long blade, which he slid between his front teeth. He looked about him, quietly taunting Peter. Behind a large, squarish plate of glass, the offices of a cotton broker were darkly elegant. "Maybe so," he said at last, then gave a whistle through his reed.

"Let's go back to my house," Peter said. "It's getting dark. The lamplighter's out already and it won't be long before it's black as pitch." His emotions were racing him. "We don't have to go into the house yet. I'll just tell my father that we're back and we can sit out under the porch again and talk."

"All right with me," said Tom. Then, when they were under way again: "Peter, I want to ask you a question."

Trembling now, Peter said, "What?"

"Maybe you'd like to be a doctor more than you'd like to be one of the men in those banks."

"Maybe I would," Peter retorted, a little easier now.

"But whose son would you rather be?" Tom asked.

Even with only a foot between them, they were becoming vague and shadowy presences, more sounds than sights to each other, as the moonless dark enveloped them. Baltimore grew still for a moment and Peter gave a long consideration to Tom's question. It was a good question, he thought. Better than the questions he asked of life. And then, suddenly, he realized the true dimension of what he felt for his friend. He did not so much want to see this boy naked, now or ever, not so much want to share with him his thoughts, his time, his secrets, or even that new and frightening instant when one erupted and shivered and dreamed. No, none of those things would suffice much longer, thought Peter. He would want more. He would want *to be* his friend. Not to be Peter Parton. But to *be* Thomas Chance.

CHAPTER

8

KATHARINE CHANCE WAS SEWING, DARNING HER HUSBAND'S socks, when Tom returned to their house. His curfew had been established at dusk—a deliberate effort on his mother's part to allow him some gray area—for Adam Chance, when sober, could be much too exacting. Seven thirty would have meant what it said to him. And Katharine did not want it that way. She had but one son, Tom, and no trouble recognizing the special qualities that set him apart from other children. As a young girl, without his acid mind, without anything like his physical beauty, she had nearly run away from her parents' house in Brooklyn. They had been strict deniers of pleasure, her parents, and their poor, small rooms had begun to suffocate her long before she was his age, long before puberty. She did not want to lose Tom this way. She looked about her. Adam, inebriated as usual, sprawled out of his chair and intermittently snored. The air in the room was visibly heavy, humid. Her own mother's doilies were draped over the rounded arms of the sofa, but, despite her washing, ancient liquor stains gazed up from them. The sofa itself was the color of dried blood.

"Tom, it's night out," Katharine said. "Not dusk, Tom. Night. Where in the devil's name have you been?"

"With Peter," Tom said.

"I'm certain of that."

"But it's true."

"I don't doubt that it is, Tom. But, shhh. . . . You'll

wake your father from his sleep. Now, where were you and Peter tonight? At his house all the time?"

"Yes," Tom said. Feeling a rush of guilt build up inside him, he added: "Most of it. We went out for a walk, too. In Baltimore. On Charles Street, by the shops, you know."

"Indeed," Katharine said, with resignation.

"I'm too late, aren't I, Mom," Tom interjected. He stared fully into his mother's eyes, blinked into a smile.

"Indeed," she repeated.

He began to move toward the water basin. "Tom," his mother said. "It's much past dusk. And I was worried for you. Your father was, too. Don't be out in the night this late again, son. Please, hear me."

Tom looked at his father. Coarse hair, but graying. Wide and open pores in the middle of his face. A third again too much weight, it seemed to him, around the waist, ballooning out as a stomach. He paused in wonder that this kind, human woman, whose very existence he took for granted, might have once given herself up to his father. He knew them both—as well as, better than anyone; and even he could not visualize it. There was thick hair on his father's chest, mats of it; he could see it beneath his father's shirt and it seemed ape-like, old and dirty. What, thought Tom, had so moved her all those years ago that she would submit to him? What? What? What?

As he poured the water from the old porcelain pitcher over his hands, he considered that, perhaps, it had been Peter Parton who was wrong, who had concocted a perverse fantasy, then rumored it as fact. But, as he calculated, there was still too much evidence in Peter's favor.

He yearned, physically, to ask his mother for the truth, but he hadn't the nerve at the moment. The questions which pounded inside his mind remained silent. "Mother," he said at last, in a louder voice now, because, at the basin, he was farther from her.

"Quiet, Tom," she said, raising a long, water-reddened

finger to her mouth. "Your father is asleep. He's had a hard day at his work, too."

Tom felt his veins fill all of a sudden. "He's not asleep," he cried. "He's drunk, Mom. Stop fooling yourself, will you!" He had whirled himself around and was staring at her now, lather on the palms and backs of his hands and on his chin.

"Pray and ask the Lord to forgive you!" Katharine said in a deep whisper.

Tom shook the soap from his hands and dunked them once more under water. "I'll ask *you,*" he said quietly. "That's all." He looked away from her, shot the towel to his face, and wiped the soap from his chin. He hoped she had not seen his tears, this good and suffering woman.

For a minute there was quiet, a sense of fright. Then Katharine gathered up her work and walked over to Tom and, before either of them could speak, they were wrapped in each other's arms, pounding each other's backs, smoothing the wrinkles of each other's clothes. Tom cried, and Katharine comforted him, suppressing her own tears. "Mother," Tom sobbed. "It's all right. It's all right. I promise you it is." But when she made no response he went on: "When Peter and I were walking, I saw a sign in a tailor's window. A gentlemen's tailor. Wanted a boy to help out, he did. If he would take me, Mother, wouldn't that be fine? I'd be earnin' you money for the house and all. Best part of a dollar a week, I expect."

Katharine held him tight against her. She knew his happiness was false. "Aye," she said. "But what makes you think he wants a boy as young as you, Tom?"

"I'm as good a worker as the next," he answered. "And a darned sight more handsome than most. Everybody says so. It's not that I'm vain, Mom." His mood rose with his thought. "I might even be able to wear a suit for him 'n sell it off my back. That would be fun, wouldn't it, wearin' gentlemen's clothes like that."

They were apart now, but very close. "Tom, you're all the time thinkin' ahead," Katharine said. "So what's a simple one like me to do for you? But aren't you putting the cart before the horse this time, son?"

At that moment, Adam mumbled something in his sleep, shifted in his chair, and then leaped up, abruptly wide awake. "Ohhh . . ." he groaned interminably. "A hellish dream it was, too."

Katharine stood fast until she could be sure of his direction. "Adam, are you all right?" she asked.

"Fine, fine," her husband answered. "Sick in the head and sick in the stomach is all! Sick. In every'n of my muscles is all!"

"Would you like me to get your bed ready?" Katharine asked. "Or heat you a tub?"

Adam groaned. "Well, if it isn't Tom," he said calmly, then raised his voice to a threatening shout. "Where in hell have you been, lad?" His breath was warm and old and smelled of malt whiskey.

"With his friends," Katharine said.

"A queer bunch, the lot of them," Adam replied. "And too late on the streets."

"He was with his friend Peter Parton," Katharine answered.

"The boy should work," Adam croaked. "I work. Always have. Does he look like a rich man's son to you?"

Tom stared at his father, and felt himself trembling.

"Yes," Katharine said defiantly. "Exactly like a rich man's son." Reaching over to Tom, tentatively only for a moment, she cupped his face in her hands and squeezed him.

"You're no damned good for him that way, Kathy," Adam Chance said. "The boy's old enough to learn the ways of the world. It's past time already."

"Where are you going?" Katharine demanded as he bounded past her, toward the small oak-doored cabinet where he stored his liquor.

"In search of sustenance," was all he said.

Tom coughed nervously. "Father," he began, "I have been looking for a job, you know. And I think I've found one . . ."

Adam swallowed and came about slowly. "What sort of work?" he asked.

"In Baltimore," Tom said.

"I hope to Christ in Baltimore. But doin' what, Tom?"

"I don't know rightly," Tom said. "But the work is in a tailor's shop, a fine . . ."

Adam turned his back on his son, his face to the cabinet again. "Woman's work, sewing," he moaned as he filled half a tall glass with whiskey.

"It's not true," said Katharine.

Adam ignored her. "Look, Tom, don't be afraid. Come here, boy," he said. Tom glanced at his mother's blank but accepting face, took one cautious step, then another, until he could feel his father's arm resting on his shoulder. It stank of sweat. Adam swallowed a mouthful of drink, but quickly wiped his lips with the side of his finger and assumed, as best he could in his present state, the attitude of a concerned guardian. "How old are you, boy? Now, I mean, tell me! Come on."

"Thirteen," said Tom.

"I wouldn't've believed it," Adam Chance exclaimed. He looked around at Katharine as though their family had never known tensions. "Thirteen? I knew a Jew once. They're a strange sort, the Jews. But this'n I knew was good enough for most things. And he told us, me and the other fellas on the wharves—you see, I don't go too far from the wharves, because I have work to do there if I want to put food on that table behind you. And I know it's where I belong, not on Charles Street, with the so-called gentlemen and ladies, 'cause, let me tell you, son, if they could, they'd chew you or me up for dessert, your mother too. So well remember that! Anyway, this Jew, he told us that when their boys is thirteen, they're taken into whatever they call their churches, the synagogue, that's it, and they have a regular worship, and after that the boys aren't considered boys anymore. They're men."

Tom was frozen.

"Are you a man, Tom?" Adam pressed, swigging the last of his drink in his glass, following the brown liquid with thirsty eyes. "That's how it was in the Bible. In the Old Testament. I should like to think you're as good as the Jews, boy, at least that."

"I don't know what a Jew is," Tom said.

"Jesus was a Jew," said Katharine.

"Simple," Adam said. "Enough of anything is enough. Too much is more than enough."

Katharine showed her puzzlement. "Wondering what I mean?" he asked. "I'll spell it out for you. It's time you, Tom, come with your father in the mornings, get a start in men's work, and, if I may say, begin to pay a share of the freight."

"I forbid it, Adam," Katharine screamed. "He's still in school, Tom is. And he's going to finish his schoolin' sure as—"

"And work as a tailor's dummy," Adam mimicked. "An old fart's hands all over him. Woman, don't be mad!"

Tom was plainly confused by this remark, but he let it go for the time being, certain that it possessed at least a tenuous connection to his experience with Peter earlier that night.

"It's his only hope to make something of himself, Adam. Give it to him," Katharine said. "You know that as well as anyone."

"The importance of education?" Adam asked rhetorically, and with another drink in hand. "All that again, eh?"

"It's a fine tailor's shop, Father," Tom said. "And the best part of a dollar each week."

"Then you have the job then, do you?"

"Yes, sir," Tom lied.

"Well, give it up, lad. Right away in the mornin'. You'll be joinin' me on the docks come fall and time enough."

"No!" Katharine cried.

"I don't mind," Tom said meekly, without meaning it, for he wanted to be done with this fight now, to face whatever he might have to later, but not here, not with his mother in tears.

But Katharine cried "No. Adam," she begged, "he's your own flesh and blood, bears your own name. Offer him, for mercy's sake, the chance to live a good life. You've worked hard, yes. Don't I know that certainly as anyone? But it's for your son to take the next step."

Adam flung his empty glass against the cornice work, for such philosophy enraged him. "That's rubbish," he roared. "Dead dreams and I'm thirty years too old to have them."

"No," Katharine retorted calmly. "That's life. The old stepping back. The young stepping forward."

Tom searched his mother's face, permanently wrinkled now, although she was not yet forty. Her eyes were fiery, but her wounds shone in them and Tom, through fear and trembling, suddenly caught a vision of what she might have been like as a young girl, when so many men had sought her.

Adam was drinking again, directly from the bottle this time. "Hope is a fine breakfast," he said, swigging a mouthful of booze, then choking on it before he could complete his sentence. ". . . a fine breakfast, but a poor supper."

"We've heard that before," Katharine said.

"Haven't heeded it."

"Lord forgive me. But you're damnably right about that, sir," Katharine exclaimed.

"Stay out of this, woman," Adam demanded. "A boy comes of age, his father's the proper one to see to his rearing, his education and apprenticeship. And it's a fine education, too, I'll tell you, that a man gets on the docks. A different sort from schoolhouse education, but I'd say better by a mile."

"The answer is no," Katharine said.

"Then you and my son. . . . You're going to take my son out of this house, away from this place I've paid in sweat to give you? And live without a roof over your heads in the winter coming? Crazy, woman. And him, there, growing up past you every minute. Don't tell me you haven't seen that look of his! The contempt he has for us. For me. Even for you." Katharine was crying now, finally broken, and Tom held her against his shoulder, wishing there was some way he, or God, might strike his father dead. Still, Adam continued: "That face of his. Unnatural. Like a girl's. That pouting, curling, contemptuous mouth. He'll want women soon enough. The likes of him won't worry too long for his parents' welfare."

"That's not true," Tom told his mother.

"Shut your fucking mouth," Adam commanded.

Katharine's soft eyes looked up from her son's side. So this was it, she thought. Adam was jealous of his son.

"Old age comes soon enough," Adam complained. "And where will I be? Or if I should take sick with pneumonia one winter, or fall in an accident?"

"You're forty-nine years old," Katharine told him. "A way still 'til the reaper comes."

"Not so far," he said. "And not so fast, woman"–for she and Tom had both taken a step back and away from him. "The boy can read and write, can't he?"

"Certainly," Tom interjected protectively.

"And add and subtract figures?" Adam's tone was momentarily milder.

"Yes," Tom said.

"Then there's been school enough, wouldn't you say? So it's settled. You'll come to work with me, Tom. Tomorrow. There's no time like the present. Or else, dear wife, would you prefer I ship him off to Lilly? Have *her* find him work.

Give him a place at *her* college." This last amused him greatly, for he was loud in laughter at his own wit, bent over, stumbling, smiling, hawing and heeing as Katharine stood murderously silent.

"Who's Lilly?" Tom asked.

"What?" Katharine said. "Oh, a teacher, Tom. Someone your father knew."

"Mom," Tom whispered, "let's leave right now. You and me. We'll be all right together. We'll make out all right together."

Katharine kissed him. "Not yet, Tom," she said tenderly. "Maybe one day. Now, while you have the chance, go up and get ready for bed. And I'll be up to tuck you in."

Benumbed, Tom ascended the narrow stairs, washed his face and teeth, changed out of his clothes and into pajamas, and slid into his bed. The muslin felt damp against his arms and feet, against the back of his neck, and only when his stomach growled did he realize that he had gone without dinner.

Light and voices came into the room from the summer night outside. Moonlight. Starlight. The faint, yellow flickering light of streetlamps. And the voices of an old woman, the neighborhood grocer, and a young man. The young man, in fact, was singing.

After his mother had come and gone, he lay in his bed for a long time, watching the shadows at play on the ceiling and far wall of his room. How forbidding they were, like phantoms. In his mind, he knew that these mysterious shapes were caused by everyday objects, that a coach passing beside a streetlamp had created the menacing shapes on the wall; and yet he wanted to cut himself off from this reality now and think only of the shadows. What if they, and not the coach, were real? What if they, through some magical power, had created the coach and the streetlamp instead of the other way around? Perhaps they would be his friends; free him and his mother. He thought briefly of Peter Parton, then of Mary Wardman again, and of his mother's sad eyes, before he fell asleep.

He awoke half an hour before dawn. It was slanting rain outside. He thought he heard a dog crying, howling as though he were giving his head's blood up in death. And, awake and asleep, he went to the window, but there was no light. Then, the rain quickened and the dog howled, louder with the rain, and Tom, in pajamas and bare feet, went downstairs and outside to look for him. He was alone in the street, drenched now, and searching frantically. He knew the water would pour into the rivulets of whatever blood the dog left behind, would dilute it pink, then wash it out; but something compelled him forward nonetheless.

The dog howled his insistence on life. Tom ran up one alley and down another, always toward the wall, but the dog was nowhere visible . . . and then, of a sudden, he gave up howling.

Tom was in the high grass in the rain when this happened. He could see his own house down the street in the distance. He wanted to find the dog and bury it or throw it, in a sack, to sea. But then, he thought, you couldn't bury someone else's dog, maybe a child's dog, so he walked on toward his house.

He was cold when he got there and he entered silently and stole his way lightly over the old, decrepit boards, and up the stairs. The door to his parents' room was closed. How could his mother be in there, he asked himself. He did not understand women, did not understand life.

He dried himself with a towel, draped his pajamas over the dining-room chair that sat beside his bed, and slid, naked, between the opened sheets. For a moment, he felt proud, happy with himself. Then, as he began to pass into sleep, the dog's blood spit through his mind. It spit in little squirts onto the white muslin, dribbled along the gray-marked wrinkles in the white. Crimson. Blood spilled in death.

Adam knocked on his door less than an hour later, but

did not come in. Tom was glad, for he had not wanted to be found undressed. "All of a quarter hour," Adam said tonelessly. And Tom understood his meaning.

On his bureau top, in a small, cut-glass pudding dish, Tom noticed a pin which his mother had given him the year he was in first grade. He had not taken at all well to school and, a few times, had gone so far as to throw fits in the classroom, beginning to cry at some hidden impulse, then continuing, ceaselessly and with no apparent reason. His teacher, Miss Thatcher, had caned him, at first on the hand and finally, in full view of the others, across his naked fanny; but not even that humiliation had corrected the problem. He had refused to speak about his episodes to anyone but his mother, and he certainly had not felt he could tell her of their true cause, which was that vague, irrational fear that would swell up in him that somehow, in his absence, she would die.

So, confronted with mystery, Katharine had replied with magic. It was a small lapis lazuli square, set in filigreed silver, an heirloom from her mother. Katharine promised him, "As long as you wear it, you need never worry, Tom. For everything will be fine then." And he had trusted in her and in it.

That seemed long ago now. He remembered a girl, part of whose ear had been bitten off by a horse, who had sat beside him that year; and it might as well have been his birth, it felt so far away. He had liked school for a long time, almost since then; and if he had never given it his best efforts, had always looked for short cuts, it was also true that most of his lessons had come easily to him; that its books had whetted his dreams; that, as an arena, it had been made for a performer of his looks and cleverness. Standing before his mirror, he crossed himself, prayed that, by September, his father might have a change of heart—or die—and that he would not have to abandon school forever.

In the awful quiet of the morning, Katharine stood over

the wood-burning stove and, wordlessly, stirred a pot of oats into mush. Behind her, facing each other across the table, but avoiding any contact of their eyes, Tom and Adam sat waiting. Tom's hands were folded. Adam's were nervous, playing everywhere: with the large spoon that had been set before him, with his napkin, with the buttons on his cuffs, along the front of his shirt, with the collar at the back of his neck. When Katharine served the meal, she said only, "Here's your breakfasts," as she put the two bowls down in front of them, and then excused herself from the room. So they ate in silence, except for Adam's cough and the one time Tom started to speak, but couldn't.

It was a gut-aching walk for Tom, the ten or so blocks to the wharf where his father worked, and, except for a pervasive sense of unreality, he would not have been able to bear it. He could not believe it was happening, that his life could change so dramatically, so abruptly, turning on the hinge of things that were clearly no more than the most trivial everyday events. What if he had not been late in coming home? Would he and his mother have spoken less loudly? Would his father have awakened in a different mood? After a different dream? At a different time? Or had none of these things been crucial to his fate? Were they merely accidents, imperfections imposed upon his own life plan by the larger power of heaven? Inside himself, he knew that the answers to these questions would elude him always. And it tormented him, seemed unfair, that he could not repeat the past.

Adam Chance worked for the firm of Pulling and Trumbull, Sugar Merchants, on the south side of the harbor; but, as a longshoreman, he unloaded more than cane. The ships which brought cane up from Cuba and the Caribbean Islands also brought whatever fruit—such as oranges and green bananas—could stand the three-week voyage. And Adam and the six men in his crew, and the dozen or so black men who worked for, with, and beside them, were responsible for removing the cargoes into the Pulling and Trumbull warehouse. As there were always two and often three ships a week destined for Pulling and Trumbull, it was dead-hard work indeed; and, however striking his other failures, Adam could honestly claim to have done it every day but Sunday, for thirty-one years.

As they approached the fence which surrounded the company on the land side, Adam turned to Tom, more than a little compassion in his face. "It's best," he said. "I wouldn't have brought you here, son, if I wasn't sure that it was for the best."

Tom attempted a smile, but did not answer.

"I'm sorry I'm not a rich man," Adam said unemotionally. "I'm sorry I disappoint you."

"I'll be all right," Tom replied.

Adam introduced Tom to a heavy, toothless man with hair the color and texture of peach fuzz. "This here's my son, Thomas," he said. "This here's Schippers." Schippers began to walk with them. "I want him to meet Ol' Phitts," Adam continued. "Maybe Ol' Phitts can use him."

"Sure," said Schippers. "Maybe." His eyes wandered over Tom. His look was puzzled. "How old are you, Thomas?" Schippers asked.

"Thirteen," Adam said.

"Um," Schippers said thoughtfully. "Thirteen."

George Phitts was scarcely more articulate, although the tone of authority in his voice compelled Tom's respect and curiosity at once. In his newly laundered shirt there was no mistaking him for one of the work crew. He, clearly, was a boss—and, Tom thought, disgustingly ugly. Owing to a vitamin deficiency, he had not one hair on his head: no beard, no eyebrows or lashes. And his ears protruded at true perpendiculars from his creased but shiny skull, making him seem older than his thirty-five years. Phitts was standing inside a shed, at a great table covered with charts and scattered small papers when Tom and Adam found him. Adam came to a halt in the entryway, gave Tom's appearance a careful once-over, and coughed intentionally. Without waiting, he followed the cough with "Pardon me." Then: "Mr. Phitts?"

Ol' Phitts looked up. "Adam," he said.

"Yessir."

"What can I do for you?" Adam was coming toward him, Tom at his side. "That your son?" Ol' Phitts said.

"My son, Thomas."

Tom nodded perfunctorily.

"Can he handle a full day's work?"

The smile fell from Adam's face. "What did Schippers tell you?" he laughed. "I say, we've only been on this wharf five minutes. No more."

"Word travels fast, Adam," Phitts said. He had a patronizing tone, Tom thought, a brand of self-importance—or was it assurance?—Tom had otherwise encountered only in the clergy.

"Don't I know," Adam stalled.

"Son, what sort of work you after?" George Phitts inquired.

Tom looked at his father. "I guess that depends," Adam said.

"What sort of work do you have?" Tom asked politely.

"Mr. Phitts'll tell you, Tom, just as soon as he's ready," Adam said.

He was clearly careful with Phitts, clearly subservient; and, for an instant, this bewildered Tom, who, for all these years, had known his father only at home, as the king of what he mockingly called his "castle."

Phitts stretched his neck in every direction. He reached into the back pocket of his pants and withdrew a worn pigskin pouch. From this pouch he proceeded to remove a small section of tobacco, which he clumsily popped into his mouth and began to chew. He was silent, except for the chewing, as Adam and Tom watched expectantly. Then, after two or three minutes, he spit a distance to his right, aiming for and hitting a small brass dish with the tobacco. There was still some in his mouth, but he slid it against his jaw before he spoke. "Thar's no regular jobs right now," he informed them. "Not by a long shot. And this here boy's too young for heavy work in any case. I could fill any such job with prize eighteen-year-old bodies, Adam, you know that."

"Start one early," Adam said, "and you'll have him a lifetime. That's what I always said. He's my son," he continued monotonously. "I can vouch for him, Mr. Phitts. Thirty-one years for Pulling and Trumbull, I oughta know what I'm talking about."

"Yes. Well, Adam, I would sure hope so," Phitts replied. "But, at the moment, I'm afraid it's a sweep's job or nothin'."

"How much does it pay?" Adam asked.

"Next to nothin'," Phitts roared with laughter. "But if he works out, we'll bring him along. Step by step. When his muscles is ready, we'll have the work for them."

"How much is next to nothin'?" Adam said.

"Twenty-five cents each week."

Adam's face fell slowly into resignation. "I guess we don't have any choice," he said. "Slave wages for a while or not a penny."

Phitts put his hand on Tom's shoulder. "Ready to start, boy, are you?" he asked, almost rhetorically.

"Yessir," Tom said.

Adam stepped backward. "Remember, son," he said, "you show 'em what you're made of. Show 'em you're a Chance. They'll expect it of you."

Tom was set to work with a broom and dustpan. He swept out Phitts' entire shed and then washed the thick film from all the windows, and the floor and the furniture, removing the cobwebs from corners and repeating whenever Phitts, with a glare, expressed his displeasure. From the shed, he went to the warehouses, beginning in the smallest first, and gave them the kind of housecleaning they had not seen in a dozen years. Each morning, at about the time he had been used to going to school, he would now raise two great caldrons of water onto a fire and, when they were boiling, pour them over the soap in his bucket. These buckets he would carry with him on his rounds, until the water went cold or black with dirt, and then he would make another trip to the stove, sometimes ten in a day. What Phitts expected by six o'clock in the evening was clearly spelled out by seven in the morning and Tom quickly grew to fear for himself if he did not complete his tasks.

"You're a nice-lookin' fella," Phitts had said peculiarly on his seventh day. "But a little soft in the wrong places. Don't you fret, though. We'll harden you up." It was then that Phitts had ordered him to haul a load of slate from one side of the yard to the other. It must have been a ton, Tom thought, and he was in constant motion for most of the day, carrying three or four pieces, as many as he could, on what seemed a thousand trips. Once, in the middle of his work, he spotted a trolley lying unused against a piling at the wharf and, noticing that Mr. Phitts was only a few feet away, approached him and asked if it might be possible for him to borrow the trolley.

"It would likely save an hour or two," Tom said.

But Phitts made no secret of his annoyance with the idea. "It's not assigned to you," he shouted abruptly, dismissing Tom with a sharp wave of his arm. "It's time you learned to mind your own work and no one else's."

By the end of that day, Tom was fully exhausted and had nearly ruptured his insides; and so, for a brief involuntary moment, he settled down with his back to a masonry wall and stretched his dead legs out before him on the dirt, trying to ease the doubling cramp in his stomach. The harbor was still in the path of the afternoon sun, and only by squinting could he make out the great mechanical clock on the Terminal Building across the tiny bay. Ten minutes until six, it read. One or two men passed, but ignored him in their haste for the gate. And then Phitts himself came by.

"All done for yourself at ten minutes before the hour?" he demanded.

"The slate's all beside the warehouse where you asked," Tom answered.

"Had you no other chores?"

Tom held his stomach. "I'm sorry, sir, I feel sick," he said.

"Get up," Phitts commanded.

Tom forced himself to stand, still using the building for support.

"Where are your buckets?" Phitts said.

Tom pointed to a distant shed and Phitts led him there. "You're lucky to have this job," he said. "When you think of all of those who don't have work. And yet you seem to want to lose it. What would your father do to you, then, Thomas, if you lost the job?" Phitts picked up a jar that had been resting on one of the rafter supports. He plunged it into the cold, soapy solution in Tom's bucket and pushed it into Tom's unwilling hand. "Drink it," he said.

"No," said Tom.

"Prefer a whip then, do you?"

Tom regarded him contemptuously.

"I'll speak to Adam if I have to," Phitts informed him. "Or it can be just between us, Thomas, and if you do your job as you were meant to, it won't have to happen again."

Tom swallowed sharply, then took the liquid all in one gulp. He handed the jar to Phitts, who replaced it against the wall. "Now go home," Phitts said. "We'll toughen you up, whatever it takes."

That night Tom took none of the shepherd's pie his mother had made him for dinner and, soon after eight, became violently sick in his room. His trips to the outhouse behind their porch became so frequent that he eventually remained there, throwing up violently, as whatever processed solids remained in his body began to flood out of him. It was as cold as wintertime for him in that stinking hut, and Katharine worried for his life and nearly went for Dr. Isadore on Holliday Street. But, by midnight, Tom seemed to have had all the flushing his insides required and, with his mother beside him, smoothing the sepia hair from his forehead, he fell asleep.

CHAPTER

9

AUTUMN CAME AND MAGNIFIED EVERYONE'S SENSE OF HIS OWN mortality. The lilac scents and leaves of summer disappeared on schedule. The honeysuckle vanished. The maple and dogwood, laurel and holly and larch leaves tumbled into piles on the grass and cluttered the pathways of Baltimore; even the grass itself withdrew into the earth.

Peter Parton came by in the evenings—although more and more seldom, as the light grew shorter—to relay to Tom the news from school: how strict the new teacher was; what the new boys were like; who was in love with Mary Wardman; and whom she had kissed. But Tom was too tired to receive or react to such information. He scarcely saw any of those involved, and, if he did, it was only casually. His poverty, his job, his father—every aspect of his situation, save his mother—shamed him; and he did not think he could bear to read that shame reflected in the perceptive eyes of his friends. Thus, his old life slipped farther and farther from him, not so much into the past as away; as if he had lived, until now, in a foreign country.

The men at Pulling and Trumbull could not replace such friends, of course; nor could the older boys he worked with. For these people were resigned to life in a way he knew he could never be. They followed the great Terminal Building clock as it wound down to tavern time six days a week, and their dreams were confined by the size of their scuttles.

On those occasions when Mr. Pulling himself came into the yard, Tom had observed their reactions, as they had, in turn, been spoken to or ignored. And it was clear to him that they had made either far too much effort, or far too little. Here was an impeccable man in fine suits, rumored to have been personally ordered in London, a man in the best Box calf boots, which Tom had noticed in the window of Livingstein's on Charles Street, at twenty dollars the pair; and, more importantly, here was their boss, the individual whose whim controlled their livelihoods—and what did they do? Most of them, his father included, behaved as though he were a sovereign. They shot him smiles. They stepped out of his way, backing off into railings or each other with the most deferential of steps. Did they not know how *un*-extraordinary this must have made them appear to him? How invisible? How dispensable? And the others, fewer, who plied him with long, flattering promises, who contorted their faces into expressions of the deepest concern as they inquired after his wife and young daughter; who repeatedly overestimated the amount of work they had processed: Could they not look around themselves at the twenty-odd acres of Pulling and Trumbull land, at the long sheds and wood-blocked wharves, the warehouses, lofts, offices, the stables, and the vast, enduring sugar plant? Did they believe that all of this would have existed had Richard Pulling lacked the guile to read the basic motives of simple men?

No. Tom was certain that he and they were ultimately different. He might do their work, and remain as poor as they forever. He might lack for schooling, as they had; his hands might callus; his hair might fall out; his body might go limp and fat with age; but, in the great interior sphere of his mind, he would always remain separate from them.

Still, there were useful items he could learn; and after a few weeks of solitary resentment, he decided to make the best of a bad bargain and try. Schippers, for one, could distinguish Cuban cane from Jamaican, and Jamaican from that of the Dutch Islands. He drank with at least a few sailors off every ship and could be easily persuaded to repeat their most exotic tales the next morning. Foster understood bananas and the hocus-pocus countries where they grew. Hurley followed storms. Keenan had worked on a railroad. Schaeffer, his favorite, had actually been a British admiral's valet in his youth and, before going into disgrace, claimed to have met Wellington at Portsmouth. And all, of course, were expert on the subject of women; although it was with Cheswit, the plant sweep and a boy of thirteen too, that he felt most comfortable discussing that sex.

Tom noticed that Adam spoke very little on the job. His father cursed as much as the next man, uninhibited by his son's proximity, and he laughed as long as any at the relentless bawdy jokes, but he had little original material to contribute. This fact became clearer to Tom during the first week of November, when Gus Keenan died of a heart attack and, short of men, Ol' Phitts assigned Tom to unload with the others. He worked in his father's crew all of a month and yet, had he been a simple itinerant instead of the man's own sprig, he knew he would have gone away with no memory of Adam Chance.

It was just after this time that Tom got himself into trouble. He and Cheswit had begun to spend an idle evening hour together each day, walking home along the blocks of shanty houses and talking of girls, keeping their eyes out, provoking the slatterns who infrequently ascended the hill from the harbor and loitered in the dim rippling pools of gas lamps. It was a winter-cold night and they were bundled against it in woolens that bore the faintest smell of an old mildew. They could see their breaths before them.

"Chet," Tom said, "I need a favor."

"Anything," came the reply. "What shall it be, Tom?"

"Can you cover my place for me?"

"When?" Cheswit asked reflectively.

"Tomorrow noon?"

"I don't know," Cheswit answered. "If Phitts don't know to begin with, there could be trouble. What's your duty, do you know?"

"I think there's an ice boat to be in. The *Olinda*. Some name, something like that."

"I don't know," Cheswit repeated. "If Ol' Phitts were to take his usual place up on the poop and see me or look around for you, there'd be trouble all right. Why's it so important to you, Tom?"

"Mary Wardman's comin' to see me, bringin' us a picnic. The school's closed down this week."

"Oh," sighed Cheswit. "You told me about her, plenty enough."

"Please," begged Tom.

"What's in it for me?" Cheswit inquired.

Tom thought long. "I'll have to owe you one," he said.

Cheswit sent a cloud of laughter into the frosty air. "Two," he said. "You'll have to owe me two. It's a big favor."

"Shake hands on it," Tom said.

The next morning, the air was even more bitter and the wind was up in a fierce squall as the *Olinda* put in to dock. The sun had risen behind thick clouds that raced, layer over layer, across the low, black sky and, only for a moment, could the ghostly winter moon be seen. The tall waves lashed at the hull, thrust it away from the seawall, and their sharp salt spray covered the men in their canvas gear. A piercing, needle-like sleet came down and stung them on their hands and faces, wherever their flesh was exposed. In the distance, among the conflicting horns, whistles, and shouts of the harbor, they could hear the captain's final command that the last mizzenmast sail be furled.

Tom's eyes shot to the sky every minute or so, hoping desperately that it would be miraculously cleared by the time of his appointment with Mary Wardman. He loved her so, at least at this moment, and wanted more than anything to kiss her. He had not seen her from the time he had gone to work, four months previously, until by accident he had found himself next to her at Mr. Keidel's butcher shop, Tom with his mother's meager order of sausages and stewing meats, Mary with her mother's list of roasts and chops. And yet, he had an instinct that their encounter had been no accident at all, that Mary had lain in wait for him. Why else, he asked himself, would she have been there at seven o'clock in the evening, a time when Mr. Keidel meant to accommodate working people, not schoolgirls? Mr. Wardman was a bookkeeper by trade, and his wife was careful, in their social connections, to avoid those who worked with their hands; so perhaps Mary had been able to think of no equally innocuous place. The Chances were Methodists, the Wardmans, Catholics. Thus they never met on Sunday, and Sunday was his only day away from Pulling and Trumbull. The more he thought, the more likely it seemed that Mary was pursuing him, and cleverly too, and, if that were true, he thought, there was a good chance she might kiss him.

So the weather threatened more than his health, and his mind was never off it. The *Olinda* had come down from Newfoundland via the coastal waters of the Atlantic and up to Baltimore along the Chesapeake ships' channel, carrying ice in its hold, great slabs powdered with sawdust, for delivery to the dark storerooms of the mid-Atlantic icehouses and storage there before the warm months. This was the ice, glacial and opaque, which would cool down a hundred thousand boxes in as many kitchens; the ice that Cooper, the Negro ice man, would bring around in March and which would soon enough thaw down to water in a base pan. Tom, for whom there were no tongs available, worked at the pit of the hold, grabbing each block between his gloves and handing it up the hatch to Schippers or Hurley.

"A damned bluster, ain't it?" Schippers said. They had been working two hours at this time.

"You're right," said Adam, who came and went, loading

the ice into a green canvas-back wagon, so that, to Tom, his voice rose and faded mysteriously.

"Any sign of a let-up?" Tom asked.

"Thunder in winter's a fuckin' strange thing," Hurley said. "Give her an hour to run her course."

"That's your expert opinion?" Tom said. "What time is it, anyway?"

"Mine. Yes," Hurley said. "It's nine thirty by what I heard last."

"Where's Ol' Phitts in all this?" Tom asked.

"Under cover. Naturally," Schippers said.

"Naturally," Tom said. Then he heaved a great exulted sigh and went about his work.

At eleven forty-five, more than an hour later than Hurley had promised, the storm had fully passed and the distant December sun once again bathed the harbor in its clean, frigid light. The outside men shed their raincoats and stretched. Lunch was near at hand, and the taste of it hung on their lips. Going last, Tom climbed the long ladder up from the hold and, once on the high deck, spotted Cheswit by the plant door.

"All that's left are a few of the heavy cakes," Tom said when they met. "You'll have to tie them fast and send them up with rope."

"What time will you be back?"

"One thirty the latest."

"Do the men know?"

"Tell them Pulling got hold of me, sent me on an errand. Somethin' awful."

"That's dangerous, Tom."

"They'll never question him," Tom said. "It's safe as safe can be."

He met Mary one block from the gate, according to their plan. She was standing against the fence, dressed in an extremely nobby green coat and wool leggings. Her cheeks, framed by coal-black hair, had been flushed by the cold to a bright pink. She had a box in her hand.

"Hello," she said.

"Hello," Tom replied.

"It's cold, isn't it? Where do you want to go?"

"I think it's nice," Tom said. "You should have seen how fierce it was all morning. I know, let's go to the old spring house."

"Where's that?"

"Up the hill," Tom said. "It's vacant now. I don't know why. I should've thought you'd been there."

"No," Mary said.

They climbed the hill at its most gentle spot and entered the tiny stone-and-wooden building. Then Mary unpacked a piece of chicken, some milk, and a large piece of chocolate-frosted cake for each of them. They arranged it between them and ate in uncertain quiet.

"Peter Parton failed the arithmetic examination," Mary said after a while.

"Really," Tom said.

"Do you like your job?"

"It's all right, for a job."

Mary paused as she bit off a piece of white meat from her chicken breast. "I wish you were still at school," she blurted out at last.

Tom saw her eyes start to fill. "I haven't stopped learning," he said.

Mary willed herself into a smile. "Oh," she said enthusiastically. "What have you learned?"

"Lots of things," Tom exaggerated. "More than I ever did in school. And a lot about life." He looked at Mary strangely.

"About life?" she asked incredulously.

"Has Peter Parton ever kissed you?" Tom heard the words as they came from his mouth, but could not believe they were his.

"That's a terrible question," Mary said.

"I'm sorry."

"Well, anyway, he hasn't. I think it's a vulgar thing to say."

"I said I was sorry."

"Still, I like Peter Parton. As a friend," Mary said.

"Do you like me *as a friend*?"

"I think so."

"You wouldn't if you knew what I was thinking," Tom told her slyly. He was beginning to feel impatient with her childishness.

"Well, I don't want to know," Mary said, annoyed.

He looked at her. Her face, at least to his eye, was the one the illustrators had used as their model when they made their woodcuts of Snow White, or Cinderella, to put beside the dull gray text in books of fairytales. Her complexion was true and young; and, bordered by lovelocks, capped by her smart, brimmed hat, he could see that it belonged to a child still, that however urgently those large, wet, black, shining eyes might beg to be kissed, they had not yet really looked on life. And at the same moment he realized this, he decided to change his approach. "Oh, Mary," he began then in a voice calculated to rise to, but not over the verge of tears. "It's just been so bad for me, being made to work here, leave the school and all my friends. I don't know what ever I'll do. I work the longest hours, as long as any grown-up and, except for Cheswit, I don't see anyone my age. My mother's flat-out tired when I get home and now, in the winter, it's dark and I'm not allowed from my house."

Mary's compassion impelled her to the bait. "Do you know what I wish?" Tom spoke on. "It's crazy. I know it. But I wish, sometimes, that we were older, you know, and maybe married and livin' in a nice house somewhere . . ."

Mary smiled at him now.

"But who'd want to marry me?" he went on. "That's years away. And I'll tell you somethin'. I'd rather be lonely all through my life than marry a girl and not be able to provide her with a good livin', in a good part of the city and all that."

Mary put her hands in his thick russet hair. "Don't think

such awful things about yourself," she said.

He snuggled against her. "I can't help it," he said. Mary's fingers touched the back of his neck then and, as if in reaction, he looked up at her slowly and their lips brushed. Mary shivered. Tom moved his tongue across her closed, pursed mouth. He was plainly frightened. Then, with a slow deliberateness, Mary closed her eyes and her mouth opened to him.

There was no heat in the spring house and Tom was eager to feel Mary's body against him, but their coats made too thick a pile between them. He remembered the bulge of her breasts against her school dress and, the more he kissed her, the more he wanted to see and to feel them now, yet every time he moved his hands lower than her neck, she twisted herself and forced them higher again.

"I love you," he plied her.

"And I you," Mary said. Tom smiled, reached softly down and unbuttoned her coat then. "What are you doing?" she asked.

"It's getting hot," he said.

"Maybe we should go, Tom." Her hands rested lightly on his shoulders. And then, with her coat opened and back, he saw the hill of her breasts and began to kiss her once more. This time his hands could not be stopped and, pinioning Mary with his weight, he rubbed them across the wool, down her sides, and back over her breasts, in gentle, circular movements. He was panting a little now and, when what conscience he had in the matter surfaced, he stopped for a second. He did not know how or where the dress was clasped.

"Oh, Tom," Mary begged then, in a sad and defeated whisper. "Why?"

Tom summoned the ghost of sadness back to his eyes. "Please," was all he said.

"Please what?" Mary asked.

"Please let me touch you," Tom stated baldly. "I love you so much. And you're the only one I have—"

"Stop it," Mary screamed in interruption. "Stop it, or I'll call out, Tom. I will. I think you're vile. And you're a bad actor, too."

"You've got a lot to learn," Tom told her meanly.

"And disgusting!"

"You'll have a lot worse than this coming to you," Tom said, "whether you want it or not." He was on his feet now and so was Mary.

"I'll tell you this," she said, anxiously connecting the buttons and holes on her coat. "I'm sorry I ever came here with you. And I feel terrible now, just terrible, if that makes you happy, Thomas Chance. But, I'm going to go to the priest and confess what I did and, then, I don't want ever, ever to see you again."

"Words spoken in anger," Tom repeated abstractedly, a phrase remembered from somewhere. "Oh, you will, Mary," he said then. "You'll want to see me again."

But when Tom returned to the wharf, despite his quick-stepped air of triumph at having stolen so much satisfaction, he was no longer in a position to smirk. Ol' Phitts met him on the gangway to the *Olinda*. "Chance, my boy," Ol' Phitts exclaimed, playing to the crowd on the deck, "have you a pocket watch handy?"

"No, sir," Tom replied.

"Gentlemen carry them," Ol' Phitts said, but his mood had turned nasty. "A block of ice fell on Cheswit's leg," he shouted.

"Oh, no!" Tom said.

"It should have been your leg," Ol' Phitts said. "Broke it, I think. We took him to old Doc Isadore."

"Oh, God," Tom said.

"Where were you?"

Tom studied Phitts. "I had an appointment."

"With a little girl friend, wasn't it? Pulling himself was here to see after Cheswit's leg."

"Yes, sir," Tom said in a low voice, which was nonetheless distinctly heard.

"So your cock's leading you already, is it. Even at your tender age. You're a hot-blooded little bastard, I'll bet. Pretty face and all. Come over here."

Tom followed him onto the deck.

"Adam," Ol' Phitts said. "Have I your permission?"

"Why, 'deed you do," Adam answered from some indistinct place in the group. "However you see fit."

"Give me a good piece a ice," Phitts demanded. "Boy, undo your coat! Unstrap your belt!"

The wind brought the temperature well below freezing as it hit one's body in this open place, but Tom saw no immediate choice but to do as he was told. He let his coat fly open and snap about him like a flag and then, with no regard for the others, he loosened his blue webbed belt to the point where he had to spread his feet if his thighs were to keep his pants from dropping.

"Give me that ice," Phitts said again; the man next to him chipped off a wedge of it and put it into his glove.

Phitts unhooked the final button on Tom's trousers then and they fell onto the moist deckboard, absorbing the thin coat of sea spray and ice-dripping that covered it. The men had begun to shriek with laughter at Tom's embarrassment, and Schippers' wail rose over the chorus to Tom's ears. Phitts tugged out the waistband of Tom's leggings and dropped the ice wedge into his crotch. "Let that cool you down," he said. "Now pull up your trousers, boy. And a week without pay if you'll keep this job."

Tom said nothing.

"Into the hold with you then. There's ice to be moved."

The men laughed, but their noise soon subsided as they broke away and returned to their jobs. Schippers was first down the hold. Adam followed him. Tom stood nearest the bow of any man and, with Hurley gone aft, third nearest to the gangway. The ice was numbing him now and he took long breaths of the thin air and released them slowly in order to suppress his spasms. Everyone watched him: the Pulling and Trumbull crew and the Canadian men who sailed the vessel. So he carefully turned himself forward and carefully slipped. For a second, he lay flat on the boards on his stomach. There were new, if diminished howls. Then he was up, again on his feet. He moved toward the gangway. George Phitts said: "Get on with it now."

But Tom cut him off. "Sir," he said.

"Are you speaking to me?" Phitts said. His teeth, as he snarled, looked yellow, and their roots were diseased.

"Here it is, sir," Tom mocked and, in one movement, flung the ice wedge powerfully at Ol' Phitts' middle and himself over the ship's railing, onto the gangway.

"Bastard," Phitts thundered down at him, when his breath returned. "You'll never work in this harbor again. Not as long as I've a breath." But Tom was running too fast to hear him.

"We'll get a horse and catch him," one of the crew hollered.

"He's a bastard," Phitts roared. "He'll catch himself soon enough."

Tom was quickly out of sight of the *Olinda,* but he had run nearly two miles before he collapsed and found himself at the junction of Charles and Pratt Streets, next to a baying coach mare. His body was smothered in sweat and he lay hard against the iced-over paving blocks, no farther than six inches from the mare's hoof. He was more completely hot than he had ever been in summer as his heart pumped blood to the surface of his face, flushed his cheeks, and brought a vein out on his temple. The mare was rearing out of control and, from the ground, Tom looked up at it, so close now that he could smell the horse. But before he could move, he felt a pair of fists bore into his armpits from behind, then felt himself being dragged back over the uneven roadbed into safety, protected from serious bruising only by the thick cushion of his coat. He looked up.

A heavy-faced Negro woman stared back at him and withdrew her arms.

"Boy, boy," she said then, in a throaty voice used to authority. "Is you all right? You ain't been drinkin' liquor?" the woman asked.

Tom shook his head.

"Let me smell you." She bent down, with no little difficulty, for she was a buxom woman.

"See." Tom struggled up now.

"Then what in Hades was you doin' to land you'self in that position?"

"I wanted to see how far I could run," Tom gasped.

The woman smiled, paused, picked up a large sackcloth bag that rested next to her on the pavement, then had another thought. "Your school closed with the holiday?" she asked.

"Um, huh."

"You goes to school, I hope."

Tom swallowed. "Naturally."

"Well, good-bye," she said, taking a first step away. "You watch out for the horses."

"Oh, I will." Tom beamed, but a crowd of merchants and shoppers and families, arm in arm and laughing, was coming up between them; and the sound of bells and trotting pairs and the high, magical notes of the carolers speedily drowned out his voice as it separated them, each into a different city.

Tom walked aimlessly along Charles and then west on Baltimore Street. In the glass windows of the shops, reflected before the green and red of holly wreaths, he recognized his own face; the want and desire inside him shone out from his eyes and betrayed him. With the mitts of his two gloves, he wiped his hair out of the bangs into which it had fallen and dried a stray tear.

Bestowing upon them only a thin slice of his otherwise preoccupied attention, and all the time moving, Tom glanced at the biscuits and Bordeaux wines displayed by J. McGowan and Sons, wholesale grocers and spirit merchants; at the mahogany grand pianos and rosewood upright pianos in the window of Knabe and Gahle; at the gleaming stoves that stretched back along the floor inside Mills and Brother, endless and somehow unreal, as if they were really an illusion, multiplied by mirrors. He walked. And minute by minute, as the afternoon wound down, the chill in the air increased and grew sharp and bit him. He might have been invisible for all the attention he attracted, yet, half perversely, he enjoyed his melancholy isolation. On a corner, a trio of plump, cheeky Irish women sang "Adeste Fidelis," complete with descant, against the commotion surrounding them; and, coming to an involuntary halt as he passed, Tom, too, began to shape his lips and tongue into the English substitutes for those exhilarating words. Low down and next to him, a vendor's fire was roasting, shooting great billows of comforting heat against his side, perfuming the entire block with aromatic chestnut. Then, when the hymn was complete, there was only an instant of silence before, on the wind, the rapturous chant of a black man could be heard:

My oysters are fresh,
  An' jist from de shell;
I can't tell de reason
  My oysters won't sell.

Tom looked around curiously, at an old and almost purple man with Indian features. He was yards away, but pushing his cart toward them, with almost witless happiness on his face, in his whistle, in his song. "Jist a-comin roun' onct moah to ecommerdate de ladies and genthem wid de elegint nice oysters," he sang, signing the air with Christmas. But, having no taste for oysters and only forty-one cents to his name, Tom merely turned and continued on.

Something about the black man haunted him—a line of resignation in his face—but Tom was absorbed in his own problems, and had no place inside him for anything reasoned. Only his feelings pressed in on him as he made his way automatically toward Monument Square.

The lanterns there had not yet been lit, but in an upstairs window of one of the finest Federal houses, three candles burned and, behind them, because the curtains remained undrawn, he could see a great, room-high evergreen, hung with reflecting objects. He craned his neck. Near him, on the common across from the great, tubular statue to Washington, a small group of Know-Nothings was gathered, huddled in the chill air while a speaker addressed them. The speaker's voice carried the wharf accent of Tom's father, of Ol' Phitts and Schippers; the pitiful men who cheered him used the rough bully-calls of those men, looked poor and frightened like those men. The Know-Nothings were a kind of political party, organized into secret cells. They were immigrant-hating, and especially virulent in Baltimore, through whose port hordes of Germans and Irish made a threatening passage into the American job market. Tom, who barely knew the words Whig and Democrat, and could not have listed one point of difference between them, well understood what the Know-Nothings wanted; for, without admitting his membership, Adam Chance had made it clear that he, a man who worked with his hands, was profoundly in sympathy with them, that he had no use for micks, kikes, krauts, chinks, or wops, and that, to his mind, by virtue of his Anglo-Saxon name, he—and Tom, if he wanted it—held something resembling a proprietary interest in America.

Tom walked silently, burying his head in his collar, and keeping as far from the group as he could. He did not want even one of the hundred or so men to recognize him. He walked, in fact, all the way to the front gate of Belvedere, the seat of John Eager Howard, which was the most beautiful and imposing residence in all the city, and the one that, in dreams, he ached to possess. At the gate, he hesitated for a minute. Then, for the first time, he began to walk down the arched dirt roadway, beneath the hollyhocks, giving no thought to what he would do if he were stopped. He reached the house quickly and passed immediately around it to its other side. There, at the border of lawn and drive, half a dozen plaster figures were arranged and, tired now, he leaned against one and gazed out at the city from the eminence of this place. The reverse view he knew: the huge house on the hill; the house that belonged to strangers with a familiar name. But this was different, and the atmosphere intoxicated him, although he could not quite make himself believe that the house was really lived in.

Winter had brought Belvedere's world indoors and, by so doing, kept Tom from being spotted. But, after a quarter hour, a gentleman wearing a top hat and carrying a walking stick appeared from the stables and called out to him. Tom was well-enough read in the popular literature of the day to sense an element of opportunity in this call. Poor boys, in the stories of Charles Dickens, were forever encountering rich men who changed their fortunes; and this man's tone was inquisitive, but polite. Tom wanted to answer. More than anything now, he yearned to know this man, to charm him, win him, and, though the instinct was so deeply buried that only its symptoms could be felt, to be his son. He stood utterly still, mute, as his blood seemed to cease flowing.

The look he gave the gentleman lasted no more than a second; and then he was off, propelled into a run by some animal reflex that his mind could neither understand nor discipline. He hit dirt midway on the big slope, and tumbled from there until the land leveled again, a few yards from the street. Then, like a fight-worn dog, he gave his limbs a quick check and recovered himself. Not for the last time, he felt that gnawing sickness that the past could not be repeated.

Pasted to the brick side wall of Lazenby and Sons, the remains of two bills advertised Whorum's Medicine and the Whig candidacy of General Winfield Scott for President of the United States in the national election of a year before. Tom read them without interest, then turned the corner and set his eyes on the window display. It was magnificent. In the center, a cape was draped over a table, with a discreet hand-lettered explanation next to it. The explanation read: "Exact Copy of a Parisian Cape. Made of fancy silk and trimmed with black lace and satin ribbon." Tom wondered how much it cost, but there was no mention of price on the sign. Dark was fast coming down onto Charles Street and, more every hour, his thoughts were of home, the dreaded rendezvous with his father, his mother's tears. He could not postpone his decision very much longer and, increasingly, he felt he had little choice but to return to his home and suffer what he would. He had no money, no friend who would take him in or give him food. And he could not desert the only love he knew in the world, no matter what man shared her house. The more he thought, the more essential the cape became to him. He knew that his mother loved the fine things life had denied her and, suddenly, he remembered an old silk dress, also with lace at its neckline, that Katharine stored in the back of her closet, a remnant of something happy in her youth—he didn't know what. If only, somehow, he could afford the cape, he could give her a true Christmas this year, make up for the anguish he had caused her. "Next year," his mother had soothed him, each Christmas, for as long as he could remember. He would try to conceal the disappointment in his eyes as the wrapping came off a homemade pair of knitted gloves, or socks. And his mother, sadder as she saw him growing out of his childhood, would simply say, "Next year," holding back her tears. But the cape would put an end to all that. Store bought and fine, it would bring them into a new world—at least for a transient moment on Christmas morning—even if he had to steal it.

CHAPTER 10

TOM PRESSED HIS NOSE AGAINST THE GLASS DOOR AND, WITH the glare eliminated, peered inside. The front room of the store was empty. Lazenby's sold clothing for both ladies and gentlemen, with the men's clothes at the rear. Tom deduced, correctly, that this was a purposeful arrangement—that a man, on his way to his tailor, might be inclined to buy his wife a present. As men had the money, Tom reasoned, this was probably more likely than would be the other way around. Then, in a burst of nerve, he tripped the latch and pushed the door ever so slowly into the store. To his relief it did not creak even once and, rather furtively, he descended the four broad steps into the showroom.

A three-sided and full-length folding mirror stood directly in front of him and he checked his appearance in it, especially his face. His own clothes had clearly not come from Lazenby's; he was painfully aware of that. But he tried to arrange his smile into an expression that said he was a Lazenby type: a certain cocky curl of the lip, an all-but-imperceptible squint on one side that he had observed in Mr. Pulling and in men like him, anonymous men who had passed him on the street without realizing that they were being studied. He copied them now, as best he could. Like the man at Belvedere, he put a little saunter into his walk and, as with everything else about him at the moment, it produced an effect of extreme exaggeration, correct in all details, but extreme and incredible. Then, content that he had concealed his true motive, he stepped lightly over the woolen carpet and floorboards and, once beside the cape, lifted it carefully in his hand. A tiny square of paper was pinned to the border and he raised this to read the small numbers. Five dollars! He gasped to himself. He could never hope to save five dollars. The murmurous sound of distant voices floated to him from the back, along with the quiet. He looked about the room, still unattended, and folded the soft silk into his hands. It would be his first theft —and his last, too, he told himself. He planned to move to the door as though bringing the garment to a salesperson and then, suddenly, when a second would see him into the street, to run. And, out of nowhere, he had an extraordinary thought. He was glad he was a Methodist and not a Catholic, like Peter Parton, for then he would have to go into a dark and confined booth and confess through a curtain that he had broken not only a law, but one of the biggest Commandments. He tucked the cape into his hand and made his way toward the door, step by step, through the still, floral-scented store . . . until, all at once, a voice boomed out at him: "May I *help* you?" a woman demanded sharply.

"Oh, ma'm."

"Or were you going to help yourself?"

"No, ma'm."

"Put it back. Just as it was."

"Ma'm, I promise, I was only going to ask how much it cost."

"Get out!"

"Please, ma'm." Some inertial force held Tom in his place. He turned and looked at the woman, about whose gaunt presence there was a faintly wilted air.

"Five dollars," she said, only a little appeased by the fact that he had chosen to confront her, rather than run. "Where would someone like you come upon five dollars?"

Chance tried his smile. "Oh, you're right about that," he

said, replacing the cape with elaborate care. "But I didn't know it would be that much."

"It's on the tag. I'm doing you a favor not calling the police, you understand. Now–"

"I might be able to pay a little each week. Or every other."

"I suppose you're going to tell me that you have a job."

"From my allowance."

"Oh, now. And how much would that be? Your payment, I mean."

Tom shrugged. "Excuse me, ma'm," he went on, bright-faced again. "Would you happen to know Mr. Thomas Pulling, the owner of Pulling and Trumbull?"

"*Of* him," the lady said. "I suppose most people around here do. Sugar man. Why?"

"I thought he bought in this shop."

"Once every hundred years. What are you getting at? How on earth would *you* know Mr. Pulling?"

"He's my–father." The word came without his meaning it to.

"*You* are Mr. Pulling's son?" She looked him up and down, approvingly at his face, but in disbelief that a gentleman would allow his son to go about in such condition.

"I didn't mean it the way it sounded. I didn't mean to say father. I meant to say godfather."

"Even so. What's your name?"

"Thomas Chance."

"Never heard of you. Never heard of any Chances. Five dollars. If it's not sold by Christmas, then you can pay me fifty cents a week and I'll hold it for you, ten weeks."

"I'll have to let you know."

Just then, a customer came into the front room from the rear; or rather, two customers did. A beautifully gowned woman of fifty or so led a young lady in her early twenties. The woman's eyes were blue and as vivid as Tom's, yet far softer; but the girl's were hazel. She had pale skin and would have been quite pretty had a certain spiritual flaccidity not already ascended to her surface. Tom imagined that she had been at her best as a child.

"Aurelia," the elder lady said.

"Coming," answered the woman who had been addressing Tom.

"We need your help. Who's this?"

"No one."

"Well, whatever you do," she said, "don't let him leave. We may need him."

Astounded, the saleslady whispered to Tom: "Wait for a minute."

"He's close to Brad's size. How old are you, son?" A note of graceful superiority in her voice.

"Thirteen."

"Mr. Pulling's godson, he says."

"Well, you're better-looking than he is," the woman laughed. "There's none of his blood in you, you can thank your stars. Name?"

"Thomas Chance," the saleslady said.

"Would you help me, Thomas?" the lady went on. "I *am* sorry. My name is Mrs. McAuliffe. This is my daughter, Clara. You see, we came, among other reasons, to find some breeches for my son, Bradford, who's about your size, and I do want to choose correctly . . ." She paused purposefully.

"You want me to try them on?" Tom finished her thought.

"If you don't mind."

"All right."

The saleslady led them back into the men's tailoring area. Tom took the breeches into a dressing room and, a minute later, emerged with them on. They fit him with near perfection and he could tell that the bulges of loose cloth at his hips were flattering. They gave him a new feeling, too, a comfortable sensation of almost military rank.

"Do you ride?" Mrs. McAuliffe asked.

"No," said Tom. "Not yet."

"For heaven's sake, don't procrastinate, with all the beautiful country around here. Get the basics down and you'll have a new freedom. In a few years, you'll want it, mark my words —to chase the girls." She laughed again then. "Won't he, Mrs. Lazenby?"

The saleslady sniffed. "Get up on the horse, please," she said, pointing to a leather mount in the middle of the floor.

"The horse?" Tom asked.

"I want to check the length of your bottoms when you're mounted." This from the tailor, who, Tom realized, was Mr. Lazenby himself.

"Any horseman knows that," Clara said, giggling to herself. "Mother, you're blind. This boy's no gentleman. Look at his clothes. If you give Brad those breeches, I swear I'll tell him that they were worn by a—"

"Close your mouth. Close it and apologize."

"Oh, Mother. Can't you see?"

The older woman stared her down. "I'm sorry," Clara said simply, then went out of the room.

"My daughter can be abrasive," Mrs. McAuliffe said then. "She hurts her own brother all the time. In even worse ways than she's just displayed. I apologize for her. Because she is pretty she has manufactured a very high opinion of herself."

"Temporary," assured Mr. Lazenby.

"I hope so and fear not."

"Please forget it," Tom said. "These are nice breeches. Your boy will like them."

"Good."

"Does he have a coat?" Tom asked.

"Do you have one to sell me?"

"Mrs. Lazenby does," Tom said. He had dismounted now and was standing by an open rack of riding jackets. "Look at this one. Why, any boy would love it." He removed it from its hanger and slipped it on.

"My husband would love you. He's with Garrett's. A banker. Always selling. How much is it?"

Tom glanced quickly at the gray square. "Seven dollars, fifty."

Mrs. McAuliffe gave him a penetrating look, then smiled

at Aurelia Lazenby. "All right. Sold," she said. "I hope it looks half as well on him."

"I'm sure it will look very nice on him," Mrs. Lazenby said, taking it from Tom with a certain astonishment.

"Well, thank you very much," Mrs. McAuliffe said then. "You've been very helpful, Thomas Chance. I'd like to buy you something if–"

Tom considered the choice. "No," he said, his eyes settled smartly on the shopkeepers. "I didn't truly do anything. But thank you, ma'm, just the same."

"Are you sure?"

"I'm sure."

"Then, in that case, I hope we meet again, young man."

"I hope so, too."

When she was gone, the Lazenbys, together smiled at Tom. "You're a mystery, aren't you? And you like it. I know you came here to steal. What do you want?" Mrs. Lazenby said.

"A job. You're both alone. It's Christmas. You need someone. I can sell. Anything. I know I can. Older people trust me. You saw that."

"There's more to this business than selling."

"When there's no one in the store, I could help you stock and clean up. Look. Ten cents a day. And the cape on Christmas Eve if I last."

"Too much."

"You'll make it back."

Mr. Lazenby looked at his wife. "You know," he said, "I have the awful feeling that we will. Eight o'clock in the morning. Can you start then?"

"Now, if you want me."

"What will your father–excuse me, godfather–say?" Mrs. Lazenby asked.

"You know better than that," Tom said.

Because of a dreary woman's futile quest for a ball gown that would reapportion her figure, they did not lock the door until twenty-five after six, nor leave before seven. Tom jumped a ride on the back of a wagon carrying firewood, and let himself off less than a minute's walk from his house. Without the sun, the air had gone bitter and Tom knew that a night in it would be enough to frostbite a man.

His mother and father sat opposite one another at the kitchen table, a plate of white beans and sausage before each of them. Steam rose, like a halo, from the food, and Adam shoveled while Katharine picked, in silence. When they heard Tom, they looked up, Adam for only a second, but Katharine until Tom spoke.

"I didn't want to worry you," Tom said softly.

"I understand, son," Katharine said. "There's dinner on the stove. I'm sure it's hot still. Let me get it for you." She had kicked her chair back and was beginning to stand now.

"I can do it," Tom said. "Don't get up. I got a job today."

Adam made a heaving sound. "Well, ain't that a piece of news," he said with his mouth full. "Fired and hired on the same day. Breaks a man's leg and another man puts him on. I can't understand the world anymore. No one mind me."

"Hold your tongue, Adam," Katharine said. "Where's the job, Tom?"

"Lazenby's." Blank faces received this information. "It's a shop," Tom continued. "A fine shop, too. On Charles Street. They sell clothes. Men's and women's, both, Mom. And they make things themselves and some of their things come from France . . ."

"And some of their things come from France," Adam mimicked him. "Now hear me out, boy, because today, what you did, you and I are goin' our separate ways from now on. Thirty-one years and nothing like this has ever happened to me until today, and do you think I can ever live it down?"

Tom studied his mother. "Father's told you, hasn't he?" he whispered.

Katharine nodded. "Have some beans and a pork sausage, Tom," she said.

". . . Cause if you got a job—be it a man's job or not

—I'll consider that I'm free of you. Thank God. And at last." He plugged his mouth with more of the starchy dinner.

Katharine said: "This is our house, all three of us, and we share it. The good and the bad. We have and we shall."

Silence descended for a moment. Tom sat down with a plateful of food and began to eat. Adam did not utter another word. As soon as he had finished and wiped up the last of the bean syrup with a heel of bread, he stood and went out into the living room. "Why don't you leave him?" Tom said. "With what you make on the washing and my job, we could live, Mom. I know we could."

His mother smiled at him gently. "I took a vow," she said.

"It doesn't mean anything."

"When we take vows," Katharine explained, "we do not do so with our lips only, Tom, but with our immortal souls. Perhaps you see more clearly than I, but this is something *I* believe, in my own heart. And whatever your feelings at this minute, I know, in that heart, that you would never have me endanger my soul."

"No, Mother," Tom said, tears coming forth even against his will, choking off his words.

"Tell me about the job," Katharine questioned him at last. "How much it pays you. How you got it. How in the world you got it in this season. Of all seasons."

"It's a long story," Tom began. "It just happened." Katharine leaned back, put her chapped hands under her chin for support and listened as Tom remembered, out loud but in a hushed and airy voice, the entire day that had passed, from its beginning in that very house that morning. He spoke for twenty minutes and she did not interrupt him, except to signal her continued attention with an occasional prod. Then, finished and searching for support in his mother's eyes, Tom got up from his chair and, on his way to deposit his dirty dish in the basin, impulsively touched and then hugged her. The support was there, clear too, Tom thought, but in a withdrawn and beaten way. Katharine loved him, sided with him, lived for his future. He knew that. And yet, more profoundly and apparently than ever, she seemed to want to avoid fanning the incident to a point of immolation. Her touch remained as tender as it had been in his childhood, but tonight it felt more cautious, more reticent. He considered the importance of a vow to someone of her age, who had been raised as she had in a home of doubt-forbidding Methodists, forever exposed, at the soul, to the clawful vengeance of an Old Testament God. He had never thought of it in quite this way before and, for the time being, and with a few perplexing edges, it made sense to him.

Together, they washed the dishes and returned the butter and other perishables to the ice chest on the porch. Then he followed her as she took six huge bundles of other people's laundry from a closet and began to separate them on the counter by the basin. She pumped a few gallons of water into a high steaming pot and Tom lifted this container onto the wood stove's burner and watched it until the first bubbles appeared. Then he poured it for her into her oval-shaped wooden tub and watched as she lathered and rung the whites, first, and then the colored fabrics. Dye from a blue shirt bled rapidly into the water and, while he heated more, Tom had a sudden impulse to tell his mother about the cape. On the one hand, he did not want to spoil her surprise, but, on the other—or so he told himself—she would enjoy the anticipation almost as much as the cape itself. He was old enough to understand the truth of this and he wanted to let it sway him, but, in the end, couldn't.

When they went back into the parlor, Adam was asleep, a crumpled copy of the *Baltimore Bulletin* blanketing his shins and a glass by his side. Katharine led Tom upstairs and when he had washed and brushed his teeth, she came into his room and found him already under the sheets. "So short a prayer?" she asked.

"I say them in bed."

"God does not answer a lazy man's prayer."

Tom forced himself over the side of the mattress and kneeled before it. His knee touched the heel of his shoes. "Our Father," he began, "which art in heaven . . ."

And, when he opened his eyes, he saw that Katharine's head, too, had been bowed; and so, respectfully, he slipped back against his pillow. His mother tucked the sheet and wool against him at last and then, tentatively, sat down on the bed, lowering it noticeably with her weight. "Thy will be done," she repeated in a soft whisper. "This is your home, Tom. And I am your mother, who loves you." She kissed him on the forehead and held him for a moment then, before she went out of the pitch bedroom into the hall.

At two o'clock in the morning, Tom awoke with a nightmare and saw the phantasmic shadows on his ceiling. He was thirsty. He tossed back his covers and walked along the chilly floor, then down the narrow steps that led directly into the parlor; and then he heard something. He looked up. Adam lay across the divan, snoring, croaking really. Tom had seen his father drunk a hundred times, but there was something strange now and, in a single, disturbing second, he realized that Adam was fitted out in his flannel pajamas, had a quilt over him, a pillow under his neck. His father ready for sleep, but not in his mother's bed! He knew instinctively what it meant; felt, in his suddenly hollow stomach, the permanence of the rupture.

As the gaiety around them swelled with the approach of the holidays, the lives of the Chances sank into a routine of despair. Adam came home some nights and remained out others. When he was present, they ate together. Silently. He paid the few bills. Katharine slept alone. She withdrew. She did her washing as conscientiously as ever and contributed the money to the household. But she was breaking inside. With Tom, at times, it was as if nothing had happened. She continued to protect him, defend him, encourage and fear for him. But she was like a woman for whom no independent future existed and, in consequence, defeat crept into her walk, her speech, and her manner.

His job became the source of all Tom's joy—and not for the profit—the dime a day or the cape—but for the things he was learning. Mrs. McAuliffe proved only the first of a legion of ladies and gentlemen who came into Lazenby's in the weeks before Christmas. Mr. Charles Fenwick came, too, and bought a coat for his wife. Mr. Brown, of the banking family; two Symingtons; a cousin of Mr. Pulling's; Mrs. Hopkins; Mr. Pratt; both the elder and youngest Garrett women; the Islings; the Rhinesnouts; Mr. Geoffrey Pershing, which was a particular event, as he was a celebrated recluse; Mrs. Walters; Mrs. Jacobs; Mrs. MacMillan; Jerome Bonaparte; and even Mrs. John Eager Howard, of Belvedere; all came, all spoke to and smiled at him, bestowing, in Tom's eyes at least, a kind of preliminary approval. And he drank in everything about them.

Their accents, for example. They were different from his and, after a short time, his own harsh voice began to make him uncomfortable. Whenever he could, he would imitate them. He soon noticed that Lazenby customers owned not one but two accents—that is, that about half owned one and the other half another. The wives of newly successful merchants, and some of the merchants themselves, spoke an extraordinarily stilted dialect, aping the English as best they could, but dropping sharp Baltimore vowels where they didn't belong. The consorts of older families, however, used a more relaxed speech. They clipped the final *g* from words like "riding"; and, perhaps most obviously, they kept their lips quite close and their teeth nearly clenched as they spoke. So did their husbands—and while, in them, it seemed effortless, Tom discovered that it was indeed a tough thing to copy. In his choice of accent, he had used a very simple device. He observed that, when they happened into the store at the same time, those with mercantile connections were often overtly solicitous of the aristocratic planters, while, in return, the planters—gentleman farmers, Mrs. Lazenby called them—were merely polite. He had asked Mr. Lazenby if this meant what he thought it did; and, once over his shock, Mr. Lazenby had told him that he was "very likely too clever for your own good." He had demurred then, but, thereafter, decided to concentrate upon the accent of the superior group.

He had been born to be looked at and, so, to model. And he was a quick success. Mr. Lazenby was amazed. Mrs. Lazenby put at least a part of it down to sorcery. But, in fact, there was very little about his manner that was practiced. He simply managed to make everyone who saw him aware of his extreme physical beauty; and, through no technique of his own, this attractiveness of person transferred itself to the merchandise. Women idealized him as their son. Men looked at his clean, open, even features and saw an even purer boyishness than they had once possessed. His contemporaries, for whom things and people were still, by and large, what they appeared to be, sensed that his approval, even friendship, were to be sought. Only a few people, such as Clara McAuliffe, continued to disparage him.

Every article he put on his back—every jacket, topcoat, and shirting, every pair of trousers—seemed at once to double its appeal to the Lazenby clientele, with the remarkable result that, by Christmas Eve, the store's entire inventory of clothing in or near his size was gone. And, what was more: Of the thirteen orders for bespoke habits, fully seven had been sold by him. With astonishment, the Lazenbys had watched his performance and, now, without regret, they folded the fancy silk cape into one of their finest gift boxes, wrapped it in white brocade paper, secured it with ribbons and bows, and presented it to Tom, along with a smaller box of homemade plum pudding and a dollar gold piece. "You're quite a young man," Mr. Lazenby said.

"Thank you, sir."

"The wife and I hope you will continue on. Christmas or not, we can always use a boy around here."

"Thank you, sir."

"You still have a lot to learn, mind you. You haven't really learned the business yet. You know that, don't you?"

"Yes, sir."

"But you've done well. So-o-o, Merry Christmas," Mr. Lazenby said, scooping up the words and, simultaneously, the reins of his carriage.

"And to you, Mr. and Mrs. Lazenby," Tom replied. Then he began the walk home, through the exhilarating hush of the suddenly religious city. He carried the box tightly against his rib cage. A carillon chimed out "O Tannenbaum" and the melody filled the dark. Jesus, it seemed to Tom, walked through the streets as couples holding hands; and he walked alone, watching Him . . . dreaming of that time in his own future.

CHAPTER

11

THE PARLOR AND KITCHEN OF HIS HOUSE WERE EMPTY WHEN he came in. Only one lantern was going. From the table beside the divan, it bathed the room with an eerie gray light, the shade and texture of shadows. He called out. "Mother," he said, in a conversational voice at first and then, more frantically, a second time: "Mother. Mother! *Mother.*"

He dropped his box and ran through both of the rooms on that floor and then bounded up the short stairs. "*Mother. Mother. Mom,*" he cried. And then, in the narrow second-floor passage, he heard something: a moan, a definitely human sound. He thrust open the door to Katharine's bedroom and found her lying on the bed, her face white, her hair astray, the muscles in her eyelids limp. "Mother," he exclaimed, kneeling down beside her, placing one hand against her forehead and the other in hers.

"Tom," she said. There was no moisture in her voice.

"What happened?"

"An hour after you left," she answered.

"You have a fever. I'd better go and fetch Doc Isadore."

"Put some water on the cloth," Katharine requested, pointing to the old soapstone basin beside her bed. It was full of stale liquid, a mixture of well water and perspiration, and there was a damp towel on its edge. "Put some more water on the towel, *freshen it* before you go."

"Did it happen suddenly?" Tom asked, as he poured from her porcelain pitcher.

"I don't know," she gasped. "Just came. Fell. Been building up to it, Tom," she had to pause, "a long time now."

"I'll fetch Doc Isadore," Tom said, kissing her lightly, but rushing toward the outside. When he was just about to turn the corner into the corridor, she called out again.

"Tom," Katharine moaned weakly.

"Yes, Mother."

"Are you all right?"

"Yes," he forced himself to say. "I'm fine."

Tom ranged frantically through the back alleys of South Baltimore, but Dr. Isadore was not to be found. His house was as dark as Tom's own and a lone maid, already sipping a holiday rum, answered the back bell and explained that the entire Isadore clan had gathered in Richmond for the holidays and was not expected to return until the second of January. She gave Tom the name of another doctor, called Richardson, but he was miles away—and at church when Tom reached his house. Tom decided not to wait. He was too frantic now. He thought of the hospital and asked for directions. Then he ran. But the situation there, in the swollen wards, was more problematic still. It seemed a fire had broken out somewhere south of the city and the injured and smoke-sick were being carted in at a phenomenal rate, inundating even the huge Greco-Roman facility of the Medical College which, because it was Christmas Eve, had only two doctors on duty. He moved hurriedly through the deep, vaulted rooms and finally tagged a young man in a bleached green gown. The man spun around. "Excuse me, sir," Tom began hysterically. "My mother's gravely sick. Could you come help her? Please, sir. Please. Please! I'm afraid she's going to die."

"Half the people here are going to die," the man responded coldly, "unless someone tends to them quickly." He was rushed, already in motion again. "Anyway, I'm only an orderly. I'm not a doctor. That's one of the doctors over there."

Tom saw the doctor and headed for him. The answer was

the same. Burned people, scarred people, people consumed with ashes and dirt and with their lungs scorched by the white heat of smoke; people crying out in the fierce rhythm of their pain; Tom looked about him and knew that no doctor would ever desert this ward to follow a small boy to his sick mother. "Bring her here," the doctor said, "and I will try and see her as soon as I can."

So Tom ran. From Greene Street to German. German to Light. Light along the water, turning with the basin. It was probably somewhere between dinnertime and church time, he thought to himself, for the streets were still vacant and the houses were lit. He had lost track of time. He ran down along the water until he reached O'Connor's Tavern. This was a squat building with a masonry base and a brown shingle top, about halfway up a rutted sand and gravel road from the wharves. He was out of breath, choking, when he got there, but he supported himself against the doorframe only a minute before going in.

The faces he dreaded were there, as he had known they would be: Ol' Phitts and Schippers and Hurley and Schaeffer. Ol' Phitts looked at him, said nothing, raised his glass, bit a huge hunk of foam from the head of the beer and spit it onto the ground. Everyone laughed. The laughter crescendoed. Hurley repeated the gesture.

Tom felt himself, for the first time, on the brink of stuttering. "Have you seen my father?" Tom said finally.

But there was no answer.

"Please," Tom said, begging. "It's important."

"He's not here," Schaeffer said.

"I swear to you. It's an emergency."

"What kind of emergency can it be? It's Christmas Eve." Schippers took a long swig, lay his head back as the liquid spiraled down his throat.

"Oh, Christ," Tom said. "Oh, please, God. Please. My mother's sick with fever."

"Is she now?" said Ol' Phitts. "Well, I'll tell you now, boy.

The great thing about being sick is that you usually get well." His tone changed suddenly. "Try Lilly's place if you want your father. All the way at the head of the road. Last place across." He laughed. Schaeffer regarded him sternly. "What the hell's the matter with you?" Ol' Phitts asked him. "There comes a time for everything in a man's life, don't there?"

Tom turned and ran out the door, pushing it so fast and suddenly that a wreath fell from its frosted panes onto the sawdust below. The narrow road went straight up after O'Connor's and he had to struggle to make it, for the cold air was thin. He had never before been inside O'Connor's, although he had known about it for years—and had an elementary idea of its reputation as a scene of brawls. Nor had he ever been this far up the road he was now on: a road bordered by decaying rooming houses of the most degraded sort, with their windows boarded, here and there, and the wind snarling through them. The wind, tunneled here, had overturned pails of old garbage, ripped strips of shutter loose, and sent rats scurrying into the street. The farther he went, the worse it became. A woman passed him. Her perfume flooded his nostrils. Then a sailor, in a foreign uniform, with another woman; the man was speaking a strange language, each word, almost each syllable, sounding to Tom as though he were attempting to clear his throat. The woman, holding the sailor at his elbow, seemed giddy. Tom continued on. The idea that he was headed for a brothel had now occurred to him, but he had only an indefinite idea of what a brothel was and something within him, an urge more powerful than curiosity, denied that it could be possible.

By the steps of the last house, a young slatternly woman, bundled in her lamb's-wool coat, stood, as if waiting for him.

"Pardon, miss," he said. "Is this Lilly's?"

"In a hurry, aren't you?" the woman said.

"Never mind. I think it is." Tom ascended the three

granite slabs and knocked at the door. The woman came up behind him.

"Are you going in?" Tom said.

"I was. Then I heard you running. I didn't know who you were. You're a young fellow, ain't you, too?" she added, as the door began to move back and the interior light poured out upon his face.

Tom recognized the man at the door, not by name; but he was clearly one of the "slickers" whose territory was the harbor, the wharves, and the neighborhoods that were tangent to them. The man was dressed up for a party, and behind him, a crowd of men and women giggled, moved about, sang to the music of a small pump organ. The young woman slid by Tom, past the man, without a nod, vanishing quickly into the group. Then the man looked at Tom. "Yes?" he demanded.

"I'm looking for my father."

"Who would that be?"

"Is this Lilly's?"

"It's cold out. Who's your father?"

"Adam Chance."

"Don't know him."

"They told me he was here. Please, sir, could you look?"

"Who told you he was here?"

"Mr. George Phitts. At O'Connor's Tavern. My mother's very sick. I'm afraid she's going to die."

"Wait here." The man closed the door in Tom's face, but it did not latch. Tom waited, shivering in the wind. A minute went by. Then another. Tom pressed against the door. Silently, it yielded on its hinge. As soon as there was a sufficient opening, he wedged himself through it, keeping himself near the wall, and closing the door again, against the chance of a draft. The hallway, curtained with coats that hung on pegs, was a sleazy, musty room, with which even the wallpaper seemed dissatisfied, for it was coming unglued at the upper molding. The rug was purple, the trim was varnished and dark, and even the background of the wallpaper, so profuse with pompoms, was purple.

Tom looked into the party room. Ten men. Twenty women. A few in nightgowns. Some thin. Most plump. A bare breast, with a man's hand on it. Everyone drinking, laughing, singing: singing "Deck the Halls with Boughs of Holly" and "Good King Wenceslaus." But his father was nowhere. He tightened his muscles, brought in his shoulders, made himself as small as he could, and, giving one more long and futile look for Adam, darted across the entryway, which was already full of shadows.

He moved with great stealth and lightness and could not be heard above the voices and music and laughter as he sped down the long, narrow, purple hallway and up the carpeted stairs. A line of tarnished brass light fixtures, jutting from the wall every six feet or so, mapped his way; and soon he was in a new corridor, much darker and more frightening. The air here was heavy with perfume and altogether quiet. And Tom moved slowly down it, past four open doors on each side, all of them leading to deserted, miniature bedrooms. He knew where he was. In his bones, he knew. Peter, a Catholic, had told him about the Dark Night of the Soul and while he had not understood it, or even tried to, the term had stayed in his mind. And now it surfaced again, for he was sure that this was it. He took step after silent step until he came to the first closed door. He listened, could hear breathing, murmurs. He leaned down, looked through the keyhole; but there were only strangers in the room—a man and a woman, both in street clothes, standing and hugging, as if about to say good-bye. He threw himself back against the wall, held himself flush against it for a minute; but the couple did not come out and his panic passed. He was almost at the corridor's end now, almost about to turn around, when he heard, through the last door, the heavy, unmistakable sighs of Adam Chance. He paused. He heard them again. A woman shivered audibly, dropping backward through the notes of an octave. "Oh, Lilly!" his father exclaimed. And, on that, Tom thrust at the handle, turned it, and flung the door open.

Adam looked around, a glacial expression on his face, a glacial cast to his eyes. "What the—"

"Mother's dying," Tom said.

Adam was still mounted on Lilly, with no sheet or blanket covering them. Lilly turned away. Adam shook in a spasm of anger. All his flesh trembled and behind it, Tom could see Lilly, pinioned, covering her breasts with one arm. She must have been fifty. Tom could see a spot of the black hair between her legs and a part of his own father's penis. It made him sick. "Mother's dying," he repeated.

"Is she?" Adam asked, shooting his hand through the air, intentionally sweeping a china bowl from the nightstand onto the floor, cracking it.

"I went for the doctor. I even went to the hospital, Father, but there's none available. There's a fire and . . ."

"How did you get in here?" Adam cried. The smell of liquor filled the air as he spoke.

"I've got to go," Tom said then, realizing, finally, that there was no help to be got from his father. But, when he turned, he saw that the doorman had come up behind him and was now blocking his way into the corridor.

"Sorry for all this, Mr. Chance," the doorman said. "He must've snuck up behind me."

"I'll say he must've," Adam roared.

"Shall I bounce him for you?"

"Not yet," Adam said. "He's my son. We have some business together."

The doorman looked confused.

"Go back to the door," Lilly told him. She had a deep, gravelly voice.

"Yes, ma'm."

Tom was trembling now.

"I guess you've seen enough," Adam said cruelly. "Have you?"

"Yes, sir."

"I won't forget this."

"No, but–"

"Quiet, boy! I can't expect you to understand what you've just done, but you'll pay for it nonetheless, I'll tell you."

"Mother is sick," Tom blurted nervously. "Please, one of you, please. If we don't get her to a doctor . . ."

Lilly studied Tom. Adam roared with laughter. "Mother is sick. Mother is sick," he mimicked, raging. "Let me tell you something, Tommy, ol' boy. You're old enough to come in here, up here, in a place like this, you're old enough to know, to understand. This here"–he turned Lilly's face; she shrieked, resisted him–"This Lilly you see me with, this fine woman has sustained me–and half of Baltimore, too, I expect–and it's this woman, just as you see her, that's your mother, Tom. Not Katharine. Lilly! Look at her! Look at her, Tom! You think we're disgusting? Well, maybe we is. Maybe so. But, like it or not, we're how you came into the world. This, right here, is where you got your start, Tom, right in this room. The two of us. Not Katharine. She just agreed to adopt you–informally, because, for obvious reasons, Lilly couldn't." He laughed again. "You're nothing but a lousy by-blow, Tom. For all of your aim, remember it!"

Tom looked at Adam, walked nearer. Lilly was crying. Her skin was wrinkled and powder had caked in its lines. Her hair had gray in it. He looked her up and down. Adam scowled at him. Tom stared at him, through him . . . all the way to hell. He put his right hand behind his back and made a fist. Then, rising onto the balls of his feet, he suddenly put his shoulder behind his punch and knocked Adam in the jowl. Adam fell over, onto his hairy back, like an upturned whale.

In a minute, Tom was out on the street again, running back for Katharine. His father's words had stunned him, but he had not yet absorbed them, not yet felt their reality in the pit of his stomach. He moved in a state of shock. And then, when he was almost home, thinking of how he would hold Katharine up on the long walk to the hospital, or of whose coach he might borrow, or steal, he saw the great arc of fire coming toward him. The fire moved on the wind, faster than the wind, over the distant hill. His house was between him and the fire, but nearer to the fire and, as rapidly as his legs carried him, the flames seemed quicker still. Every minute a great clap resounded through the neighborhood as something that had been torched exploded. And the scent of burning cedar was like a flood in the streets. Crowds were forming. Men drenched their houses with water. Women, bundles and children in hand, made their way toward the wharves. And Tom had increasing difficulty getting through. A policeman tried to stop him at one point, but Tom ran and the man had too much to do to pursue him.

Past the Partons', the Wardmans', all vacant now, Tom ran toward the glowing arc of flame. He was half a block away, out of breath, at once chilled and overheated, when he looked up and saw that it was no use. A whole wall of fire was falling now, erasing everything in its path. A dog scurried by him; two cats, with their backs singed. He pushed himself forward. At her window, weakly pressing her face against the glass, he could now see Katharine and, for a moment, hope swelled in him. But before he could reach the door, the flames fell from higher ground onto the roof, spiraled down and ignited the house, and in less than a minute, while he watched, it was gone.

The shock was complete, as if ice had suddenly been touched against the open endings of his nerves. For an instant, he thought of the cape. Black silk, lace, and satin: ashes now. For another, of Katharine; then Adam and Lilly; then Katharine again, fevered, helpless. He had failed her, but he was too weak now to assume that guilt. He had to be pulled back, dazed, by a stranger; and when he ultimately faced the fact that he had nowhere to go, no one to go to, he began, out of habit, to run.

His emotions tore at him and only the running, the strain of it, seemed to vent them. He ran along Warren Street to Fort Avenue, then three miles out that thoroughfare to Fort McHenry, where he fell asleep in the middle of a wide, frozen lawn until, some moments later, the chill awakened him.

Christmas morning. In a few hours, he thought suddenly, the young McAuliffe boy would rise and open his presents, those wonderful breeches which he, Tom, had sold to his mother. Most of the world would awake to such happiness, and yet he was so desperate, so incurably miserable.

He had to move to keep warm. He went to the edge of the parade grounds, and looked back from that point at the old brick fort, which had weathered British cannon in the War of 1812. All but the guards were asleep. Then he turned and looked out at the Chesapeake. It was black now, cold and immense and truly black, for the moon had already settled down behind the city, away from the water. The fire was far off and, from here, where the steeple-topped waves rushed turbulently to shore, only a faint horizontal glow betrayed its existence. A veil of winter stars was spread across the nighttime sky and Tom regarded it carefully. Although he was not, in the ordinary sense, religious, he cast his eye about until he found what appeared to him the brightest planet, the Christmas Star; and then, for a moment, moving his lips, he spoke directly to it, and made God a promise.

CHAPTER

12

The Reverend Hugh Alexander, pastor of the Wesley Methodist Church in South Baltimore, stepped back from the window of his parsonage into the light of the kerosene flame. Outside, high above a windblown veil of snow, great clouds raced before the moon. But, turning from them, he took the marbled covers of a book in both palms and looked down through his reading glasses at the small, crowded type. It was a thick book, an almost brand-new edition of a classic religious manual entitled *Holy Living and Dying*, whose author, Dr. Jeremy Taylor, had been chaplain to King Charles I. This new and revised text had been published recently in London—to much applause from an expanding community of professional Christians—and sent to Hugh by a Welsh cousin.

Hugh picked up where he had left off, on page forty-three, beginning a section on "Sobriety in the General Sense," and by the time he read two paragraphs farther, to "The Evil Consequences of Voluptuousness or Sensuality," he was fully entranced. He sat back in his high cracked leather chair, stretched his feet onto the small stool which his wife, Emily, had covered in a needlepoint of flowers, and drank in every word: "The nature of sensual pleasure is vain, empty, and unsatisfying, biggest always in expectation, and a mere vanity in the enjoying, and leaves a sting and thorn behind it." He liked these words and decided now that he would use them in a sermon. For they were soft and soothing words to him, and whatever his regrets, his sense of opportunities missed, these were words which made it all worthwhile, which erased his doubts and justified the life he had decided upon. Hugh was not a stupid man. He saw his own failings as well as those of others, with the same brutal clarity. More than once he had actually reviled himself for feeling jealous of his own sons' youth, or handsomeness; for housing, however involuntarily, an unmistakable lust in the presence of some young woman; for giving too many of the Lord's minutes to thoughts of worldly pleasure—thoughts no less sinful because they were only thoughts. And yet Dr. Taylor, by devaluing all Hugh feared he had missed, almost magically renewed his sense of purpose. Feeding him rhetoric, Dr. Taylor nonetheless satisfied Hugh's appetites, or rather, in some medicinal fashion, removed them. And Hugh read on: "Sensual pleasure is a great abuse to the spirit of a man, being a kind of fascination or witchcraft . . ." In mid-sentence, he looked up at his wife's bony chin, her too-translucent skin, and a terrible thought occurred to him.

"Where's the young Tom Chance?" he asked her suddenly.

"In the guest room. Where we put him. It's late. He's probably asleep."

"We're going to have to make some decisions, Mrs."

"I fear it, sir." Emily had knitting in her hand.

"Are we to keep him here? With us?"

"Those are your decisions, Mr. Alexander. It's either that, I take it, or the orphanage. There's no word of his father?"

"He—and that despicable woman—have gone. Only Satan knows where."

"He is a fine-looking boy," Emily said, "and clever enough. I think we could manage with him here. For a time anyway."

"As you wish."

"Why don't we wait and see?"

"I was thinking of our daughter, Frances," Hugh said.

Emily raised her eyes, hesitated for a moment. When she

was sure she had caught his meaning she said: "I hadn't thought of that, but they *are* young. Thirteen. Both of them. They were side-by-side in school ever since we came here from South Carolina—and that's been two years already—until . . ."

"It is better to conjecture such things in advance. I tell you, I see some red in those shimmering eyes of his."

"In all of us," Emily said.

"I pray not."

"He has a job. But, rightly, he ought to be in school still."

"One thing at a time," Hugh suggested. "What is today?"

"The twenty-seventh of December. He's been here two days. Since Christmas morning. Poor little thing, coming in like that, after a night like that."

"I am as aware of that as you are."

"If he puts you off so . . ."

"He doesn't *put me off*," Hugh asserted sternly. "He is a part of my flock. Tomorrow is his mother's funeral. After that, he may stay here as if he were one of our family. For a while. But we must watch him closely, do you hear? We will minister to him, for the sake of Jesus Christ our Lord, but we will not accept any less than we have from our own children."

"What about his schooling?" Emily asked.

"That will come," Hugh said, and he lowered his eyes to his book.

He considered his own ambivalent feelings toward Tom. He was now in his forties and it was natural, he thought, that he should see this boy through a father's eye; but, try as he might, something troubled him. The boy was clearly helpless, but he seemed, also, worldly. And this was peculiar. Perhaps Tom was simply too handsome. While Hugh felt compassion for his past, there was always the future to think of and envy—the long earthly future of a man with those looks. He coughed and, with great, practiced discipline, forced the thought from his mind.

* * *

Tom took the parsonage's spare room, two doors from Frances; but, ordinarily, they kept more distance than that between them. Frances, angular in body and plump in the face, exuberant, struck the major note of the household. She was, in turn, quiet and rambunctious, feminine and boyish; but Tom did not care for her. She had entered his school, in his year, only two years before he had left it; and the sight of her with a book, or with a quill pen and a sheet of paper prompted deep memories that gnawed at his insides. In men, as in boys becoming men, Tom had learned to value a variety of qualities: a cunning appearance, of course, and a natural manner, but, as much or more than these, loyalty and honesty and brightness, an animated spirit, an imagination full of twists. Yet in girls of his own generation he could still prize only one thing: their physical beauty. To his mind, this was the starting point, without which there could be no beginning. And either, like Mary Wardman, one had it, or, like Frances, one did not. Tom did not think of this attitude as a failing on his part anymore than he saw his own bad luck as a failure on the part of God. It was simply the way the world was. Some people were poor. Some rich. Some lovely. Some not. Frances's eyes were too big. There was a silly quality to their watery gaze. There was too much flesh on her bottom and not enough up front: she had no breasts. And, because of this, her ambitions struck him as ridiculous, like blooms without a stem.

"Are you going back to school?" she asked him one day in January, during the first real conversation they ever had.

"Why do you want to know?" Tom replied. They were outside the parsonage. Snow had fallen and, as Tom shoveled, Frances swept the loose powder from the slate and, in the glove of her mittens, formed balls of ice, which she threw ever so lightly at Tom's feet.

"Father says you can," she continued.

"He didn't say it to me."

"I know. He said he'd have to consider the matter. He always says that, about everything. But I heard him talking to Emily and he said that you could. That is, if *you* wanted to."

"Since when do you call your mother Emily?"

"I don't."

"Only behind her back?"

"I suppose. Anyway, do you want to go back to school, or not? You'd probably be behind."

"I doubt it."

"Suit yourself!" Frances dropped a ball of snow in the center of the walk.

"Damn you," Tom said. "I'm going to leave that right there for you to sweep away."

"If you do," Frances said, "I'm going to tell my father that you cursed." Tom studied her. Frances continued. "I'll tell you what you ought to do, Tommy," she said precipitously. "You oughtn't to go back to that school. It's terrible. I mean it. You already know enough, anyway. What you ought to do is to go into the theater. You're handsome enough. I don't need to tell you that. And you'd make good money once you were known, and travel. As soon as I'm older, that's what I'm going to do. I'm going to be an actress. I already sing in choir."

"Sure," Tom said. "Well, I think I'll probably be better off not counting on it. I'm learning about as much as I can take in at Lazenby's anyway."

"I have friends who are actors and actresses," Frances said calmly and without revealing that they were imaginary.

"Really?" Tom's voice was strong with disbelief.

"It's true."

"And where did you meet them? At one of your father's other churches, I suppose. In South Carolina?"

"That's not your affair, Tom Chance. But, I'll tell you this. One of them's a boy and he's a magician. He trains wild horses and he's the most beautiful boy in the world."

"I'd like to see him."

"Well, you won't. That's for sure. And two others are girls. One's Dutch. Blond. Prettier than that Mary Wardman you like so much. She travels all over the world."

"Dreams," Tom said. His words pierced her awakening heart for a moment. "And you're wrong about Mary Wardman."

Tom did not return to school, then or ever. Being unsure as to how long Tom would remain with them, Hugh did not raise the matter until the following summer, by which time Tom felt too secure and successful at Lazenby's to want to make a change. He had the luxury of money in his pocket, of the fine clothes the Lazenbys provided him for free, and of contact, day after day, with the genteel and monied class to which he aspired. And the thought of relinquishing all these things for reentry into a schoolhouse where he would find himself a year behind his former equals filled him with anxiety. Money, not some academic riddle, was on his mind, and his agenda. "The only difference between us and them is their money," he told Frances, and Peter, and even once, Emily. And he decided to pursue it with everything he had.

It was quite extraordinary, and widely remarked upon that a boy of just fourteen should have a personal clientele only a handful of names shorter than that of the store's proprietors. But it was, nonetheless, true. Starting with Mrs. McAuliffe, her son, her friends, even, eventually, her abrasive daughter, Clara, he had cultivated a following by providing huge and equal measures of service and flattery. No detail escaped him: no hemline, neckline, cuff, waist, bodice, trim; no promised date. But there was more to his charm than efficiency. He quickly learned how much could be gotten with a single, well-placed compliment: "It suits your nice skin, Mrs. Barrow"; "Matches your eyes, Mrs. Carroll"; "Makes you seem taller, Mr. Brown." His face gave him a mask of innocence, made him easy to believe; and no one suspected, or wanted to, the guile that lay behind it.

He had another trick, too. Among the rich, he had noticed, not uniformly, but often enough, a pronounced urge to expiate some of the guilt they felt at possessing so much. They betrayed this burden most obviously by the excessive courtesy they bestowed on those they thought below them: on servants, on Negroes, on him. It was as if it were important to them that they be thought "good" by their inferiors. And, instinctively, he understood this knowledge for what it was. The rich could be an arrogant lot when they chose, and he knew that very few of them had any fear of revolution, that it was not a desire for self-protection which prompted them to ingratiate themselves with those of lower position. No, it was something different. It was a conflict between their two faiths: their natural belief in the rightness of an economic and social system that had buoyed them to its summit and their Christian faith in the equality—indeed, divinity—of every human soul. Having dwelt, though faithlessly, half a year in the house of a minister, he saw their dilemma with absolute clarity. One could live a Christian life, but that was hard, and its reward far off. Or one could compromise, could live, if he had the wealth, in a great house, as he pleased, and salve his conscience by dispensing smiles, pieces of silver, the most trivial favors and courtesies. This was a life of Christian manners and, understanding this, Tom played to it, supplied it an outlet. He presented himself as a humble, hardworking, striving boy, a nice young man who knew his place, who wanted, one day, to get ahead (for this was America after all) but who, for now, was not afraid to wait, or work. And this technique was almost totally successful and seductive. People felt good simply because they had bought an item from him.

Peter Parton had come to his mother's funeral, despite the fact that Roman Catholics were expressly forbidden from entering Protestant churches. And, thereafter, Tom had begun to see Peter more often than he had done since leaving school. In the winter, just before dusk, Peter would come in to Lazenby's and, for ten minutes, he and Tom would share a cup of marshmallow chocolate or tea, or else, together, they would go out again and walk a square block, during which time Peter would give Tom the news of school, and Tom, with a certain calculated exaggeration, would dwarf it with news of the store. Peter said that Mary Wardman had failed a history examination. Tom said that he had recently met, and spent an entire morning talking to and outfitting, a man called Chamberlain, who was reputed to be worth one million dollars. Peter said that Frances Alexander had almost been caned for singing in class while the teacher was talking. Tom said that Clara McAuliffe was being married to a man called Regenault and that, although she was "a bitch," she was ten times prettier than anyone they had known at school. And so it went. When spring came, they met and passed the long evenings together; and life was much of a piece for the next several years.

Tom remained at the Alexanders', dutifully attended services every Sunday, and Bible school before them, and automatically performed his chores. His father had vanished, Lilly with him. And Tom, who had no roots, knew it. He was aware, always, that he might, at any minute, be tossed out of the parsonage and into an orphanage; and, although it was conceivable that he might then turn to the Lazenbys for help, he did not want it to come to that. Hugh was a distant man, demanding in his way, and specific about what it was he required. And this suited Tom, for it gave him a good idea how much of his life he still owned and removed the uncertainty which would have otherwise plagued him. He liked his room. He liked the warm meals, particularly the roasted beef that Emily laid on her table. He liked the prestige, albeit limited, of being the minister's charge. And, oddly, though he was still not attracted to her physically, he increasingly liked Frances.

He did not really believe in the Methodists' God but he pretended to.

"At six o'clock," Hugh had explained, "we rise. Fifteen minutes to wash and dress. And we meet for morning prayer in the parlor. No lateness. My eldest son is twenty-one now and for all the time he lived in this house, he was never late. Never. You understand? Mrs. Alexander will expect you to be prompt from prayer to breakfast . . ."

"Yes, sir."

"Don't interrupt. And to help her, both you and Frances, with her pots and dishes, with the refuse and whatever other morning chores she has for you. Following that, Frances will leave us for school and you for your work.

"Dinner will be served at six. We shall make that concession to you. Until now, we have always taken dinner at five exactly, but that, you tell me, will not accord with your employment and it is better that we take meals together in a true Christian spirit. Evening chores after the meal. Then psalmody, on most nights. And you're to be in with the dark. When you see your friends, I don't care, so long as you've fulfilled these obligations. Have you anything to ask?"

"I shall be fine, sir," Tom had said. And that had become the routine by which he had lived.

His job paid him nearly four dollars each week now and he was careful to save all of it that he could. He gladly contributed the first envelope of every month to Hugh and Emily for room and board, but, apart from this obligation, his expenses totaled next to nothing and he was able to watch his nest egg grow by more than a hundred dollars each year. The act of paying his own way appealed to him quite as fervently as it did to the Reverend and Mrs. Alexander. To them it provided a sign of Christian character, not to mention a certain usefulness with the grocer and butcher. But for Tom it bought an even more precious sense of security, a feeling not unlike that he had long ago known with Katharine, in that happy time he could scarcely remember.

At night, after they had sung a psalm together and each retired to separate work, Tom got into the habit of borrowing her schoolbooks from Frances, and so assiduous was he that, at one point in April, he had gone two weeks ahead of her in her mathematics lessons.

If he had settled on a certain beneficial and practical friendship for her, she had reserved, for him, a much higher affection. Impelled by rebellion, propelled by the sheer look and smell and sound of him, she devoted the largest thoughts of every minute to him and soon could not escape, even for a second, the feeling he produced in her. It was terrifying. She could not confess it, for she knew that Tom would balk and feared that Hugh would banish him from their house for good; and so she mentioned it only secretly, to her imaginary friends.

Tom, of course, sensed it immediately, but had another person on his mind. He was still in awe of Mary Wardman. She, not Frances, was the golden girl to his eye. She was the girl whom everyone wanted and no one had had—the prize—and he had no compartment in his dreams for anyone else, anyone less. Since Katharine's death, on the few times they had met, she had been civil to him, even coy; and now he found that the mere thought of her was enough to make him grow wildly excited. But there was no opportunity for him. He had considered it thoroughly. He could not yet dare to try for her. He feared that she would refuse him again. He feared that she would accept—and become pregnant. He thought endlessly, feared endlessly, and, until the spring after his seventeenth birthday, did nothing.

Then, in March, as he sat with Peter under his father's porch, having their usual conversation on a late Sunday afternoon, watching the great bay boat of the Baltimore Ship Packet Company as it slid out from the harbor, the first of three events shattered his adolescence.

"Chamberlain was in again yesterday—no, Friday," Tom

had just finished saying, "and said he might consider me to be his assistant in a year or two."

"Good," said Peter.

"Can't say if he really will or not, but wouldn't it be something?"

"Sure would."

"You're quiet tonight."

"Something's happened."

"Something big, I hope."

"Yes, it was big," Peter said. Tom did not like the tone of Peter's voice.

"Very capital," Tom bluffed.

"You really shouldn't say things like that 'Very capital' business," Peter stalled. "Everyone knows you're just acting when you say it."

"What happened?" Tom asked.

"Just like when you used to say 'noblesse oblige.' Frances thought it was awful. And you really ought to pay more attention to what she likes and doesn't, because she's becoming very pretty."

Tom bored his eyes into Peter's.

"All right," Peter said. "I'll tell you. Mary Wardman and I. We did it."

"I don't believe you."

"It's true. I swear it. I'm—"

"Jesus Christ!"

"I'm sorry, but we did."

"Jesus Christ!"

"I know you like her, but we couldn't help it. You'll find someone else, Tom. Some rich girl probably."

"She's not dead, you know, just because you and she—"

"I'm graduating from school in June, Tom."

"And you don't have a job. I know that. So what?"

"We're going to be married."

"You and Mary? I see." Tom thought out loud. "You're both the same religion. You're both Catholic."

"That has nothing to do with it."

"Jesus," Tom said. "You never know about anyone, do you?"

It was now 1857. When Katharine had died, three years before, Tom had had a fire, the memory of dead bodies and evil men and a drunken father's words, the image of a fat and graying whore to come to terms with; and he had managed, totally alone and with surprising quickness, simply by putting them out of his mind, by suppressing them the moment they surfaced. Hugh had credited Tom's recovery to "the boundless love of our Savior," but Tom knew, even then, that the strength had originated within him. Sometimes, in the dark, he would see the flames again in his mind, see Ol' Phitts and the hallway at Lilly's, see his father and the woman, smell them, hear them. . . . The scenes would occur in a flash: when one came the others would follow and could not be stopped. But once they had all passed, he had learned to throw his mind immediately onto other subjects: his job, his chores, a book, or Mary, or the glorious future he imagined before him, and thus bury what, in any case, could not be exorcised. He had resisted every temptation to search out his father and determine the truth; for he told himself that he knew the truth already. He was Katharine's son. He looked too much like her. Simple as that! He had healed the open wound of doubt with the balm of a faith as rigid as Hugh's; and any man who could do that, he assured himself, could certainly survive a wounded pride, the loss of a love and a friend.

As rapidly as possible he purged Mary Wardman from his thoughts. And she was all but dressed and gone when, in June, the second event occurred.

It was late in the month, a slow season for dressmakers and tailors, and the Lazenbys had left him alone in the shop half an hour before closing time. They had had an important appointment to keep at the home of a favored customer and had gone out together, expecting that Tom could deal with whatever arose. Then, with less than ten minutes until he would have put the key in the door, Clara Regenault came in. She was very plainly dressed. Her hair was up and back. Her expression was as smug as ever, but he could not deny her beauty.

She stepped—much too daintily, Tom thought—into the showroom. "Is Mr. Lazenby here?" she asked, in a lifeless monotone.

"No, ma'm. I'm sorry."

"Mrs. Lazenby then?"

"They went out together."

"Perhaps you can help me."

"Certainly."

She looked at him. She always did. He was aware of it. Now, at seventeen, he was a full six feet tall, with a man's frame and a hard body; and he knew she liked what she saw, but was sure she would never admit it.

"There's a dress in my name. In work, I expect. I wanted to try it, if I might."

"Of course, ma'm. I know it by heart."

"Good."

Tom darted into the back of the ladies' section and emerged with a hanger, on which was hung a great white cloth, rather like a linen sheet. He placed the hook of the hanger onto a stand in the showroom, and when the falling cloth had straightened, he removed the cover from the dress.

"That's it, exactly," Mrs. Regenault said.

"Let me help you." Tom took the garment again in hand and led her back to a small dressing room, where, in the manner of a bellboy at a good hotel, he checked the light and furniture. As he moved, he could feel her eyes on his neck, and it made him nervous. Then he closed the door behind him and went back to the front of the store, where he had merchandise to check and stock. Five minutes passed. Ten minutes. It was nearly closing time when he heard the sound of the dressing-room latch.

"I'll only be a minute," Mrs. Regenault called from the dressing room. "You're not in a hurry, I hope."

"No," Tom answered. He was adjusting the drape of a wool coat on a mannequin.

"No dates?" Mrs. Regenault called amusedly. "No lovely young girls?"

"What?" asked Tom loudly, almost certain that he had heard her correctly, but surprised.

"I should have thought the girls would be all over you now," Mrs. Regenault continued, coming into the showroom as she spoke, wearing the pale gray silk dress with the hint of rose color in it. "The girls your age. Aren't there some?"

"No," Tom said. "That fits you very well, doesn't it?"

"There aren't?" Mrs. Regenault exclaimed.

Tom smiled. "I mean there are girls my age," he said seriously. "And I know them, but they're not 'all over me.'"

Mrs. Regenault gave him a spoiled, pouty, but intensely sad look. "Then the world's certainly changed since I was your age."

Tom started then, turned on his heel, and looked at her head-on, with a fierce, disturbing directness. "It's because I don't want them to be," he told her.

"I see," Mrs. Regenault replied. She had not moved a step from the time she had come into the room; her eyes were fastened to him now, candidly trying, with all their moist beauty, to draw him in.

Tom blinked. "Why do you look at me that way?" he demanded after a few seconds.

"I'm sorry. I didn't mean to."

"Do you think I'm beautiful? Is that why?"

Startled, Mrs. Regenault answered "Yes."

"And that's all you care about, isn't it?" he asked.

"No," she protested anxiously. "I think you're a very nice

young man, everyone does, very clever, that you've done very well since . . ."

"Don't be nervous," he said. "And don't worry about it. I don't give a damn about it myself. It's all right as long as you understand that. I don't belong to you."

Briefly, Mrs. Regenault smoothed her dress. Then, with a tense smile, she said, "I'm not nervous, Tom; but I really am confused."

Tom moved nearer to her, reached out and touched her cheek with his soft palm, and turned it toward him. "Don't lie," he said. "Agreed?"

"Yes," she whispered, a bit frightened. And then, with a surprising, manly force, he put his lips impulsively against hers, kissed her until their teeth touched, forced his tongue inside her mouth, and stepped back. It was instinctive for the first time in his romantic experience. Thoughts and words were coming to him now more quickly than he could absorb them, and he felt that his own actions were somehow beyond his control.

"Do you want me to undress?" he asked, anxious at the reality of her, of an act he had imagined so many times alone.

She shivered, hesitated. "Yes," she said meekly.

"Is that why you stayed here after everyone had gone?" Now it was his eyes which would not release her. "Tell me!"

"Yes," she admitted.

"I thought so."

"What are we going to do?" She seemed a little humbled now, and not far from tears. "Have you ever made love to a woman before?"

"What about your husband?"

"I don't want to think about him."

"I'll lock the door," he said. "And put out one of the lights. We can use the big dressing room. It's quite safe. No one will come by this late."

When Tom came into the dressing room, Mrs. Regenault

was standing. He touched her lightly in passing, and dropped himself onto the tufted seat of the French Provincial divan. It was a small room, of course, but with a cozy charm. "Take off your clothes, Clara," he said then, using her Christian name for the first time. "I want to watch you."

"Just like that?" she protested, stunned by the sudden authority of his voice, and irritated.

"Just like that," he repeated without expression, his boldness astounding even himself, but sounding like fire to his ear.

Clara tried to bring out her smile. "Then help me with my dress, for God's sake. You can certainly do that, can't you? These aren't the easiest things to get on and off."

"I'd rather watch," Tom replied, "if you don't mind. Mr. Regenault, does he have other women?"

"He does, if you must know."

"He's crazy then."

Clara looked at Tom sweetly. It took her a minute to undo all the hooks of the dress and she tried to seem as if it were not an effort, to hide the work of her fingers. Then, when the last catch came apart, she reached down in one unbroken and rapid movement, pulled the dress up over her head and let it fall into a great puffy bulk on the floor. She stood facing him in her bodice and, with equal pretense, began to work on its pink ribbon fasteners.

"Do you recall," Tom asked her, "the first time we saw each other?"

"I don't think so."

"You hated me."

"That's not true."

"Don't apologize. I hated you too."

"That's an awful thing to say."

"If anyone had ever told me that I . . . that you . . . that *we* would ever—"

"Don't use that word," Clara interrupted. "I hate that word."

"Well, you know what I mean."

"Yes. But you've grown up a lot, too, Tom, remember that. You're a man now." In an almost dance-like gesture, Clara now removed her corset, spread it apart, up, back and off her shoulders. He breasts tumbled out—and she shook for a second with her new freedom. Tom studied her. In the mirror, he could see her back, smooth but taut, with the riding muscles plainly visible beneath the pearl skin as she moved her arms. Her breasts were firm, not small, not large. They came to a tiny point at her nipples. Clara looked down at them, and then at Tom.

"You have nice breasts," Tom said.

"Thank you."

"Too bad you have to wear them in all that corset. It makes them red. I wouldn't if I were you. I'd just wear my dress and nothing underneath."

"I'm afraid that wouldn't do," Clara laughed.

"Take off your pants now," Tom said. "Come on."

"If you were any older, I'd slap you," Clara replied. "You're so sure of yourself."

"It's my youth," Tom smiled. "Tell me something. How long have you wanted me anyway? A year?"

"Not that long." Clara, by this time, had removed her stockings and was now sliding her small, laced panties down over her thighs, slowly, to tease him, revealing a dark triangle of hair above her crotch.

"Well," Tom announced when she had finished, "there we have it. You're a beautiful woman, Clara Regenault." A random laugh. "But why spend yourself on a young salesboy, clearly of no consequence?"

"Please stop it," Clara said. "You're embarrassing me. You're making me feel cheap."

Tom removed his jacket and tie, loosened his shirt. "The answer to your question is no," he told her then. "I've never done it before—with anyone."

"I wasn't sure," Clara said. She straightened up, began to come toward him.

"Now you are."

She leaned over him now and kissed him. Tom felt her breast with his palm, the tips of his fingers, ran his hand down along her side into her hair, through it, below it, finding the crack, and held her. He shivered nervously. Clara paused, sighed. "Let me take off your shirt," she said.

Tom released her, leaned back slowly. "How old were *you*?" he asked.

"Seventeen," she whispered. "Seventeen, too." She pulled his boots, then his trousers all the way off, caressed him with her fingers, kissed his chest. Tom's penis sprung out from the cotton waist of his pants as she withdrew them, hard now and throbbing as she touched it. She stood over him, just an inch beyond reach now, the first naked woman he had ever known. Not a girl, but a woman; and though a last romantic part of him might have preferred to experience this moment with a virgin, a tight-bodied girl of his own age, there was an even stronger instinct inside him which fed on the power he felt commanding this much-desired woman. Her breasts were soft and he could see her tiny nipples growing wider and erect as the air hit them and falling with gravity as she bent over him now. Her hands stayed on him lightly, holding back his foreskin as, inch by inch, she began to slide up over him. In half a minute she was on top of him, kissing him, her mouth at his, her breasts at his; and she was about to put him inside her when, suddenly, causelessly, he broke away.

"We could go to hell for doing this," Tom said gravely.

"You don't really believe that," Clara said. But Tom slid out from beneath her nonetheless.

"Turn over," Tom told her. "Let me have a look at you. You're a good-looking woman. How old are you, by the way?"

"Twenty-six."

"You ought to be ashamed of yourself," Tom laughed.

Clara was shivering. "I know women aren't supposed to want it, but they do, Tom, so will you please—just please *do it*?"

Tom stood silently then, thirstily. He moved on top of her and followed her directions.

Moments later, Clara looked up at him and saw, for the first time that day, how perfectly young he was. No hair on his body; not even a beard. "My God, I wish you were a man my own age," she sighed in a spent voice.

But Tom stared into space.

"You wish too much," he said.

CHAPTER 13

THAT NEXT AUTUMN HE DISCOVERED THE THEATER.

Clara, smartly dressed, her face mature and emotionless but her eyes full of the memory and embarrassment of their last meeting, came into Lazenby's again several weeks later and immediately informed him that she would be sailing to Europe. "To France, to be exact."

Tom's face betrayed his anxiety. "Nothing's the matter, I hope."

"My husband and I have decided"—Clara hesitated—"to reconsider the hasty decisions of our past."

Tom drew himself closer, whispered, "Not because of me?"

"That's vain, isn't it?"

"I was afraid you were pregnant."

"Were you?" Clara laughed to herself. "Well, thank you awfully much for your concern, but there's no need for it."

"Don't be sarcastic! I didn't sleep worrying about you."

"About me? Or yourself?"

"If you want, I'd, we'd—"

"No," Clara said.

"You know I need you," Tom said, though the words rang false from his tongue.

"The stage," Clara exclaimed suddenly, "that's where you belong. A star. And you would be. I have no doubt about it at all."

"You can't just leave," Tom said. "I want to see you again."

"I took advantage of you. And you gave me what I deserved. I don't regret it. Nor will I repeat it. There's no future possible between us. You must understand that. For many reasons, not to mention age. Though I admit that you pleased me. But if we continued, once more, twice more, something terrible would happen. So *no*. No. *No*."

She opened her eyes in a passionate scowl. "You're faithless, Thomas Chance, like a magnificent alley cat. And you're no gentleman. There's only something about you. . . ."

Tom smiled.

Then, in the first weeks of September, an astounding thing happened. He was in his room, about to go to sleep at ten o'clock, but still reading, by candlelight, the last few pages of a business text. His window was raised about a quarter of the way and, through it, riding a slow and dew-dampened breeze, the intoxicating scent of evergreen washed about him. There was a chill, too; and he liked the sensation, pulling the great wool covers and quilt up about his neck. Suddenly the latch on his door moved upward, both wood and metal creaked, and, before he could guess who was there, Frances had entered his room. She was still in her day clothes. She pressed the door behind her. She took a deep sigh. "Oh," she exclaimed, "I've got to tell you something."

"Get your breath first," Tom said. He had watched her and could not deny that, over the past years, she had grown into a beauty.

"I'm all right," she pronounced at last, calming, but no less full of excitement.

"If you put your hair back," Tom told her thoughtfully, "—maybe up, not back, I'm not sure—but if you did something with it, you have a nice line to your cheek, do you know that?"

Frances gave Tom a quizzical look. "Like this?" she asked, taking the whole shock in one fist and pulling it backward, away from her face.

"Well, a little more carefully, but that's the general idea."

"I don't know."

"I'm in that business, remember. It's my job to make women look beautiful."

"I could never look beautiful."

Tom thought. "I think you could," he said genuinely.

Frances smiled.

"Straighten up a little. There. Look at you. You have a wonderful-looking body. I'll agree it's recent, but there it is, you have it!"

Frances dropped her eyes to the ground. "I'm glad you think so," she mumbled. "I'll need it. That's what I came in to tell you. I've gotten a part."

"A part?" Tom seemed astounded. "As an actress, you mean?"

"In a show. I don't speak, but I'm on stage almost half the time."

"That's wonderful!" For the moment he felt outdone.

"Don't you want to know which play, Tom?" Frances prodded.

"When. Where. Everything," Tom said.

"Well, it's not Shakespeare, so don't get too excited. It's a musical. A revue. I'm just one of twenty girls. Or twenty-one, I can't remember. We come on stage right, go off stage left. Dance around. But you have to start someplace."

"Of course you do."

"And a lot of people wanted the parts."

"I'm sure."

"It's at 'Old Drury.' The Holliday Street Theater—that's its real name—John T. Ford's. You've probably heard of it. And it's called. . . . Isn't that awful, I can't remember what it's called."

"You *are* nervous."

"No, it's not that. It's just that it's new, something they just wrote for this theater. *Paris in Springtime,* or *Springtime in Paris.* I guess I *am* nervous."

"Why not? It's the start of great things."

"You know Miss Evelyn and that recital our choir gave six weeks back, the one where I sang 'Jesus Is My Heart's Salvation' solo, and there was such a terrible fuss about it? That's where Mr. Ford saw me. Don't ask me what he was doing there."

Tom lay his head back and stroked his neck along the pillow underneath it. "What about your father?" he asked. "Do you think he will—like the idea?"

"If I tell him, no. He wouldn't like it one bit coming from me. But if Miss Evelyn tells him that it's a proper thing for a minister's daughter to do, he'll go along wholeheartedly. And she's promised to drop a word in his ear."

"Still, in a way it's dancing," Tom said. "The Church doesn't hold with dancing. Neither does your father."

"The Church buries its head in the sand. If there's a decent paycheck to be made, my father will see it Miss Evelyn's way." Frances paused uncertainly. "Tom?"

"Now there's an odd look for a happy girl."

"There is going to be a party. Mr. Ford is giving it and he's invited everyone in the cast."

"Good."

"I want you to escort me."

Tom smiled. "I don't think your father would approve of that."

Frances's face set determinedly. "Look. I know you have a girl already, Tom. If you don't want to take me, say so."

Tom's eyes darted about the edges of the ceiling, tracing the four walls of molding in a continuously clockwise direction. "How do you know anything of the kind?" he demanded, his attention quickly reverting to Frances.

"Only from you. You're more obvious than you think. I've known it all summer. You have talent, but you're not a trained actor."

Her sentence struck Tom. He snapped, "If you must know, she's a woman, not a girl."

Frances felt a sudden throbbing in her head. "I don't care—if *you* must know."

"Forget it."

"I shall." Silence fell between them; then, from Tom: "Where *is* the party?"

Frances was momentarily stunned. "At Barnum's Hotel. Next Thursday."

"Now, that's very fancy."

"I wouldn't know. I've never been there."

Tom took another careful look at her face. Very English in color, smooth and pink. Her hair was down again, over her shoulders, in front and in back. Her lips were only vaguely parted, so that none of the bone-white of her teeth could be seen. Her nose was short, straight, perfect from the front; her brows wide, brown, and young; her eyes like almonds and larger and more moist than he had ever seen. He looked down her body, slowly; it was, he guessed, of medium height—five feet five inches, perhaps, or maybe five feet six. Being a haberdasher, he thought in these terms. Bosom: thirty-four, he suspected. Waist: twenty-five. Hips: thirty-four. Weight: one hundred twenty, at the most. She had, in the past year, changed so totally, and yet he could not purge the memory of her former self from his appreciation of her now. He wished, in a curious way, that he had not known her until now.

"Well, I've been to Barnum's Hotel," he said at last. "And it's wonderful. Look, I'm sorry I growled at you. And I'd be glad to *escort* you. There's nothing I'd rather do. If you'd like, I'm sure the Lazenbys would let us borrow some clothes from the shop. And I think it *is* going to be formal, too, because I know we've had some customers who've ordered dresses for Mr. Ford's party."

Frances bit her lip.

"Come here for a minute," Tom said.

"What for?"

"I want to kiss you goodnight."

"What about your g–*woman*?"

"She's gone," Tom replied.

Frances moved slowly toward him, bent at the bedside and brushed her lips quickly over Tom's. "Did you kiss her? I'll bet you did."

Pink coats. And red coats. Black worsted dress suits and military uniforms with gold braiding and flatboard epaulets. There were women in white, ladies in blue and green velvet, and Frances in a splendid blue gown. They swirled about the small lobby of Barnum's Hotel in the cool dusk, beneath the light of party torches and a full, orange, harvest moon. And it was like no real thing had been in all their years of experience. Tom glanced at Frances. The dress fit her perfectly, and he drank in the look of it as he drank in everything else about him. He, himself, was outfitted in straightforward tails, bow tie and weskit, all borrowed, like Frances's gown, from the Lazenbys' stock, and slipped into only minutes before the party in the same dressing room where he had entered Clara. Frances had secretly come to the store and changed there too; and, like Cinderella, they would both go back to the shop on their way home, strip in the dark, and return to their street clothes, so as not to run any greater chance than necessary of soiling the garments.

Through the lobby, they followed the crowd into a large reception room where they were first asked their names, and then presented with a silver tray holding glasses of champagne. "No, thank you," Frances told the waiter.

"No, thank you?" Tom repeated incredulously. "Why, I've never tasted champagne in my life and neither have you. We should certainly try it." He removed two of the glasses and handed one to Frances.

"Champagne is liquor," Frances said.

"If you're going to be an actress, you'll have to experience everything you can. Including liquor. Ask anyone."

"I wouldn't dare."

"That's because you know I'm right."

Frances turned somewhat, gazed about the room, and began to walk. Tom followed. She held her glass waist-high. When a moment and the immediacy of the subject had passed, she lifted it and sipped a bit of the wine, grimaced some, then sipped again and a third time. Everyone in the room seemed to know, if not everyone else, then at least a fair number of those present. Yet she knew no one. A few men smiled at her as they passed, but did not stop or speak. One woman frowned. Frances could not place her. Tom, on the other hand, had several customers among the guests and, with these, he exchanged a few pleasant words, but too much in passing for him to introduce Frances.

"Look around, Tom," Frances announced suddenly. "Won't it be wonderful when we're famous? Do you know what I'm looking forward to? I'm looking forward to the day when I will be able to meet a complete stranger, someone I've never seen before in my life, and someone will say, 'Have you met Frances Alexander?' and *they,* not me, will get numb all of a sudden and say, 'No, but I've seen her on the stage.' "

Tom took up the thread of her fantasy. "It was in *Romeo and Juliet,* wasn't it?" he added in the most sophisticated voice he could imitate.

"I don't know," Frances whirled on. "Oh, Tom, won't we have fun?"

"I'm having fun right now."

"I'm having the best time in my life," Frances said. "Imagine us being here with the most important people in Baltimore."

"Don't get too carried away," Tom said. "These are only working people. Just like we are, most of them, only they get paid more. But they're by no means the most important people in Baltimore."

"Of course they are."

"They're theater people," Tom said. "You should hear what the bankers say about them."

Frances lost her smile. "You're a bucket of cold water. How in the world do you know so much about everything?"

"The same way I know about plays and business accounting. I read. I listen. I read your books even."

"Well, it's too much for me," Frances said. "So let's just *pretend* they're important, all right?"

John T. Ford was constantly at the center of one clique or another and they could not maneuver their way to him gracefully. Frances wanted to thank him. Tom wanted to meet him. Ford was a young man, not yet thirty, and already renowned as the manager of the best minstrel troupe in America. Besides that, it was well known that he had put up, from his own pocket, a third of the capital which had brought a shuttered "Old Drury" back to life. And this impressed Tom, who thought it no more than sensible to make the acquaintance of every rising personality he could.

Their opportunity came on the way in to dinner, when, accidentally, they found themselves stalled directly beside Ford's group of the moment.

"Mr. Ford," Frances interrupted.

"Yes."

"I just wanted to thank you."

"And you are?"

"Frances Alexander."

"Of course. Meet Mr. Booth, Mr. Robson, Mr. Albaugh."

"This is Tom, Thomas Chance, my . . . friend."

Mr. Ford, beginning to move now, stretched his hand out limply, almost behind him.

"I, too, want to thank you very much, sir," Tom said in a full voice, "for having us."

Ford looked around, startled at first by the strength of Tom's voice and then, more profoundly, by his first real glimpse of Tom's face. "And you are also an actor?"

"No, sir."

Booth and Albaugh—and another man called Williamson—were now studying Tom as well. Williamson, effete, almost pretty, regarded him strangely.

"That's too bad," Ford said lightly. "You'd look so perfect as my Ferdinand."

"Wouldn't he?" Williamson cooed.

At dinner, where people from the cast were meant as decoration, there was a mix-up of place cards and Tom found himself next to a large, theatrical widow named VanDurand who had a broad mouth and dead-looking skin. Mrs. VanDurand, he discovered, "adored theater," "knew Frances," "died with happiness last summer at Stratford-on-Avon" and was "absolutely sure you can't be telling the truth. The clothing business! I've never heard anything so wonderfully funny. Hysterical, really! You're much too handsome not to be on the stage."

"You flatter me," Tom said. "But it isn't true."

"Nonsense."

"Well, I have thought of it," Tom admitted. "But I understand there's very little hope for an unknown."

"Nonsense again."

"And I've not trained."

"A good year under your belt, with Ford, learning the ropes, and that should carry you. Not another word now. *I* shall see to it."

Mrs. VanDurand, Tom understood, was motivated less by an altruistic heart than by the wish to play a part herself. He suspected that she was one of those people who, having few worldly demands upon her time, found it necessary to be perpetually in the process of discovering something, or someone. He did not know why he suspected this—it was out of his experience—but he did, instinctively. And he knew, too, that Mrs. VanDurand would be able to gain Ford's ear, for he knew that she was rich. He had discovered the type in Lazenby's, memorized and catalogued it, and he could spot it anywhere. Even if he erred, he thought, there was her jewelry as evidence: a large round diamond ring, a diamond necklace, and a tiara, with the most enormous pearl he could imagine in its center. Smooth. The color and opaqueness of cream. The size of a dove's egg.

"I can't help admiring your pearl, Mrs. VanDurand," Tom offered finally, about to begin on his aspic of lobster now and stalling in order to follow her choice among the forks.

She smiled. "I'm glad you like it, my dear. It's the only thing I have left. I gave a dinner two weeks ago and, while it was going on, some thieves—I could call them worse names —entered my bedroom window and made away with absolutely everything else. Luckily I was wearing this pearl." The thought evidently amused her, for she laughed.

"I'll say. This is delicious, isn't it?"

"Indeed. *And* it's my favorite. My late husband, God rest his soul, gave it to me. After one of our fights. Everyone has them, they don't mean a thing. Did you know that pearl is the only gem which does not require the human touch to become beautiful? All the rest do. That must mean something, don't you think? They say pearls descended from the clouds, as rain, into the sea. And I believe it."

"That's fascinating," Tom said. "It must be so . . . valuable, so expensive."

"I shudder when I think."

"Oh, don't," Tom exclaimed, "or you won't enjoy it." It was a stock phrase of his, from his work at Lazenby's.

Mrs. VanDurand moved closer to him. "To tell the truth," she whispered sotto vocé, "I'm pleased as pleased can be that it *is* expensive, because *I'm selling it*. What I mean is I've sold it."

"Really?"

"To Goelette and Company, have you heard of them? Absolutely the finest jewelers on this side of the Atlantic."

"I've never had any dealings with jewelers."

"I shouldn't expect so. At—how old are you?"

"Seventeen."

"But this is its last fling, tonight. On this old head in any case. My marvelous friend, the Pearl of Macao."

"Pearl of Macao?"

"The finest jewels have names, young man, and mine—Monsieur Goelette's now—has a beauty, wouldn't you say: the *Pearl of Macao*. When Willard bought it they assured him, in writing—they don't often do that—that it had been stolen—gotten, anyway; I don't like the word stolen—from the crown of a Nepalese princess. And, all things considered, there haven't been too many owners, really, between her and me."

At this moment, two waiters appeared, differently costumed. The one in red removed the dish upon which the now-devoured aspic had rested, whereupon the one in black replaced it with a plate of turkey. In front of each diner, its base clasped into a small silver stand, there was a white card with the menu set forth in splendid black calligraphy. Tom deduced that the dish before him was "Boned Turkey on Pedestal," and that the dessert to follow would be "Plombière, Ornamented with Ice Flowers." He did not know what "Plombière" was; nor, for that matter, had he ever tasted an ice flower.

"This Monsieur Goelette," Tom quizzed after a pause. "Will he sell the pearl in turn, or keep it? Who will he sell it to?"

"That's his business," Mrs. VanDurand said, delving heartily into her asparagus. "What he tells me is that he wants it for his own collection. I don't believe it for a minute. He's in business to make a profit, what?"

Frances, watching across the table, met Tom's eye and grinned.

"Lovely girl," Mrs. VanDurand said.

"Thank you."

"Don't lose her to the stage. It's a danger, you know."

Tom remained silent.

"But then not for you, I shouldn't imagine." Mrs. Van-Durand smiled once more, a lambent coyness in her aging face.

Tom grinned too. "I truly cannot get over your pearl," he said.

CHAPTER

14

FRANCES MADE HER DEBUT IN *Parisian Spring*, FOR THAT WAS the revue's true title, the following Tuesday. It was the first, though not the principal attraction of the autumn season and the house was full. Tom, alone, tired from a day's work, the desires of his body and mind increasingly fixed on Frances now, and frustrated, sat in the orchestra, in a seat for which she had given him a ticket. The lights in the house went out gradually, as, one by one, the individual flames were extinguished. Then, following the theater's long custom, an immense illumination appeared on the screen: Fort McHenry, bright beneath the bombardment of enemy ships; and a great baritone voice began to sing, to the tune of a drinking song, "Anacreon in Heaven," the verses of Key's poem: "O, say can you see, By the dawn's early light . . ."

The music shot a shiver down his spine. He had heard it only once or twice before. Yet, from his program, he knew that it had been introduced here, that the audience at the Holliday Street had stood and sung it every opening night since 1814. Secured by the hundred voices of the crowd, he too sang out and, for a moment, as the chords swelled ". . . And this be our motto . . ." he felt again the presence of something larger than himself. On the spot, he put it down to patriotism, pure and simple. But afterward, with a kind of whole sight as he lay in his room, he decided that it had neither been the image of America nor the God of Hugh

Alexander that had moved him, but a simple magic trick of music and language and light.

Revues were rare at Old Drury. Most theatergoers, brought up on classics, preferred to see their favorites over and over again—and, if not their favorites, if not even the familiar, they at least required a story. *Parisian Spring* closed after eleven nights, three days prior to schedule. The cast was let go and the strikers loosed on the set.

Tom stood in the wings, next to Williamson, waiting for Frances's return from the final curtain call. Williamson—it was he who had given Tom permission to be there—watched him suspiciously. "Your girl friend," he said finally. "Attractive, in her way."

"Yes."

"So, one might say, are you?"

Tom looked surprised. He mumbled, "Thank you."

"Untrained, though. You like the theater, don't you?"

"What I've seen of it so far."

"Will it embarrass you if I tell you something about Frances? For her own good?"

A slow anger began to burn in Tom. "Please go on."

"Richards—you know him? He's a director. Doing *Tamburlaine* at the Perregrine around the corner. He offered her a part. As the virgin of Damascus."

"And."

"Not 'and,' 'on.' *On* condition that she not be." Williamson had a silly laugh to himself. "You understand, don't you?"

"I think."

"He wanted to lay her. To use the king's English. As it turns out, he found someone else."

"I'm happy for him."

"She'll never get ahead, though. No good parts, until she does. One either plays or one doesn't. I promise, it's the fate of every aspiring talent."

"I think we should conclude this conversation, Mr. Williamson," Tom said, "before I feel inclined to bloody your already rather crooked nose."

Williamson seemed unthreatened. "In the rest of the world, Mr. Chance, this is the Victorian Age. But not so much here in the arts. Not so much as you think."

The crowd had delivered a last, polite applause, and the curtain was falling. "The most important performers," Williamson continued, "are paid in gold at the end of each performance. Hundreds, or thousands, of dollars. For a single night."

"What do you want?"

"Not Frances Alexander."

"You *are* sick."

"Then so were Socrates and Michelangelo. You could be a great star. Rich beyond your dreams."

"No."

"Any girl you wanted then. Don't think I haven't done that, too. Look at that line. All the best of them I've had."

"Mr. Williamson," Tom whispered brutally, "if you so much as smile at Miss Alexander in the future or at me, I am going to see to it, personally, that . . ."

"That . . . *what*?" Williamson goaded.

"That you are killed," Tom said, then did an immediate about-face.

The twenty-one girls now swirled about the wings. With the curtain down, they began to remove their petticoats and skirts and Tom marveled at their immodesty. Smiles dropped automatically. Two girls giggled with Williamson. Frances, sausaged into a lace-up corset that was too small for her, stood next to Tom. The tops of her breasts were squeezed up from it and Tom eyed her cleavage for the first time. He moved her hair back with the palm of his hand and kissed her on the lips.

"What a naughty look!" she laughed.

"This is a naughty place."

"I don't think it is. I think it's a wonderful place. Oh,

Tom, just before we went on, I got the best news. I'm going to be in *The Tempest*. A nymph. It's the very next play."

"Oh, God." Tom sighed. "What is the price of that?"

"Do you mean how much will I be paid? You don't mean that, do you?"

"Williamson, not ten minutes ago, suggested to me that you could be in some damn play if and only if you . . ."

"I've heard that line," Frances interrupted. "So has every other girl, I expect. But Mr. Ford himself offered me this part. With no strings."

Tom kissed her.

"He asked me about you."

"Me?"

"If you could handle the role of Ferdinand. I don't know what it is."

"I don't either. What did you tell him?"

"I told him you'd talk to him."

Tom was given the large part of Ferdinand in the same production of *The Tempest* in which Frances was to play a nymph. No conditions had been attached to the part and, though he knew that, like most things, it had come to him purely on the basis of his looks, he was prepared to think that fair enough.

"Miranda, daughter of Prospero, the Duke of Milan, and very beautiful in her own right, is meant to fall in love with Ferdinand the *moment* she meets him," John Ford had emphasized. "So Ferdinand must project—*project*—not simply have a very strong physical appeal. I wouldn't be honest if I didn't say I was taking a big chance on you, no pun intended."

Thus a new phase of their lives began. Frances's dream in the open, she left school. Tom adjusted his hours at Lazenby's, no longer worked nights or during afternoons of matinees. He learned to speak from his chest rather than from his throat, to "boom" his voice, to walk gracefully, to stand straight, to fence, to sound, move, and seem like a gentleman. Frances, similarly, learned to dance, curtsy, sing, and recite. Two or three times a season she would completely change identities, submerging herself in her new parts, however small. Within two years, she had played: the nymph; a young shepherdess in *Figaro's Marriage*; Ehea, a maid, in Marlowe's *Tamburlaine*; then Zenocrate; Silvia in *Two Gentlemen of Verona*; Cordelia in *King Lear*; and minor parts in the works of both Sheridan and Goldsmith. Tom's roles during the same period were, on the whole, fewer, but more important, and once, when the intended actor had become ill with typhoid, he had had a ten-day run as Romeo, although the reviews had later called him "wooden."

Both were popular among the others in their set, though Frances was thought, by far, the more serious. Both were fairly often propositioned, though Tom was thought, by far, the more available. Indeed, no matter what their source, Frances refused all such overtures and had a reputation for so doing; while Tom, if his mood was right, could often be counted on for fun. Even among a theatrical crowd this seldom went farther than an hour of heavy kissing and embraces; actresses, particularly young ones with aspirations, feared the certain death a pregnancy would put to their careers. But two women had found Tom worth running the risk and he had gladly gone along for the experience.

It was odd. Every time he touched another girl, he wanted Frances more passionately than before. And yet he could not say that he loved her; could not, in conscience, promise to commit his life to her. Was she merely a challenge? He thought it was more. "When I'm ready," she had said, over and over. And it had become almost a joke between them.

Williamson had exaggerated the case, but there had been a kernel of truth in what he said. Frances was passed over for several parts—one as Ophelia—in favor of another actress who soon thereafter married the director. But Frances was competent and she managed to work without personal concessions, if not in starring roles. Tom, who had had his shot as Romeo, was simply not so practiced as his competition. This was the age of John Wilkes Booth and Edwin Booth in *Richard III* and *Hamlet*, of Stuart Robson playing Tony Lumpkin in *She Stoops to Conquer*. These supremely talented men were all a few years older than Tom, all devoted to the theater, with years of experience stretching back into their adolescence. And beside them, Tom, though many thought him more exquisite, seemed entirely less professional.

"Take Booth, for an example," Ford explained to Tom at one point. "Take Edwin. He's the most talented. He'll surpass his father, too. Now, like any successful actor, he has his mind on one thing: his work. He withholds nothing of himself. Damn it, Thomas! With you, I can't make it out, there always seems to be something *in reserve*. Withheld, by you, from the audience, and even from the character you are supposed to be playing."

Tom was silent.

"Why?" Ford asked.

"I haven't any idea," Tom said.

But he did. And it was very simple indeed. He had no long-term interest in the theater—no interest at all for its own sake now, but only as a means to something else. He did not want to be the greatest thespian who had ever lived and, by not wanting, he knew that he had relinquished the chance. At the beginning, dressed in a splendid costume, hearing applause, seeing his own name in print in the Baltimore *Sun*, he had fantasized an actor's life, a director's, a producer's. But his eye, even from the stage, had been too keen, had put its sights too high. It was a dictum of the theater that one must act as though the audience were nowhere to be seen. And yet, while his mouth spoke Shakespeare, Tom's eyes could not help scanning the rows of the orchestra, the dress circle, and the boxes. His thoughts could not help playing with the people there. They were as much a show for him as he was meant to be for them. Whenever he noticed a young couple in their own box, a man of his age in a fine gray suit, or a young woman, smiling prosperously, in a long, romantic dress, he would fret with jealousy. His imagination would romp. He would picture the man at a great desk, handling fortunes; conjure the woman on her estate with her ivory-faced children and their English nurse. And this distraction would appear in his performance, take the edge from it, leave him only his face on which to depend.

The more poetry he learned, recited, and was paid for, the more convinced he became that he was not a natural artist, that he belonged, instead, in the world of affairs. The ladies and gentlemen he idealized in Old Drury's audiences or Lazenby's clientele were people of affairs and property who had been tracked for success from birth, as he had been tracked for despair. He accepted this, understood that he had to make his own luck, find his own path, even to approach their privileged world. But he had not relinquished the dreams of his boyhood when he used to walk the bankers' streets with Peter, and he knew now that he was stronger for it, tempered and ready, in the giant storm he foresaw, to make his move.

In no time, it was 1861.

On a wind-wild night in March, he and Frances dined at the apartment of Jeremy Dearrdorff, a twenty-five-year-old actor in the Old Drury company. Jeremy occupied the entire second floor of a fine Federal house on Bolton Street, and they met him there for short whiskeys in his sitting room at six o'clock.

"Care to talk a minute of business?" Jeremy said after two

sips. He was a dedicated actor, the next most handsome male in the company after Tom, but, to many, suspiciously effeminate.

"Prefer not."

"Never-the-less." Jeremy stretched the word. "I've been over the *Volpone* again. It's fearsome. Infinitely clever, of course. But terrifying."

"You think so," Frances offered. "I haven't read it."

"Have a little topper."

"Only a quarter of an inch. I rather admire Volpone," Tom said. "Everyone loves a good, gulling rogue."

"Perhaps next time around you'll be old enough to play him." Jeremy swigged a full swallow of bourbon.

Frances gazed into space.

"Not me," Tom said. "I'm not long for the theater, Jeremy. Haven't I told you?"

"Not because you were passed over."

"No. I'm too young for Lumpkin. And, anyway, Robson has it for life—at least until he's fifty."

"Why then?"

"Why do you think?"

"I know some people say there's going to be a war, but I scarcely think . . ."

Frances, all of a sudden, burst into a smile. "Good for you, Jeremy."

Tom became solemn. "I guarantee you, Jeremy Dearrdorff, there is going to be a war," he declared. "And soon. There is going to be a war because there has to be."

Jeremy lit up genially. "Don't take it so seriously. I'm no one to rely on. I never follow politics."

"You follow poetry, my friend. Plays." Tom laughed to himself. "Well, all that is about to be swept aside." He raised Jeremy's tiny Istahani carpet. "Swept under the rug, as they say."

A polite, yet precarious smile from Jeremy. "You are *about* to ruin my dinner!'"

"Yes, Tom. Stop, why don't you?" Frances said.

"Follow politics or not, when 'The Star-Spangled Banner' is sung, before curtain, you must have heard it: Everyone stands and they sing 'Dixie.' They overpower poor Francis Scott Key, don't they, Jeremy? 'Den I wish I was in Dix-ie. Hoo-ray! Hoo-ray!' You've heard of Sumter?"

"Yes."

"And 'Bleeding Kansas,' 'The Missouri Compromise,' 'Dred Scott,' and Mr. Jefferson Davis."

"This man Lincoln hasn't been in office a week, for Christ's sake, Tom. And he's a good man. Give him a chance."

"You know what they say in South Carolina, don't you? About the South."

"Tell me."

"They say it's too large to be an insane asylum and too small to be a nation."

"I was born in South Carolina," Frances said. "I love it there."

"You never owned so much as a plant of cotton," Tom snapped.

"I can still love it, can't I?"

"It's the tide of history, my friend," Tom said. "Coming up from the South. And down from the North." He laughed. "Into our lovely, little quiet Baltimore." Tom raised his whiskey, then swallowed it. "Why, this is such a bracing time to be alive, Jeremy. Shakespeare never knew such a time. I wouldn't miss the chance for anything in the world."

Then, on the nineteenth of April, the Sixth Massachusetts Infantry fulfilled his prophecy. Twelve hundred men strong, the regiment arrived at the President Street Station of the Philadelphia, Wilmington, and Baltimore Railroad and waited there to be drawn by horse (locomotives were forbidden on Baltimore streets) to the Baltimore and Ohio's Camden Street terminal where its cars were to be attached to a new locomotive to Washington. But, midway between the stations, with its rifles down, it was attacked by an angry mob of Confederate sympathizers and seventeen people were killed.

A few weeks later, President Lincoln called for seventy-five thousand three-month volunteers, and it was in the emotion of that moment that Tom, over the objections of Hugh, Emily, Frances, both Lazenbys, and John T. Ford himself, gave his notice to both his employers, and Baltimore, and enlisted in the Union Army.

He was scheduled to leave Baltimore on June thirtieth. Thus, in the late dusk of the twenty-ninth, flush with two severance checks, he escorted Frances to dinner at Barnum's Hotel and, afterward, for what seemed an interminable walk along the harbor of the city, past a pier of small boats.

"No stars," Frances declared nervously, after a long silence.

"The clouds are low."

"No moon either."

"No."

"Listen to the boats. Splashing with the tide." Frances hesitated. "They're all empty for the night, don't you think?"

"I suppose they are." There was a small chill and Tom walked briskly.

"Let's go aboard one." Frances turned her head up.

Tom remained silent.

"Can we?"

"Why?" Tom stalled, seeking time to gauge her meaning.

Frances's voice was low, intense, and barely audible. "Oh, my God," she said. "It's such an awful time to be alive. It's our last spring. It is. I know it is."

"The last spring of our youth." Tom smiled as he studied her. "That's all. Not even that."

Frances's hand slid out from Tom's and gently squeezed his wrist. "I'm . . . ready," she promised, then thought. War, even as an idea, was the closest to death she had come, the most persuasive reminder that neither life nor youth was permanent. "I've been thinking of it for a while now," she added anxiously. "Ever since . . . ever since the crocuses came out. Don't ask any more now, Tom. Please. I love you."

They decided on a deserted, beamy, gaff-rigged sloop at the far end of the pier and stole their way down through a hatch into the single stateroom on board. It had a wide bunk, a thin sliver of a cushion, no sheets, a canvas tarpaulin, and a small paraffin lamp which Tom lit, after shielding the portholes with canvas.

Frances laughed. Tom kissed her.

"I've imagined this so many times," she said while Tom undressed her, "believe it or not. Only I couldn't until now, and don't ask me why, because I don't know."

Tom kissed her again, traced the line of her body with his hand. "*You've* imagined it," he whispered.

She was staring down, on a shy angle, away from him. He pressed his lips along her shoulder, took her whole smooth nipple in his mouth. He held her, lowered her onto the bunk in the yellow, flickering light, parted her legs. He lay his face at her stomach, her nipple again, almost cried, spasmed; and then, after a minute, slowly and without words, he went inside her.

Frances spread her hips, brought her feet together behind Tom's knees and tugged him as he pumped. Gold light, in a shallow, elliptical pool, bathed their faces from the tiny lamp beside them and, for an instant, she could see the last trace of old stage makeup, powder caught in cold cream, against Tom's sideburn. Impulsively, she ran her tongue across it, but its taste was too sweet and saline to enjoy. When Tom had finished, Frances snuggled against him, brought his arm more tightly around her, and massaged, with the very tip of her forefinger, the hard and tiny circle of his breast.

"So that's it," he said at last, searching for her reaction.

She nodded "Yes."

"The dance with no steps." He smiled.

"We belong to each other now," she said deliberately, reverting, as she often did at serious moments, to the musically pitched voice of her Southern childhood.

Tom wanted her. He felt at home with her. "Yes," he answered. "That's true, isn't it? In a way."

They lay together two hours. Neither slept. Then, a little before midnight, after Tom had placed a pillow beneath her and made love to her twice again, they came up onto the deck of the sloop in the iron-black night. "'I love you," Frances said into the wind. "You don't have to go. Why do you have to go?"

"Wars make boys into men." Tom smiled. "Everyone knows that," He hugged her close against him, calmed her.

"Don't tease."

"I'm not." He was serious now. "If all goes well, I'll be an officer–and a gentleman. I've read of these things, Frances, all my life. Wars have a way of propelling people farther ahead than they would ever have gotten without them. Smart people. Clever people. The war will be my college. I won't die in it. In the back of my mind, I've always believed that a man knows if he's going to die. And I know I'm not. Not now. I'll be someone you'll be proud of."

"I understand plays, I guess. But I don't understand life. I don't understand you."

Tom gazed at her. "Courage," he said with soft detachment. "That's what life's about, isn't it? And the fight against laziness, of course–energy. But, mostly, courage."

Frances's eyes held back their tears, but, in a minute, they shot suddenly upward. "Look at the sky," she declared. For there, in the Southern night, a great comet shone, brighter than any star, with a long tail and a head the size of a full autumnal moon. "What is it?"

"I don't know."

"It's an omen. And it frightens me."

"If it's an omen," Tom replied gently, "it's the omen of a

new age." He watched it silently, transfixed for a minute. "And a new age is bound to be our age." He kissed her forehead. "Wouldn't you say, Frances?"

She smiled. "Why, you're a genuine romantic, Thomas Chance, and no one would ever know it by looking at you."

"Come on," he said. "Look. There's a telescope on the bow. Why don't we use it?" He pulled the cover from around the brass instrument.

"Me first." Frances pretended to be happy.

"It'll be a blur still."

"Fix it, then."

"So you think that little comet's prophetic, do you?"

"Little! Our poor country."

"Yes. But we'll be fine, you and I. And do you know why? I'll tell you. Put your eye to the glass. Now move it to the right, very slightly." Tom paused. "That's why. Because we know how to use a telescope. All there is to it."

Frances nodded. "Really," she asked, "what in the world are you talking about?"

"Kiss me first and I'll tell you. . . . Good. . . . Now, I'll show you: You see, the way to use a telescope is like this, with the small end at your eye and the large end facing the object you want to see. That way, an object that would be very small to the naked eye becomes much larger. But, as sensible as it is, most people don't use that method."

"They don't."

"No. Most people do exactly the reverse." Tom twirled the device, squeezed his whole face against the large screen. "They want to reduce not mysterious comets, but very obvious, everyday things. They don't want to enlarge them, but to make them smaller to fit the scale of their own petty imaginations."

"I see," Frances said, though she didn't quite. All the sky was illuminated now, with a yellow mist of phosphorescence.

"Then how can we have anything but wonderful futures

before us?" Tom coaxed. "If you don't trust the stars, look at your hands." He raised them, stared at them. "You have such beautiful hands."

Frances waited. "I'll always love you, Tom," she said. "Always." She struggled to regain the earlier note of laughter. "But I don't have beautiful hands. Just capable hands. Like my mother."

Tom bit his lip. His eyes ran up the sky dome. "Yes," he said absently. "Capable hands. Like my mother, too."

BOOK III

THE LEGEND

(1868–1891)

CHAPTER

15

JUNE, 1868.

With an extraordinary, delicate touch, as though it might crumble in their grip, the long, tapered fingers of Henri Langlois, the Belgian jeweler, removed a square-cut diamond ring from one of the Goelette and Company vitrines and delicately held it up to the window's light for appraisal. For a long moment, this ascetic-looking young man—he was thirty-two, very tall, gaunt—stared at the stone and seemed to hold his breath until, suddenly, as a spoiled child might forsake a toy, he dropped his hand back into the case, slipped the ring again onto its pad, and took up what appeared to be its twin. Behind him, silent but curiously poised, Thomas Chance and another man, darker, shorter, watched him as he worked.

"Regular surgeon's hands," the other man whispered appreciatively into Chance's ear.

"I told you," Chance agreed. He had removed his coat and was working in only his cotton shirt.

Langlois, who had not been meant to hear, continued to study the new diamond. "Artist's hands," he said absently, without diverting his ice-blue eyes from the jewel in his hands, and without smiling.

Chance laughed. "Yes," he said. "I suppose there are all sorts of artists, aren't there? We're all three artists in our way. Henri Langlois, may I present Felix Hardenstein, Goelette and Company's new accountant."

Langlois looked up at Chance, thought, rose to his feet, and extended his hand to the dark, intensely bearded Hardenstein. On his forefinger, above the knuckle, he wore the ring he had been inventorying. Chance noticed it.

"Monsieur Langlois," Chance proceeded to tell Hardenstein, "is from Belgium. From Antwerp. In fact, he has a very successful business there. He and I did some business recently, very satisfactorily, involving the Pearl of Macao that I showed you."

"Oh?"

"And he has, very kindly, agreed to come and direct this shop. For a time." He looked at Langlois. Langlois nodded as his eyes fluttered.

"Excellent," Hardenstein said in a deep, rich voice.

"Mr. Hardenstein was on Wall Street," Chance explained. "After considerable investigation he was recommended to me as a man who is as discreet with private information as he is clever with figures. You're both about the same age. I hope you shall work well together."

"I was certain you were from Wall Street," Langlois replied. "One can always tell a man who works with money, can't one?"

"Yes. I imagine that's right."

Tom took a few steps and surveyed the empty store. "I see you are already around to that side of the room. You're moving fast. How is your inventory progressing? Better than you thought? Or worse?"

Langlois took his seat again. "Many fine pieces," he said. "Two exceptional sapphires. Kashmir. Oooh, what I'd have given to have had them in Antwerp! I had a Russian client who would have snapped them up. There's a ruby, too, fit for the Czar. But it doesn't belong to us. And, of course, many good diamonds, a few of which are large—quite large, in fact. But, sadly, nothing like the Macao."

"All these belonged to Goelette?" Hardenstein asked.

"Almost all."

"You bought them at a few cents on the dollar, then?"

"It was a distress sale, of a kind," Tom acknowledged. "Surely, Chamberlain told you that story."

"Yes. But I don't work for Chamberlain, Mr. Chance," Hardenstein declared. "I work for you. Someday, I'd like to hear the whole story from your mouth."

"Someday you will. Right now we have some plans to make. It's important that Goelette and Company not seem, to the public I mean, not seem—what?—*disrupted.* In any way."

"No," Langlois offered sagely. "It would be better if it didn't."

Chance flung out a chair from beneath a showcase and leaned his weight against its back, balancing himself on the balls of his feet. "It's imperative for what I have in mind, if we're going to make a go of it. Let me ask you something, Mr. Langlois, for Mr. Hardenstein's benefit—I already know the answer myself. How many jewelry shops, equal to this one, exist, now, on the continent of Europe? Your guess will do."

"Well, Chaumet, in Paris. And Pierre Cartier, probably, though I doubt he has the stock. And Garrard, in London, or Asprey. Either, I should think. Although I haven't been in London for a while. Antwerp and Amsterdam, more for the stones themselves—for the trade—than great pieces. Vienna has two, and, of course, the Russian houses *can* be excellent." He mumbled. "A guess? Half a dozen. Eight at the most."

"How many here?"

"In America? Tiffany's your biggest competition, isn't he?"

"So I'm told."

"But he's a little more everyday in his approach. Not quite what we are. Not quite so—exclusive."

"Well, I wouldn't underestimate him. He's very good, and very well established, but I think you're probably correct. And so you can see, Hardenstein, just what a rarefied world we've moved ourselves into. And how easy it would be, with a new management, for people to say that we didn't quite fit. They'll be looking for changes where there aren't any. So it's very important that we not *disrupt* anything, as I said."

"Right you are. But I still say that once a principal is gone, as Goelette surely is, any firm must make adjustments."

"Have a seat."

"Thank you."

"And I'll outline those adjustments you're so eager to see."

Hardenstein shot a glance at Langlois, who did not return it.

"First, Mr. Langlois," Tom asked, "when will our inventory be complete?"

"Today is Monday," Langlois answered. "Wednesday morning, positively."

"Now, Mr. Hardenstein, I asked you earlier for certain information. When do you think you will be able to give it to me?"

Hardenstein's coal-black eyes lit up. "The list of receivables is already on your desk. Names and amounts. Some of them will surprise you."

"Good."

"What I mean is that some of those who owe us the most are the richest people in New York."

"Or thought to be," Chance added, smiling.

"Now, as for the bank matters: Goelette and Company has always done business with The Bank of Manhattan. That is, on a regular basis, one day to the next. On an irregular basis, certain financings have been arranged through Drexel and Childs."

"But there is nothing outstanding with them at the moment?"

"No."

"And Mr. Anthony Drexel is a client here, is he not?"

"A very good one. Seems he always pays by check, at the time of purchase."

Chance felt a sudden, internal laugh. "The only things I ever really *bought* here I paid for in cash," he said.

"Excuse me, sir."

"Nothing. Go on."

"Well, there's nothing outstanding with Drexel, as I said. Actually, there are no loans due anywhere."

"Tomorrow," Chance said, "I want to remove, say, a quarter of the funds we have on deposit with The Bank of Manhattan and put them in the Tenth National."

"That's Chamberlain's."

"And Tweed's. Correct. Don't tell anyone where they are going."

"No, sir."

Tom said, "If they ask at The Bank of Manhattan, say you don't know, but you think it's for a purchase of jewelry. They're an old institution in this town, with a useful imprimatur. They can be useful friends. So don't offend them. Don't start them thinking. Then, when you go to the Tenth, have the people there get as much financial information as they can on anyone who owes us money: what they own, what else they owe."

"I'll be very quiet about it, too," Hardenstein, the man from Wall Street, said.

"That's right."

"Now, Mr. Langlois, the first time you see a large piece that you think is good value and that this firm should buy, I want you to come to me immediately, because I want to make whatever arrangements have to be made through Drexel."

"As you wish. I can only pass on the value of gems. Not banking houses."

"I want them to trust us." Tom made an elaborate travesty

of a pause, then continued. "I can read your face, Felix. You want to ask me, but you're not sure if you should. You want to know how, considering the manner in which this company was taken over, can I ever hope to expect any truly honest firm to trust us. Don't you?"

Hardenstein, instantly flustered, answered: "That's a good way of putting it, sir," and stretched the muscles of his neck.

"Well, I will answer that for you, very simply. By letting them make a little money off of us. That's how."

Hardenstein's suspicious eyes were more intense than usual. "On the theory that even the best businessmen forget when there's a profit involved?"

"On the theory that most people live for the future," Chance said. "Now, first thing in the morning, I want to meet with the staff. Before we open. Right here. They're crucial to us at this point and I don't want them to spend their time worrying about their jobs when what they have to be worrying about, what we all have to be, is making sales."

"I'll arrange it," Langlois said. "Although, the floor manager, Mr. Thistle, is considering leaving, as you know. He mentioned it to one of the others and word got to me."

"He's too loyal," Chance said. "I know that. I'll take care of him. Any other questions?"

Hardenstein cleared his throat. "Not about the immediate future, really, but we haven't talked at all about anything farther away than day after tomorrow."

"Mr. Langlois?"

"I can't think farther ahead than that. I have all I can do to finish this inventory."

"Yes," Chance said, in a new tone, half sensitive. "One day at a time. No visions. No direction. Not yet. Until we see which way the wind blows. All right?"

Confounded, Hardenstein said, "Yes, Mr. Chance."

And Thomas Chance, for an instant flashing the white of

his teeth, the old, reliable, beguiling smile of his youth, said: "For God's sake, Felix, call me Tom."

Counting the men in the shop, of whom there were nine, and not counting Langlois or Hardenstein, Goelette and Company had twenty-four employees in all: four women—the youngest nineteen, the oldest seventy—in the office; the imperial floor manager; five salesmen; a Prussian doorman; two Irish maids; a short, but especially solid-looking Chinese man who performed double duty as a janitor and packer; and the floor manager's eviscerated nephew who ran general errands, without large valuables, about New York. On Tuesday morning, promptly at a quarter before nine, they were all assembled in the store. The safes had been opened at eight thirty sharp; the last of the jewelry had been put on display in the showcases; and the staff, having been more than usually quick in its rounds, waited nervously for Thomas Chance to begin. As a matter of courtesy, the available chairs had been left first to the ladies and then to the older men present. But by the time Chance cleared his throat most of the employees, though not the Chinese, the errand boy, or two of the shop men, were seated.

Thomas Chance himself, dressed in a gray country suit with a faint blue overcheck, and looking more like a man who planned to spend his day beside the fashionable new track at Jerome Park than tending shop, took a seat on the top of a solid-looking walnut desk and crossed his legs.

"Good morning," he said, pausing immediately afterward, uneasy in the quiet. "As many of you know, I am Thomas Chance. I am the new proprietor of Goelette and Company. I'm not from New York. Although I've spent a considerable amount of time here, I'm from Baltimore, Maryland—two hundred miles south, smaller, but a city not altogether unlike New York. A port city, and more cosmopolitan than most.

But, putting that fact aside for a moment, I'm sure that there are more questions about me than those having to do with where I come from . . ."

A murmurous hum, like the rising, then descending scales of a musical exercise, passed through the showroom.

". . . And I think it's only fair of me to try and answer them. So let me begin with the first, that is the first question I would be asking if I were out there where you are sitting. Am I a jeweler by trade? That is, do I know anything about gems and jewelry-making? Well, the answer to that is both yes and no. Yes, because I do have some knowledge of gems, but it's an amateur's knowledge compared to yours: I've been a client of this firm's, for instance . . ."

A second hum: a single note, released almost chorally, then caught.

"And no, because I've never really been in this business before. Until now, it hasn't been my life. However, I have been in the retail business since the age of thirteen. And I think I know not only that business, but the special part of it that has to do with what we call 'the carriage trade'—*that* business—about as well as anyone could. I've sold at the counter and been very successful there too, enough to know that it's the most important part of any store, because that's where the life-and-death decisions are made, the decisions of customers to buy or not to buy."

He took a theatrical breath, passed his deep green eyes about the room, engaging, in turn, the eyes of each of those present, some for longer than others. Thomas Chance was, once again, on stage, fashioning a mask, presenting it, selling it.

"But I don't want anyone here to misunderstand me," he continued, "because anyone who has worked at selling knows that it is impossible if he doesn't have the merchandise in his case, or if he can't get it. As quickly as the customer demands, he has to be, must be, backed up in every way by the rest of his company. By the craftsmen. The office. The other salesmen. And, not least, the proprietor. So, before I go on, I want to tell you that I intend to give you all the support, all that you'll ever need—*and more*! Both through Mr. Langlois and personally. That's another promise I make you.

"Back to questions, for a minute. If were you, I'd want to know just how much capital this new man, Chance, was putting into the firm. Not out of simple nosiness, but because that level of capital might mean the difference between my having a job and not having one." For a moment, everyone sat up. The youngest office girl, like the oldest, held her hands in her lap, but so tightly together that her knuckle cracked.

"One thing about me is that, even though I'm young—twenty-eight is the correct age, whatever you've heard: I was born on Leap Year, 1840—I'm old-fashioned in some ways. For instance, I don't like to talk, or even to hear too much said about my business arrangements. So I'm going to be general rather than explicit with you. But I'm going to tell you that there is enough money presently in and available to this company for us to be sure of . . . well, I think you know that what I mean is that money will not be a problem if we, all of us, do the best jobs of which we are capable.

"In that connection, although I realize it is unnecessary, I want you all to know that you shall continue to have your jobs, if you want them. We are starting with a clean slate and I can promise you that when you are later judged, it will be upon what you do after this day and not on what has happened, if anything, before it. Of course, if anyone wants to leave for any reason, that's a private decision, which I will respect. But we are planning great things for this company, you should know that—real movement forward—and I would hate to think of anyone walking out on that kind of success without giving it half a chance."

Then the postman knocked at the front entrance, bearing the morning sheath of letters and packages. Mr. Thistle spotted the shadow of his uniform through the pale curtain of the door and glanced over his shoulder for Chance's approval, which he got at once, before turning the key.

"Well," reckoned Mrs. McCorquadale in a hushed, almost intimate voice, "he has plans at any rate, whatever they are. He seems to be a builder, not a destroyer. That's a good sign, I'd say." She dropped each word lightly, as she might have dropped small stones into a pond, hoping to contain the ripples within a certain area. Three inches on the plump side, about fifty, with her hair in a bun and a ne'er-do-well husband in Brooklyn, she meant to address only those immediately around her, the remaining three women who worked in the office, particularly Miss Doolan, the youngest.

"He's a good-looking fellow," another woman said.

"He's a piece of work all right," whispered Mrs. McCorquadale. "Wouldn't you say so, Edith?"

"Yes," answered Miss Doolan shyly. "Oh, yes, I'd say so."

"Then we're all betting on you," continued Mrs. McCorquadale in a magnificent conspiratorial rhythm. "We're, all the rest of us, too old for him by a good bit. Why, I'm old enough to be his mother. Well, not quite . . ."

Another woman smiled. "Darn, McCorquadale," she interrupted. "He's twenty-eight, he said. You could have even had him late in life."

"Foolishness!"

Miss Doolan smiled.

Under camouflage of the general noise, the gossip of cliques continued until the postman left and Thistle snapped the door shut.

"All right," Chance said then. "So, the matter of jobs being settled—because you have them, they're here—only one thing else remains to be asked. If you're truly as clever a firm as the population of New York seems to think you are, then you will ask how I, not being a jeweler, can hope to continue the glorious record of my predecessor, Laurence Goelette."

He crossed the legs of his trousers again, stared for a moment at the reflection which played on the brogue of his shoe. With the tip of a finger he removed a long lock up from his forehead and grinned.

"And the answer is yours for the asking. And simple. By hiring the best people I can find. Hardenstein, our grumpy genius of the books." He laughed. "Monsieur Langlois. Each and every one of you. No one knows Goelette and Company as you do. No one could. On no one will I rely more." He paused then, suggesting, perhaps, that he might have suddenly concluded without warning. Then he looked about again.

"One more thing," he added, "in order that you will know where I stand. When I worked for someone else, I never allowed that fact to color my thinking. I worked as though the business were mine and I would be putting all the profit from everything I sold straight into my pocket. *But,* I wanted to be paid for it. I expected to be. *Demanded* to be."

"Here, here," said one of the younger shopworkers.

"That's as it should be," said Thomas Chance.

"Three cheers for you," said another.

Chance laughed. "Therefore, I'm going to make you a deal. For the summer, through September, all of your salaries will continue to be paid exactly as they have been. I know that Mr. Goelette was French and demanding and more extravagant with himself than he was with you." Here, the perfect demagogue's smile. "But that kind of thinking, if nothing else, has come to an end here. And, starting October first, when we go into our Christmas season, the biggest time of the year, every one of you who has convinced me that you really *mean business* and want to work will have a raise of ten percent—with other raises following later."

His voice trailed off as applause drowned it and, in a quick but considered pivot, he was down from the table.

All that morning, lunchtime, and afternoon he spent in

his office, behind the protective glares of the women in the outer room, interviewing each employee individually. He averaged fifteen minutes with each; enough time to have the man or woman sit, drink a cup of Brazilian coffee or English tea, and begin to talk. "Since you, in many ways, bear the most responsibility of any member of this firm," he told the owl-faced Mr. Thistle, "I'm going to effect your raise—fifteen percent—immediately. Somewhat larger than the others. In consideration of your position." And Thistle, who, as Chance knew from the company books, had not had a raise in salary for almost a decade, smiled gratefully, extended his hand, and never again spoke of leaving.

Chance told the foreman of his workshop that "everything" would depend on him and his men. "If you don't have it, you can't sell it." Then, an hour and a half later, he told the youngest salesman that "everything" would depend on *him*. "If it's not sold, what good does it do you? What's the value of anything if you can't turn it into money?" Although he knew it unnecessary, he confidentially told Hardenstein to "keep an eye on" Langlois because "he may have more artistic sense than business." And Langlois to do the same on Hardenstein because "all he can see are dollar signs. And we are not in the dollar business, we're in the jewelry business." He asked for a running, personally conducted inventory from each man and from Thistle. He instructed the Chinese to use whatever force was necessary to prevent a robbery, to call the police in from the street first, but to shoot if he had to. And he promised all four of the women that they were his right hand.

"I remember when I was twenty," he told Miss Doolan, who was the last to be seen.

Having a china teacup at her lips, she did not answer.

"What do you think I was doing then? I'll bet you'd never guess."

She swallowed. "Some kind of businessman?" she asked.

"No, I was an actor."

"An actor?"

"But then the war came."

"And terrible it was."

"Yes. Well, where are you from? Where do you live?"

"Brooklyn. That's on my sheet. I know it because I filled it out myself."

"Brooklyn. Well, I hope you're happy coming over here every day."

Miss Doolan trembled a little and replaced the cup and saucer onto the coffee table. "Oh, I am, sir. Very."

"I'll bet you have many beaux," he said, not understanding why himself. She was not a pretty girl according to either conventional standards or his own. But the very qualities which kept her from being pretty—too-thick lips, a certain skin and bones quality to the rest of her—nonetheless struck him as erotic.

"No," she said. "Not me. I don't have even . . . well, one of the boys in the shop likes me, I guess you could say, but that's all. And he's crazy to . . ." She tried desperately to hide her feelings in laughter.

Chance played along. "Tell me something," he asked, coming around from his desk. "What do you like to do?"

"Like to do? . . . I don't know. My job? My housework?"

"What do you do well? What one likes to do is often the very thing one does well, if you understand what I mean?"

She thought suddenly. "Well," the words sprang forth from her. "I like to dance."

"I don't blame you. I love to dance."

Mrs. McCorquadale opened the door then. "Excuse me, Mr. Chance."

"Yes?"

"Mr. James Fisk is in the store. Mr. Thistle thought you'd want me to inform you."

"Thank you very much."

"He's the Erie Railroad man," Mrs. McCorquadale ran on. "There's also a pair of dealers. A Hebrew. And a Persian.

They travel together. The Hebrew cuts diamonds. The Persian only deals in colored stones. Mr. Goelette had a fixed appointment with them, every Tuesday at about this time."

"Fine, then ask them to wait."

"Very well." Mrs. McCorquadale stepped back a little as he passed her on his way into the store, seeming, with the motion of a wave, to deposit Miss Doolan once more into her care.

Goelette and Company, on the east side of Fifth Avenue just below Fourteenth Street and Union Square, was unusual among the retail establishments of its day in that it owned its own real estate: a squarish marble vault of a building, smaller than the new iron-fronted stores, but vastly more enduring to the eye; more substantial, with an open passageway of space on either side, a pair of exquisitely reticent frosted-glass lamps at the entrance, and smart, blocked awnings in the French style. Except for the awnings, which Mr. Goelette had called "sportive," the premises reminded Thomas Chance of a bank.

The night after his meetings with his staff, he made a personal tour, by candlelight, of every inch of it, including the third-floor storerooms. Then, on the following morning, before he took even one message, he asked Miss Doolan to call the Chinese into his office.

"The third floor," Thomas Chance said. "It was an apartment once. I can tell. Someone lived there."

"Mr. Goelette live there. Until his wife die."

"That was three years ago?"

"I think yes, sir."

"Well, it ought to be all right still. Here's what I want you to do. Take the maids and Mr. Thistle's nephew, John, and give the place the best cleaning you can. I mean *the best*. Verbena wax the wood and take a good soap to the glass. Take a good soap to everything, in fact, before you wax it."

"Oh, yes!"

"Right. I don't care if it takes all week. But I want it to be ready to live in. To entertain customers in. Do you understand me?"

"Not take all week, Mr. Chance," Mr. Li said. "Two days all."

"But you understand what I want?"

"Will be suit-able for best customers," Mr. Li responded. He was smiling with an effusiveness Chance found hard to understand.

"Can you move the storage rooms somewhere else?"

"To the back. What not go there, I put down low in basement."

"Good. Well, thank you, Mr. Li."

Mr. Li stood fast. "'Scuse, Mr. Chance—"

"Yes?"

"If you live third floor, you need cook an' women take care your housekeeping? Yes?"

"That's putting the cart before the horse," Chance laughed. "Do you have someone in mind? Someone in your family?"

"Older brother finest cook in Mulberry Street. Both young sisters, obedient housemaids."

"Well, I'll strike a bargain with you, Mr. Li. You put those rooms in truly first-class shape, and we'll try your family beginning Monday."

"Very good, sir."

"You've been here twenty years, I know you wouldn't put me wrong."

"No, sir. Thank you, sir."

True to his promise, Mr. Li had the old apartment prepared by Friday morning, and Chance moved in on the weekend, after lunching with Frances in the dining room of the Fifth Avenue Hotel.

"Aren't you afraid?" Frances asked him over a plate of jellied consommé.

"What on earth of?"

"Well, I'm certainly not if you're not," Frances said. "But ever since we've been back here, you've seemed so concerned about making the right impression. You're in business now, I understand that. So the way some of these old women look at us, I'm surprised it doesn't bother you. I guess it does bother me, a little."

"Men and women go to restaurants together all the time now," Chance said.

"Men and women who are married," Frances interjected, "or else the women are coquettes. You know that. And so does everybody else who sees them."

"You're *not* a coquette, as you put it. I've told you that. How many times?"

"Sometimes I wonder. If *I* wonder, what must other people think?"

"Try and think of the apartment, if you want a problem to worry about. I want you to take a look at the furniture, then get hold of some good woodcuts. See what the best styles are. So we'll have a proper place. That ought to be done as soon as you possibly can."

"Oh, Lord. My show begins Tuesday . . ."

"All the better. Worry about that and I'll have Thistle or McCorquadale take care of the flat. All the walls are fine as they are. The damask only had one tear in it, but there's a landscape hanging there, so it doesn't matter. It's only a question of a few missing pieces."

"I thought 'flat' was an English word."

"English–and American," Tom said.

Frances laughed. "I was going to say you'd changed in the last week. But underneath it all, you were always pretty serious. I suppose I got too used to Bermuda, to having you, I mean."

"You still have me," Tom answered solemnly.

"Oh, for God's sake, Tom. I'm a woman of twenty-eight. I ought to have children."

"The way we're doing it, it's the only way I can for a

while, for the time being," Tom told her gently. "I can only live for the moment." He hesitated. "Don't think I don't know how that sounds and it's not what I mean, actually, but what I mean sounds even more false. Of course, I live for more than the moment. I'm always planning for the future, calculating. But you've got to believe me, Frances: I don't know what that future's going to be, and I can't marry you—or anyone—until I have a better idea."

Frances looked across the room at a large party to whom a squad of waiters was just then serving a highly glazed game bird. Tears burned in her eyes. "No one knows the future," she replied abstractedly, averting her glance.

"No," Tom said. "Of course not. But that's not what I mean at all and you, who've known me more than half my life, know it isn't. By God, I'll say it. I'm different. One word: *different*. And I have a destiny. That's what everything's gone to make: My good luck in some ways, and all the terrible things in my life. Now, you'll say 'the fellow's mad.' "

"When I was a child I had a destiny," Frances said. "Just like you. But now I've achieved it. And you have, too, Tom, if you'd only try and see. I have a career. You have your business. You said yourself that it was the finest jewelry business in the whole country. And I've heard others say it."

"So you think I should settle down into the jewelry business, making lavish baubles, talking my heart out to sell them." Always to Tom, the very words "store" or "shop" evoked a picture of Lazenby's, of kindly proprietors besotted with trivia: waist sizes, lot sizes, sleeve lengths, shoe widths.

Frances stared curiously. "If that's how it's done, naturally. If not, whatever was the whole thing for?"

"I can scarcely believe what you've said just now."

"Poor Tom," she replied sarcastically, deliberately derailing him. "Order us another claret, will you, when he's by next."

"The whole risk was not undertaken merely to get hold

of a store, Frances, and then leave well enough alone at that."

"No. Then perhaps you want too much."

"Perhaps. You've said that before."

"Shall I tell you how I see it? No, don't answer. I *shall* tell you, whether you like to hear or not. I'm not so facile as you. I start at the beginning of any problem. So I say to myself, Tom wants to be a rich man. Very well. So do most men. And I admit it's a quality I'm drawn to myself. But what is a rich man? That's my next question; and that's where we're different, you and I. I ask it. You don't.

"A rich man is someone who can have what he wants. Or very largely so. Correct?"

"Yes."

"So, I ask *my*self, aren't there two ways of getting rich: one by finding money; the other by wanting less."

Tom laughed. "Damn the theater. You belong in a university."

"It's not as stupid as you think, what I said."

"I didn't say it was stupid." Tom straightened his chair. A waiter hurried over. Tom signaled him away. "Now, listen to me, Frances. Very carefully. We're not there yet, where you think we are. We haven't come the whole way by a long shot. Remember your father's sermon about some people being pint containers, some quart, some gallon. And each man had to fill himself. The parable of the talents, remember. Well, I have always known, even before he said it and I thought of it in that way, that I was a gallon container." He flashed his smile again. "Or a barrel. And I always thought that you understood that and that, in your own way, you were too. Don't you want to be the *star* of the show?"

"But less than before. There are so many people better than I could ever hope to be. The English girls are much better trained. And some of the Americans are so pretty. One week at Wallack's again and I already see how much tougher it's become since last year. The best actresses from all over the country come here. It's not like Baltimore, but this is where you have to succeed, isn't it? I mean if you are going to succeed on Tom Chance's scale."

She took a long drink of the wine, tossed her head back, and watched the lights, the globes of milky white glass in which they burned.

"America is changing," Tom resumed, his eyes keen and sharp, his voice rhapsodic. "Any fool can see it! It's the age of iron. And steel. Most of all, railroads. The country's opening up. Just since Appomattox. And there are kings' fortunes waiting to be made. You don't have to go far to know that. It's as clear as—as Colonel Harvey's new elevated over on Ninth Avenue.

"And Goelette is just our nut, that's all. Just a ticket into the game so that I can play with the money men. You know how I think of it? Not as a store, but as if that nice marble building were a bank and in it there was only one account and it belonged to me. Of course, it's my job to make it run and give me all the profit it can, but that's only the half of it. I have another job, too. I have to use that money—like a pry: borrow on it, let it work for me until I'm in the really *big* deals. Not selling one pearl to one man, that's not a big deal. Even for a million dollars." He laughed, then wiped his forehead with his napkin. "It was only a start. The country's got to grow now. And I'm going to build it, Frances, as much of it as I can. That's the kind of big deal I'm talking about."

Frances clenched her teeth. For an instant, involuntarily, they shivered. "Sometimes," she said, "I wonder what would have happened if we had never left Baltimore."

"Dreams change one minute to the next," Tom told her. "Right now I'm having a new one. I wouldn't say it's smaller. But it's surely more immediate."

"Honestly." Frances looked up. "In midafternoon?"

Tom teased, "Sounds almost cheap, doesn't it?"

"I was a chorus girl," Frances laughed. "I have a taste for the cheap side of things."

"Make haste to my new premises," Tom said in a plain imitation of a theatrical voice.

Frances put her hand across the table, resting it for a moment on top of Tom's. Her eyes regarded him through a long pause, at once projecting all the eagerness she felt and masking the tragedy. A breeze, from nowhere, flurried across the great room and touched her skin. And, as she raised her hand to the down on her neck, she felt, in the transitory summer chill, the unmistakable death of something precious.

CHAPTER 16

As proprietor of Goelette and Company, Chance had an impeccable entré into the beau monde of post-Civil War New York. Fashionable women streamed through the shop, some almost weekly. And, in their wake, husbands, consorts, and would-be lovers often followed, money in hand. The Astors came. The Stuyvesants. The Connages, Cutlers, Coxes, and Coffins. The respected Joneses. The Madison Barts. Old Mrs. Hoggenheimer. Young Mrs. Hergenroeder. The ballerina, Madame Sacha Brizzard. P. T. Barnum himself. The Seligmans, Kuhns, and Goodmans; the Schleisners, Strausses, and Reginald Strongs of J. The Hills, Harrimans, Headleys, Haywards, and Hays. The theatrical Murdochs. The meat-packing Murdochs. Tom Thumb. The lady with two heads, from the Barnum Museum. Even the celebrated Madame Van z Panz, whose true name was unknown, but who, by even experienced accounts, presided over the finest brothel in New York.

Auras of perfume drifted across the room. The whispers of old women, the laughter of young, eddied out from hidden corners, past the mannered traffic at the gold jewelry counter. People stepped lightly, wore beautiful clothes. And the atmosphere—an intensely stronger proof of Lazenby's, more intoxicating because this was New York—grew heady by noontime, particularly with the onset of autumn.

There were still rumors about Chance, of course. Someone said he had killed a man. But, with astonishing rapidity,

Tom Chance and Goelette and Company had become one in the minds of people who counted. Those on the outside had little interest in anything more than the glamour of the Goelette name, to which they had been accustomed for decades and from which they would not waver so long as the new proprietor maintained its standards.

Thomas Chance conducted most of his daytime business in the elaborate office where he had first bought the Pearl of Macao. The word of his interest in "propositions" had not taken long to get around the city, and soon the pages of his appointment books had become almost solid blue with ink. Throughout the day strangers came and left—well-dressed men carrying briefcases, men with plans, seeking Chance's advice and backing. One might have guessed that they were all attorneys-at-law, or bankers: sedate, brisk, professional.

Yet despite this, and despite his personal cachet, as Christmas approached, Tom was increasingly aware that he seldom saw the best families after six o'clock. And, after a time, he made it his business to find out why.

New York society was then divided between "nobs," whose ancestries were most often Dutch and who represented the entrenched wealth of the city, and "swells," who, like him, had grown rich in the Civil War era. The boundary between these classes, like a well-grown hedgerow, was observed and respected, but, nonetheless, far from solid. Industry, looks, and temperate manners had propelled at least twenty men Tom could name (if not recognize) across it, established them socially once and for all. And even these, he imagined, would be hollow assets when compared to the right girl's affections.

But there was a problem in that approach. The most conspicuous heiresses of the day resembled cows, or so it seemed to him, and he had no interest at all in selling himself to such a female. They were wide-hipped, fat-jowled; their mouths seemed full of mush when they spoke. The hour-glass figure was indeed the fashion, but these young women seemed to Tom to be hiding their excesses behind it. They had little to say; less, in the way of body, for a man to be curious about; and yet, in an alternating current of giddiness and complacency, they made it impossibly clear that they knew who they were.

Only rarely, at one of the counters, or seated with her family in a box at the Academy of Music, or driving in the park, had Tom been attracted by the kind of superior young woman whose subtler beauty, softer manner, and finer accent reminded him of Clara and suggested that, in Mr. Thistle's phrase, "very few of heaven's gifts had been withheld." Yet these situations had never lent themselves to exploitation.

Until, in March, he met Elizabeth Evarts Pope.

It was a limpid morning, almost Mediterranean. A blizzard had fallen two days before and great wave-shaped drifts of snow still remained in the streets; but the sun, angling out of cloudless sky above the East River, felt once again near to the skin. The thermometer showed sixty degrees.

Ice had begun trickling down into streams that puddled the mud between paving blocks and flooded and ran in the gutters, and dripped, steady as rain, from the eaves of a hundred buildings. Horses still missed their step on hidden patches of startling slipperiness. Carriage wheels, though very few, still went dead on their axles, making sleighs of the coaches they supported and producing, usually for no more than a frightened moment, a chorus of high-pitched screams. And yet most men were hatless. The collars of their coats were down for the first time in months. All at once, after the endless interior winter, people were coming unbundled, chancing hazards, going out. Like a mountain prospect from which one can see, across a border, the landscapes of two profoundly different countries, it was a day which looked forward and back. The air, like summer ocean, grew cooler the lower down one felt it, the farther from the sun, and great buildings cast shadows that made pools of gray winter again. But the soft, intoxicating perfumes of the false spring had come unfrozen: salt at the piers, grass in the farmlands; and there was pollen in the virgin springtime light.

Until noon, the showroom was empty of clients. Mr. Li and the maids busied themselves polishing English tureens and repoussé tea sets. Mr. Thistle and the others conducted a full-scale inventory. And Thomas Chance paced quietly about, throwing a keen eye on each case and checking each jewel against the record in his memory.

Then, suddenly, the door opened, flooding the tired must of Goelette and Company with the fresh, ripe promise of the day, and two women, mother and daughter, entered. Behind them, at the curbside of Fifth Avenue, Chance could see their victoria waiting and, harnessed to it, a pair of exceptionally handsome bay horses. The coachman and footman were liveried in buff and, under the whip, a spotted Dalmatian had come to rest like a porcelain statue.

Mr. Li hurried to the door and took it, by the inside handles, out of their grip.

Thistle, more than ever like a smiling owl, approached them at a politic pace and distance.

The elder lady smiled. "Mr. Thistle," she said. She enunciated the name with an imperceptible movement of her jaw, as pleased with herself for recalling it as Thistle was flattered that she had.

"Indeed, Mrs. Pope. And good morning to you ladies. May I be of some assistance?"

Mrs. Pope walked a step forward and her daughter followed. Next to the younger woman, a small white poodle heeled obediently.

Chance did not take his eyes from them.

They appeared, to him, rather like Alice and the Queen

of Hearts, as Goelette and Company had recently sculpted them in gold for an eccentric English client. And yet, Mrs. Pope projected more softness, less shrillness and severity; she smiled. The Popes were descendants of George Garrick Pope, who had amassed a fortune trapping and trading furs, much as the original John Jacob Astor had done. Chance knew this, just as he knew that they lived in a fabulous Italianate house on Lafayette Square near Nineteenth Street and that they often traveled abroad. For these facts were an essential part of the lexicon of a certain class in New York at that time; and, besides, the *Herald* reported them.

Thistle offered an even more obsequious smile and waited. The young woman, fair-skinned and blond, and entirely covered by a blue dress, thought that such a smile would hurt the muscles of her face if she were forced to make it, and no doubt give her wrinkles prematurely. Under her breath, she was starting to explain this feeling to her little dog, when her mother turned to her and said, "Mr. Thistle, Mr. Goelette is no longer here, is that my understanding?"

"Quite correct. He's . . ."

"No matter. My daughter, Elizabeth, is about to have her nineteenth birthday, Mr. Thistle. And, for her party, Mr. Pope and I thought she might have a piece of jewelry entirely her own. More to the point, *I* did. Inherited pieces can be splendid, naturally. But I think I remember that, at eighteen . . ." Her voice trailed off.

Mr. Thistle considered her appreciatively. He liked the arch of her back, the exacting clip of her speech. "Right you are, madam. And it's a very generous sentiment on your behalf."

"Of course, Mr. Pope wanted to choose it himself, but what's the point in that, what?"

"No," Thistle demurred. "Although Mr. Roderick Pope's taste is well known in New York, what we are concerned with here, I take it, is the young lady's, don't you know."

"Within bounds. My suggestion was a necklace. Something fine." Mrs. Pope flicked her wrist for emphasis. In the language of the day, and especially among her own set, she was what was called a "character." "Fine, but discreet. Not one's bank account on a thin gold rope, you understand."

"Nineteen," Thistle repeated thoughtfully.

"I was in Europe last year," Elizabeth interjected. "I was what is called a debutante—"

"I'm sure Mr. Thistle knows what a debutante is, Elizabeth. Honestly."

"I don't see why. They don't have debutantes in America, do they? Not really. But I'm sorry, Mr. Thistle, if—"

"No, Miss Pope. You needn't apologize."

"Well, anyway, the English girls had lovely pavé necklaces. The diamonds were set in silver on gold. I know that doesn't sound like it makes the simplest sense, but I asked one and that's precisely what she told me it was."

"To the contrary, it makes all the sense in the world. Let me show you such a piece, and you can tell me if the look of it seems right to you. Don't think of the design, but the materials, and then we'll come back to whatever we have to."

"There's a man over there who's been staring at us the whole time we've been talking," Elizabeth said abruptly. "I think that's awfully rude, don't you?"

Mr. Thistle looked around at his staff. "Which—"

"Don't turn. He's wearing gray. Just over your shoulder. Very handsome, too. And one scarcely sees fine-looking men anymore. Beautiful women—but the beautiful men are few and far between."

Mr. Thistle's face was blank. Mrs. Pope said: "I'm sorry, Mr. Thistle. It's the new sort of small talk, I imagine. What they're using in England these days. Or I don't know where my daughter would have learned it." Her stare and the even flatness of her tone were direct reprimands to Elizabeth. She paused, then added: "Even if it's a compliment one's paying, one learns it doesn't always do to be—direct."

"Yes, Mother. But *he* was staring. And he still is."

Thistle bridled, turned, and quickly turned back. "The man in gray," he smiled, "is Mr. Thomas Chance, our new proprietor. I'm certain he only means to see that you were taken care of properly."

"How old is he?"

"Elizabeth!"

"Twenty-nine, I think."

"He looks younger. Still, twenty-nine doesn't seem very old. It's young, I should imagine, to be the proprietor of a famous firm such as this."

"Very," Mr. Thistle said, having caught his employer's eye a moment before. "Allow me to introduce you. Mr. Chance," he continued in a raised voice. "Excuse me, Mr. Chance. I wonder if you have a moment for us."

Tom regarded Elizabeth once again across the distance before he began to move. It was as though, in a moment he had never really expected to live, he had, by accident, come face to face with someone he had thought alive only in his imagination. And it made him nervous. He looked for defects—anything to prove that this was not the girl he had dreamed of for years—but there were none. Her Dutch blond hair, straight from the roots, burst out into lovelocks by the side of her face. Her skin was smooth, young, vulnerable, and yet, like an athlete's, flooded with pink. Her brow arched naturally, a little aloof, superior, not a kind brow, but a symbol of will; and her eyes, darker than the rest, peered out below it through the most suggestive squint he had ever seen. The mouth was a wide, ready Cupid's bow of exceptional redness. Because of the hair, and because her young skin fitted tightly over her bones, the first impression was almost Hellenic, but she was more pretty than strong. Tom knew this instinctively, sensed that she had been made, like a hyacinth, to bloom in her spring.

Her high blue dress accentuated the childhood which she had only recently left behind and gave, to the press of her body against it, a look of mild and pleasant sinfulness and, to the moment, especially for Tom, an air of poignance, even urgency.

He smiled evenly as he joined their group, awaiting Thistle's introduction, which was immediately forthcoming.

"Mrs. and Miss Pope," he said, "it's a great pleasure."

Elizabeth's dark eyes drank him in. "Mr. Thistle was about to show us some necklaces," she said. "Mummy, myself, and Horace."

"Horace is your little dog?"

"I brought him back from France with me last autumn. Don't you think he's the most adorable poodle you've ever seen? Do you have any others as customers, Mr. Chance—poodles, I mean?" She fluttered her lashes, out of her mother's view.

Tom smiled. "One or two," he replied. "I hope that doesn't disappoint you."

"You know perfectly well that it does," she continued. "But I warn you, I'll not buy anything at all unless Horace approves it."

"Did you hear that, Mr. Thistle?" Tom said. "We must be very good to Horace."

Mr. Thistle looked surprised. He was behind a case now, holding a necklace up for Mrs. Pope's inspection, and she was moving toward him, leaving Tom and Elizabeth behind for what she thought a harmless moment.

"How old is Horace?" Tom asked.

"Not quite two years. He wasn't a puppy when I got him. Obviously."

"Oh." Tom stumbled for time as Horace sniffed, dismissively, at his cuff.

"You'll have to forgive him." Elizabeth smiled. "He's not really shy. They cut his moustache off by mistake and he's very embarrassed about not having it anymore. Are *you* embarrassed about not having a moustache, Mr. Chance? You must be the only clean-shaven man in New York."

"I've had them from time to time."

"Well, don't grow one on my account," Elizabeth stated provocatively. "I think they're plain awful. And you, of all people, don't need one. I guess I shouldn't have said that."

"I'm glad that you did."

Elizabeth hesitated. Tom looked sideways at her mother. He bent over a nearby case, hoping to gain, by the appearance of business, more time alone with Elizabeth. And Elizabeth, sensing his unspoken intention, played along. "These are all meant for dinosaurs, aren't they?" she inquired. "Another reason that Horace is nervous is that he's just been divorced, poor thing."

"I *am* sorry." Tom left his mouth wide open.

"He was married, quite briefly actually, to an apricot poodle. We Popes aren't prejudiced, you see. Apricot poodles are fine, Father says, if one happens to like apricot." As though she had been discoursing, all along, on a matter of the highest seriousness, she opened her hands in a small gesture of apology for something she meant one to feel she'd been fated to say.

Tom straightened, considered her with a long, mock-professional gaze. "Diamonds, absolutely," he said suddenly. "You're the most obvious princess I've ever seen."

"Elizabeth," Mrs. Pope called then. "Mr. Chance. . . . Mr. Thistle wanted you to see this, dear. I won't say anything. Why don't you try it in the mirror before you decide?" It was a scrolled Victorian design, diamond on silver on gold, and Tom helped her with the clasp, remaining on the client's side of the case as Elizabeth pondered the matter.

By the word "character" her friends had meant that Adelaide Pope had been known to smoke a cigarette in public, rumored to have puffed a gentleman's pipe in private (as to what it contained there was still further speculation) and, as a girl of Elizabeth's age, to have ridden bareback, in a most untraditional habit, along the bridle paths of Bloomingdale on the Upper West Side. But the veneer of formality was no less occlusive for the playfulness of the soul it hid; and Chance was awed by her rule-like posture, her direct carriage, the wide, netted bouffant of her hair. What faint hint he found of her more sympathetic side resulted less from anything she did or said than from her vague resemblance to Mrs. McAuliffe, in Baltimore.

Nonetheless, behind the most reserved of faces, her experience decided that he was handsome; more importantly, that he was interesting; and that he was "going places." It was one of her beliefs—deeply held, but not often discussed—that the aristocracy, above all, required the best of the "new blood" if it intended to survive. And though it was precisely this opinion which differentiated her from the model grand dames, Chance did not yet know her well enough to sniff it out and work it to advantage.

Elizabeth made a little, unhappy smirk. Tom looked at her. The necklace lay awkwardly against her dress.

"No," he said. "You're right."

"Maybe for some great duch-ess," she smiled, "of about ninety, with a good, big chest to rest it on. I might as well wear my mother's parure, do myself up like one of the Bourbons—which, believe me, I'd have no objection to, if there weren't so many, well, social reasons not to. At my age."

"A parure is a possibility. To scale, of course," Mr. Thistle said.

"Or a ferronière," Elizabeth suggested, referring to a fifteenth-century ornament for the forehead that was then enjoying a strong revival in fashion.

"Or a necklace," Mrs. Pope said finally.

"What fun it is to josh you, Mother!" Elizabeth said.

"Mr. Thistle," Chance asked, "is Monsieur Langlois in our workrooms? If he is, would you be kind enough to send for him, please?" He turned to Mrs. Pope. "When is the birthday?" he inquired gently. "That is, by when would you need the necklace?"

She answered his question with one of her own. "Could you do it in a month?"

"Mr. Langlois is our chief designer, the very best man in Belgium before we hired him away. Let's sit down together and I think we'll come up with something more original, personal, and suitable. After all, nineteen's a better age than most to commemorate."

"I suppose," Elizabeth agreed.

"A very possible idea, Mr. Chance."

While they awaited Langlois, Tom showed them one extraordinary piece of jewelry after another and chatted with a brand of idle inquisitiveness.

"We've made jewels for European debutantes," he assured them.

"It's a tradition there," Elizabeth replied. "Americans aren't sure enough of themselves to have a tradition."

Tom looked. "Some Americans are very sure of themselves," he confided.

Elizabeth paused. "Now that's something for my taste," she said, turning the conversation by the hinge of her own impetuosity. "What a lovely emerald pin!"

"Here. Hold it?"

Elizabeth did. "What do you think, Mother?"

"Exquisite. But too much too soon, if you take my meaning, my dear." Another stage-like flick of her wrist. "Perhaps when you're older and established on your own."

Elizabeth looked at Tom and smiled.

After the best part of an hour, with the assistance of Langlois and his sketching pencil, they had decided on a simple confection of small pear-shaped diamonds. They would hang like tears from what would seem an invisible rope, all mounted in silver.

"C'est un très important collier en diamants des tailles poires, serti de vingt-et-un diamants, dégradés," Langlois murmured, half to himself, tilting the elected sketch toward both Popes.

"C'est très bien," Elizabeth rattled off. *"Oui, ma mère?"*

"Absolument," the elder lady said.

Tom listened intently. He did not speak French, but the earnestness of his concentration suggested an internal conviction that a clever man, if he had to, might learn it on the spot, as he might learn anything. He wiped his brow. Mrs. Pope, from a tray of a hundred, selected four of the twenty-one stones before deciding to leave all choices to experienced workmen. She did not mention price. Off and on, taking an obvious last minute in which to be sure of her decision, she would touch a tiny diamond with the point of Langlois's tweezer, move it in the light, smile at its reflection, and there would be something in her manner, the very casualness with which she could luxuriate in executing such a gesture, which distinguished her from all around her save her daughter. These were fragile objects, Tom thought. Men valued them, counted them, earned their livings with them. Only a certain kind of human being could play with them this casually, as though, like all beautiful things, they were meant only for her pleasure. Like the shining golden mane of a lion, these exquisite little touches, smiles, and "thank you's" defined her and Tom knew, with piercing suddenness, that, whatever else he might acquire on earth, he would never master them, that, if they came at all, they would come to his children.

Mrs. Pope rose and Tom felt at once hollow in his stomach. He did not want Elizabeth to leave. He wanted to show her every jewel he possessed, his office, the Pearl of Macao, his apartment. He wanted to tell her his plans, watch as those imperious eyes came alive to his dreams. He feared that his own impression had not been indelibly enough struck, that she had taken, by a sheer posture of entitlement, the upper hand in their conversation. He feared, too, that she might be merely flirtatious by nature, that there might be hundreds of other promising men in her life, that she might kiss them—or marry.

"Well, good-bye," he said when they had gotten to the

door. "We'll put the necklace right into work." Then he gave her a long smile.

Mrs. Pope made a faint bow-like nod. "If you'd be kind enough to send a copy of the order round to Mr. Pope's office for his approval," she said, "I know he would appreciate it."

Mrs. Pope nudged her daughter out of the door, but, at the last second, with the spring air rushing in about her, Elizabeth turned abruptly full-circle, looked at Tom and said: "I envy you. Being here all day with all these beautiful things."

That night, Tom and Felix Hardenstein went together to Niblo's Garden, where Frances had the second lead in *The Black Crook,* the most successful and controversial "ballet show" of the past three seasons. They sat in one of two large private boxes that flanked the stage on its own level. These boxes, decorated with exterior, life-size figures of nearly unveiled young women, drew almost as much attention from the orchestra and galleries as the set itself. The house, as usual, was sold out, and as the lights about it dimmed and the music began, the soft murmuring of the crowd came together and swelled into a kind of choral panting. Everyone knew that *The Black Crook,* splendid spectacle though it had been billed, contained more simple nudity than any competing attraction in New York. And so, urged on by the outrage of churches, young men and old men, some with their ladies beside them, came out night after night, to be beguiled by the glitter of silver and jewels, the magnificent choreography of feminine figures and light, the front and center views of Frances's thighs, and all of her breasts but the nipples.

Tom had not wanted her to take the part, but he had had little time left over from his other business to work, seriously, on dissuading her. And the farther they had drifted, the more crucial it had become to Frances to get on with her career. The great dramatic roles of the New York stage had seemed, in light of at least twenty disappointing auditions, to be receding ever more surely beyond the cutting edge of her talent. And yet, she hoped this scanty costume and risqué role would draw public attention back to her and charge her career with new possibilities.

Tom watched her. She was weeks short of her twenty-ninth birthday, yet she was finer looking now than she had ever been. Still on the thin side, but better fleshed, more ripe. His emotions confused him. First, because he loved her, envied her in a perverse way, though he could not admit so, even to himself. Second, because he detested the distance at which this place and play existed from his lofty social goal. His foothold in New York society was not so secure that his acknowledged girl friend could parade herself like this without affecting him. He could come to Niblo's Garden, he believed, but she should not act there. It was "Haymarket," and embarrassing. He knew that there was not a man present, including Hardenstein, who would not have been glad of the chance to remove those final, dazzling cups about her breasts, those panties, but, as much as he ached for a woman, some latent moral guilt prevented him, told him that *he* could not go on using her. He was not a moralist on the point, but a man. He felt free, and expected to use other women, women whose business it was, women who understood certain things about men. But he could not use Frances. He could not hurt her without hurting himself.

After the last curtain, when Frances arrived at the box, Felix stood, bowed, kissed her hand, and quickly excused himself. Then a moment lapsed in which she caught her breath, oriented herself. A stageman brought a plate of oysters that Tom had ordered for her and she smiled at them as though they were about to save her life. She took a heavy swallow of champagne.

"Well," she began finally. ". . . Hello. This is a surprise, isn't it? *I'm* truly surprised." She had a quick, foreboding sense of his quiet, then sipped her champagne once more as she tried to read him.

"I surprised myself," Tom said. Against the background of Elizabeth, he was judging her afresh.

"Well," Frances exclaimed softly, "there's nothing like a full house to overcome whatever other misgivings an actress has." She looked out as the last aisles cleared. She had drawn a pale rose-colored robe about herself and let down her hair, so that even those few who had turned had failed to recognize her.

"It was full, all right."

"Were you . . . scandalized?"

"What do you think?" Tom smiled.

"I don't think anything would ever scandalize *you,* Thomas Chance!" She forced a laugh, touched him. "Cheer up," she said. "Was it an awful day?"

For a long moment, glimpsing his weakness, Tom hated himself. This woman knew him perfectly. And loved him, had given herself to him. He asked himself what he would have become without her, then shrank from the question. For he loved her, too, although he could not take her as a bride. He was—he had thought of this during his walk—like a frontiersman on the social and economic landscape of the new age, so that to marry anyone but a certain class of girl would be to put a lid back on his dreams, to contain them before they were tested. He knew that he could never do that, although he did not know exactly why.

"It was a very quiet day," he explained. "No deals."

"No deals?"

"Well, one, if you call it that." He gazed off abstractedly.

"Oh."

"For a play."

Her eyes lit. *"Oh!"*

"At Wallack's. *Macbeth.* You're to play Lady Macbeth."

"That's mad."

"It's fact. A three-month run. The backers wanted you."

"*You* wanted me, you mean!" She smiled, slid suddenly over and kissed him on the lips. Tears rushed to his eyes and he dammed them as fast as he could.

"The agreement was made at five o'clock," he said. "Felix will have it signed tomorrow, the next day at the latest. It'll get you out of here and Pike's and Tammany. Back on the real road that you wanted to travel when you began. I've always hated myself a little for sidetracking you."

She smiled compassionately. "Whatever I did," she said, "was because—"

"No," he interrupted anxiously. "Don't say it! I know it. I *know* why."

"Tom—"

He looked at her ominously. "Macbeth's a lot of work. It's a good break, but you'll have to eat and sleep your work the way I do." He paused, swallowed. "I think it would be better if you took rooms at the St. Nicholas."

The muscles in Frances's face fell limp. She was silent. Finally, looking upward after tears, she asked: "Tonight?"

And Tom answered "Yes."

She yearned to know why, but could not bring herself to ask him. She straightened her slumped body as quickly as she recovered strength and poured the wine into her. "Well, I knew it was coming," she said. "And dreaded it. I won't deny that. But you've given me so much. I guess it doesn't do to be greedy."

"No," Tom said. "I'm sure it doesn't. In the end, it never comes to anything."

"I love you," she said. "I'm sorry, but I have to say it."

A little startled by her stoic acceptance of the situation, Tom added: "Don't be sorry. You met a bad actor, Frances. You'll meet a good one one day."

But, emotionally, she was past him. "Do you know what I've learned, Tom? Starting when I was a little girl, in South Carolina, and then when you came to live with us and, worse, in that cursed war? I've learned that human beings can get along, strange as this will sound to someone like you, that this life the Lord gave us is so precious that we can even enjoy it without having everything we want."

Tom did not answer.

"Sometimes," Frances added wistfully, "I wonder if that's not the only way we can."

CHAPTER

17

IT WAS A MISTAKE. ALMOST IMMEDIATELY AFTERWARD HE knew it: a sudden premonitory shudder, then a long gnaw at his intestines. And it lasted for days, until, like a pilgrim on a first and solitary voyage, he could bring himself to realize the impossibility of trying to inhabit two continents at once.

The man, Scudder, was young, with sand-shaded hair, even features, innocent eyes, and an indefinite, affable way. Twenty-three, he was the bottom sibling of one of Chance's partners in the paraffin deal and had come down to New York only a few months before, after four years at Yale. They had dined together, and he had struck Tom as guileless and lonely. So when, over port, he had looked up with puppy eyes and asked Tom if he knew the names of any available women, Tom had mentioned Frances. A small thing, really, Tom decided: a favor for both of them. But it bothered him.

Scudder waited a little before acting on Tom's advice, but by the time the next week was out he presented himself at Wallack's Theater and, bouquet in hand, asked her to join him for supper. He had gained access backstage by introducing himself as "a friend of Tommy Chance's" and his manner was so complaisantly harmless that Frances saw no reason not to accept. She had no idea how much he knew of her past, or, for that matter, for what age he took her.

But if he were a friend of Tom's, she deduced, it was probably sufficient. She did not like to think of her life as checkered. Sometimes, though, she could not help doing so. There was a residue of Methodism still in her blood, coursing from mind to conscience and back, so that whenever she encountered a certain kind of person it troubled her for a moment. She was glad enough not to be a virgin at most times, but she wished she knew what this boy expected. She refused to believe that Tom had sent such a young boy to spy on her and, therefore, accepted the date as a message, a kind of final offering from Tom, as if he were seeking to give her back her twenties. She put the spring flowers in water and went through an especially vivid performance as Lady Macbeth. Later they dined in a small cafe on Twelfth Street, where they got drunk on two carafes of cheap Bordeaux.

Tom's business was uniformly successful. Like the oracle at Delphi, he worked, shrouded by mist, protected by sycophants, at the farthest reach of a cave. And, from this office, a flow of secret ventures began to emanate. He dealt in commodities: cotton and grains of all kinds; timber; stones; even obscure items such as the bellies and coats of animals; and the insides and skins of fishes, most especially whales, whose teeth he began to collect. He also dealt in: real estate, New York and New Jersey farmland; jewels; theater; precious metals; and, above all, money. To those who were permitted to see only its separate parts, his process was a maze of confusion. Those who brought money had no idea where the investments they were making had come from. Those who brought ideas could never actually identify the source of their funds. Those who sought to fix Chance as a power in one particular field, or even two, were frustrated in their attempts. Those who sought to prove his honor could never quite vindicate him, except to say that many men with perfect reputations had made handsome profits on his account. Those who sought to prove the reverse failed as miserably. And so enigma both marked and magnified his operations, as he had known it would, attracting more deals than a straightforward financier might have dreamed of.

In truth, of course, the mechanism was simple. Men with propositions that were too speculative for orthodox banks and without the collateral or desire to guarantee a loan, had to find alternative means of raising the capital they required. While other men, willing to accept a higher risk for a higher return, were ambitious to invest and multiply their fortunes in the boom that had followed the war. What these separate groups required was a conduit that could bring them together—and, since the members of neither group ordinarily knew those of the other beforehand (or often afterward), a conduit they could trust. This was the role of Thomas Chance. The better merchant banks—Seligman, Drexel, Belmont—took the cream of such deals, but New York was building at a phenomenal rate, capitalizing the country and the movement west; and there were more than enough opportunities for a man like Chance. He was careful, suspicious, selective. But when he once found an idea or parcel on which he believed he could realize a profit, he set out doggedly to secure the money to back it, "always too much, never too little, always enough to hold until the market comes round, and only from the kind of persons who can wait and will." Then, for his effort, he would take a share, often as large as twenty percent, of the enterprise or syndicate formed. He had been astute in his first choices, and lucky, and the word had spread.

One April morning, Tom and Felix Hardenstein had just concluded a review of Goelette and Company's monthly accounts when Mrs. McCorquadale rapped at the door of his office and told him that there was a gentleman in the store who said he was waiting for Mr. Fisk and that the two of them would like, if possible, to have a few minutes of Chance's time.

"Did you get his name?"

"Mr. Thistle did. It's Mr. Jay Gould. I'm sorry, but I had to see the look on your face."

"Very well," Tom said, bursting into a brief grin. "And as you can see, it's smiling. Tell him I shall be with him presently." When she closed the door, he sighed. Gould in the store? Jay Gould, the terror of Wall Street and wrecker of Erie, a man renowned for his frugality, his obliviousness to comfort or luxury? It couldn't be on a matter concerning jewelry. Or could it?

Railroads were the premier investments of the day. They accounted for more than three quarters of the shares traded on Wall Street, were being built, and sabotaged, one after another, even along competitive routes. And, like practically anyone who had money, Tom had speculated in their shares and profited. But his old dream of a more principal role had begun to haunt him as his capital had reached the point where he could contemplate such scale. And Gould and the Erie were large. Tom knew that Gould, with the ebullient Fisk as his front man, had stolen the Erie out from under Commodore Vanderbilt and a group of Bostonians the year before. He knew that the pair had watered its stock, later propelling its price with their proceeds, and had found immunity from prosecution in the same place he had—through Chamberlain, Tweed, and the corrupted judges of Tammany: Cardozo, McCunn, and Barnard.

Chance looked about his office curiously. He was eager for propositions, sure that he could be as wily as any man. But he wished that Gould had chosen a better morning, for he had not rested well the night before and, with the first light, a little after six, had come down to his office to work. His mind had raced him all during the dark, preventing dreams, dropping fragments of his deals onto the screen of his imagination, melting hard numbers into fluid shapes that he could neither add nor reckon with. For months, work had been his life. He had eaten to work, slept to work, partied to work, made love to work—and a part of him was fragile because of this.

He studied Hardenstein. "Anything else?" he asked in an unhurried voice.

"Not at the moment."

Tom stood and walked out into the store.

"Mr. Gould?" he inquired quietly of Thistle.

And Thistle pointed to a frail man with black eyes, black hair, and a black beard who was looking into the watch case. His hair was receding, but his brow made a thick line straight across his forehead, giving an immediate impression of directness and intensity. His clothes were neither fashionable, nor even very good—much less fine than Mr. Thistle's, for example—except that he carried a splendid beaver-skin hat, high and with a wide brim. "That's he, don't you know?" Thistle said.

Chance approached him. "Mr. Gould?"

Gould looked up. "Yes. Mr. Chance, thank you for seeing me."

"My pleasure. Do I understand you are expecting Mr. Fisk?"

"Any moment. I hope I haven't—" He stretched a small hand spasmodically forward.

"No. I was just going over our accounts for March. I had just finished when they told me you were here."

Gould offered a perfunctory smile. "I hope you liked what you saw."

"Very much."

"I should think you would with fine things like these. These are railroad watches, aren't they?"

Chance glanced down. "On the right side, yes. Minute repeaters."

"Whose?"

"Ours."

"I misspoke," Gould commented carefully. "I meant to ask who makes them."

"The basic watches, we do. On the second floor. We buy a more expensive brand in Europe and a less expensive one in London."

"The more expensive is Patek-Philippe, correct?"

"Yes." Chance needed all his shrewdness here, could feel the spider commencing to beguile him, to net him in the first web of some dark arabesque. "It's not an old name yet, but we feel it's the finest. Our watchmakers do, and they've been with Goelette and Company . . . well, let's just say rather longer than I have."

Gould laughed politely, made a deliberate hesitation. "Railroads, as you might imagine, have a great need of railroad watches." He laughed again. "How would it be if the Erie were to buy two of each from you? We'll give them to our men, discover how well they like them, which they prefer, and then, perhaps, we shall order more."

"That would be fine," Chance said. "As a matter of policy, I never discuss the affairs of my clients, but I don't think it would be a breach of any confidence if I told you that the New Haven uses all three, as well, and has had wonderful luck with them."

Gould's attention stirred at Chance's formidable canniness. "Minute repeaters," he mused. "They're wonderful things, truly, aren't they, Mr. Chance? In the dark, those chimes when you press one. So reassuring. One always knows precisely where one is . . . according to one's plan."

"Only on the Erie," Chance complimented him. "On the Central, Bill Tweed tells me one is as apt to be late as not."

"Yes," the dark man nodded. "Well, here's Fisk now."

Outside, six horses, black down the left, white on the right, had brought an enormous open barouche to the curb and, from it, between gargantuan coachman and footman, Fisk and two striking women now descended. Fisk, in military regalia, was a colorful sight: tall, stocky, and blond, with a long waxed moustache and his hand thrust Napoleonically inside his waistcoat. He was instantly gregarious, immediately recognizable from the newspaper cartoons of the day, the antithesis of Gould's sallow presence. The ladies, who walked behind him, were voguishly plump, giddy or not depending on his mood.

Fisk acknowledged Gould with a grin, then shook hands with Chance. He spoke to Thistle, inquiring about an arthritic joint the latter had mentioned at their last meeting, and to two of the other salesmen, with whom he deposited his ladies while the trio retired to Tom's office.

"I promised them each a little something," he laughed, a trace of the circus roustabout still in his voice at the age of thirty-five. "I wasn't going to bring them. I was going to come alone. But when they found out exactly where I was going . . ." He took up a Havana from Tom's box and lit it. "No man ever had a problem getting a woman to follow him here."

"No," Gould agreed. "I wouldn't think so."

"Jay's married," Fisk continued. "Since how long now?"

"Six years last January."

"I won't say anything. I don't usually. He doesn't like it."

Tom smiled.

"He's a regular family man," Fisk said. "You should see him up at our new place. We moved the Erie, you know, into the old Grand Opera House, all marble and iron and the prettiest woods and inlaid in gold. Gorgeous! We want you to come visit us, too. I don't know how much you've been around theaters—yourself, that is—but it makes for a nice place to spend the day, I think. If you're going to give your all to something, it's nice to have a good place, some women around, a little tit. Cheers you up. But Jay keeps his vows, all right. Never gives one a second look."

Gould's eyes, having catalogued the room, had settled patiently upon the single display case in which the Macao was shown.

"The famous Macao," Tom said, reading his thoughts.

"I imagined so." Gould looked toward Fisk.

"Beautiful thing!" Fisk exclaimed. "Seen it before. Mr. Chance was kind enough to show it to me. I'd say it would demand a woman of some—pulchritude," he went on.

"And you like a little . . . pul . . . chritude," Gould smiled, wanting, in this room of acknowledged philanderers, to seem less than prudishly sober—wanting, and yet not completely succeeding.

"Once in a while," Fisk concurred, in diminishing voice.

Gould's black eyes were darting now, ready. "Let me ask you some questions, Mr. Chance."

"Whatever."

"What is the price of a fine Burmese ruby, one carat?"

"Five hundred, about."

"Retail?"

"Yes. In this store."

"Of a similar sapphire?"

"Four hundred."

"And a pearl?"

"A good one? Much higher. Eight hundred, I would say, to give you an average."

"And gold?"

"One hundred thirty-three at the market closing yesterday."

Gould quickened his pace. "Lumber. Building lumber."

"Four hundred a carload."

"Soybeans?"

"Two hundred."

"Potatoes?"

"Twenty cents, each." Tom smiled.

Gould looked puzzled.

"Over the counter at Park and Tilford," Tom said. "You pay for the name and the salesmen's frock coats."

Gould smiled. "I think you understand what I was getting at," he said. "It's plain to me that you understand." He crossed his legs, held his stomach just below the rib cage, as though, for a second, the old tubercular trouble had set him back.

"I'm not a connoisseur," Chance said. "I'm in business to make money. This business. Any business."

"Exactly. Never take your eye off of the main chance. I learned that as a boy. I must have been thirteen, so that would be twenty years ago now. And I never have." Gould paused. "I want to buy gold, Mr. Chance. Steadily, secretly, in very large amounts."

"Gold has fallen recently," Tom suggested. "It was nearly two hundred fifty during the last years of war. And so much prosperity as we've known since—well, it hasn't much reason to rise, in my opinion." He paused. Gould was silent. Fisk puffed his cigar. Tom sensed that this picturesque horse trader, for all his effervescence, was listening for even one deviation from perfect pitch. "But you are more accustomed to that business than I, so my question to you, Mr. Gould, is why?"

"You're a jeweler and you ask me why?" Gould said. "I'm sorry, but I couldn't resist that. Here with your pearl staring at me. One would think such treasures were all that concerned you." He paused, then went on. "There is, approximately, fifteen million dollars of gold circulating in this country right now, Mr. Chance. Of which, approximately, seven million dollars belongs to me." Chance breathed a deep and incredulous sigh.

"Merchants need this gold, sir," Gould continued, "for the transaction of their foreign business, for specie payments. It's a must. You'd agree?"

"And you want more?"

"It's a year of bumper crops," Gould elaborated. Chance strained to follow his logic. "That's a certainty. I can promise you that it will be a year of bumper crops." He paused, allowing each man time to think, to be tested. "We live in cities," he said then. "And so many men like us are prone to forget that America is really an agricultural nation. It always has been and it still is. The best way for farmers to get the highest value for their crops is, therefore, to sell them abroad. The higher the price of gold goes, the more valuable these crops are going to be with respect to paper money, and people in Europe will be encouraged to buy them."

Thomas Chance listened alertly; a first impression of the puzzle was forming in his mind.

"Where is the center of our agriculture?" the small man pressed.

"New York?" Chance answered automatically, but, seeing that Gould's blank expression remained unbroken, added: "Or do you mean Chicago? Because it's closer to the source."

Gould shrugged. "London," he said. "The price of grain in New York is determined at any given moment by the price that grain will bring in London."

'So," Chance said exuberantly, "as gold goes, so goes grain?"

Fisk, who had begun to seem tired and bored as he toyed with the pink sapphire ring on his little finger, came suddenly alive. "Yes," he said. "As gold goes, so goes grain: East, aboard the Erie Railroad."

The three men laughed.

"But there's more," Gould explained. "What if we were to buy all the gold on the market? In that case, we could set the price wherever we wanted it. We could make an unprecedented fortune."

"We have to buy quietly," said Fisk, "or the price will go out of control."

"Naturally."

"That's where you come in, as I trust you've figured out by now. We would like to make some of our purchases through Goelette and Company, to . . . maintain their confidential nature."

This seemed reasonable to Chance. "We could do that,"

he said. "Without, I think, arousing any undue suspicions."

"I was certain you could."

"Both through the firm and some of the other accounts with which I'm associated. But let me ask you, Mr. Gould—"

"Jay."

"Jay. Let me ask you: Surely Seligman—isn't that your regular banker?—could handle such a matter as this with discretion. Why have you not left it to him?"

Gould was frowning. "We are buying through Seligman Brothers," he said. "Plus other channels."

Chance thought rapidly. "I'm correct, I think, in assuming that the plan will also depend on two factors still more important than discretion? We shall need huge resources—"

"We have them," Fisk interjected.

". . . And," Chance announced with an only slightly subdued ring of challenge in his tone, "we will need some assurance that the federal government itself subscribes to the agricultural policy you recommend, that it will not begin to sell from its own stockpiles in order to lower a rising price. If I'm not mistaken, they have, what, one hundred million dollars worth of the stuff in Washington, give or take."

"You're a shrewd man, Tom," Gould offered. "Absolutely correct."

"The Treasury Department, to my understanding, has never looked with too much favor on gold speculators," Tom said.

"No," Gould said. "It hasn't. But it's a new Treasury Department, Tom, a new administration. Johnson's gone now. Ulysses Grant is President."

"I met Grant once," Tom said.

Gould squinted.

"It was during the war."

"Only the once?" Gould asked.

"Yes."

The frail man seemed vaguely relieved, but Tom thought

that it might have been as much in reaction to some cessation of pain in his stomach, for he straightened a bit, stretched.

A new silence filled the room until Tom asked: "Are you trying to tell me something, Jay?"

At which point Fisk shrugged, dropping one of his medals onto the thick carpet, and Gould coughed.

"Everyone's in," Gould said. "It goes as high as it possibly could."

"Grant himself?" Tom marveled.

"When we move, they move with us."

"Do you know when that will be?"

Gould did not like this question. "I—and our mutual friends—shall see to it you have ample time," he stated adamantly. "We'll begin with some small purchases next week, in your name. I will be in contact with you before then."

"Excellent," Tom said. "Thank you." They were standing now.

"Not at all," Jay Gould said. "I look forward to working with you." They shook hands firmly. "Oh, and Tom, if you'd have your man send those watches around to us. Twenty-third Street at Eighth Avenue." He smiled and, putting his walking stick to the floor, was quickly gone.

Mrs. McCorquadale, following him with her eyes, said, "So that's The Scarlet Man of Wall Street. Always the same, is it not, Mr. Chance? They're never too much in person, these famous men. More holes than colander, he is, I'd expect."

But Tom laughed to himself. Gould had Grant in his pocket, he thought, and this silly woman was busy writing him off. So much for her! He was trying to remain calm about the news these two men had brought him, to keep his dispassionate view, but he lacked the constitution at the moment. He was electrified by the very idea of such political power, of such proximity to the President of the United

States—intoxicated by the cunning of Gould's scheme. He glanced casually at the pixieish bump in Miss Doolan's nose while, Midas-like, his mind surveyed the fortune he would make. Not since he and Peter Parton had walked the streets of Baltimore together had he allowed his dreams such space to romp.

When Tom's blood slowed from this rush of impending glory, he thought again of Elizabeth Pope, who seemed above it. That pretty, pastoral girl, always with him in imagination, nearer to being a princess than anyone he had known before her. He was glad he had said that when she had come to the shop, glad that he had established himself and his interest on that rather more than mercantile footing.

For nearly a month now, as part of his daily regime, he had followed the progress of her necklace through the workrooms. He had studied Langlois's sketches, rejecting two for a superior third. He had stood behind Langlois, pretending to learn, as the latter had selected the twenty-one graduated pear-shaped stones that it called for. He had given it precedence over every other job in the shop, dealt it out personally to the senior jeweler and checked the man's green wax models at every stage. The most skillful setter, a temperamental Persian who had been reared in the North of Italy, had been allotted three pressureless days in which to complete it, twice the time he would have ordinarily had or needed. And the finishers had spent the whole of a Thursday bringing up the color of its metal, smoothing its delicate prongs, boiling away the dirt, the dust, and the light, filmy grease that adhered to any piece after so much handling. But the final product was commensurately exquisite, betraying the care with which it had been invested; and that was exactly how Chance wanted it to be. He held it, in a soft chamois, up to the light shining in from Fifth Avenue, let it hang by its clasp, turned it, smiled. Then, from Mr. Li, he secured one of Goelette and Company's finest purple boxes, saw that its satin pad was fresh and free of threads, and laid the bracelet out, snapping the lid gently closed on top of it. Immediately, he put the box into his personal safe, beside his personal ledgers, and left instructions with all staff in the showrooms that he was to be advised the very moment Elizabeth came for it—that, under no circumstances, was anyone, including Langlois, to take it upon himself to locate or deliver the necklace.

But it was not until several days had passed that Elizabeth returned to Goelette and Company and was shown into his office.

Tom was alone. He made a quick fuss over his papers and stood. An awkward pause enveloped the room.

"Have a seat," he said. "Please."

"Thank you." Elizabeth was also alone. As she lowered herself into the chair, he realized that she was still wearing a light spring coat that reached her throat.

"I'm sorry," he said nervously, standing again and coming around behind her. "I didn't take your coat. They really ought to have done that in the office."

"Oh, no," Elizabeth replied. "They did. They asked, but I didn't want them to. Here, I'll show you why." She gave a soft, conspiratorial laugh and, as Tom removed her coat, he saw that she was wearing an evening dress that exposed long, symmetrical V-shaped areas of her creamy skin both in front and in back.

"You *are* a princess, aren't you?" He laughed. "In this prim city, only a princess would have the plain good sense to try a new necklace with the dress she meant it to go with."

Elizabeth gazed up at Tom, assessed whether she believed that had been his meaning. She seemed to be holding something back. What it was, she wasn't sure of herself, but finally she replied, "No, Mr. Chance, this isn't my party dress. That's being readied, silly. But it has almost exactly the same neckline."

Wordlessly, he went to his safe, procured the necklace, and

opened the box before her. The moment he did, she jumped a little in her seat, clapped her hands, and took it from him. "Absolutely magnificent," she exclaimed, playing with it in the light, just as he had. "I never believed it would be so beautiful." She leaned up suddenly and kissed him on the cheek.

Tom smiled. "Where's your nice mother?" he asked. "I rather thought she would come with you."

Elizabeth looked at the large gold-sculpture clock on Tom's cabinet: Perseus and Andromeda holding up the hour. "Eleven o'clock," she said. "I imagine she's gone to the hospital to visit my sick aunt. She sent me with a maid, but I sent the maid to Stewart's. I'm old enough to make my own decisions. Mother's wonderful really, but once she's done with something, like this necklace for example, she loses interest. She doesn't care one whit for any jewelry unless it happens to be her own."

"Interesting."

"Not very. Let's try it around my neck."

Chance helped her with the clasp, instructing her fingers how to work it in future, then adjusted the necklace so that it was centered just over her collarbone. He brought her a silver hand mirror and, once she had it working, it was as if, suddenly, he had ceased to exist. She studied her skin with extreme care, regarded the new jewel from every possible angle. "Sometimes—often, in fact—" she continued at last, "I have the feeling that my mother's jealous of me. My aunt, too. Even my father, occasionally, and that's strange enough, you'd agree."

Tom said, "Nineteen years old. Beautiful and clever as you are." His eyes devoured her. "I don't know."

"Everyone thinks it's such a joy to be young and have no responsibilities but looking after one's own fun all the time. And I imagine it is, in a way . . . but, well, one thing: All these boys my parents surround me with—even when they're men, they're boys. Even when they're your age."

"Yes," he agreed.

"And no girl in her right mind wants that. At least I don't. I want some experience"—she paused—"at living, before I settle down. I will say they were better in Europe."

"Oh?" He wondered what that meant. Had she been in love there? Was she not the virgin he had thought her?

"Much. But it will all be over soon," she sighed. "This party, anyway."

"When is it to be?" Chance asked.

"Why, tonight," Elizabeth answered in a surprised voice.

The thought struck Thomas Chance dumb. He had had no reason, only an impression gathered from her tone, her occasional wink-like smiles, some of the things she had said, or, rather, the inviting tones in which she had said them. He had hoped, nonetheless, to be asked to that party, had watched his mail, and, when there had been nothing in it, had imagined that the day was even farther off in the spring, or that, at the last minute, she would urge him in person. But now the news, simultaneously, that he would not be asked to come and that this object of his most persistent fantasies would be subject to the attentions of two hundred eligible young men in barely a few hours stunned him.

"What in the world is the matter?" Elizabeth remarked. It was the same voice, the same manner of a moment before, yet now its old, kind melody rang as callousness in his ears, as if he had discovered some unutterable lie at the base of his universe.

"I haven't any idea," Chance recovered. "I just felt dizzy for a moment. I shall be fine."

CHAPTER

18

THAT NIGHT CHANCE STALKED THE CITY. UP FIFTH AVENUE to Fifty-ninth Street, past the squatters in Central Park, their dilapidated lean-to hovels, their weary junk wagons, parked and soundless in the after-dinner hours. Down Madison on the bedraggled one-horse rapid transit. Across Twenty-third Street to Eighth Avenue, making a thoroughfare of the quiet public rooms of the Fifth Avenue Hotel, a torture out of every passing gentleman who looked as if he might be destined for the Popes'. He walked into and out of the Astor House, past the St. Nicholas. And then, on impulse, remaining aloof, without a morsel of lunch or dinner to carry him, he ferried himself to Lafayette Square and saw that old Isaac Brown had already taken up his station at the porte-cochère of the Popes' house.

It was then the queer custom of ladies and gentlemen not to use their personal carriages after dark, and Brown stood, tall and smiling, as he received the first of his fleet of landaus. Brown was the majordomo of New York. He greeted every arrival by name, in a loud voice, so that the names could be passed along by pages to the receiving line inside. And Chance listened for an hour, secreting himself in a narrow pedestrian alley, for he knew Brown from his usual post at the Academy of Music.

He watched the flurry of crinoline disappear into the mystery of lighted, curtained rooms, studied the young men's walks: Too sensible, he decided, flat and springless, with no hint of assertiveness in their step. Some were bearded. Most wore Dundreary whiskers. They prattled and postured as they moved from carriage to house. And, for a short time, because he had not yet deprived himself of the belief that most women inherently wanted to have him, he was able to salve his hurt with condescension. He remembered Clara Regenault. How many effete young gentlemen, polished in their dance steps, had tried in vain for so much as a kiss? he asked himself. He knew the answer.

But the more carriages that arrived, the longer he waited, the livelier the current of music that escaped into the pungent springtime air, the sharper his pain became. The glittering social beast had stung him, all right, and he knew it. It had called a final halt to his assault at the very moment he had gotten his quarry in sight. Fortune, it seemed to be saying, was one thing; love, and especially marriage, another. Perhaps, in some too-obvious way, he had revealed himself before Mrs. Pope. Or, perhaps the barriers were Elizabeth's own, emanating from some genetic center within her, beyond control of her will, like the shape of her face, or the color of her eyes. The trouble was, he had no way to tell. He did not know whom to blame, whom to hate, on whom to seek vengeance.

When he had surfeited himself, he walked back over to Wallack's Theater, where Frances Alexander had become a considerable success in *Macbeth*, and was on the point of entering by the stage door when he saw the young man—the Yale man was all he remembered, for he was tired and had drunk a flask of bourbon—to whom he had given Frances's name.

"Chance," the young man called across the alley full of flowers. And Tom, sensing his dead-end, looked back over his shoulder.

"Yes," he said. "Who . . . ?"

"Scudder," the young man said.

"The light was faint. Sorry, Scudder. Of course."

"What brings you to this neighborhood?"

Chance did not hesitate. "I've only just left dinner with some business friends," he replied. "I was just taking some air on a walk home. Would you care to walk with me? Which direction were you going?"

"No, thank you," Scudder said. "I'm waiting for Frances."

"Oh," said Chance.

The pleasant young man sensed that all was not right, and continued. "Why don't you wait too?" he suggested. "Frances would love to see you. She shouldn't be long."

"I can't tonight," Chance explained, inhaling a whiff of his own strong breath. "But sometime in the future."

Scudder smiled. "We should," he said and, as Chance began to walk, called out again: "We really should. You know we're to be married two weeks from Saturday."

Chance turned, unquestionably startled by this news. "No," he said. "I hadn't known."

"Some people've told us it's a bit . . . hurried, but it's what we both want, so—" He raised and dropped his shoulders.

"Well, everything splendid to you, Scudder . . . you and Frances, both. We'll be in touch," Tom cried, the cave of the alley transporting his garbled echo back to him, beside the heavy scent of a thousand unsold geraniums.

Tom, moving fast, thought then of searching down a whore. He also thought of death. In a trance, he walked all the way to Longacre Square, at Forty-second and Broadway, then, with little more awareness, back to his apartment.

A lamp flickered in his office, behind an ornate slice of frosted glass. So Tom pressed his eye against the design and spied Miss Doolan working at her desk. He reached into his pocket, found his key, and let himself into his own room through the back door. Then he came out, frightening her so that a scream caught in her throat.

"Miss Doolan," he said.

He stood at a distance of at least six feet and it was not clear to her, in the dim light, whether he had come home from a party, or merely downstairs from the apartment above. "Mr. Chance," she said.

"Writing at eleven o'clock. You'll ruin your eyes by that wretched old lamp." In fact, the lamp gave an effect much like the flattery of candlelight to her soft, imperfect Irish features.

"Mrs. McCorquadale left only half an hour ago," she explained. "*She* asked me to stay—not that I minded. We were so far behind, and Mr. Hardenstein wants the inventory ready on Monday. She locked everything but the back entrance. The safes, as you can see, are locked, and the showrooms and—"

"Quiet, girl!"

"You're not angry."

"No. On the contrary." He looked at her.

"Good."

"Where will you stay?"

"With a—friend of mine, a few blocks from here. I sometimes do, if it's too late to go back to Brooklyn."

Chance let the remark pass. "Have you eaten?"

"Yes, sir."

"Boiled beef at five o'clock at Childs?"

"Boiled chicken." She smiled. Her nervousness was fleeing her, thank God.

He fixed her with his eyes, making his intention as plain as he possibly could in the circumstances. "Well, then, would you care to come up and have something to drink?"

Miss Doolan parted her lips into the start of a smile. "Mr. Chance," she said directly, "is that a—proposition?"

"If I told you yes, that it was—" he said.

"The answer would be 'yes,' that I would," she replied.

"Very well, then it is," Tom said.

On the landing, she told him: "You know, as long as I

have been working here, I've only been upstairs one other time, to bring you some papers once."

"Is that so?"

"You probably don't remember it."

"No." Tom, a step behind her, was staring directly at her buttocks, and feeling dizzy again from the bourbon. "Miss Doolan," he inquired gently. "I hope my curiosity will not offend you, but I don't think I had any idea, until tonight, that—"

She looked around and gave him the kindest smile he had seen all day—in weeks, perhaps. "Where I grew up," she explained, "let's just say that most girls didn't and a few girls did—and I was one of those. I mean it's a poor neighborhood. You never lived in no place like it, I'm sure. And, well, I've always been a little too independent for my own good. From things like churches, I mean. My mother wasn't Queen Victoria."

"I see."

"I'll bet you thought that any Catholic girl was going to be a virgin."

"No."

"That's funny. You sound like you thought that."

"No." When they came into the gallery and Miss Doolan had had her first breath of the heady atmosphere, Tom lit a candle and said, "Miss Doolan, I'm going to ask you for a very big favor. Ordinarily, I would ply you with some witty story, some gossip, some delicious food, but, as you know, the staff have all gone home long ago, and I've had a truly beastly night until now. So, I was wondering if you would mind if I just slipped into my library, poured us a pair of whiskeys, and, in the meantime, perhaps you could prepare, and meet me in the bedroom, which is right there." He pointed to the door at the left head of the gallery.

"Why not?"

In the library, Tom teetered senselessly for a moment,

then poured three whiskeys, downed one, and carried two, on a tray, through the window-lit darkness back to his bedroom. Miss Doolan, totally naked, her clothes piled squarely on the seat of one of the Regency chairs, was sitting in one corner of the small sofa when he got there. She had let her hair down. It fell to her waist. In the glow of the candle, it had taken on an auburn tint.

Tom sat beside her, handed her a glass. They made a quick, silent toast, without touching glasses, then she placed hers on the side table next to the candle. Tom swallowed another shot, then removed his coat. He slid down onto the sofa, laying his head in her lap and throwing his own legs up over the distant side. It surprised her. He looked at her and smiled. He was very tired and she could see that now, with him so close and directly in the light.

He reached up and gave her breast a weak cupping in his hand. Against his cheek, he could feel the smooth crease of her stomach and, above it, on his forehead, the sphere of her breast as she bent over him and opened his shirt. Her lap was tight. His eyes opened and closed again. Her hands lay flat on his chest. Tom was almost asleep, but not quite, and he could still feel the light touch of her fingers against him, like the touch of a nurse, concerned in each new movement for the effect they produced, asking no pleasure for themselves. From this tenderness, he inferred a quality of niceness. But he could not bring himself to turn and kiss her.

He felt feverish, as if he were floating on air, high above the furniture about him, bobbing. She placed a finger at her lips, kissed it softly, touched it to his. This simple girl. Not pretty, not a princess, but so wonderfully uncomplicated. She reached down, then, and squeezed him—tiny amounts more pressure until he came awake. She took him in both hands, massaged him, and then, as he had known she would, tried to force him up against her. He could feel a soft hand in his hair. The other hand grew firmer by the second . . . and it must have pressed some exposed nerve, she thought, for suddenly Tom screamed in terror, just as she was beginning to take him.

"No," he cried out. "No. No. No—" There was a shrill, infantile chord in his cry, and, after its first bellow, he convulsed in tears and fell drunk onto the small, Aubusson prayer rug beneath him. His body, clearly by reflex, huddled in against an imaginary cold and Miss Doolan, more than a little shocked herself, could think of nothing to do save throw a blanket over him. Then she hurried to dress.

That Tom, weakened, in a second between waking and sleep, had been borne so realistically back through the shocks of his past, that he had virtually walked a second time into that purple room containing Lilly and his father, could not have occurred to her.

Then, just as she was leaving, he looked up at her again and, gathering all the strength he could, begged her to forgive and understand. "I'm sorry," he said finally. "It's just that you're much too kind a girl for anyone to use, Miss Doolan."

And she looked back at him, aware for the first time of how great a blessing it was to be ordinary, and said only: "No, I'm not."

She went off then, presumably to her "friend's" and, in a few seconds, Tom was asleep.

He never saw her again.

Tom awoke in his bed, feeling a curious elation with the early dawn. He had climbed up onto the great mattress sometime during the night, but he could not remember when.

The Chinese brought him a tray of waffles and kidney stew, a glass of fresh, unpasteurized milk, and a wide Imari cup of Lapsang Souchong tea. Mr. Li had always worked either for English exiles or Anglophilic New Yorkers and this, along with a mixed grill, was his specialty. Tom so liked it that he swallowed it nearly whole. Then he ran out of his bed, shedding his poplin pajamas on the floor, and took cover in his bathroom, behind the wooden door of his shower. There, standing on the morning-cold tin of the tub, he shivered, reached above him, and tilted the spray-headed can by its rope until the water hit him, lightly and pressureless, with its soft, baptismal suggestion of new beginnings.

He worked all day in his office, but he did not see Elizabeth again until Monday, when she came in to say that her necklace had been "even more successful" than she'd hoped and to ask that its clasp be tightened. Tom, who had been listening, wearily, to Thistle's suggestion for a new window ("yellow for May, after purple for Easter; but not a vivid yellow, don't you know: more that of certain roses") turned sharply when he saw her, disturbing, with his elbow, a bowl of floating orchids, splashing some of the fragrant water onto the glass of the vitrine below it and onto the mahogany. But he ignored the spill in Elizabeth's favor.

"I'm glad," he said intensely. There was no doubt at whom he was looking, nor in what manner. And his staff, as quietly as they could, seemed to separate from him, move out and away.

Elizabeth did not budge. "Everyone loved it," she said.

Tom's eyes, fiery, but a little pitiless now, unmoving even as his lips rose into a smile, watched her. "And your party?" he inquired.

"Was lovely."

"I wish I had been there." His voice was deliberate, almost chilly.

Elizabeth, sure now of that which she had only suspected, tried futily to match the immenseness of his expression. "Yes," she said. "I *too* wish you had been."

Tom knew that the next moment was crucial to him, that, in future, he would either live on its memory or regret it forever.

"I would like to see you," he said, summoning all his

courage against the adolescent fright that still lived inside him.

Elizabeth handed him the necklace. "My parents sail for Italy on Saturday," she said, "if you would like to come then."

Tom paused. "I didn't think your mother would mind," he replied awkwardly.

"Not Mother. Father." Elizabeth smiled. "Father would mind."

Tom did visit Elizabeth on the Saturday of her parents' departure. She was provisionally under the chaperonage of her aunt, but the woman had not taken her role to heart and when Chance arrived, at dusk, only the servants stood guard: a reduced staff of three "Biddies" and a "Pat" who were without authority to challenge Elizabeth.

It was curious, Tom thought, that now, as the light fell across the open square, the great Italianate house appeared so much less formidable. Perhaps its diminution had come with access. Perhaps, in the nature of things, dreams inevitably surpassed reality. The thoughts occurred to him, but did not linger. He was simply too pragmatic. He looked carefully at the four sides of Lafayette Square and, measuring for the first time, saw that the Popes' was by no means the largest, or even among the half dozen truly grand houses there. It had, of course, that impressive carriage entrance and, above it, in the original stone, a weather-smoothed escutcheon charged with the family's armorial bearings: a book, a candle, a lance, some Latin words. But it was not the palace he remembered, and he breathed, before knocking, a small sigh at the fact that he could have afforded one like it himself.

The "Pat" answered the door and admitted him at once. The "Pat" had a good-humored, Irish smile and looked, perhaps, only ten years Tom's senior. He lacked, altogether, the haughty and unspoken conversation of an English butler, and this surprised Tom and put him at ease. After he had given over his coat, one of the Biddies showed him up a flight of stairs and into the drawing room where Elizabeth, sitting quietly, wrapped in great folds of woolen skirt, with her legs folded girlishly beneath her, sat peering at a sheet of music.

"Mr. Chance, Miss Elizabeth," the Biddie said.

And Elizabeth looked up gratefully. "Oh, wonderful," she said.

The Biddie held fast.

"Well, that's all, isn't it?" Elizabeth asked her. "Except for our tea. Don't stand there, Kathy, like a piece of starch."

Tom smiled. The Biddie shook her head faintly and withdrew.

"My aunt has gone over to Fifth Avenue," Elizabeth said calmly, extending her hand. "She has a friend there with whom she shares a common interest."

"Oh."

"Yes. An English whiskey. I forget its name. It's a very bad thing for her, of course, but, for me, it's splendid that she likes it so."

Tom blushed. "May I sit?"

"Here. Next to me."

"Thank you."

"I'm not so cruel as I seem, Mr. Chance. It's quite simply that–"

"You've been brought up in a certain way." He paused.

Her eyebrows arched. "Yes–"

"And now you see yourself in a somewhat *different* role."

"Different? Role?" Elizabeth asked. "You sound more like an actor than a jeweler, Mr. Chance."

"Do I?" Tom smiled.

"Yes," Elizabeth laughed. "But, here's our tea coming. Quite real and quite hot. No stage business about it."

A large silver tray was put down before them, and, resuming a more conventional posture, Elizabeth set about the business of preparing them each a cup.

"Cream?" she asked.

"Lemon," Tom said.

"Not very English."

"*Very* Southern."

"I wouldn't know. I love tea," Elizabeth went on. "Don't you? Do you know what I think is the best thing about it? Not the tea itself. I could as well take that as leave it. But what we're doing now, all this juggling about of plates and kettles and cups. I think it's marvelous. You know, just when you've swallowed your watercress sandwich, you find you have the jam from a jam bun all over your fingers."

"Indeed," Tom laughed.

"That's the fun: the ritual of the thing."

Tom smiled at her innocence. "If we're lucky," he said, "I suppose that it is. In a way."

She handed him his saucer and cup, thrilling to the sound of his spoon against it, the precise splash of his sugar. "What?" she demanded.

"I was just being philosophical," Tom apologized. "As you were."

"I wasn't being philosophical for an instant. I was just stating a simple fact, which is that I adore tea. For one thing, I'm not clever enough to be philosophical."

Tom moved closer, regarded her slender face in the slanting, sinking light.

Elizabeth smiled, looked down at the dish of pastries that had been presented with tea, hesitated. "Mummy says that we practically keep Monsieur Griffou in business," she offered nervously, "with all the French rolls and cakes that we buy. Why don't you stay for dinner?"

"Why don't we dine out? At Delmonico's, or—"

"That's a naughty thought, the two of us alone in a public restaurant. People would gossip."

Tom smiled suddenly, but hesitated. "Then I shall accept your invitation," he said finally.

"Good."

Between tea and dinner, they talked considerably more, but with the same evasive curiosity that had characterized their previous conversations. Elizabeth was falling in love, or rather had fallen and was now deciding to risk the consequences. Tom was awaiting his moment, but not nearly sure enough that it would come. He was nervous, soothed only by her presence, afraid, in the most desperate way, of their impending moment of parting.

Elizabeth took him on a tour of the house: her father's study, his scientific books, his telescope (for astronomy was his avocation); the long vaulted hallways; the drawing and ball rooms—all haunted, eyed by the ashen portraits of former family patriarchs, furnished with their boxes, their tables, their silver and gold. Tom, in the nighttime quiet, could all but hear the ghosts and read their minds as he followed their progeny through the dustless reliquary, marveling at the hold the past exerted on such humans as the Popes, at their clearly curatorial devotion to its props and symbols; it was as if, without such present and tangible links, they feared that the whole iron chain of their past might slip suddenly out from the tenuous hold of their consciousness.

Elizabeth took a seat on the needlepoint bench by the harpsichord and, by heart, hidden in shadows, played soft, measured Bach: "Jesu, Joy of Man's Desiring," then "Siciliana."

They dined on clear soup, chicken, and spring vegetables, drank a bottle of Mr. Pope's private Medoc, exchanged short words, long glances, and breathy, metronomic pauses; studied, like lapidaries, the reflections of candlelight in their glasses, twisting their stems, marking blue prisms, white prisms, red prisms out along the white lace cloth. And then, a little before ten, they arranged to meet again the next night . . . and the one after that. . . .

The following Thursday, on the way out of a small dance to which Elizabeth had had him invited, Tom told her that he was in love with her But she said nothing. Then, on Saturday, he told her a second time and again she did not reply. They were alone in his apartment.

"You must like me," he pressed. "You come here. This is the second time. And you have me at your house. What do the servants say?"

"I tell them anything I want. Anything that comes into my mind. All sorts of crazy things," Elizabeth laughed. "Of course I *like* you."

Tom began to kiss her and she yielded to him, took hold of him. "*Like* me?" he protested then. "I love you. *Love* you. Do you *love* me, Elizabeth?"

Her heart skipped a beat. "Yes, Tom," she said finally. "I *love* you."

Their romance, with those proclamations made, continued into and then through the summer, rejuvenating Tom, maturing Elizabeth, but, even so, unconsummated. Not since he was seventeen had Tom felt anything like it, not since, at the Holliday Street Theater, an old Lebanese magician, with a double wart on his eyelid, had pressed a small leather ball into the hold of Tom's fist, waved his wand, invoked his words, and Tom had felt the ball multiply—not simply seen, but felt it. He had not understood then. He did not understand now.

CHAPTER

19

"It's the last day of May," Jay Gould declared thoughtfully. "Monday, the thirty-first. Tomorrow Boutwell's to announce how much gold the Treasury will release in June."

"How much do you expect?" Chance inquired. He sat quietly at his desk, studying his senior partner in the weak light, for the windows had been shuttered against the afternoon sun.

"Only the usual," Gould replied.

"I thought you wanted him to announce for three months ahead."

"Never," Gould said.

Fisk raised his glance. It was coming to be called "The Flash Age" and he personified it, uniformed but coatless, with mustachios copied directly from Napoleon III.

"Then *I* misunderstood," Chance suggested.

Gould hesitated. "How much gold have I bought in your name? Through your accounts, I mean?"

"Two million three hundred sixty-five thousand," Chance recalled at once and from memory. "So far. That's what you've spent."

"Handsome," Fisk allowed.

"And you, Mr. Chance? You personally are in for—"

"Less than one million."

"But *just* less."

"That is correct."

Gould smiled at Fisk, gave Tom a sideways glance. "We would be better off if Boutwell announced for three months. Tom's right. We'd know where we stood. But, of course, so would everyone else in the Gold Room."

Tom thought carefully. "I'd rather know he wasn't going to sell in July, in August, or before the harvest," he insisted. "I'm willing to let another man make a dollar too."

Gould seemed emotionless. "Noble," he said flatly.

"Gold is one hundred forty," Fisk announced out of the blue. "If anyone gets out now he won't take a beating."

"But he might trigger something," Tom said. "A bear run, for instance. And that could hurt his partners."

"Undoubtedly," Gould concurred. "And besides that, he'd regret it for the rest of his life."

"Why, Jay," Fisk said, "I've never heard you use that tone of voice before. It sounds so much like a—a threat."

"Not at all," Gould said. "What I meant was that gold is not going to stop at one hundred forty. Neither Boutwell, nor any other Secretary of the Treasury, is going to stop it there."

Chance looked at this dark, solemn, and yet somehow electric presence. "Why not? Is Boutwell in or out of our calculations? If he's in, why won't he announce the Treasury's intentions three months hence? If he's not in, how can we be certain what he will do?"

"Abel Corbin," Gould offered then. "Mr. Abel Corbin. Is that a familiar name to you, Mr. Chance?"

"Corbin? Corbin? Should it be?"

"I don't know." Gould wheezed for a moment, waved his small, pallid hand through the smoke of Fisk's cigar. "One meets many people in the course of one's business, but one accumulates few friends. And Abel Corbin, I'm glad to say, is as true a friend as I've known. Despite the fact that he's twice my age and more accustomed to life in Washington than in this city."

"You have a point," Chance said. "Don't tease us. Make it."

"Very well," Gould said. "Mr. Corbin married last year. I don't know from what firm he purchased his wedding ring, but the lady upon whose finger it rests is the President's sister, the former Jenny Grant."

"I see," Tom said.

"A little more than before," Gould suggested, "but not everything."

"Corbin is–involved?" Tom asked.

Gould smiled broadly. "Yes. And Mrs. Corbin–a very avid investor."

"Does it run in her blood?" Chance asked.

"Those things always do."

Tom's eyes grew calm. "Then you're true to your word, Jay. And, as I told you before, for as long as you're in, I'm in with you."

Gould nodded. "Yes. Now, the President hosted the Corbins a week or so ago at the White House and, I gather, he was very much impressed by the argument for higher grain prices that they made. He relies on them, you know, quite heavily. That's a well-known fact, if you'd care to check it through another source."

"Unnecessary."

"But being a canny fellow yourself, I'm sure you're wondering just what incentive we've arranged for our political friends. Certainly, I think you're entitled to know that, if you are buoying our market with so much of your own capital."

Chance laughed guilefully. "Their capital, I take it, is not their own."

"They are, after all, salaried people." Fisk smiled. "Public servants. We are indebted to them. All of us. Why shouldn't we be?"

"I have collected a portfolio of gold bonds," Gould explained. "Very substantial. With the understanding that any profits realized through a rise in the price of gold will accrue to . . . I trust you will take my meaning if I say only that they will *not* accrue to me."

"Perfectly."

"The fifteenth," Gould said, "of June. At the Corbins'. West Twenty-seventh. Six in the evening. The President and Mrs. Grant will be there, Mr. Fisk and I, Chamberlain, Bill Tweed. I should like you to have a word or so with President Grant. As a matter of reassurance. One never knows when that can be useful—for a jeweler." He laughed.

"Thank you," Chance said.

"Have you a young lady?" Fisk asked exuberantly.

"Very much so."

"Then bring her along."

The hallway, into which the bouquet of a fresh potpourri drifted from an adjacent closet, was flooded with strangers, almost impassable at six o'clock when they arrived. It led directly to the Corbins' dining room, to a sideboard full with cold roasts and warm sauces, jellies and aspics; but, except for the small cucumber sandwiches, open and pungent with vinegar, Elizabeth was not much impressed by her surroundings. Her glow was bright, but her eyes were condescending. President Grant, looking especially worn, red-faced as though his afternoon razor had had need of further stropping, prompted no awe from her. She thought him, amidst his circle of hangers-on, even more vulgar than her maid had suggested.

Grant was huddled with Gould, Fisk, Corbin, and three anonymous men.

"McCulloch, when he was Johnson's Secretary of the Treasury, always had his hand in the market," Corbin was saying.

"*On* the market," Gould replied.

"It frightened investors," Fisk added.

"Too much so," Grant said.

"They couldn't make their plans with any certainty."

"I'll have some herring," Grant said, "if you don't mind, Mr. Gould."

Gould smiled broadly. "Of course, Mr. President. Allow me–"

"George Boutwell's a gent," Grant said once the slippery fish had been washed down his throat with bourbon. "But all's right now. All's right!" He gave a wink.

Chance was introduced to the President by name then, but had time only to shake his hand before another man, a friend of Tweed's, appeared for the same purpose. Grant regarded both at an angle, politely, but without engagement.

Fisk was even more brilliantly attired than usual. Like a monarch, he possessed a wardrobe of legitimate uniforms; and tonight, mustachios waxed, he had elected to appear as Admiral of the Fall River Steamship Line, which he owned. This costume fitted to perfection, for immediately following the Corbins' reception, he, Gould, and the presidential party and family were to sail, aboard that line's new steamer, *Providence,* for the Peace Jubilee in Boston. Tom talked with Fisk, and his friend, Josie Masefield, for ten minutes as the President, just behind them, received one guest after another, with Corbin and Gould apparently stationed at his elbow.

"Extraordinary, Miss Pope," Fisk offered, pointing in Grant's direction. "Wouldn't you agree?"

"Yes," Elizabeth said. "Extraordinary."

The President's party sailed from the East River, on the last ebb tide. Tom and Elizabeth, employing one of Brown's landaus for the night, joined a small group which saw them off at the pier and then returned alone to Lafayette Square, where Elizabeth provided warm milk and music and Tom tried to fathom the sudden breadth of his own good fortune. Settling into a dead Pope's Adam chair, he closed his eyes for a moment and dreamed the whole party over again in his mind: the President; Gould; Fisk; Chamberlain; himself in a mirror. He heard Elizabeth's Mozart; felt, on his tongue, as a pressure in his veins, the delicious rush of adrenaline.

Four days later, Grant returned to New York and was entertained again by Gould and Fisk, this time at a performance of *La Périchole* at the Fifth Avenue Theatre. The centerpiece of that entertainment was the exuberant can-can number, but that small clique of politicians and tycoons presented a rather solemn sight to those who saw them in their box: private, few in number, businesslike. Tom, who had been made aware of, though not included in these festivities, nonetheless heard the reports. And then, within twenty-four hours, came the news from Gould that "Grant remains solidly in our pocket." By that time Tom had already doubled his own investment in gold and gold bonds, as well as encouraged a few of his clients to do the same.

Tom did not know, because Gould had not told him, that the overnight sail had collapsed into a near fiasco—that Gould's one-track insistence on a government hands-off policy toward gold had offended the President, as well as perplexed him and caused him to raise his guard. Nor did Tom know—here, because Fisk had not told him—that the latter's seedling doubts as to the wisdom of the corner had finally bloomed, and that he had not yet committed more than a token stake on its behalf.

Events soon afterward began to race. Gould brought the news that Major General Daniel Butterfield had been appointed Assistant Treasurer and therefore head of the Sub-Treasury at New York.

"Butterfield, eh?" Chance said. "Army of the Potomac Butterfield? Life's a hell of a small thing, isn't it? A real circle! I gave him a cut once, I remember. I had to, of some of the things I was selling his men."

"I too have given him a cut," Gould said more somberly. "People don't change."

"No."

Gould removed an envelope from the inside pocket of his

coat and handed it to Tom. "Open it!" he said. "Inside you will find two certified checks, drawn against our bank."

"Two million dollars?" Tom exclaimed on finding them.

"One million each. I want you to go into the market with them. Tomorrow. Then the next day. Take your usual commission."

"Who else is buying?"

Gould snapped: "You shouldn't ask that sort of question. It's not what they call 'ethical.' But Speyer is. Seligman and Company. Heath. Nevertheless, buy as low as you can."

"Always," Tom agreed. He seemed about to continue, but caught himself suddenly, even as he sensed Gould watching him.

"Something the matter?"

"Nothing. These are big stakes for me. It's turning out I'm betting everything I have."

"On a winner," Gould said reassuringly. "On a winner."

Afterward, Tom asked Hardenstein how much of Goelette and Company's money was on deposit at the Tenth National Bank. And Hardenstein immediately told him. "An imprudent amount. Sixty percent, as you wished. One hundred fifty thousand, plus or minus. It's not such a sound bank either, rumor has it. Of course, I—"

Tom cut him off and thought in the silence. He could not remove the deposit without Gould knowing that he had, without endangering the confidence of the dark man on whose scheme he was betting so heavily. On the other hand, he suspected that Gould, in control of the Tenth National, was issuing checks far in excess of its reserves. The Tenth, he knew, had a city charter. Its regulators were his friends, but also Gould's friends: Tweed and Chamberlain—Tammany. If the corner failed for any reason, the bank might fail with it, and Goelette and Company, along with the other depositors, might lose its entire account.

Gold rose still further. By the end of August, it had reached one hundred forty-seven—and Gould owned nearly forty million dollars in contracts for it, calling on just less than three times the extant supply. But the cannier speculators had begun to sniff a raid, and the bears were increasing along with the panic.

Then, on the twenty-sixth, an editorial, signed by Corbin, appeared in *The New York Times*. Entitled "Grant's Financial Policy," it enunciated Gould's to the letter. Continued prosperity depended on a high gold premium, Corbin declared. "The President will not send gold into the market and sell it for currency."

Chance read the article with rapid exhilaration of spirit; re-read it; went to see Gould at the Grand Opera House, but found him out of the office. He recognized Gould's hand in the editorial and, on the pretense of congratulating him, wanted to evaluate his opinion of the bear resistance. Chance, with many contracts at prices above one hundred forty, did not want to remain for long in a market that might fall ten points lower—or, as some said, twenty. But Gould had apparently vanished from sight, and taken Fisk with him.

Now, Chance found it hard to digest his food, difficult to devote to Elizabeth the attention she required. It was the crucial gamble of his life, with many times his entire fortune risked upon it. Therefore, he awaited the harvest with all the restless passion of a new Swede farmer tilling the long plain of his adopted country for the first time. The harvest, he knew, would bring the climax to this adventure. The western crops, sheathed, bagged, and trained into the eastern ports, would be off to their destinations in only a few weeks' time, to be sold in London, in Liverpool. He understood that once these sales had taken place, the bulls would no longer be able to argue, as Gould had, that a high gold price would make American crops more valuable with respect to paper money and thus inflate the prices paid for them in Europe. And yet he had not put so much on the table merely to make the modest profit he could realize if he pulled out now. He was "in" until the moment of the corner, when he and Gould and Fisk would be able to bring the market to bay and, by controlling the supply, force a vastly higher price for gold than could ever be reached through open trading.

Early in September, Grant, passing through the Corbin house on his route to vacation at Saratoga, wrote Secretary Boutwell that he considered it unwise for the government to sell substantial amounts of gold while the crops were being transported to market.

"I," Gould told Chance, "was standing directly outside the dining room when he gave it to his secretary. Abel came and told me at once. The President felt it more . . . decorous that way, I imagine. At any rate, I had the letter a good day before Boutwell."

They were standing in the black marble hallway outside Gould's office. "Fisk?" Chance said. "I've heard he's on the fence. I was surprised. I had thought, naturally, that he was with us."

"He is."

"I can't go in anymore. Neither can my people. We're heavily bought," Tom said. "And I don't want to sell. But—"

"No, don't sell, whatever you do. Fisk is coming in. I can assure you of that. One hundred percent."

Tom cast him a long and severe look. "I believe you," he said.

But for nearly a fortnight, prices plummeted: down to one hundred forty-five . . . one hundred forty-one, and still no buyers . . . down to one hundred thirty-six . . . one hundred thirty-two. Until, on the thirteenth, evidently convinced by Gould (and the government's failure to sell its stocks) of Grant's complicity, Fisk made the great commitment Chance had been waiting for—and entered the market with eight million dollars. That great and resonant voice, ultimately indiscreet, walked the rim of the Gold Room, shouting orders to buy. Mrs. Corbin, he confided to Chance, had promised him that her brother would never allow the government's gold to be sold. And Chance was not the only one to whom he so confided. The lithe bronze Cupid and the arched bronze dolphin cavorted at the center of the amphitheatrical Exchange, but, all about them, the mood was changed, charged by Fisk's electricity, enthusiasm, fortune. Chance was delighted, while confounded. For Fisk, he remembered, had helped to hatch the plot to corner, had helped to seduce the presidential family. Why, so late out of the quiet, had he come forth with the frenzy of a convert?

In the fever of the moment it didn't matter. Gold began to rise at once—and, for a while, by more than a dollar an hour. So that Chance's losses, though only on paper, were quickly made good again. He was ecstatic. Everyone was buying—a broader base of the market than had ever before been involved—as if, playing crew to Fisk's admiral, these watchful traders accepted his actions as a signal of the commander-in-chief's intentions. By the twenty-second, gold had returned to one hundred forty-one and showed no sign of a slide.

"We'll see it one fifty," Fisk said, after they had returned to the Grand Opera House at the close of trading.

"And higher," Tom said. "The crops are en route now. Two hundred's not impossible."

"Not at all," Gould said. A servant handed him a message, which he opened, read, and closed immediately, with no change of his perpetually grave expression.

"Anything wrong?" Tom asked.

Gould managed a smile. "To the contrary," he sighed. "But I must go and pay a personal call—of all things, at such a busy time." He stood from his chair, wheezing for a moment, coughing, and then he turned.

"Well, good night," Tom called.

"Yes. Goo-night," added Fisk. "Fare thee well, Jay."

"Good night, gentlemen," Gould said.

There was a pause. "Two hundred?" Fisk asked Tom wistfully. "I think so too. In my heart, I think so—"

"And yet it took you a while to come around."

"Only until Jay assured me that Grant himself was going along."

"I thought he knew that in June," Tom said.

"We knew Corbin was going along. But we didn't know for sure that Grant was. Anyway, we do now! Jay's talked with him. And I've talked with his sister. It's going to make us money, Tom. Money, money." He laughed. "What a wonderful thing that is!"

Gould, following the message he had received, proceeded directly from the Grand Opera House to the Corbins', hurrying his coachman, ordering the whip, shredding paper as nervously as any schoolboy bound for his examination.

It was a warm evening. There were still leaves on all the trees along the New York streets and they were still green. But the summer scents had suddenly gone, and the ripe, heavy air had disappeared.

Corbin was direct, solemn, and weak in his step; ghost-like, Gould thought, and smaller, as if somehow punctured, drained of a previously defining flatulence. His wife stood beside him. He nodded politely, but before Gould had time to take a chair, he handed him a letter. "Jenny received this" —he paused—"only an hour ago. From Mrs. Grant."

Gould's eye shot straight from the letterhead—"The President's Mansion"—to the signature—"Sis." Then he read the body of the note, muttering out loud as he reached the crucial sentence. "Tell Mr. Corbin," he read, "that the President is very much distressed by your speculations and you must close them as quickly as you can."

"He's giving you time," Gould said after a moment.

"Yes," Corbin said. "I think so."

"But how much time?"

"He's onto us. I don't understand this, I thought he was with us," Corbin rambled frantically. "You've got to close out my account. You've got to give me my profits."

"*Your* account?" Gould laughed.

"Yes."

" 'I am the power behind the throne,' " Gould mimicked furiously. "Those were your words. There will not be any profits once this is known. I'll be a ruined man. And so shall you be."

"No!"

Gould thought. "Has anyone else seen this letter?"

"No."

"Then burn it. Tell no one."

"No one," Abel Corbin said in a frightened voice.

"Mrs. Corbin?"

"No one," she said. "This was our great chance, Mr. Gould."

"Not a word to Tweed. Or Butterfield. Or Fisk–or Chance. No brokers, relatives, friends. Not a word to *anyone*."

"Can you save us? Do you think–"

"Very few people will get out of this alive," Gould said. "It all depends on when he acts. There's very little time. We have to remain together, think of ourselves."

"Only ourselves," Corbin assured him.

"Because there's no other way," Gould said, "to avoid being ruined."

CHAPTER

20

RELAXING, OVER CHOCOLATE, IN THE SMALL YEW ROOM AT THE base of the stairs in the Popes' house, Elizabeth turned to Tom and, a little precipitously, said, "It's so typical of them, isn't it, of Father especially? Says he's returning in the fall and, like clockwork, here he is due in on the equinox. It's the astronomer in him."

"I don't think I'd ever care too much for stars in themselves," Tom said curiously. "Unless I could use them to gaze into the future."

"How awful that would be." Elizabeth stroked her poodle's coat. "How boring!"

"Of course I'm as romantic as the next man," Tom promised her. "You know that."

"Yes."

"But everything always seems to happen at once and. . . . Anyway, when *you* imagine the future what do you see?" Tom asked. "Let's talk about you, not me, tonight."

Elizabeth smiled, sat up a little on the slipcovered sofa. "I don't know," she said. "Really I don't . . . unless it's the past."

The servants, not Elizabeth's aunt, reported her friendship with Tom to Mr. Pope, who was most emphatically not amused. He had neither met Thomas Chance, nor ever previously heard the name in any but a business connection;

and it was to these failings, as much as to the occasional rumors, that he objected. For Roderick Pope, the lineal descendant of George Garrick, was an individual governed by a complicated set of interior laws, the most general of which was that one should always deal in known commodities: old firms, old friends, old neighborhoods; one should avoid mysteries.

He was a handsome man, athletic of build, graying now, but with the old brown still back behind the temples. He rode to hounds two mornings of each week, in New Jersey. He had an office on Broad Street which he attended with sufficient regularity to convince casual acquaintances—and himself—that he was a banker; but his real devotion was not to money, but to form. Of that religion he was a priest and, like a priest, a servant. He believed, with all the fervor of an archbishop for his deity, that the civilized, if not the physical world, depended upon men's exercise of certain basic rites. And to the perpetuation of these traditions he had, although rather painlessly, committed his soul. A doctor gave himself to medicine; a scholar to truth; an aristocrat to . . .

Who could argue, after nearly nineteen centuries of confusion, that the values of Christ should not be one with the values of the established churches; the established manner; the established wealth? Honor. Family. Courtesy. A brand of discriminate warmth to one's equals. An arm's-length compassion to those who were not. The propagation of one's name, one's genes. The preservation of one's treasure. These were the tenets of his creed and, about them, he was humorless. Roderick Pope, so eager to systematize all experience, even the visual experience of starlight, was almost totally uncritical of his own attitudes; and, as a consequence, like most men whose principles exceed their intelligence, he had become especially suspicious of everyone else.

He waited no longer than the salad course of their first lunch since returning before raising the matter of Thomas Chance with Elizabeth. Seated at the inside of the small round table they kept in an alcove off the dining room, he put his fork matter-of-factly into the greens and held some leaves up to the light. "Beautiful lettuce," he said. "Lovely *emerald* color."

"It's Bibb lettuce," Mrs. Pope said. "I always prefer it."

"I know," said Roderick. "I thought perhaps Elizabeth might notice it too, now she's become an expert on jewelry." He seemed more than usually dour. "Did I say jewelry? I meant to say jewel*ers*."

Elizabeth remained silent. She was used to his callous indirection. She could scarcely believe that he did not see it himself, the farce he was acting. But she could not play him, as most girls could their fathers. She had never been able to. Her flirtations, now as always, had to be reserved for others, for she knew, from experience, that there would be no response from this judgmental man.

Mrs. Pope scarcely looked up from her plate. She continued deboning the last of her bass, with something very like surgical attention.

"Mr. Chance," Mr. Pope said finally. "Have you been seeing him? Is that true?"

"Is it all over town, Father? Is that what you mean?"

"Is it *true*?" he repeated.

"Yes." Elizabeth frowned.

"Good Heaven," he said. "I don't know whether to be glad for your honesty, or sorry for your lack of judgment."

"He's a very attractive man," Mrs. Pope explained softly. "But how *old* is he, Elizabeth?"

"Twenty-nine," she answered quickly.

"Twenty-nine? Yes, I remember. He seems older, I suppose. He's a handsome man, no doubt about that."

"I wish you would disentangle yourself, Elizabeth," Mr. Pope suggested flatly. "There's no future for you with Mr. Thomas Chance."

"He's not an aristocrat," Elizabeth said. "I'll grant you that. He's not a member of your precious club—"

"No. And he never will be," Roderick Pope said. "I know more about him than you imagine. He's a criminal, daughter. Or the next thing to it. He stole that jewelry business right out from under Goelette. That's common knowledge. He's wired into Tammany–Tweed's gang. And also Gould, and that indescribable Fisk fellow."

"Jim Fisk?" Mrs. Pope inquired with half a smile.

"The same," her husband said.

"He *is* indescribable. Of course, I've only seen him in the papers."

Elizabeth sat very straight in her chair and said nothing. Mr. Pope swallowed, then spoke: "*They* stole the railroad—the Erie, you know—out from under Vanderbilt and Drew. They're a pack of jackals, those railroad men. But I suspect your friend's friends are the worst of the lot. They bled the Erie's treasury dry to do what they did. They watered down the stock. People lost their whole lives' savings while they let the stock price go to nothing. Then they ran a bull raid, drove it up—and secretly, out of vengeance. Because Drew was selling short and they knew it. They set out to break him. They succeeded too."

"All of this means nothing to me," Elizabeth said. "Nor has it anything to do with Mr. Chance."

"It has everything to do with Mr. Chance. Remember, Elizabeth, you're the only Pope in this line. And you must be careful, with whomever you see, that he has at least as much to lose as you have—which very few people do."

Elizabeth squinted at her mother and her mother smiled and touched her lips with her napkin. "I rather suspect that I have more to gain, as well as lose," she said. "Let's try another subject, why don't we?"

"Because the present one has not been brought to completion," Mr. Pope snapped sharply. His jaw was rigid now, military; and, for an instant, Elizabeth could read in his steel-gray eyes the contradictory sources of her own ideal and fear of men. "Mr. Thomas Chance is out of the question, out of the question," he continued. "When you lie down with dogs, you get up with fleas. It's an old proverb, but the Popes have always lived by it, much to their everlasting benefit. I forbid you to see or speak with him again. And that is that, I trust."

"No, Father," Elizabeth said. "I'm afraid it can't be. Before you go on, I think you should know that Tom Chance and I are engaged to be married."

Mrs. Pope took a sudden bite of her fish. "Elizabeth!" she exclaimed.

"Wait, Adelaide," Roderick Pope interrupted. "I don't believe the girl has heard me."

"I was going to tell you anyway, today or tonight. But you jumped me so quickly."

"It's impossible."

"Not at all," Elizabeth declared quietly.

"For want of everything, consider the matter, Elizabeth. It's the Age of Newton. You're not being sensible."

"And what has Mr. Newton to do with Tom and me? No more than Mr. Gould or Mr. Fisk, I suspect."

"He has this to do with you. Certain things are absolute. Time and space . . . quite a number of things. Do you understand where I'm leading?"

"It's always to the same place, isn't it?" Elizabeth replied. Something about her father did not seem to originate in quite the right place, as if his emotions came but obliquely from his heart and always through the filter of his reason.

"I don't want to be too technical," he continued. "But if you remember, when you were a little girl, I taught you Newton's First Law and, for a while, you could recite it: 'Every body will continue in a state of rest or of uniform motion in a straight line unless it is compelled by some external force to change that state . . .' " He paused. "So, you see, it's my duty, as your father, to keep you away from such external forces. Because what is true and right for physical bodies is also, in a manner of speaking, true and right for families like our own. That they should proceed in a straight line, lest they cease to be what they were."

"Father," Elizabeth began, holding her smile, but with a new, firmer voice, "I know more about Tom, I think, than any of your Union Club friends could possibly know. He loves me. I love him. And we are going to be married. Next spring. With or without your blessing."

Her father stared at her. He inhaled deeply. "Shall we worry about that *in* the spring?" he said.

"As you wish."

Roderick looked at his wife and began to mutter through barely parted lips as if unsure of even her attention. "If there *is* an impressed force," he recited in a slow speech from memory, "the time rate of change of momentum is proportional to this force and takes place in the direction in which the force acts . . .

"Thomas Chance," he whispered conclusively. "No. No. Never!"

Gold rose all day Thursday, closing at one forty-four. Fisk bought heavily. He had a girl on each arm and looked more like a renegade from one of his own operatic productions than a true investor. Gould also bought. He was neither so loud nor so ostentatious in dress or gesture as Fisk. But he knew that the market's eyes and ears were settled upon him and he kept up his front, releasing substantial orders to buy at crucial moments. Alone among those in the Gold Room, he knew of the President's intentions to break the market. His selling was being conducted in secret, through an entirely separate set of brokers, and on a much larger scale than his buying. He was selling for his own account, for the Corbins', and for Butterfield's, the latter having agreed to inform him when the government order finally came through and to provide an interval before its execution. To everyone else, including Chance, he struck the posture of a charging bull, stern, confident; so that, through their own brokers, Tom—

and men like him—felt encouraged to buy even more heavily than they had.

By dawn on Friday, Tom owned nearly five million dollars in gold contracts, a figure representing more than six times his personal wealth. He had not seen Elizabeth the night before, owing to her family's return. And, besides the uneasiness that event had produced, he was agitated from another night without sleep as he prepared to drive to the Gold Room. All through the dark, from midnight until the small Perpetuelle had chimed out one, one thirty, two . . . and on to six, he had tried to lose himself in sleep, but his mind had refused to come out from the counting house. It was too busy totting up his new, phantom fortune, visions of which made him anxious, excited, and tired.

He felt so very sure of what he was doing, of his associates. Gould had taken him aside on Thursday. "Our moment's coming," he had said. "Another week or so and—"

"Yes," Tom had said. "We'll have sailed past two hundred."

"Every hope. Every hope," Gould had said.

And Tom was prepared for that now, that week, as he moved out into the quiet streets, alone and full with thought as the sun rose and threw the morning shadows westward. It was a splendid day. High autumn.

He traveled, by victoria, to the Metropole Hotel where, in the company of two floor traders, he breakfasted on oranges, kippers, and a variety of breads. He had decided to forgo his usual eggs at the sight of them, but he drank two cups of black coffee and half of a third before he got up from the table and drove down to the brokerage offices of Heath and Company on Lower Broadway.

Almost no one was there when he arrived. The door had been unlocked only minutes before. The desks of the traders were still clear from the night before. He could see their wood-grain surfaces, their inlaid leather pads, the neat stacks of order slips that were made each day at closing in preparation for the day to come. He rubbed his hands against the chill, then thrust them quickly into his pockets. In a few minutes, Fisk arrived.

Fisk had even more women than the day before. Chance counted three immediately. They had insipid faces, small with button noses, and large busts gathered up by their costumes. Tom and Fisk shook hands, smiled, laughed for a minute like teammates before a match: competitive, but not directly; hoping, perhaps, only for greater degrees of relative success, but the same general outcome. Then Fisk went to his corner. Gould took another corner when he came in a few minutes later. He smiled perfunctorily, but no more. He was constantly, nervously tearing papers into confetti-like strips and dropping them onto the floor. Also, he had a sheaf of documents which he seemed to be reading.

The price of gold reached one forty-seven by a quarter to ten. And it showed no sign of turning, or weakness. Down the street, at the Stock Exchange, shares were tumbling in reaction. The dollar was worth less every minute now, and the prices of commodities were falling in the panic of uncertainty; firms with weakened treasuries were going bankrupt.

"Buy," said Gould quietly.

"Fifty thousand, I'll wager," exclaimed Fisk, "that we'll be over two hundred by the end of trading today."

Yet no one took his bet.

"Buy," said Tom. He was sure that the corner had come, that they were on the point of controlling the supply of gold.

"How much?" asked his broker.

"As much as you can."

At ten o'clock, the price was one fifty. At ten thirty, five points higher still. Fisk's broker, Speyers, was ebullient. Others, depending on the positions they had taken, were either frenzied now, or paralyzed with fear.

"Look at them," Tom's broker said. "They've gone mad. It's madness in here."

"It hasn't ended yet," Tom said.

"I bought you all we could get at one fifty-five. The price is moving now. We'll have to pay—"

"Whatever," Tom said.

"Are you sure?"

"Just *do* it!"

"There may be a corner—but what if it breaks?"

"No," Tom announced. "It can't."

"I've seen them break, these corners," the broker said.

"Don't be stupid," Tom said. "No one's seen anything like this before. Now, buy or I'll find someone else who will—"

"Yes, sir," the broker replied. "Seligman has some. I'll get over to his man if I can only find a way. It's a madhouse in there. Far worse than here."

"Yes," Tom said, then suddenly stopped short.

"Excuse me," the broker said, pushing his way into the crowd now.

"Seligman?"

"Yes, Mr. Chance."

"That's strange."

"He's been selling all morning."

"Not to you, has he?"

"No, sir. I only just discovered it myself."

"Where is he?"

The broker pointed in the direction of the Gold Room.

"Has he been selling to Gould?"

"I haven't an idea, sir."

"To Fisk?"

"I've no way to—"

"Whose gold is he selling?"

"Seligman is very secretive. Very discreet. No one will ever know from him."

Tom thought.

"Does Mr. Gould know you?"

"No, sir. I've not had the pleasure."

"Good."

"I don't understand."

Just then a voice boomed over the crowd. "One hun-dred sixty-two," it cried, its message repeated at once by those who heard it, borne on sudden whispers across the human tide of the room.

"One hundred sixty-two!" the broker said, astonished.

"Listen to me," Tom said. "And do what I tell you. It's very important. Everything depends on it." His eyes fixed the broker now. "Everything. If I hear you've breathed a word of of this, I'll—kill you."

The broker nodded.

"I will," Tom said.

"I believe you."

"Go as near to Gould as you can."

"Done." The man was shaking slightly.

"Try and spot his brokers. Who's coming and going. See if Seligman's man is one of them."

"You want to know if Gould is selling."

"Yes."

"Secretly?"

"Yes."

"I'll do what I can. Shall I continue to buy—in the meantime?"

Tom paused. "I don't know," he said.

"One sixty-three," the loud voice called.

"Yes," Tom said. "Buy. Buy. I'm probably wrong."

"Fisk is buying," the broker reminded him. "And they're the Erie boys, both of them."

The crowd in the Gold Room was shoving against the railing now. A part of it, having broken off, swayed toward the fountain itself. But the great mass was trapped, hysterical, barbarous. Gold reached one sixty-four at eleven o'clock. And Tom, unaccustomed to trading in the open market, to the life signs—particularly the pulse of it—did not fully imagine it could turn on him at once. He had the distance from the

Gold Room to Heath and Company as insulation. And he continued to buy.

Gould, however, quietly and furtively, went about his selling. He had salvaged the Corbins' profits and Butterfield's and most of his own when the messenger arrived, just before eleven thirty, to say that General Butterfield had finally received an order from Secretary Boutwell to sell five million dollars' worth of gold.

Gold was hovering at one sixty-four when Tom's broker returned. It was eleven thirty-five. "You were right about Gould," he said.

Tom's face lost its color. "He's selling?"

The man nodded.

"The fucking son of a bitch!"

"He's *been* selling. In fact, I bought some of his gold."

"You idiot!" Tom exploded.

"But I stopped as soon as I realized it was his."

"Clever," Tom said sarcastically.

"Why must you do what he does, Mr. Chance?"

"Why? Why? Why!" Tom repeated. But his mind seemed suddenly elsewhere, distracted, pathetic.

"Gould's been wrong before. He doesn't run the market."

"Doesn't he?" Tom asked with cold anger still edged in his voice.

"Shall I sell?" his broker asked.

"Yes."

"How much?"

"Everything," Tom said. "Immediately. Will the market absorb it?"

"I don't know."

"Use everyone you can."

"I want to say, I think you're wrong."

"No," Tom said. "I'm not wrong."

Tom was out of the market by twelve thirty, having sold

all but a few hundred thousand dollars of his holdings at prices above one sixty and the remainder at one forty-five. A few minutes later, the price, in response to Butterfield's noontime announcement, had tumbled all the way to one thirty-three and the crowd, escaped from the Gold Room, was swaying toward Heath and Company, chanting, preparing to lynch Jay Gould.

Tom had seen Gould, weak and exhausted now, nearly broken, slip out through a rear door that gave access only to an alley, followed by Fisk, of all people. And he had seen a few of the angrier brokers stare them down with ready vengeance. He felt the emotion himself, felt betrayed, abandoned, thirsty for the salty taste of his betrayer's death. He looked around at the frantic crowd. Men rushed in every direction. Papers flew. Shoes were trampled. The air hung, fogged with smoke, thick and expired. And, somewhere in the distance, he saw Fisk's women, young and whore-like and alone. Tom moved slowly, glanced cautiously, appeared, to his relief, to be the focus of no one's attention. He wiped his hair back from his eyes, the perspiration from his lower brow. And, though his heart thumped to the song of sudden triumph, he masked himself in an expression of dejection, the hunched walk of one who had lost—and made his way out of the brokerage into the bright and autumnal afternoon.

Gould might retreat to the fortress of the Grand Opera House. And Fisk, relentless in his gullibility, accepting his patron's explanations, might go with him. Their thugs might even protect them from the jeering crowd outside, a crowd that chanted murder. But Tom Chance would walk alone through the stunned financial canyon, unremarked; and there neither was nor would be any mob outside Goelette and Company. His participation in the corner had not drawn the light of public attention. Like certain dull gray fish in a sea of blue-white sharks, he had been saved by his relative inconsequence. And, he knew, it was a lesson to remember.

CHAPTER 21

TOM AND ELIZABETH MARRIED IN THE SPRING.

About a week before the ceremony, Mr. Pope paid a call on Tom and, indirectly, attempted to buy him off. Tom was cordial—offered the elder man a chair, which he accepted, and a cigar, which he refused—but he did not allow the subject to come to a head.

"Elizabeth is quite young," Mr. Pope said.

"She will be twenty soon. Her mother, I think, was married at twenty."

"Yes. Well—"

"Nor am I yet ancient—" Tom laughed. "Mr. Pope, I beg you, if we don't bring youth to our marriage, what do we bring?"

Mr. Pope, impervious to most constitutional differences among people, was not much moved. "I'm afraid I don't know—"

"Elizabeth's young. I'm young. She loves me and I love her. She loves New York and I love New York. We're both of us healthy. Both Episcopalians . . ."

"As of recently."

"Is it not a man's right, in this country, to choose his religion?"

"And his church," Mr. Pope said. "Even Trinity."

"Indeed."

"Mr. Chance," her father began in a more moderate voice

now, "as one man to another . . . I want to talk to you not about what Elizabeth will *bring* to her marriage, but about what she will *not* bring."

"Go ahead," Tom said. "Although, for me, all that is necessary is that she bring herself."

"The Popes, as you are undoubtedly aware, are an old and established family in this city. Quite naturally, we are jealous of that position—our good name, going back over the generations. Most of us, but not all, are descended from George Garrick Pope, who came from England aboard the *Dove* in 1620 and later built his business as a fur trader in the North. You probably know that."

"I've heard it," Tom said.

"That was—nearly—a dozen generations before us. Please follow me now. I'm going to do some mathematics for you. I said a dozen generations. So let's suppose that each person in each of those generations had three children. The truth is that many had considerably more and a few had less. So let's use three. That's three times three for twelve times. Three to what is called the twelfth power." From his breast pocket, he then removed a small card upon which all of the calculations had been worked out in a neat hand. Three times three was nine, times three was twenty-seven, times three was . . . all leading up to the ultimate figure, three to the twelfth power, which the card showed as: 772,641. Roderick Pope considered the number gravely, then announced it: "Seven hundred seventy-two thousand, six hundred forty-one," he said. "And add one more for the original George Garrick. That's how many Popes there have been in this country, on this continent, since— It's more than you thought, isn't it? For one small family. What you've thought of as an . . . exclusive family. Many more than you thought. Of course, they're all not alive now. But thousands of them are. All legitimate descendants of George Garrick, but not legitimate heirs, if you understand the difference."

"Not quite," Tom said.

Mr. Pope faced him directly. "A family like ours would not be able to survive if we kept dividing up our fortune every generation. Clearly, you can see that. As many Popes as there have been—even into a large sum, a royal sum, it just wouldn't go."

"So you must marry your children to those with fortunes in their own right. Mr. Pope—"

"And . . . *and* select who among us are to inherit. You've heard of primogeniture. That's rather our way. I say 'rather' because we don't confine it to eldest sons, Mr. Chance, though they receive more than the others, but we do confine it to sons."

"Confine?"

"Elizabeth will receive a stipend. She will not inherit."

"She is an only child."

"With male cousins."

"I see."

"I'm glad. It is obviously a rather private piece of business, but I thought it might color things for you."

"I told you that I love your daughter. And I do. Inheritance or not. Stipend or not."

"Well, then—I suppose it's 'Good day'!"

"I have, now, considerable means of my own," Tom said. "I don't expect that fact to impress you. I don't mean it to. But perhaps it hasn't escaped your attention."

"No, sir," Mr. Pope said. "Neither my own, nor anyone else's."

It was a large, flower-filled, particularly fashionable wedding, held at Trinity Church. Elizabeth wore her grandmother's gown, had seven bridesmaids, and both a maid and a matron of honor. Three of the bridesmaids were also named Pope. Two were cousins from Philadelphia. The maid and matron were also cousins, but closer for the fact that they had gone to school with Elizabeth at Miss Prippit's. Tom had thought of asking Langlois and Hardenstein to stand as ushers for him, but decided against it. Not having attended one of the Eastern colleges, he had few friends in any purely social sense, although he knew that that was what was called for. He knew that the bride's guests—her family's guests especially—would judge him partly by his ushers, and so he had looked about for faces that would fit and had come up with enough, including Scudder's older brother. All of the men asked were surprised that they had been, and said so to one another. Two or three would not have thought to invite Tom to their own weddings, and two or three hadn't. But he was an attractive enough fellow, they told themselves, a good man to know even if, before this, they had never considered him quite as a friend.

The organ began at half after ten. The Popes' Biddies were the first to arrive. Trinity was not a Catholic Church and, strictly construed, this was a sin and would require confession later; but, for Elizabeth, they were willing to make an exception. They had been up all night for three nights preparing the house, the family's clothes, the biscuits and punches and roasts, catching sleep only when they could, an hour here, another there. And they had no intention of missing the "vows," as they called them. Walking down the long nave on the arms of the well-bred young gentlemen Tom had pressed into service, they shuddered a little in awe at the magnificence of the limestone walls, the gold brocaded tapers, the huge arches of the English perpendicular-Gothic style. They marched humbly, but as far as they could, to just behind the family pews. There they turned left into the bride's side, each motioning, with exaggerated, noiseless courtesy, for the others to go in ahead, each praying for that valued seat on the aisle.

The organ carried Elizabeth's favorite hymn out among the entering crowd: "Fairest Lord Jesus, Ruler of all nature, O thou of God and man the Son . . ." and Elizabeth, in the rear vestibule, even amid the preparations, could feel the words on her tongue. Her mother's favorite followed: "A

Mighty Fortress Is Our God"; then more Bach, and a pause. It had been Elizabeth's idea to do away with the bridal-march entry and have the ushers enter singing, hymnals in hand, exactly as the choir did on Sunday mornings. So at precisely the moment when the congregation expected to hear the familiar Mendelssohn, it heard, instead, the voice of the rector from the front of the church. "Hymn number two hundred seventy-nine," he announced.

And then the first pair of ushers, the shortest, appeared in the doorway and the procession began as everyone joined in the hymn:

Praise to the Lord, the Almighty, the
King of creation;
O my soul, praise him, for he is thy health
and salvation.
Join the great throng,
Psaltery, organ, and song,
Sounding in glad adoration. . . .

It took four verses to bring Elizabeth to Tom, and by that time the music had cast its spell. The church, to Tom, had become enchanted ground and he looked out no farther than Elizabeth before he realized it. Her father's face remained straight and pious, but, dimly in the background, he perceived a conquered city—five hundred smiles—as if that many Popes and Astors and Stuyvesants were offering it up to him now. And, beside them, he could sense the comfort of familiar faces: Chamberlain, Fisk, even Mrs. McCorquadale. The old ferments were active in him, and desire was not the least of them. Desire of this soft and rarefied woman: physical as well as verbal possession now. Desire, in the final sense, of a permanent end to loneliness.

"Dearly beloved," the rector began. And then, in a quarter of an hour, it was over.

That evening, with the organ song faint in memory, they

retired to the Prince of Wales' suite in the Fifth Avenue Hotel. The final light of their wedding day was dying out of the sky over Madison Square. For a moment, from their window, they lost themselves in that pale froth of lavender and gold with the Eden Musée silhouetted out against it; the low, magic city reaching its way to the Hudson. The thrilling rush of their carriage rides was passing from them now. And so, too, the religious elation of their vows, the enchanted stir and murmur of their half a thousand guests, arriving, departing, whispering, in low and rapturous voices, as they waited out the long reception line, and danced. They were alone, Tom and Elizabeth, human again. Only the gay scent of freesia, spreading out from the management's bouquets, startled their privacy.

Elizabeth sat on the edge of a chair, a trifle exhaustedly, and allowed herself two long, deep breaths. "Would you like something?" she asked.

"What, for instance?" Tom smiled.

Elizabeth sighed once more. "Tea. I don't know, or–"

"No, thank you," Tom replied. He was standing still and almost over her.

"Just a glass of water," Elizabeth said. "That's really all I need. Just a simple glass of water."

Tom moved directly to the small Chippendale table just inside the foyer and poured her one from a carafe that rested there. "Here's to Paris," he said as he handed it to her.

"We shall be there in a fortnight, shan't we?" Elizabeth smiled.

"Indeed we shall," Tom promised. He was on the point of coming close to her, to sit for a preparatory moment along the arm of her chair, when, suddenly, the wet tumbler slipped out of her grip and cracked into powder on the hard floor between carpets.

When the noise had passed he noticed she was crying. "Oh, Tom," she begged, "I'm not sure I can."

He smiled and touched her lightly. "It will be all right," he said.

"Not tonight, anyway. I just don't think that I could—tonight."

Now he said nothing.

"Do you understand?"

He looked stunned. He regarded her hungrily, but without making a sound.

"I just don't think that I can sleep with you, Tom."

"We're married," Tom said quietly. He could not believe the beast that, second by second, she was revealing to him; as if, with a solitary paragraph from The Book of Common Prayer, the whole Victorian cage had suddenly come down from around her, abandoning her to a codeless world in which she was not prepared to survive.

"I beg you," he said, yet knew it was wrong even as the final syllable came off his tongue.

"Beg me? Why, look at you."

He put his hand on her shoulder. It trembled beneath his touch, as if from some internal war of personalities he had never previously guessed at: too much paradox; too dark an interior to have been glimpsed through such bright gowns. Not for the first time, he sensed the hollowness of dreams.

Elizabeth sprang to her feet and gave him a frightened look. She loved him and knew it, and yet there was another power driving her—a black, chthonic relic of her childhood. The seed of this terror had been planted so close to her soul, and so long ago, that she could barely separate them now. And so her instincts told her that *it* must be real, as the overlay of charm which surrounded it must be false, as her voice was false, her fetching smiles, her little jokes. The nearer Tom came to threatening her virginity, the more urgently her instincts insisted on this and fought her desires; the more her trembling became like shivers and passed beyond her control.

"Elizabeth!" Tom announced then, with enough voice to bring her still.

"What?"

His eyes pierced her—vivid, but cold now, unforgiving.

"All right," she cried. "You want to have me? *Have me,* if you want."

"What are you doing?" she demanded after she had fallen back onto the mattress and caught her breath.

"Turning out the lamps. That's obvious enough, isn't it?"

"Oh, no," Elizabeth said. "I want them on."

More shocked than surprised, Tom did as he was told, for, in his heart, he still believed that the act itself would ultimately resolve everything.

She was feline, he thought, fragile under pressure; that was all. She was quiet now and he regarded her cautiously. He had dreamed of more of a prelude. Naturally, he had expected the evening, in the warmth of a hundred kisses, to reduce itself to this moment, but he had not anticipated the element of challenge that he found. Slowly, silently, garment by garment, he undressed her and then himself. He studied her: the blond, defiant mane, the icy brow, the graceful and patrician neck, the small but firm and jaunty breasts, the narrow waist. . . . He had married a woman, he knew—maybe a princess; but the old vision seemed far away from him now.

Elizabeth frowned at him, a grimace collected from a little bit of every feature she possessed. Only for an instant at a time, and then in artful flickers, did she permit her eyes to roam down lower than his waist.

Tom approached her slowly.

She slid away.

He turned and caught her, held her head back, kissed her. He forced his tongue inside her, meeting no resistance, for this was familiar territory, already yielded.

She struggled. She turned onto her stomach. He rotated her back.

"Elizabeth," he said.

No answer.

He drew himself up into a kneeling position then, placed a knee between her legs, and spread them.

"I've ruined your life," she cried. "I'm—"

"Frightened and young," he told her. "I . . . love you, Elizabeth."

By the time they returned from Paris, he knew her body perfectly and considered, more or less, that this completed his knowledge. He was sure, after a year and one month of courtship, that he knew her mind as well as any man ever had or would and that a good deal of what he knew he liked. He and Elizabeth still had fine times together, and private moments, and the soft sense of shared dreams, even if the old, flirtatious winks were gone. Those winks had had to go; he knew that. They were like youth, and he was glad that in their place he had the right to touch her now, and to lie in her bed. So the more time passed, the more inclined he became to consider her old fright as a wound that had healed—for he wanted it to be gone from her life and from his.

Frances had been his friend and Elizabeth was his idol. When he compared them that was what he saw. With Frances, when the physical had ceased to be exciting, he would have been left with a companion, someone who loved and understood him at his source: with Elizabeth, he told himself, it would be right to start a family.

They were given a modest Georgian house near Gramercy Park as a wedding present from the Popes. The house was made of bright red Holland brick and had a wide porch with tall iron railings rising all the way around it, and a pair of bronze coach lamps at the entrance. The sitting room on the first floor and the master bedroom above both opened on twin exposures, so that, in spring, the breeze brought the scent of dogwood in from the park and ruffled the sheets and the covers on furniture. Tom had been reluctant to leave his apartment for Gramercy Park, but the house had appealed to something domestic in Elizabeth, some buried memory of her own childhood—a doll's house, she thought—and he had agreed and had brought the Chinese along.

In the summer they had use of a large cottage on the

East River at Eighty-sixth Street where the air had the cleanness of country and the danger of malaria was less than downtown. But apart from these changes of residence, Tom's routine was not much affected. One day he took stock of his financial dealings and found, at the age of thirty, that he had assets of almost three and a half million dollars.

On their first anniversary, Tom gave Elizabeth the emerald pin she had admired on the day he met her. Then, in 1872, she gave birth to a daughter, Katharine Evarts (after his mother's Christian and her mother's maiden names). And he gave her a sapphire.

In 1873, their second child was born. This was a son. They named him simply Pope Chance, and he delighted his father as nothing ever had. As soon as he had been allowed to see the baby, Tom ran, singing, from Gramercy all the way to Central Park. Delirious, he was nearly stampeded by a delivery carriage, then mistaken for a fleeing thief by a policeman, for whom he was lucky to have a cigar.

"What's the name again?" the Irishman asked.

"Pope Chance. Born today."

"And it's a damn good thing," the officer smiled. "Us Catholics need a few more in this country."

Roderick Pope proved equally and spontaneously fond of his grandson. He had no sons of his own and was glad that Elizabeth and Tom had carried on the family name. Glad and rather monstrously proud. So that afternoon, for the first time (yet as if it had been the hundredth), he invited Tom to dine with him at the Union Club.

"Fifth Avenue and Twenty-first," he said. "Adelaide wants to stay with your wife."

"I know."

"Fine, then?"

"Yes. Let me ask you, though, is it dress suit?"

Mr. Pope smiled. "The Union Club? Can be. I'll tell you, Tom, how I approach a dinner like this. I usually have a nap first. Heaven knows I need one today. So do you. Then I have a tub—a nice lukewarm one on a day like this. And I slip into whatever is around and comfortable. And it's usually a dress suit."

Tom smiled. "Yes, sir. I understand."

Always before, because he had been looking from the outside in, he had thought of clubs—the Union Club, the Maryland Club, any club—as a kind of compensation for the ravages of age. He had seen the old men, the imitation English, on the steps of these buildings, their canes in hand, disguised as walking sticks; and yet, in answer to their privilege he had had his youth. He had envied them a little—but no more, he suspected, than they had envied him, and probably less. So he had worn his youth defiantly as he passed them, picked up his step a little, and left the matter there. He had, since his marriage, felt connected to the Union through his father-in-law's affiliation—but, at the same time, more disconnected than most men for the fact that it was never mentioned in his presence. He knew that men his age were members now, because he had heard two of Elizabeth's cousins mention it to one another when they had not thought that anyone was listening. And he had deduced from their tones, and quite correctly, that it would remain unavailable to him until Roderick Pope decided otherwise.

Thus, though it was only for dinner, the invitation brought with it a feeling of triumph. And it was with more than ordinary curiosity that he remarked the great lantern and the scripted names on the bronze postal boxes that lined the front hall. He and Mr. Pope took a drink in the bar. There were perhaps twenty other men in the room, drinking and gaming beneath the reproachful eyes of a Tanganyikan moose, and all but one or two of them nodded politely. Mr. Pope talked of the new baby through two English whiskeys and recorded a bet about the child's athletic abilities in the betting book by the bar. The bet was for five dollars and had been taken by an old friend of Roderick Pope's, whose name Tom had failed, even on a second try, to get correctly.

They dined at a private table, at such length that the rigid slat-back chair had put Tom's right leg to sleep by the time they stood, and he was forced to limp away into the drawing room.

"Cramp?" Mr. Pope had asked.

"Just asleep. Feels like pins and needles."

"Happens to me all the time. Something to do with the height of a chair, they say. You're tall, though. Perhaps—well, of course, there's no way to know with any certainty. There seems to be a theory for everything these days."

"It was a lovely meal," Tom said.

"Working it out? Good. Have a seat on that plush thing. Have a brandy, why not?"

"Thank you."

"Napoleon?"

"Thank you."

Mr. Pope pressed a small bell and, almost at once, a waiter appeared and took the order.

"So the cuisine was satisfactory? Your meats were as you like them?"

"Oh, yes. Exactly. More than satisfactory."

"It's a fine club."

"I can agree with you on that. I've never known, never *seen* a nicer one."

"No. Neither have I. You know, you ought to consider joining." The same familiar voice in which the invitation itself had come, as if no obstacle worth the name had ever presented itself.

"I don't know what to say."

"Don't dissemble, Tom. Just say yes."

"Yes, then." Tom laughed.

"And Pope too, in his time. Here are our brandies. To Pope."

They touched glasses.

"Waiter," Mr. Pope interjected before sipping the cognac.

"I'd like a glass of cold water on the side. No ice."

"Very good," the waiter said.

Tom hesitated. "To Pope," he repeated.

"May I live to see him in this club," his grandfather said. "May we both live!"

As soon as Elizabeth was recovered, Tom presented her a small scarlet box as casually as if it contained lagniappe from Goelette and Company. It was her first day up from bed and they were alone in the drawing room, having come down from the nursery on their way to dinner.

"I have to admit," Elizabeth said, "that I've been expecting this. Though I can't, for anything, imagine what it is. I admired that emerald pin—and you were so sweet about it. And the sapphire. Although how you knew I loved sapphires, I don't know. I don't think I'd ever mentioned it." She took a swallow of her sherry as she removed the wrapping paper. About a week before the birth she had had her hair cut short, to just above the neck, and it made her seem older now, less fully in bloom.

"Blue eyes," Tom said.

"What?"

"Blue eyes. All babies have blue eyes, silly. Sapphires are blue. So—"

"Why didn't I think of that?" She reached for an instant to her hair, then carefully raised the top of the box on its hinge. For a moment, her eyes seemed puzzled; then, gradually, they began to swell, not so much "to pop out," as the current expression would have had them do, as to retreat in awe. "How beautiful it is!" she exclaimed, with total sincerity, but without that knowledge of gems—of this gem especially—which would have permitted her to fully appreciate the magnificence of her husband's gesture.

Tom explained that this was "The Pearl of Macao."

"The Pearl of Macao," she repeated slowly. "It was in your office, in that special case. Oh, Tom—"

"I first saw it as a young boy," Tom said.

"And I as a little girl."

"You weren't a *little* girl."

"Compared to what I am today, I was. And that was only four years ago. A little more."

"And one husband. And two children. And a house. And goodness knows what else–"

"I've tried for you, Tom," she said. "I know I'm not the kind of lover a man dreams of. And I don't s'pose I ever will be–what some women are, I mean. I've never talked about this before and, really, I don't want to now, except to say that I *have* tried for you. And that I know you've tried for me. And I appreciate that. Very much.

"You love me very much, don't you?" she asked, glancing down again at the Pearl of Macao.

"Since the day I saw you."

"Shall I wear it?"

"You can't wear it yet. It hasn't been set. If you want we'll do that for you in the morning. And you can hang it on a pendant. Or however you like. Langlois could do it. Or else you could keep it in its box for a while, look at it–that might be nice."

"I love you," she said. "And our children. And that's just what I'm going to do: I'm going to keep it in a box and whenever I look at it, I'm going to think of how lucky I am, of what a lucky woman Elizabeth Pope Chance is, and of all the people I love, starting with you."

CHAPTER

22

"CAMPAIGNS," TOM SAID, GRADUALLY EXHALING THE WHITE smoke of his Havana. "That's what life is, a series of campaigns."

"That's a damned realistic way of looking at it," C. C. Chamberlain replied. He smiled, dipping the mouth of his cigar into his snifter of brandy. With age, Chamberlain had developed a chronic cough. "In that respect, you've done as good as anyone I know. I mean, here we are in the library of the Union Club, of all goddamn places, and, to be frank, it's hard to believe that twenty years ago you were just a kid peddling haberdashery."

Tom reflected for a moment. "Not even twenty. It's 1873 and I went to work at Lazenby's in 1854, so it's been nineteen. But that's what I mean. From then until now, I've always been on one campaign or another. But I don't know anymore. It's as if my entire life has become a holding action."

"There's nothing wrong with a holding action. What you have achieved already is well beyond the dreams of most men, Tom. Every so often a man has to catch up with himself."

"You're right. But I can't help wishing that I had one more *big* deal in the works. The way I see it, I'm just one step down from the top of the ladder."

"Well," Chamberlain interrupted, "you have the money.

So all you're lacking is the idea. A lot of people are making money in steel—and railroads," he added. "I'll wager that if you took the fifty biggest fortunes in this country, twenty-five would be from railroads."

"Certainly one would be from shipping." Tom's face suggested he was joking. "I wouldn't credit any list that didn't include you, C. C."

The older man gargled his brandy as he swallowed. "Not me! I'm small potatoes. An angle here, an angle there. I own a few ships and I've put a few dollars away, albeit in a lot of places. But I'm still a speculator and I know it, an opportunist with a fistful of cash. I'm no industrialist, for God's sake. I'm not the kind of man who builds empires. That's what you want to do, isn't it?"

Tom nodded.

Chamberlain smiled. "Well, you have a son, so it makes sense for you. I never had any children. Tried, but—"

Tom's eyes widened, their usually fierce green growing darker and more moist, letting Chamberlain know easily that he understood his problem and yet respected the privacy of its nature. "I guess it has a great deal to do with Pope," he interrupted. "With Katharine too, of course, but mostly with Pope. Although that's not the only reason. A good bit of my drive—"

"Your *hunger*." Chamberlain laughed.

"I wouldn't fight you on that word. I've never believed that people were very good at judging their own motives, but I see mine well enough to know I have to satisfy myself before I even begin to consider anyone else."

"That's what got you out of Baltimore. You could have satisfied your father by working on the docks."

"By God, I'm ready for another leap."

"Do you want some advice?" Chamberlain asked.

"From you? Any time."

"The chance will come." For a moment, Chamberlain's cough overtook him; then, when his calm returned, he added: "Set your affairs in order, get yourself into a position where, when it does come, you'll be able to see it. But, for Christ's sake, Tom, don't work yourself into a state that keeps you from enjoying the love of your family. That's the most important thing."

Tom nervously tightened his cravat. "My affairs *are* in order," he replied. "The best they've been in in years."

"All the better," Chamberlain continued slowly. "All the more time to spend with Elizabeth, and the children." A wistful tone crept into his voice. "Such comfortable children you have, Tom: with Katharine already chattering away and that baby Pope, with those wonderful dreamy eyes, just like his mother's. The moment a person comes near either one of them, there's a fire in the hearth."

For three years, until 1876, Tom followed Chamberlain's advice. He continued to rise each morning at six, to spend the first half hour of his day with his ledgers and the next hour in a rigorous regime of exercise—push-ups, sit-ups, weights, and a run totaling thirty flights of stairs—culminating in a three-minute shower of frigid water. At a quarter before eight, he breakfasted—more than half the time alone, for Elizabeth did not like to rise before ten—with the morning newspapers spread beside his place setting. And at eight thirty sharp, he departed for his office.

Goelette and Company prospered under the combined care of Hardenstein, Langlois, and Thistle, each of whom now enjoyed a small percentage of its profits, though Tom still insisted he be called from his office to close any sale of more than five thousand dollars. Although the store's inventory consisted entirely of precious gems and jewelry, Tom applied to it the latest merchandising techniques of the department stores. For two days in the early fall and spring, a fortnight before the first estimable party of the Season, Goelette and Company would offer a leisurely, private preview of its forthcoming collection exclusively to its regular clientele. During the winter—on the first Thursday of November, December, January—Tom would call in Delmonico's to cater small dinners in the store's main showroom.

"Each dinner is to be strictly limited to fifty guests," Tom admonished Langlois at the beginning. "We don't want to say so flatly, but it should be understood that the fifty guests are those whose accounts have been most active in the month immediately prior. If asked, naturally we'll deny this, but you can see how it is in our interest to have our public understand that this is our criterion. It will engender a certain amount of social competition that will benefit us if we are not too blatant. There's something about exclusivity that appeals to New Yorkers, and the thought of dining among these cases of jewels, if we make it seem a privilege, ought to entrance them. They'll want to come here, but, more than that, they'll want to be *seen* here."

"Thursday is a good night," Langlois had agreed. "Many of our clients allow their servants Thursdays off."

"You've gotten to think exactly as I do." Tom smiled.

From his office, and occasionally from the apartment above it, Tom carried his private business farther each year, gradually multiplying his interests. But for all his success, he understood that he remained no more than a substantial investor in most arenas. Only at Goelette and Company did he enjoy the role of a principal.

"The problem is the nature of the business I'm in," he told Elizabeth one day as they sat reading in the wainscoted library of their house on Gramercy Park. "It's not basic enough."

"Jewelry?" she asked. "I suppose it's not like food, if that's what you mean by 'basic.' Although it seems only just less essential to many people."

Tom smiled. "To a few, but not many. In the whole country, I wonder how much jewelry is sold every year."

"By everyone? Is there any way to know such a thing?"

"None, except to guess."

"But you've obviously thought about it."

"In a very general way, taking everyone's business and lumping it together, I'd estimate a couple of hundred million dollars. But of course there's no way to take over control of the market."

"If you did," Elizabeth said, "you'd have a monopoly. Then you could charge even more—'whatever the traffic would bear.' Isn't that right?"

Tom glanced up. "I had no idea you were so well informed about economics."

"It's a case of do or die. If I'm going to talk to my husband for more than a few minutes at a time I have to learn these things."

Tom grinned apologetically. "If that's true, your husband must be mad."

"I suppose all dreamers are a little mad." Elizabeth smiled.

"Only when they're momentarily out of dreams."

"You're a jeweler who's really a banker," Elizabeth responded as a fresh thought shot through her. "If the jewelry business isn't truly what you want, why don't you sell it, or let the others run it for you. Then you could go into the banking business. You could open an office downtown."

Tom began to rock in his chair. His eyes narrowed. Outside, against the window screening, the first flies of springtime pressed toward a bright interior lamp. "Or we could move farther," he suggested. "We could look at the future, decide that, for example, steel is going to be a coming thing, gather up our resources and simply move to Pittsburgh."

Elizabeth returned her teacup to its saucer and studied Tom's expression. "Pittsburgh," she said. "I don't know, Tom. I've never been there in my life. I'm a New Yorker. That's how I was brought up to think of myself. And I rather like the thought of bringing up my children here. I want them to be New Yorkers, too."

"They'll always be New Yorkers."

"Not if they don't grow up here. Not if they don't learn to love it at a very young age. Mother says it's a special taste."

"Nothing special about it," Tom said. "I'm a New Yorker and I didn't set foot in the city until I was twenty-seven years old. That's what makes New Yorkers different from other people, Elizabeth. You don't have to grow up here to be one. All you have to do is to come here looking for something that you couldn't find wherever you were."

"Father would dispute you."

"The original George Garrick Pope was a New Yorker in the way I mean."

"Even if you're right, if you're so romantic about New York and New Yorkers, why on earth do you want us to move to Pittsburgh?"

Tom stared at his wife. "I'm not sure I do," he explained. "But I do want to put us in the path of opportunities. The railroads are expanding across this country, all the way to the Pacific Ocean. Believe me, anyone making steel is selling all he can make to the railroads."

Elizabeth forced herself to smile. "No more Huyler's ice cream if we leave New York," she teased. "No more Park and Tilford lobsters. No more of Monsieur Giffou's little tarts."

"Of course there would be," Tom promised.

Elizabeth smiled. "But couldn't we do just as well staying where we are? We must know a hundred men who are making fortunes in New York."

"There's a Scotsman called Andrew Carnegie," Tom continued, "who's growing the richest of all. He's the one that brought back the Bessemer process from England. He started a dozen or so years ago and all he had to put up was eighty-three hundred dollars. So think of the opportunities for people who have what we do!"

"I'm trying to, but I'm also thinking that people make fortunes without forsaking everything they have. Downtown, don't they? On Wall Street? Father never spoke about business, but I always gathered that the men who wanted what you want were able to find it there. Was I wrong?"

"No. Some of them were and are. But mostly it's for people who have decided to stop risking their money on themselves. For one reason or another, I guess, some people get to a point where they'd rather stop risking it on their own ideas and start putting it into other people's businesses. But I'm a long way from that point. All you get then is the return of the market. A little more if you're lucky, less if you're not. Elizabeth, the decision needn't be made this week, or this month, as long as we both understand that it *is* in the offing and prepare ourselves for it. The first order of business is for me to arrange my affairs so that they're not simply conducted out of the bottom drawer of a desk in a back room at Goelette and Company."

"*Chance* and Company," Elizabeth declared. "That's what it should be called."

"Too much time is wasted selling rings and necklaces. Any woman who purchases a jewel worth more than a thousand dollars supposes she's entitled to the top man's time. But the distraction always comes when I'm in the middle of something a hundred times more important." His glance wandered along the rows of gold-tooled, leather-bound books. "I'm thinking of selling Goelette."

CHAPTER

23

SPRING, HAVING ARRIVED LATE IN 1876, DID NOT LINGER. AND the summer which replaced it, although clear and bright by day, was the hottest and most humid in years. So after fifteen minutes beneath the cold-water shower in their East River cottage, Tom called out to Elizabeth.

"The heat's brutal," he exclaimed, lathering the thick, black coal-tar shampoo through his long hair. "This is the only escape."

"Apparently you're going to stay there all day," Elizabeth answered in a pleasant voice from across their bedroom. "I rather expected we'd be out and downtown by this hour."

"What time is it?"

"Eight o'clock already. What time do they expect us?"

"Whenever we get there," Tom said. "Are you all ready?"

"All I have to do is put on my dress. I'm going to wear gingham, it's so terribly hot outside."

"It won't be a long ceremony. You cut the ribbon and we'll walk inside together. After that you can do what you want with the rest of the day."

"You mean it's going to be business as usual from then on. Chance and Company's first day—and a new building to boot—and you're going to dive right in? What about champagne? I thought we were going to celebrate."

Tom's voice grew wry. "Let's celebrate right now."

Elizabeth took his meaning at once. "There *are* other *ways* to celebrate."

"I have a little story for you," Tom called as the steady drizzle of the shower began to let up.

"I can wait until you're decent," Elizabeth replied.

"It's about a couple who had been married for half a dozen years. The woman was beautiful. Some people thought the man was handsome. And they were very much in love—"

"When you come out of the bathroom, darling, will you close the door behind you, please?" Elizabeth suddenly interjected. "Any more moisture than there is already and my hair will surely lose its curl. I'm sorry—back to your story."

Tom cleared his throat. "For the first two years of their marriage, every time the man made love to his wife, they put a marble into a glass bowl beside their bed. Then, after their second anniversary, instead of adding a marble every time, they would take one out. And do you know what?"

"I can't imagine," Elizabeth answered tensely.

"Even after six years, the bowl was still half filled with marbles."

An even cloud of haze diffused the sunlight as Thomas and Elizabeth Chance arrived at Twenty-one Wall Street at ten o'clock. A small crowd awaited them at the door while a single workman, his feet wobbling on the utmost rung of a ladder, chiseled the final letter of "Chance and Company" into the marble lintel above the entrance. Below the lintel, and parallel to it, a ribbon of blue grosgrain silk stretched across the doorway.

"This is a very big day," Chance said, handing a long pair of shears to Elizabeth, but facing the assembled group.

"Hear, hear," rose Chamberlain's voice.

"Some of the faces I see were with me right from the beginning." Tom's glance roamed from Chamberlain to Tweed. Then, suddenly, he remembered Frances. He knew that she had abandoned Scudder the night before their intended wedding and later married a doctor in Baltimore, and a part of him ached with her absence. "Others came along shortly thereafter. And a few have joined us only in recent days. But we are, all of us together, about to enter upon an adventure—the kind of adventure that is peculiar to America, an adventure of commerce and industry. Money is the blood of this country. The banking system represents the arteries through which it flows. The great industrial companies now emerging and the little one-man shops alike are the organs which keep the United States alive, healthy. So I say to you that it is a noble objective that we share. And I promise you no less than King Henry V did his comrades-in-arms: 'That gentlemen . . . now abed shall think themselves accurs'd they were not here.'"

As the applause diminished to Mrs. McCorquadale's lone clap, Elizabeth severed the ribbon and the group made its way inside. "It's straight to work," Mrs. McCorquadale proclaimed. "We've all been inside before with the movers. If anyone needs anything, the girls and I will be around to help him find it."

"She's a fine hen for your chicken coop," Chamberlain told Tom as the two of them retired to Chance's office on the second of the new building's three floors.

"I'd rather have a good secretary than two good customers' men," Tom said.

Chamberlain ignited his habitual cigar. "I counted four columns and a dome. This is some building, all right. What do you call its style of architecture?"

"Greco-Roman," Tom replied.

"I've never seen anything go up so fast."

"That's because it didn't really 'go up.' The essential building was here. We just altered it a few places inside and laid a veneer over it. At first the idea bothered me, but the more I thought about it, the more fitting it seemed."

"There's no veneer about you, if that's what you mean. You're a genuine tycoon. But what are you going to do with

Goelette now that you're over here and your financial activities are out in the open?"

"They're not all 'out in the open,' " Tom laughed.

"Of course not. Still, the question is: Will people want to buy jewelry from a man who doesn't tend his shop?"

"I don't know the answer to that," Tom said. "I do know that it's far too tempting and simple to steal from an absentee owner. That's why I asked you to come in here just now. You were instrumental in my purchase of Goelette and I wanted you to know that I am planning to sell it."

"Sell it?"

"To the Katzenstines."

"For a pretty penny, I hope. They're rich as Croesus, you know."

"A very pretty penny."

Chamberlain grinned. "You'll be looking for a place to put that money."

"I want to try to find a steel mill," Tom said.

"But you're not a factory man. How would you run it?"

"I don't have to be a factory man. I can read a balance sheet."

"Maybe," Chamberlain said. "But my advice is to stick to something that you know. At the very least to something that's nearer home."

"Have you been talking to Elizabeth?"

"My word of honor," Chamberlain promised. "Not a word."

Tom, out of nervousness, began to breathe heavily. "Deals have been coming to me for years. Every shape, size, and variety. You know that, C. C. I've invested in real estate in places I've never been. I own shares in mines I've never seen. I've made money in rare diamonds and pitch black coal."

Chamberlain applied his open palm to his belly. "The bladder," he complained. "It doesn't age well." He coughed, dismissed Tom's offer of help with a wave of his hand, and continued: "Sometimes the most obvious deals are like great luscious cakes. Have you had that experience? They're marvelous to contemplate, but once you put your fork into them, you find that there's nothing there."

Tom smiled. "I've found that. Not too often, thank God, but enough to know what you mean."

"We have to guard against our own ambition," Chamberlain said. "What men like us want is always all and always now. But that can often be both too much and too soon. Times haven't yet recovered from the panic three years ago."

"Put your thoughts in one word," Tom asked abruptly.

Chamberlain's expression ripened slowly into a smile. "Ships."

"Ships?" Tom repeated the word as a question.

"I own two shipping concerns," Chamberlain elaborated. "Front Street Shipping and South Street Steamship. Front Street is mine entirely. Its boats sail to and from Bermuda, the Caribbean Islands, and a few eastern and gulf ports, such as Baltimore, Charleston, Savannah, and New Orleans. South Street has the same routes, but more vessels. The problem is that I only own forty-nine percent."

Tom studied the older man's face. "And you want a . . . congenial partner to buy up two percent more. I owe it to you a hundred times over. How much is involved?"

Chamberlain sighed. "Two percent, three percent, *ten* percent, it wouldn't do me any good at all at this point. But I'll tell you this: a man who jumps to conclusions that quickly could lose his ass in the steel business." He sat back into his chair, adding a polite request for whiskey.

"There ought to be some bourbon in the cabinet," Tom said, rising and going for it himself. When he located the decanter and a glass, he began to pour two fingers full.

"That's enough," Chamberlain cautioned almost at once. "It's still morning, you know. Sun and yardarm and all that business."

"I wasn't going to say anything," Tom said.

"I'm dying," Chamberlain announced abruptly. "So I feel a little more entitled to my pleasure than I otherwise would."

"We're all dying," Tom replied with mock humor. "What makes you think you're going to get there any sooner than the rest of us?"

"The doctor told me. Then, can you believe it, he had the bad taste to croak himself."

"Serves him right for—"

"He wasn't wrong. I came within a hair's breadth. If you'd looked at me then you'd've said I was dead."

Tom rested his head in his hands and shook it. He returned to the liquor cabinet, poured himself a shot glass of bourbon, but ignored it. "How long?"

"Not long."

Tom swallowed deeply.

"I want to tell you two things," Chamberlain said. "First about bananas. There's a Captain . . . Baker, I think his name is, who's been bringing bananas from Jamaica to Boston for five or six years now. He's expanded the trade ten times over since then. And he's still only a local fellow with nothing like the cargo space that I have. The second thing has to do with a little country called Costa Rica in Central America. Its president is a general named Guardia. He and another man, Minor Keith, have been trying to develop rail connections between the country's inland cities and its coastal ports. They've been cultivating bananas in order to have freight. But they need funds badly. They're exactly where our own railroads were thirty or forty years ago."

"Proving what?"

"That the right man could blaze a trail! With this new bank of yours and my two shipping lines, you could build an international transportation network that would have it all over anything Gould or Vanderbilt could imagine. If you got into the business now, on the proper scale, you could throttle the competition. You'd wind up owning the cargoes *and* the means of bringing them to market. In time, you'd even dominate the governments of the countries where you did business."

Tom considered Chamberlain's proposition. "If you don't want me to buy up the missing two percent, what do you want? Let me guess. You want me to buy you out entirely."

"I don't have any children," Chamberlain replied, "nor any wife left. I'd have no one to leave the money to."

"I don't follow you."

"It may be the first unselfish thing I've ever done, Tom, but I'm going to give you my stock in the Front and South Street Companies–*if* you want it, that is."

"Give?" Tom gasped.

"Give. Not bequeath. I'm going to assign you the stock sometime in the next few days. On two conditions, of course. You'll have to assume my expenses, which I assure you are modest, for the rest of my life–that means for a matter of weeks. And you'll have to swear to me that you won't simply turn the stock over and take your profit, that you'll give my plan a good, hard try."

"I can't just take the stock from you, C. C. Why, it must be worth considerably more than a million dollars."

"Considerably," Chamberlain said. "And, if you don't take it, who will?"

CHAPTER

24

C. C. CHAMBERLAIN DIED FOUR WEEKS LATER TO THE DAY. "Luckily he went in his sleep," Chance told Elizabeth.

"Still, I'd rather not know when I was going," Elizabeth replied.

"I forgot," Tom said. "You don't like anything unsettled on your horizon."

Elizabeth bridled. "That's a very sharp remark."

"I know. I had no business making it."

"Yes, you did. I haven't been a very obliging wife lately."

"Well, I'm glad you're aware of that at any rate."

"Do you want to know why?" Elizabeth demanded.

"Naturally."

"Because what comes easily to you comes harder to me—and to most women. For you it's a physical thing . . ."

"That's not true," Tom interrupted.

"I think it is," Elizabeth said. "When you're excited you think it's more. But once the moment has passed, you kiss a woman a few times on the cheek and disappear out of her life as though that were all she needed."

"I only have one woman, and that is you," Tom admonished.

"No," Elizabeth said angrily. "You're married to your work."

"You wanted to stay in New York," Tom said. "C. C. wanted me to run his companies. And I wanted to do something on a big scale. Very well, I thought, I could combine all three and everyone would be happy. But you don't seem to understand that nothing happens in this world unless you work for it."

"Not for sixteen hours a day!"

"That's over," Tom explained, "now that I've bought out Chamberlain's partners in South Street. I told you how I went in there with two percent more stock than they knew I had. And the one fellow wanted to count the votes—"

"And you said 'Sometimes we count the votes and sometimes we weigh them.' But I don't care about any of that, Tom. Why should I? Why should I just wait here and talk to the servants all day in order to . . . to *service* you when you feel like it?"

"Pope and Katharine," Tom said. "Aren't they here to talk to?"

"For God's sake, Tom. Pope is three years old. Katharine's five."

"Where are they now?" Tom's voice fell to a whisper.

Elizabeth shivered. "In the nursery. Asleep."

Tom moved toward his wife. "The other night at dinner I said to Mr. Delmonico . . . I looked around his restaurant and there wasn't a table to be had. Food coming on fifty trays. Wine being poured everywhere, waiting chilled and in those baskets. And his prices are certainly dear; so I said to him: 'You have a veritable gold mine here, Mr. Delmonico, haven't you?' And do you know what his answer was? 'At the price of eternal vigilance.' And he's right!"

Elizabeth gave Tom a frightened look as he began to remove his frock coat, waistcoat, and tie. "If you need something to occupy your mind," he said slowly, "then find something. Plan a house or a garden, if you want. But one thing we are not going to do is to go on even a moment longer the way we have been." Having unfastened its buttons, he now snapped his shirt from his body so fiercely that it cracked the air. "I'm your husband and—"

"You have rights to my body."

"Yes," Tom said. "Although it'd be nice if you put it some other way." He placed his hand firmly on her shoulder.

But she pushed it away. "Nothing else would say it so accurately." Her eyes were intense and feline, the lines of her face and posture, resolved. "Use the word and I'll do it."

"What word?"

"The vulgar one. I want you to understand that's all you want."

"I won't use any such word," Tom said as, beneath his hard new grip, Elizabeth let her body go limp.

"Whatever you say," Elizabeth said flippantly. "Your–"

"My wish is your command," Tom interrupted.

"That's what I was going to tell you."

"I know it was."

CHAPTER

25

LIKE A GOOD MEDIEVAL KING, THOMAS CHANCE INCREASED HIS power at the expense of his barons. The mixture of Chamberlain's plan, his own business acumen, and the predisposition of some Latin American governments to favor those who made it worth their while proved a fortuitous one, and it was not long before Chance had gained control of nearly two dozen corporations. Among them were two foreign railroads, the Azurean in Panama and the Nutrian in Costa Rica; two domestic railroads, the Cumberland and the Blue Rouge; once cocoa importer, the San Ambrosia Tradewind Corporation; one gigantic banana grower and importer-exporter, Hispañola; one trust, called Port d'Antigua, which held control of sixteen plantations in the Caribbean Islands and Central America; a Jamaican boat builder, Lafalier; the North Atlantis Port Company; the Coach and Carriage Company of America; the Chance Steam Engine Company; two American real estate concerns, Belvedere Hill and Holliday Street; and one general importer, Lazenby, which did a particularly large trade in sugar even as it continued to handle smaller quantities of expensive European textiles.

On Wall Street, by 1880, Chance and Company had emerged as one of the three most successful houses on the gentile side of an increasingly polarized financial community. But on Fifth Avenue, where Elizabeth was applying her finishing touch to a replica of the Chateau de Côppet, success, on any scale, seemed more elusive.

"I'm told it's the largest house yet built in New York," Elizabeth said the day they moved in.

"By whom?"

"The builder."

"Builders always want to make contests out of these things," Tom said. "They hope that some other family will feel moved to compete."

"No matter how much they spent, no one could achieve anything more beautiful," Elizabeth said, resting her hand on a bow-fronted secretary. "Don't you think it's beautiful, Tom?"

Tom studied the old Lyons silk whose folds framed each window. "If it makes you happy." He smiled. "I doubt if there's another woman in the world who could have made a room so beautiful."

"You used to call me a princess. Do you remember that? I'll bet you said the same thing to everyone."

"Only to you," Tom said. "Don't let Katharine walk in the gallery, by the way."

"Why not?"

"The Italian stuccatori are working on the ceiling. In the nude. I just came from there."

"I saw them yesterday," Elizabeth said. "I suppose it's logical enough that they don't want plaster all over their clothing, but I have to admit I was a bit shocked, particularly by the young good-looking ones."

"Really?"

"It isn't just out of duty, you know," Elizabeth said oddly. "That's not the only reason I sleep in your bed. Even when we've had our differences, I've never said I didn't love you."

Tom remained silent, puzzled.

"But I have to admit," Elizabeth went on, "that when I walk through this enormous house, I begin to wonder what kind of world we've built for ourselves."

"The best of which we were capable," Tom said.

Elizabeth smiled faintly. "Love and hate are very close, Tom. And as long as my feelings were darting from one to the other, I never worried much. But, being apart almost all our waking hours, we've grown into quite different people. We don't know each other anymore. And the frightening thing is: I'm not sure how much I care."

Tom's heart skipped a beat. "You just said that you loved me."

"I don't deny that. You're the father of my children. Until last week, you were the only man who had ever made love to me."

Tom's thoughts froze in his mind.

"I had to tell you," Elizabeth said nervously. "I'm sorry." She choked on the word for a moment.

"Who?" Tom said at last.

"A boy," Elizabeth replied.

"I said who?" Tom said.

"And I told you," Elizabeth snapped. "It was a boy. Barely in his twenties. He needed love. And so did I. It won't happen again. I promise."

Tom's icy stare appraised her. "For the love of God, you have to give me a name. You can't expect me to go through life wondering, every time I look at a man twenty years younger than I am, if—"

"Don't ask me any more questions," Elizabeth said. "It's as much your fault as mine, or his. You can wonder whatever you want."

At that moment, Pope and Katharine entered the drawing room a step ahead of their nanny.

"It's a castle, Mummy, isn't it?" Pope asked, blond hair falling before his calm blue eyes. Even at seven, his speech possessed his mother's rhythms.

"Nearly," Elizabeth told him.

"Will I have friends in this neighborhood?" Katharine asked. By this time she was sitting on the edge of a Louis

XVI sofa, observing a pair of long bronze sculptures in an adjacent hallway. The sculptures took the form of nude young males and, in the dim, interior light, Katharine looked remarkably like Tom as she studied them.

"Of course," Elizabeth said.

"Cousins?" Katharine's eyes were Tom's eyes, young again. Her russet hair was Tom's hair. She would have been a beautiful boy. Instead she was a handsome girl.

"A few," Tom said. "But mostly friends."

Katharine smiled. "I guess that's almost the same thing."

Tom reconsidered his wife's cool and fragile beauty, weighing its old intimation of purity against his new knowledge of her, and judging her both more repellent and desirable for the fact of her value to a young man. He wanted to punish her. But, at the same time and even more urgently, he felt a compulsion to have her. There was a long, awkward silence, during which Tom thought he discerned a hint of regret in Elizabeth's eyes. But, defensively, for the sake of the children, his glance continued about the room. From the pictures which hung on every wall, the past bore down with particular intensity; and it occurred to Tom that, in earlier times, any one painting might have been the pride of a church.

CHAPTER 26

To Tom, it came as a surprise. But after the shock of Elizabeth's admission of infidelity, their life together, rather than exploding, resumed a familiar shape that continued nearly through the eighteen eighties—the decade of Elizabeth's thirties and his forties. Initially, Tom required her more consistently than he had in years, as if a part of him now demanded constant proof of her presence. And entwined about his tense and beautiful body, feeling and smelling him, a penitent Elizabeth would often forget how degraded it had once made her feel to be taken for granted. But gradually, as the children grew into their teens, it became not sex or contrition, but Katharine and Pope who exerted the most cohesive force in the family's life.

"There's absolutely no mystery about which one of them takes after which one of us," Elizabeth told Tom one day in 1885. The remark was prompted by her discovery, in the back of one of Katharine's drawers, of a small portfolio of erotic Oriental drawings.

Tom said, "The normal thing when a girl is about Katharine's age is for her mother to take her aside for a talk. That satisfies the curiosity."

"We've had a talk, as you call it."

"Only when it was forced on you by biological events beyond your control. And you told me yourself that you hardly scratched the surface."

"I can't help it if I'm shy, Tom, when it comes to these matters."

"She's a fiery sort of girl. Someone has to take her in hand."

"Oh, she's fiery all right. Just like her father. Tom, you do it, please. Talk to her?"

Tom stared at his wife. "You're right. Pope's more like you in that way."

"Yes," Elizabeth suggested. "There's a passive streak in both of us. It's funny. And too bad in a way. I mean fieriness works much better in men than women. And passivity is just the other way around."

"Nature may not be so eager as the rest of us to conform to social customs," Tom responded with a smile. "As I remember it, you could be rather determined when you wanted to."

Both of his children shared with Tom a love of the waterfront and, at least once each month, he made it a point to bring them along as he visited his fleets, docks, or cargoes. One day in the warm summer of 1886, Tom took them out aboard one of the Front Street schooners and they watched as workmen raised a gargantuan statue of a lady upon a granite pedestal on Bedloe's Island in the mouth of the New York harbor.

"I've seen that statue before," Pope said. "It was in Washington Square months ago."

"They were assembling it, silly," Katharine said.

"I think it's very rude to give someone something that has to be assembled," Pope replied nonchalantly. "I've forgotten its name."

"Liberty Enlightening the World," Katharine answered proudly.

"I still think it would be better if the French had given us some land," Pope offered. "It wouldn't have to be as much as the Louisiana Purchase. Maybe one of their islands. Or some country in Africa."

As a light wind raised her hair like a flag, Katharine said, "Think of all the Dutch and English sailors whose ships passed alongside that island before this country had even gotten started."

"People are still coming," Tom said.

"I know," Pope added. "And they're crazy, too. My teacher said that those Irishmen and Germans actually think our streets are paved with gold."

"Don't you?" Tom asked.

"Of course not," Pope said.

"When you're older," Tom told him, "you'll learn that they are."

"Pope's embarrassed," Katharine said. "Watch his eyes."

"What are you talking about?" her brother demanded.

"When we were little, whenever you were embarrassed you would close your eyes very tightly—like this," Katharine said, squeezing her face with considerable exaggeration. "I believe you thought no one would see you when you did that."

"Well, I can tell you one thing," Pope said. "I won't mind not seeing you next year. I'm becoming kind of glad you're going away to boarding school."

"That's cruel," Katharine snapped.

"I don't think so," Pope said.

"Another thing you used to do," Katharine continued, "was to draw pictures of the world and put yourself at the North Pole."

"So what?"

Katharine glanced at her father's watchful expression. "I don't know." She began to smile. "It's just that you're my brother and I love you and that's what you used to do, so I remember it."

Pope's eyes came back from the great metallic statue to his sister. "Virginia," he said wistfully. "That's a long way for you to go to school. I'll go to Boston, won't I, Father?"

"To Groton, if Reverend Peabody will have you two years from now." Tom took a breath. "Why, Pope?"

Pope smiled as a wave of salt water burst over the seawall and splashed his face. "No reason. I was just thinking."

CHAPTER

27

By Thanksgiving of 1888, Thomas Chance was as powerful as any man in New York. His empire, in the dozen years since Chamberlain's death, had fulfilled the older man's promise and grown to rival, then eclipse that of Vanderbilt. His name had acquired the first aspects of legend. Whenever circumstances brought them together, all the great businessmen, even the ascendant Pierpont Morgan and the dying August Belmont, confronted him with deference. And, as often as not, when he and Elizabeth attended the Patriarchs' Ball or one of Mrs. William Backhouse Astor's dinners, Tom would find himself seated directly at Mrs. Astor's right. It was a rich and comfortable life, the life of a man for whom self-initiated challenges had replaced an older and more natural necessity to struggle. And, in many ways, it both suited and beguiled Tom. For as the light went out of the early winter's afternoon and the wind whined above Central Park, he had no notion of the danger that awaited him, no sense that, like a serpent lying just below the surface of a still, black sea, its poised and poisoned fangs were all but within the distance required for attack.

Katharine had sailed back on Tuesday from a summer-through-fall adventure in France that had followed her graduation from boarding school. And Pope, now a junior at Groton, had returned late the night before on the train from Boston.

Still full from a lunch of turkey, oyster dressing, and pumpkin pie, Pope searched thoughtfully about the room. "Every time I get off the train, it seems they've hung another wire above the streets. There are so many of them now that you almost feel there's a roof over you."

Tom looked up. "It's the telephones. Everyone with two cents wants to subscribe. It doesn't matter if they have anyone to call."

Elizabeth put down her newspaper with a sudden, rumpling sound. "Tom," she exclaimed. "Did you see who died?"

"No. Who?"

"Laurence Goelette."

"Let me see."

Elizabeth passed the obituary section to her husband. "It's sad."

Tom did not answer for a minute.

"Who was Laurence Goelette?" Katharine asked.

"I see he stayed in France," Tom said.

"An old man," Elizabeth explained. "Your father bought his jewelry firm."

"Oh, yes," Katharine said. "I remember hearing about that. Why do you read the obituaries?"

"Habit," Elizabeth responded. "Ever since your grandmother and grandfather died."

"That's been two years ago," Pope said. "I don't know about you. But obituaries scare the pants off me."

" 'Scare the pants off,' " Elizabeth repeated. "If that's the sort of talk you've picked up at Dr. Peabody's, I'm afraid I don't like it."

"Sorry, Mother," Pope said.

"Don't let them scare you," Katharine said. "They're just a lot of ink on newsprint."

Pope laughed. "But the people in them always seem to die alphabetically. And Chance is pretty far forward to the—"

"You should put your mind to better use than thinking up such foolishness," Elizabeth said.

"Your mother's right," Tom agreed. "Here, Pope. If you want a problem to think about, I'll give you one: If you could buy a shipyard for five hundred thousand dollars, and you needed to earn at least three percent on your investment, how much—"

"I read an article about you, Father," Pope interrupted. "The author said that you were never content with less than fifty percent interest."

"There are sentimental reasons in this case."

"So there *is* a shipyard."

"In Baltimore. It's called Pulling and Trumbull. I had my first job there. Of course I didn't buy it only out of sentiment. If we use it for our fleets, there will be quite a savings."

"Don't put us through hoops." Elizabeth's voice had an edge to it. "Who's going to Baltimore? For how long? And when?"

Tom lit a cigar. "I'm going alone the first time. Only for a day or so. I'm leaving in the morning."

From the entrance, in the crisp November air, the long sheds and wood-blocked wharves, the warehouses, lofts, offices, stables, and the vast, enduring sugar plant of Pulling and Trumbull were intolerably vivid to Tom and, for a moment, he looked away in reaction.

Richard Pulling, now seventy-five, but still tailored and booted to perfection, turned to Tom and smiled. "Ghosts?" he asked.

Tom passed his tongue over his lips. "I wasn't sure if you would remember."

"It's no use to turn away from ghosts," Pulling said. They'll stare at you from every side."

"I'll be all right in a second," Tom said. "I suppose I'd only thought of the pleasure. I expected that the pain would be duller by now."

Pulling smiled sympathetically. "Most of our people are

new since your time. Hurley's still around. And Cheswit."

"Cheswit?"

"Dark-haired fellow? I'd say middle forties. Walks with a limp. And, of course, Phitts. Only now there's two of them in a way. Trouble."

"Phitts," said Chance, "is about to be out of a job. What do you mean there are two?"

Pulling began to step forward, digging the point of his walking stick into the ground a few feet ahead of him. "There's George Phitts. They've called him Ol' Phitts since he was twenty-five. And now there's Charles Phitts, his nephew. He's not employed here actually. He's a lawyer. His uncle sent him through college and he apprenticed here in Baltimore. But he's with the union, at least part of the time."

"I've been involved in companies where there were unions before," Tom said. "The thing is to nip them in the bud. Then you come out smelling like a rose."

Pulling's stick was trailing them now as he lifted it and thrust it ahead. "I don't want to be dishonest with you. I'm not up to it anymore. A man gets to an age. . . . All my life, I've had a credo. I've tithed to my church and I've tried to give my men a fair shake. But a few of them—it's the old story: two rotten apples—don't seem to want that anymore. They seem to want the skin off my back instead."

At that moment a boy's shriek pierced the stillness and faded, followed quickly by the crack of leather and a still more penetrating cry.

"What's that?" Tom asked.

"What?" Pulling asked. "I didn't hear anything. You'll have to pardon me, Mr. Chance, but my ears are not—"

Tom waved him silent and listened attentively. The leather cracked once more, but this time there was no scream. Tom stepped lightly but rapidly in the direction of a shed. He waited. There was a long silence until the whip cracked, but then he was sure that the sound originated from inside. He opened the door at once, almost expecting the scene upon which he came. George Phitts, his raisin-skin aged by weather and sun, was standing, belt in hand, over a young boy who had been spread-eagled across a workbench. The boy's hands and feet were bound; but two men still stood guard at either side of him. The men had apparently been laughing, for the last lines of a sadistic smile had been frozen onto their faces.

"Close the fucking door!" Phitts commanded as he reeled toward Tom.

But Chance caught him in the sight of his pistol. Gradually he began to squeeze the firm trigger of the Colt.

"Don't you give a man a chance to explain his side of a story?" Phitts pleaded nervously.

"You always were an ugly son of a bitch," Tom said, letting up for a moment. "I think God made you that way to protect other men from you."

One of the men beside Phitts began to smirk.

"Chance," Phitts declared suddenly. "I remember now. Adam Chance's boy."

"Who's going to tell me what all of this is about?" Tom demanded.

"I will," said one of the men. "This fellow here was trying to throw us out of work."

Tom stared at the man. "How?"

"We'd refused to work until they gave us better pay. And shorter hours. We work twelve or more each day as it is. And this'n here was fixing to break our strike."

"He was going to do your work?"

"Yes."

"So you beat him?"

"He's younger and stronger," said the other man. "If we let him get away with it, the owners'd expect us to do as much as he did."

"I see," Tom said. "What if you'd killed him?"

"We weren't going to kill him," Phitts said.

"You're not a union man," Tom said. "You're a hoodlum.

Long before anyone had ever heard of a union, you were a hoodlum."

"It's the gun gives you courage," George Phitts said. "We've all heard about you. Rich man now and everything. I guess you've come so far you can't talk to people like us without a gun in your hand."

"You're on my property." Chance backed away from the door, allowing them room to exit. "I bought this company day before yesterday. And I'm ordering you to *get off* and *stay off*."

After the three men had left, Chance turned to the boy on the table and began to unbind him. The boy's breathing was only now returning to its normal rate and he was writhing with the pain of two long, crimson welts.

"What's your name?" Tom asked in a paternal tone as the boy struggled to pull on his shorts.

"Parton," the boy said. "Wardman Parton."

"Peter's son? Mary's your mother?"

"Yessir."

Tom paused involuntarily. "Tell them I'd like to see them sometime."

Later that evening, through the mellow smoke of O'Connor's Tavern, George Phitts regarded his nephew, Charles, and said: "That Chance is a bastard. His father was a no-good bastard and he's worse. His mother was an old whore who had a place up the road here, before you were born. At least that's what Adam Chance used to say when he got good and drunk."

Charles Phitts smiled. At thirty-two, he had a pleasant, open Irish face which was rescued from prettiness by a great splash of freckles and a too-wide nose. And he was enormously tall. Even seated, the trunk of his body rose nearly a head above his drinking partners. "Thomas Chance is a very powerful man. In one way, you're lucky he didn't pull the trigger."

"A man like that could commit murder and get away with it, if that's what you mean," George Phitts said. "And that's what frightens me. Pulling would have caved in sooner or later. That's why he sold out."

Charles Phitts thought. "I don't know what to tell you to do, Uncle George. I'm for the union as much as you are. But we're only a small part of the company as it is, and if he fired you, it's going to be tough."

"You're a lawyer," George Phitts said. "No offense meant, but, I'll tell ya, lawyers think within the law. 'N' sometimes that can be a disadvantage."

"If you go too far outside the law," Charles said, "the men won't follow you."

"And if I don't? I'll tell you what then. The union will die. And I'll not even be left with my job. You know, I don't have but two hundred dollars put away."

"What other choice do you have? Ten percent of the men at most will stay out on strike. The others are too scared, or stupid, or they owe too much to the company store."

George Phitts wiped the foam of his beer from his mouth and grinned. "I'm afraid we're going to have to do the dirty deed," he said. "It's us or him. We have a right."

"A reason," Charles said. "The law must give you a right."

CHAPTER 28

From New York to Baltimore all the land lay frozen-brown and flat near the coast, white and hilly as the train moved a few miles westward. Now, in Christmas week, the frost was already a month old and as deep as the root of an oak. It had solidified the running streams, made them, in the moonlight, from the window of the Pullman, seem as one with the fields through which they were passing. It had glazed the stone fences, petrified the wood, frozen the trees . . . everything except the sky. At a little before six o'clock, Tom, Katharine, and Pope were startled from their sleep: a sudden flash of winter lightning, three claps of thunder, then a second glow as bright as a summer noon. Pope flung his cheek back from the glass, inhaling the putrid scent of steam. "Where are we?" he asked.

"Half an hour out of Baltimore," Katharine replied.

Pope yawned. "That's right. You must have covered this track dozens of times on your way to and from school."

"It's exciting, isn't it?" Katharine said. "I'm so glad Father asked us to come along. After all, we know so much about Mother's childhood and so little about his. I'm glad to be coming to Baltimore finally."

"And going to the waterfront." Pope smiled. "Together. The same as when we were small. Mother should have come."

At the station, they took a large meal of hot cereals, sausages, and griddle cakes, then boarded their coach in the gray light an hour later. The coach was narrow, but covered. It was pulled by a single speckled-gray draft horse, driven by a single speckled-gray man, both of whom avoided tracks and chuck holes as best they could; but whenever they passed onto side streets, the ride was rough. Katharine grimaced, shifted in her seat as her breakfast rose and fell in her throat. She glanced about. Beside them now were two hotels, and at the corner of one with an alley, Katharine observed a tall man urinating. His face was sooted. He was dressed raggedly. She averted her eyes.

The faster the pace the more severe the chill—until, suddenly, they turned and were no longer headed into the wind. . . . Tarred rooves. Loose stones. Broken brick. . . . Baltimore lay like a ruin in this quarter, still and ashen in the empty morning.

"The hill to your right," Tom said after a minute. "The house I was born in stood just behind it."

Pope studied the white slope with cautious deliberation, watching his father while he measured his own thoughts.

"Was it . . . awful?" Katharine asked.

Tom shrugged his shoulders, but grinned. "Not until I had something to compare it to."

After an hour's tour of Federal Hill and the Pulling and Trumbull grounds, Tom dismissed the coach and they walked to the end of a long wharf to which a harpoon-laden whaling ship was tied.

"There aren't whales in the Chesapeake Bay, are there?" Pope asked.

"Not that I've ever heard of." Tom regarded his watch. "You don't see an old gentleman around, do you? It's out of character for Pulling to be late."

"No," Pope said after looking. "No one. Can we go aboard?"

Katharine shivered. "I wouldn't want to."

"Nothing to be afraid of." Tom took a tentative step toward the gangway. "Hello. Hello? Anyone—"

The sound of creaking wood rose to their ears as the large, deserted ship swayed in the icy harbor; Tom could hear the rhythmic, tidal flow of the bilge. Finally a faint voice spoke from deep within the hull. "Ahoy. . . . Help. . . . Down below."

Tom glanced at Pope. In a moment they were fully on deck, where Tom searched out the hatch and, lowering himself through it, led Pope and Katharine down a steep ladder into the cabin. "I say," he called out at once, "where are you?" But there was no reply.

"How strange," Pope said. "Hello. Hello! Can you hear us?"

They had come, quickly, into the lowest section of the cabin, ten feet at least below the vessel's gunwales, when Tom noticed a long rectangular hatch that led to the hold. Motioning for silence, he withdrew the hatch cover far enough to peer into the dark and shapeless space. "Are you all right?" he demanded, as he ignited a paraffin lamp and descended toward the keel. Automatically, and partly out of the fear of being left behind, Pope and Katharine trailed him. The small lamp cast a dim and abstract puddle of light whose sudden flicker alternately hid and exposed them, projecting limp, indefinite shadows against the bulwarks.

Katharine trembled. Pope sighed heavily. Then, after a scuffle too brief to register in memory, the light was extinguished, and a new, more powerful lamp shone from George Phitts' right hand. His left wielded a harpoon.

Katharine, confronting the grotesque and hairless creature, cried out involuntarily. But a younger man came out from the shadows and gagged her.

Tom swallowed. "There's no need to harm the children."

"Ain't there?" Phitts demanded.

"Children?" the man with Katharine asked. "This don't look like no child to me."

"Maybe you'll understand what Pulling didn't, Mr. Chance. It's a matter of survival. You *or* us."

"Be reasonable," Tom said.

"Would a reasonable man bargain with the likes of you, sir?" Phitts said. "Not on your life! With Pulling dead, the moment you got free of here, you'd have me gunned down."

"That's not my way," Chance said. "My way is . . . money."

"She's on fire," the man beside Katharine declared. "Look at her twitch when I touch her." He laughed.

"Take her astern," Phitts said.

"Money," Chance repeated loudly, his eyes fixed on the floor. "Let me show you." Slowly, cautiously, he began to reach down until his hand was next to his boot.

"It had better be money," Phitts said, "and nothing else." His two men, now curious to see whether, in fact, Chance was carrying a fortune on his person, began to approach Tom.

"It's a trick," Phitts said. "I ought to—"

Suddenly Tom removed his pistol from his boot and fired directly up at Phitts, felling him. The two accomplices rushed Tom, knocking him over. The man who had subdued Katharine took up Tom's pistol. But before he could bring it level, Pope sprang upon him.

Tom's heel thrust upward into the other man's temple, knocking him unconscious. There was no light now that Phitts' lamp had been darkened, but as he wrestled with Pope, the young man was still in possession of Tom's gun, and he began to fire now, betraying his position only by the sound and the sparks that flew from its hammer. Tom was just coming up behind him when he fired the shot that struck Pope.

By the time Tom reached the house of Dr. Chapin Welch, he had run more than three miles. The long muscles ached in his shins. The cold air had begun to feel thin and painful as his lungs inhaled it. And his breathing had become tired. He rang the bell on the porch, but did not wait for the door to be answered before twisting its knob and going in. A black maid in a white dress met him in the front hall.

"My son's been shot," Tom gasped, propping himself against the parlor partition.

"Dr. Welch," the black woman called in a deep voice. "Emergency in the hall, please."

A pause. Then a sliding door of heavy walnut panels rolled immediately back into the wall at the rear of the corridor and Dr. Welch stepped out from his examining room. Behind him, Tom could see that a blond woman in her later thirties remained at the side of the doctor's desk, sitting patiently with her legs crossed as though her conference had not been interrupted. Dr. Welch appeared to be a few years younger than Tom, and one or two inches shorter. His frame was wider. His wrists were as full as the wrists of men who did manual labor. His hair was wiry, long, and red; and his beard was full.

"Gunshot," the maid elaborated.

"My son," Tom repeated as the doctor, gathering his bag but going coatless, followed him out of the door. "In a ship's hold at the Pulling and Trumbull wharf."

"Is he conscious?"

"He was." Tom's words puffed like tiny clouds before his face.

"I see." They mounted the doctor's wagon and brought the single mare to a quick gallop over the dirt and pebbled roads.

Tom managed a deep breath. "Two other men have been hurt. One badly." He hesitated. "And a third is dead."

The doctor's eyes were a more diluted green than Tom's, but they were filled now with circumspection. Tom's glance met them head on. "It was self-defense," he said, breaking the silence.

"Do you know the name of the dead man?"

"George Phitts."

Dr. Welch betrayed no emotion. "How did you know to come to me?"

"You're the nearest. I'd heard that you had set up practice in old Doc Isadore's house."

"Doc Isadore?" Welch smiled. "That was a long time ago. Twenty, thirty years. Are you from this area? I don't think I've seen you around here."

"I haven't lived here since . . . the war," Tom said.

The doctor drew in the mare's reins, applied a light whip. "I see."

"But we know each other, Doctor. In a way. My name is Thomas Chance. Does that—"

"Oh, Gawd!" Welch swallowed sharply. "Of course it does."

Tom sensed the uneasiness of the doctor's tone. "How *is* Frances?"

"My wife is . . . as well as can be expected," the doctor replied as they entered the Pulling and Trumbull gate. "Which ship?"

"The farthest," Tom told him anxiously.

Dr. Welch removed the bullet from where it had lodged, below Pope's lowest right rib. The operation was painful, largely because of the lack of adequate anesthetic, but the doctor assured Tom and Katharine that it had been a success. "Your son's need now is for rest. If we move him before he has regained his strength, the danger of infection will be too great. I recommend that he stay on in our hospital for another week. And then we'll talk about a train ride to New York."

Tom telegraphed the news to Elizabeth, and he and Katharine took rooms in a hotel. It required less than an hour to convince the police of the circumstances surrounding Phitts' death. And with that matter resolved, Tom returned to the small hospital in South Baltimore where

Pope lay, watching the sharp winter shadows reel across the ceiling.

That evening, after Dr. Welch's last round, the door of Pope's room opened tentatively and, still obscured, Frances asked: "Tom?"

"Frances."

She came around the entryway slowly, studied and smiled at Pope, and stood silently: a woman of forty-eight with the color of salt in her temples and lines in her forehead that Tom had never seen. Her eyes were still moist, her figure trim; and, in her voice and carriage, Tom saw, at once, the residue of her theatrical past.

Tom appraised her carefully, and in silence. Always, he had been afraid of time, of its diminishing effect on passion.

Frances kissed him warmly on the lips—the same tongue-touching young woman's kiss she had always given him. "My husband says he will be fine," she began, glancing again toward Pope. "And he looks it, doesn't he? How old now?"

"Seventeen."

"Seventeen," she repeated nostalgically.

Katharine regarded her cautiously, but with a definite curiosity, sensing the strength of the unmentioned bond between this woman and her father.

"And you?" Tom asked. "Children?"

Frances smiled, an older smile than he remembered, resigned and sad. "No."

Late that night, long after Katharine had retired, they met and walked together by the harbor.

"They're marvelous children," Frances said.

"Thank you."

"Pope has his mother's coloring. Does she know?"

"I expect her on the train tomorrow."

"Good."

Tom smiled. "She's changed, Frances."

Frances's heart skipped a beat. "Changed?"

Tom walked faster in the tense silence. "Withdrawn."

"You loved her so," Frances said. "You were almost funny. I'm sure I would have thought you funny if you hadn't shattered my heart."

"The stage misses you," Tom said.

Frances laughed. "If it hadn't been for all this awful business, would you have looked us up, or come and gone as though we weren't anywhere nearby?"

"Sooner or later I would have looked you up."

"You might not have found us then."

Tom felt suddenly frightened. "Not have found you?"

"We aren't living together, Chapin and I. In the same house, yes. But not as man and wife. We haven't for a long time now. Chapin has his practice and–"

"And–"

"He has a woman. A girl. Twenty, I think she is. I expect it's only a matter of time."

Tom took her gloved hand in his. "People make awful mistakes in life," he said slowly. "But the worst mistake is not knowing love when you have it."

Frances bit her lip. "It was always you, Tom. Always."

Tom reflected for a moment as they walked the desolate December night. He gazed at the sky, at the black and lonely border of sea and land. "When I told Elizabeth I wanted to bring the children down here with me, even though it would be just for a day, she got very angry. She said I was trying to take them away from her. You don't know her, but there's a fey streak in her. A lot of women like that have it and it's attractive when they're young, but then, sometimes, it hardens and spoils them. We haven't been much married either." He stared at her.

"Isn't it too late?" she asked.

"It's never too late."

Frances drew him close. "That must be right. It has to be."

On the first day Pope was permitted visitors from outside his family, Charles Phitts came in to see him. Tom was sitting in a large cushioned chair in the light of the window.

"Excuse me," Phitts asked. "Is this Mr. Chance's room?"

Tom stood. "Yes," he said. "Who are—"

The tall young lawyer extended his hand and Tom reached out automatically. "Charles Phitts."

Tom stared up into the freckled face with a mixture of suspicion and alarm. "I'm afraid—"

"This is very difficult for me," Phitts began. "But I've come to apologize for my uncle's action and to tell you how sorry I am." His tone and expression were deceptively benign.

"Thank you very much," Tom said curtly. "Now if you'll excuse us."

"Father," Katharine reproached him, "I'm surprised at you."

"Thank you," Pope said.

Phitts nodded. "I also wanted to tell you that my uncle and his . . . 'friends' were acting alone. He was a leader of the union, but he was *not* the union. And except for those who were with him, the men did not share his passion for violence. They are good men, Mr. Chance. I hope you won't feel any instinct to penalize them for his crime."

"I know the men," Tom said. "I've known them—and what they are—before you were born."

The meeting ended and Tom did not think of it again until a month later, when he came back to Baltimore for Pope. Pope's stay had lengthened over Dr. Welch's original estimate, but by the last of January he was ready to travel. Katharine had remained behind to care for her brother, and was packing her suitcase when Tom confronted her.

"Katharine," he said, "I've been back here a little over three hours and hardly a person I've talked with hasn't mentioned seeing you with Charles Phitts sometime in the last two weeks. Do you deny that?"

Katharine looked at him silently, then turned away.

"I'm your father, Katharine."

"I didn't know it was a crime to be seen with him."

"Has he made advances to you?"

"Father!" Katharine blushed.

"You're an attractive girl. It wouldn't be unnatural."

"He's an attractive man. And a gentleman. I don't care what you say. He wouldn't force his attentions."

"But he did try to kiss you, didn't he?"

Katharine felt a great swell of anger. "I kissed him," she said loudly, "if you must know, Father. And held him, if you must know everything."

"It's only because I love you," Tom said.

Katharine was sobbing. "It's not fair to ask people to be responsible for their feelings."

"You're weak now," Tom said. "But spring's coming. You had a nice time in France last year. Maybe you should go back."

That October, in Monte Carlo, in a garden of olive trees and orange and lemon blossoms, beside the rock promontory and the jade sea, Katharine impetuously married the Duc de Fontainville, then set up housekeeping in Paris. Marriages to foreign nobles were, at that moment, the rage among New York heiresses. Pauline Whitney, Consuela Vanderbilt, and Anna Gould had each made one.

BOOK
IV

THE LINE

(1892–1918)

CHAPTER 29

ALL NIGHT FOR THREE NIGHTS THE GREAT, DRY SNOW FELL ON New England; and Pope, looking out from his bedroom in Claverly, could see no line between the marsh and the Charles River. The sky was white and opaque, less refractive than the land, for the powder dropping through it did not appear to be crystalline until it had come to rest. It was to have been the night of the last full harvest moon, but the clouds were much too low and thick. And Pope watched, unable to sleep, as the famous streets of Harvard stood silent and still and the limbs of ancient trees wept and glimmered with ice.

Behind him, through the open door, Arthur Forrest came into the room. He was a stocky boy, with a low, protruding, almost sinister brow, and of less than medium height. He stepped silently toward Pope, until, over Pope's shoulder, he could see the white ribbon that was Mt. Auburn Street, where two young men were throwing snowballs in a stream of lamplight. Pope sensed Arthur's presence at once, but did not acknowledge it until Arthur said: "It's ten minutes before three."

"I know," Pope answered.

"If you're this nervous," Arthur said, "I should be shaking visibly. If anyone in this suite has no reason to be nervous about club elections, it's you, Pope."

Pope turned about slowly. "I don't care for myself," he said. "But my father sets great store by these things."

"Aren't you a legacy?"

"Not for the Porcellian Club. My father didn't go to Harvard."

"But there've been so many Popes. I mean, not to let you in would almost be more of a comment on the people who kept you out than it would be on you."

"That's the viewpoint of a loyal friend," Pope said.

"You can count on that," said Arthur carefully.

"We've known each other more than a year now, you and I and Phillip."

"Fourteen months. Since our first day as freshmen. I was surprised when you ended up as our roommate. Groton people usually stick together."

"I suppose," Pope said. "But there wasn't anyone in my class I felt that close to."

"I'm not complaining. Whatever the reason, I'm glad it happened. I hope we'll stay together, all three of us."

"That's another thing that's been on my mind," Pope told Arthur. "I don't want this matter of clubs to drive a wedge between us."

"Phillip and I have been punched by the Fly," Arthur said. "I know he's going there, and I have to confess I'm leaning that way."

"Are you? I rather thought that you would. You know so many of the members."

"No more than you do," Arthur Forrest said.

"But you know them better," Pope said. "That friend of yours from Cleveland, for example."

"That's true."

Pope paused. "I think we should make a point, even if we each go into a different club, to lunch together three times a week at least, and as much as we can at The Pudding."

"It's a good idea," Arthur said, "but I'm sure there are fifty promises just like that that are made and broken every year. Clubs are only the first thing that separate people, Pope. Wait until one of us finds a girl."

"I thought Phillip already had," Pope said.

"Phillip has found a receptacle," Arthur replied.

"All the same, she consumes a good percentage of his time."

Arthur grinned. "Don't show your fangs over Gloria," he said. "There are millions of girls like her, and any one of them would jump at a Chance . . . you know that as well as I do."

"But I'm so spoiled," Pope said. "I want so much more than that, and the awful thing is that unless I have it I can't be happy."

"Still, you ought to try a girl like that. The old saw about 'sowing wild oats.' "

"I know."

"A man our age ought to be laid at least once a month," Arthur Forrest said. "If you ask me, it's a goddamn sin if he isn't."

"More easily said than done."

"My rich uncle in Cleveland gave me good advice," Arthur told Pope. "My father told me to study hard, graduate with honors, and join a good New York bank for a few years before coming back to Ohio. My mother told me to eat a solid breakfast every morning. But my rich Uncle Bob said, 'Arthur, when it comes to houses, yachts, carriages, or screwing, my advice is rent them all.' "

Pope smiled. "If you like that advice so much, why don't you take it?"

"For one thing, I don't have any money," Arthur said. "For another, I'm afraid of getting syphilis."

"Well, you're not alone there. More than one of my ancestors has died from that."

"I saw a man who had it once," Arthur replied. "It was probably the worst thing I've ever seen."

"I don't think I could bear to be sick like that for very long. I'm much too vain."

"That's understandable," Arthur said. "You know, it's not the idea of dying that frightens me, but the idea of a long, miserable, drawn-out death, particularly with sores all over me . . ."

Pope shifted his view back to the window. "You think of the most awful subjects, Forrest, at the most peculiar times."

"I'm going to bed," Arthur said, turning to the door. "Let me know when you get the nod from the P.C."

"*If* I get the nod," Pope corrected.

"And when you get that off your mind, let's pick a night and tell Phillip to have Gloria find us some girls."

The following morning, a boy in a charcoal suit and waistcoat arrived at the door of Pope's suite and, finding him in his bathrobe, handed him a small doubly folded invitation and a cigar. Pope nodded cordially, put the cigar into his breast pocket beneath his monogram, yawned, and took the envelope into his room before opening it. Raised at the top of the stiff merino letter sheet were a small silhouette of a boar and the letters P.C. He took a deep breath and read the offer to join.

He placed the paper face down on the blotter of his desk, went into the bath, and drew a tub of hot water. Outside, the sun had not yet come above the horizon, the snow continued to fall, and in the fresh drifts along Plympton Street, he could make out the vanishing tracks of his visitor.

Arthur Forrest wore alpine boots and knickers for the hike to his Classics lecture across the yard in Sever. The class was a large one, compulsory for undergraduates, given by a Wykehamist with almost perfect elocution and enormous, puffy eyebrows. The professor had commenced his first address by relating his view that the true purpose of a university education was to reduce the time one devoted to thoughts of the opposite sex from 90 to 75 percent. And, a tone thus set, he had played to full houses twice a week thereafter.

Coming onto Massachusetts Avenue, Forrest turned to Phillip Grainger and said: "Pope's going into the P.C."

Grainger was taller than Forrest by several inches. His complexion was lighter, drier. And though neither was conventionally handsome, Grainger had always had better luck with women. "That's not news," he said.

"He was elected last night."

"I wish we could have talked him into coming to the Fly."

"We didn't try very hard," Arthur said.

"There wasn't a chance in the world to begin with. Not with his father's heart set on the P.C. His father dominates his life—you know that."

"I do," Arthur said. "I also know that Thomas Chance is one of the four or five most powerful men in this country, and I don't want to lose that connection."

"A person would be a fool if he did." Phillip's laugh had a conspiratorial ring.

"But I don't think there was any way he could have carried us into the P.C. on his coattails. Oh, they wanted him, but he's not tough enough to use his power. It's a shame. He has that extraordinary charm—"

"Known as a hundred million dollars," Phillip interrupted.

"And he couldn't be brighter. Or nicer. Or better looking. But there's just that little bit of grit missing."

"They're all wonderful-looking in that family. But, you're right, it is a pity."

Arthur laughed. "From his point of view, of course. But looked at from ours, isn't it marvelous?"

Phillip's smile was cruel. "Still, it's almost too much as it is, isn't it? It's almost enough to kill for."

* * *

After the initiation night in February, the Club came to play a larger part in Pope's daily life than anything else at Harvard. He breakfasted and dined there. He completed those of his assignments that did not require the use of a library, read for pleasure, conducted his correspondence, and, weather permitting, played a daily game of "club squash" within the archly private walls of the new brick clubhouse. He was attractive and funny, and soon developed a full circle of friends to whom he told witty stories about his French in-laws and about the glamorous life of his parents' house in New York.

"They're very grand, my sister and brother-in-law," Pope told Bobby Homans, who was a year older than he. "Much grander than any of the English."

"Oh, really?" replied young Winthrop Ames, who had overheard Pope's remark from farther down the dinner table. "I'd been led to believe that the English were about as grand as any people could be."

Pope laughed. "Let me tell you the difference." He gave a contemplative look at his knife and fish fork. "In England the upper classes all have marvelous silverware. But in France they have gold."

"Too much splash," Ames responded automatically.

"I'll grant you," Pope agreed. "But, still, there's something dazzling about it. Katharine's American, of course. So she doesn't have it in quite the same way Edmond does. But what *he* lacks in substance he certainly makes up for in style. He owns a great house on the Isle, a stable at Deauville, and a vineyard somewhere else, I don't know where precisely. It isn't in champagne, and that's the only thing worth drinking, as far I can tell."

"Hear! Hear!" Homans said. "But speaking of wine, our bottle of rather ordinary grape juice isn't so cold as it should be."

"Twirl it." Ames touched the bottle lightly with his palm.

"I'm not sure that will work," Pope said. From the center

of the long table, he removed a water pitcher and two salt cellars, then silently emptied the contents of each into the free-standing wine cooler.

"What will that do?" Bobby Homans asked.

"Change the freezing point of water," Pope ventured. "Make it chill faster."

"I suppose you learned that in France," Ames teased.

"That and how to make love the Latin way," Pope retorted.

"The Latin way?" both asked at once.

"As opposed to the English, or American." Pope smiled. "You see, the English put it all up in front. Just the way they do in speaking: all up in front and then they cut themselves off. Before they should. They say 'fee-let.' Once they've got the first syllable out of their mouths they're practically through with a word. Not the French, though. They say 'fi-lay.' They follow through. If you understand what I mean."

Pope acquired a facility for epigrams; and, as often as not, would try out at least one in any sustained conversation. "Amory," he would say, "has a soul like October weather: clear but not cold"; or "Hypocrisy is the lubricant of social intercourse." He began to read James, devoured Johnson once he discovered the *Rambler,* and became enamored of a three-year-old novel by a young English writer named Oscar Wilde: *The Picture of Dorian Gray.*

He fell under the sartorial influence of a clique of upperclassmen who took their cue from Britain, and began to order his clothes from an Italian tailor on Brattle Street who had once served an apprenticeship on Savile Row. He commissioned boots, black and brown oxfords, and Albert slippers from Peale's. He had his ties cut from silk squares and rolled into seven folds by the London firm of Edouard and Butler, and from them, too, he received shirtings and collars, bathrobes, and silk pajamas. The monogram on his handkerchiefs duplicated that of his club. And, for two years, until the fall of 1894, he inhabited a world in which, as Wilde's writings assured him, his first duty was "to be as artificial as possible."

He tasted his studies with occasional pleasure and frequent boredom, but never with relish or terror. His own position in the connected societies of Cambridge and New York was too securely predestined for that. In devoting by far the greatest number of his hours to matters of clothing, food, and social preference, he did not accept the notion that such frivolities were a young man's right merely because, in the later years, more serious concerns would overshadow them. Instead, he defended these superficial sources of pleasure as highly serious in themselves. His rearing had included precious little instruction concerning the making and spending of money, but quite a lot in the art of how to stride gracefully, speak without chattering teeth, separate good furniture from bad. He knew that such tasks were essential ones in the life he would live and, much like a prince, he saw his future clearly, without the romantic distortion of a misted eye: One great man of affairs was sufficient to any family. And Thomas Chance occupied that position as though it were a large, physical space; not Pope nor Katharine nor Elizabeth nor Frances had ever been permitted to invade it, even temporarily. Pope had neither the will nor desire to compete against his father in that arena, for as surely as he knew that age must lose to youth, he understood that mortals seldom triumph over legend. Therefore, he was content to be what he was: a rich man's son, pleasure-seeking but unself-serving, affable, with less guile than most.

Through his sophomore and junior years, he continued to share a Gold Coast suite with Arthur Forrest and Phillip Grainger, and to lunch with them most days. Then, in the early fall of 1894, his senior year, Phillip, his voice gruff and husky from a cold, suddenly said: "I suppose this is the beginning of the end."

They were in the crimson-paneled bar of The Hasty Pudding Institution and Pope sat forward on the cracked red leather chair. "What on earth?"

"A year from now, who knows where any of us will be? I can remember a year ago so clearly. It doesn't seem very far away." Phillip gulped his port.

"No." Pope filled the silence as he gathered his thoughts. "But neither is it imminent."

"That's life," Arthur announced. "People's paths converge on a point, linger awhile, and broaden."

Phillip looked up and at Arthur on cue, for, unbeknownst to Pope, this was a conversation that the two of them had contrived and rehearsed in private. "What are you going to do?" he prompted.

"I don't have any idea," came Arthur's line, in a sober voice.

"Neither do I," Pope added innocently.

"You'll go back to New York," Arthur told Pope.

"Not right away."

"I would if I were you," Phillip said.

"That's because you grew up in Cleveland," Pope replied.

"Perhaps."

"Well, if you do go to New York, go to Chance and Company," Pope suggested. "I don't want two of my best friends in some competing firm. Particularly since they're both geniuses." He laughed.

Arthur tilted the edge of his low brow toward Phillip and smiled from the side of his face.

"That's why you have so many friends, Pope," Phillip said. "You always overflatter them."

"Well, you've never had anything less than an 'A' in mathematics. And Arthur, not me, is the number one politician on campus. Bound to be class marshal."

Forrest and Grainger glanced approvingly at one another.

"There's plenty of time to talk the whole thing out," Phillip said after a pause.

"One day when you're visiting the house," Pope promised, "you can talk it over with Father."

"Yes," Arthur said. "If you wouldn't mind, that would be fine."

CHAPTER

30

In the early spring of 1895, Pope married Laura Molyneux, a pretty girl a year younger than himself who had been studying to be a nurse in Boston. He had known her since freshman year, but the relationship, at least to others, had seemed platonic. The news of the engagement surprised Thomas and Elizabeth Chance, but did not discomfort them. Apart from his advice that Pope might want to wait until he was older before marrying, Thomas Chance had expressed no misgivings. Laura's mother and Elizabeth had, in fact, been together in school, and scores of Popes and Molyneuxs had known each other for generations. In one of their rare substantive conversations, Tom even told Elizabeth that he suspected Pope might be the sort of boy who would be "best off with a wife." And Elizabeth agreed.

Pope graduated in June of that year and, on the evening following the ceremonies in Harvard Yard, Tom hosted a small stag dinner for him in the large private dining room at Locke-Ober's. Tom made a few deliberately unmemorable remarks after the Lobster Savannah had been cleared, raised his Taittinger, and called on Pope, eager to watch and judge his son's performance. But even when Pope stood, the conversation at the far end of the table continued for a moment, so Arthur raised his spoon to his glass and struck it.

Pope laughed politely and cleared his throat. "There's an old story," he began, "that takes place in the days when the good Romans were feeding the Christians to the lions. And there went out a decree from Caesar that any Christian who was rejected by a lion would be given his life and freedom. Now the Christians, of course, were very excited by this prospect and each day, in the Coliseum, when they were lined up, they would discuss with each other the various tricks they thought they might use. . . ." Pope's eyes rose and gazed over the brim of his glass at the twelve gentlemen in evening dress.

"One man applied a rare ointment to his person, but, as the crowd and his fellow Christians looked on, he was quickly gobbled by the beast. Another man tried prayer, and a third tried magic; but all were consumed immediately. Finally, a very quiet and sullen Christian was brought up before the lion and, as the huge animal began to charge, this Christian stepped aside and whispered something in his ear. Suddenly the lion grew tame and sat down like a playful household cat!

" 'This man is saved,' cried Caesar. 'This man is *free*!'

"Naturally, all of the other Christians wanted to know what it was that the man had said, and when he was paraded past them, the man about to enter the ring leaned over and asked him.

" 'It was simple,' the saved Christian explained. 'I simply told him that after the meal he would have to give a toast.' "

"You were very fine on your feet tonight," Tom told Pope as they stood alone in the June moonlight on Tremont Street, with the wide Common beside them.

"Thank you, Father."

"I had no idea that you were already that polished as a speaker. I liked your story."

"It's the first time I've used it."

"You did it very well." Tom paused. "You seem to be interested in Roman history, so let me quote you something:

'In the second century of the Christian Era, the Empire of Rome comprehended the fairest part of the earth, and the most civilized portion of mankind.' Do you recognize it?"

Pope considered. "Not at once."

"Gibbon," Tom said. "*The Decline and Fall of the Roman Empire.*"

"I'm ashamed to say I've only read bits and pieces."

"That isn't why I mentioned it," Tom said. "I mentioned it because it has a bearing on us."

"Chance and Company?"

"Yes."

"I had hoped, actually, to have some time to myself before I decide if . . . that's the kind of work I want."

Tom listened patiently. "In life," he said, "certain responsibilities fall on us."

"Phillip and Arthur are certainly pleased that you offered them jobs. I hope it didn't pose a problem for you."

"Not a bit," Tom said. "When a man gets older, it becomes very important that he throw out lifelines to the younger men around him. It keeps *him* young. But, bright as they are, Phillip and Arthur are not Pope Chance, and they can't be—because you are the 'rightful sovereign.' "

"You make it sound like a country instead of a business."

"It is bigger than some countries," Tom said.

"I suppose it is." Pope smiled. "And yet I have a feeling about my life, almost as though it were that ballet by Tchaikovsky where all the stage is set and dark and there's a very thin curtain in front of it, hiding it, until suddenly the light goes on behind that curtain and the audience can see everything. That's what I'm doing, Father. I'm sitting in that audience. The stage is my life, but the room is still pitch dark. And I'm waiting for the light to go on."

"Waiting?" Tom reflected. "Nothing comes to those who wait, Pope. Least of all, happiness."

Pope nodded for a long moment as he thought. A slow

breeze, rich with honeysuckle, blew from the direction of the Public Gardens and Pope inhaled it in deep, extended breaths.

"There are only two things in the world that I desperately want, Father," he said at last. "I want to be happy, and to make you—and Mother—happy."

"Take my word," Tom urged him carefully. "In the long run, you will achieve both if you come back to where you belong."

It was only four weeks after that conversation that Tom gave a second dinner, at the Union Club, in order to celebrate Pope's return to New York and his new association with Chance and Company. More than half of Wall Street's titan-bankers were seated at the long Brazilian walnut table and, after the brandy had been poured and the snifters warmed, Tom took Pope aside in the gentlemen's card room and presented him with a small, purple-satin box. Inside was the Pearl of Macao.

Pope started for a moment. "Why, Father!" he exclaimed.

"It's part of your heritage," Tom said.

Pope considered. "But what about Mother?"

"Don't be ridiculous, Pope," Chance said through faintly nervous laughter. "I didn't steal it from her. She . . . and I . . . both want you to have it."

Pope gripped the loose pearl with exaggerated care. "May Laura *wear* it?" he asked at last.

"Of course she may," Chance replied. "And she will do it justice."

Pope was assigned a small, prismatic office, around a corner and two doors removed from his father's. It was a high room with a single twelve-pane window that looked onto a sunless cobblestone alley. Its plaster walls and cast-iron molding had been coated, too many times, with a dull gray paint that absorbed most of the available light. Opposite the window, the top half of the wall containing the door was constructed of glass whose scroll-etched border framed a view of the accounting department. There, beneath an arched ceiling and three gigantic electrical lamps, twenty employees, in four rows of five desks, worked silently over their ledgers. And Pope, whose mind invariably wandered from the details of the financial statements that were put before him, often looked up in wonder at the concentration of those in the next room.

Grainger's desk was the farthest away, but, in no time, it became a lure for Pope's eye. All day, from considerably before Pope's arrival at eight o'clock until after his departure at six, his friend remained poised over his work, shifting in his chair only to adjust his visor or dip his quill pen into India ink. And not the least effect of this visible persistence was to produce, in Pope, continual and disturbing questions about his own adequacy for the job he had taken on. He had no more idea now than he had ever had of what might fulfill him in life. And yet, in a paradoxical way, he understood that it was because he did not that he had felt compelled to return to his father's bank. For he had no strong, competing ambition with which to challenge his family's wish. Thus, the spectacle of Grainger's diligence challenged him the moment he gazed up from the eighteenth-century partner's desk at which he sat; and, at times, he wondered if that were by accident or by his father's design.

Lunch was the sole release from duty that Phillip Grainger allowed himself each day. At precisely five minutes before twelve, he would stack his papers, line his pens in vertical rows, remove his visor, stand and walk the long way—to be certain that his colleagues saw him—to Pope's office door. He would give a ceremonial rap on the door jamb, Pope would join him, and the two of them would go off together, usually laughing, to collect Arthur Forrest, whose office was on the floor below. Unless a new place had opened that they wanted to try, they would lunch in a rear booth at Spike's, where Phillip Grainger liked two of the waitresses. Spike's offered a special lunch at thirty-five cents, which they invariably took. One November Thursday when their plates had been filled with sauerbraten, red cabbage, and potato dumplings, Phillip turned to Arthur and said: "What's this about the Azurean Railroad? They're operating three times over their budget."

"It's the Latin Americans," Arthur said. "They're different. It's hard doing business with them. Money sticks to their palms."

"Too *much* money," Phillip replied. "The way they're going, they'll bleed it dry."

"What do you mean money sticks to their palms?" Pope asked.

Arthur smiled at Phillip, then turned. "The Latins require tips," he explained. "Just like the waitresses in this place. Just like Lucy there."

"You mean bribes," Pope responded.

"It's their custom," Arthur continued. "If you tried to do business with one of those fellows and you didn't offer him a little something on the side—"

"I don't care how you put it, it isn't right," Pope said. "But the way it sounds to me, neither of you cares about that. All you seem to be arguing about is the cost."

"I'm in the accounting department," Phillip answered. "Costs are what I'm paid to think about. Your father doesn't want me minding his business for him. Or Arthur either."

"You can be sure your old man knows what he's doing," Arthur said in the tone of an older, more experienced man.

"Oh, yes," Pope said uncertainly. "He does. About this and—everything. I only wish that the right decisions came as clearly to me."

Arthur studied him. "Well, never mind that now," he said. "You're still growing in this business. We all are."

Two months later, in January of 1896, Laura gave birth to Pope's son, Eliot, a playful, ringleted child who restored

at least some commonness of purpose to Thomas and Elizabeth Chance: a sense of prolonged generativity, of dynasty.

Laura, however, was too restless, energetic, and open-eyed to remain simply a wife and mother for long. At the hospital where she did volunteer work, she had heard Jacob Riis deliver his famous series of lectures: *The Other Half and How It Lives*. And she had read his articles in the *Sun*, grown nauseous at thoughts of the poverty that cursed the Bowery, Hell's Kitchen, Mulberry and Hester Streets. She helped found the Children's Aid Society, which provided night school for a hundred thousand people.

"There's only one thing I'm sure of," she told Pope the following summer: "That a life designed for yourself, no matter how grandly you seem to succeed, is nothing more than a prescription for unhappiness."

"I know," Pope concurred. Though he lacked her faith, he was still too aristocratic in mind and youthful in appetite to want to abandon thoughts of himself completely.

Referring to Pope's father, she said, "I do wish Dad would help us with the Society. There's so much he could do."

"I'm sure," replied Pope. "But, as Arthur says, you have to understand him. He was reared in a different time."

"Still, I'm going to talk to him. The world's been good to him and he owes it something in return."

Pope quickly thought of his mother, of the sleet-like wall between his parents. "Has it?"

"That's such an extraordinary question. I'm not even going to bother to answer it," Laura said.

"If I remember," Pope smiled, "you're the one who's always said that riches aren't everything."

Laura returned his smile. "If I hadn't been sure that you believed that just as much as I, I would never have married you, Pope Chance."

Pope leaned over and kissed her impulsively.

But after the initial touch of their tongues, Laura pushed him away. "Pope!" she exclaimed.

"What's the matter?"

"You're on fire."

Pope looked at her, puzzled. "Oh, come on. This is no time to be teasing. I was just beginning to get in the mood."

"I don't see how you're even standing up. I've never felt anyone so feverish in all my life."

Pope raised his hand to his forehead. "I don't think it's all that bad," he told her. "I suspect it's nothing more than the same old summer cold that haunts me every year."

"Maybe so," Laura said. "But where is our thermometer? I want to take your temperature just in case it's not."

"Upstairs," Pope said. "In the medicine cabinet where it belongs. I saw it this morning."

"Then I'll get it," Laura said.

"I don't want it stuck up my rectum."

Laura laughed. "No one's going to insert it in your rectum unless it's the doctor."

"Laura," Pope called a few seconds later, when she was a third of the way up the flight of stairs.

"What is it?" She turned and paused.

"How would you feel about leaving New York completely? I don't mean for the summer. I know you didn't want to do that this year because of the baby. But I mean for good." He came up to stand next to her. "We could find a place in Europe, live in England one year and Scotland the next. That sort of thing. Arthur and Phillip are a hundred times more interested in Chance and Company than I could ever be. And, if anything happens to Father, I'd be a damned fool to try and run it when they're so . . . hungry to."

Laura scratched her wrist. "I don't know," she said. "We can talk about it later, can't we? It sounds wonderful the way you put it, but it's not the kind of decision I like to make in the middle of a flight of steps. Now, which way are you going? Are you coming up with me, or shall I bring the thermometer down to your study?"

"I'm coming up with you. I told you, I was just beginning to get into the proper frame of mind."

"After we take your temperature," Laura said. "Think of your friends who aren't married yet. Think of Arthur and Phillip, if you must."

"I'll never understand why you don't like them."

"I'll never understand why you do," Laura said. "They do nothing but use you. But, even then, there must be times when they wish they were married, and what can they do? Nothing."

Pope smiled. "Phillip always has a girl or two on the string—waitresses and working girls mostly. Arthur's more particular. He has very big dreams he's not about to compromise."

"I'll say," Laura said, returning from the bath with a thermometer in her hand. "And that's what I'm afraid of. Here we are. Now, open your mouth."

After four minutes, the mercury had risen to just below one hundred one degrees.

"I want you to see a doctor immediately," Laura said as she read it.

"One hundred one isn't all *that* uncommon," Pope said.

"It's plenty of cause to call the doctor. And we have Eliot to think of. It would be a good idea if you got into your pajamas and stretched out under a cover."

"What are you going to do?" Pope asked.

"I told you," Laura said, going out of the room. "Call for the doctor."

By the time Dr. Ashton arrived, the sun had been down for an hour and Pope's temperature had risen by another degree.

"How do you feel?" the doctor asked.

"If I weren't dressed like this and lying here, I wouldn't know I was sick."

Dr. Ashton smiled. "I can't believe that's quite the truth."

Pope motioned toward the door and Dr. Ashton pressed it closed. "I feel a little dizzy. It's true that I felt fine until an hour ago. I imagine it's just coming over me now, whatever it is. Probably a summer cold, wouldn't you think?"

"Very likely. See if you can stand up, Mr. Chance. . . . Fine. Feet together. Now just breathe normally. . . . Take a deep breath and—let it out. Once again . . . fine."

"Find anything?" Pope interrupted.

"When I do, I'll tell you," Dr. Ashton said. He listened again to Pope's heart, pressed here and there on his body. "Cough, please. Can you cough? Thank you." He raised the lid on Pope's eye, then placed a long wooden stick into his throat.

Pope gagged.

"Raise your arms over your head. Let them down. Now, bend your head back, can you?" The doctor's fingers searched the glands of Pope's neck. "Tell me if I'm hurting you." When he finished, he directed Pope to the edge of the bed and said, "You have influenza, Pope. Not a severe case, but not a weak one. I want you in bed for a week's rest at least."

"I'm not sure my father will be pleased," Pope replied. "There are quite a number of things he's asked me to do."

"I'll have a talk with your father." Something in the doctor's tone suggested that he had left his diagnosis incomplete.

"That won't be necessary, Doctor. Thank you very much anyway." Pope paused and stared into Dr. Ashton's large brown eyes until they flinched.

"You have a goiter, Mr. Chance. A lump in your neck." He took Pope's hand and raised it to a slight protrusion that extended from the side of his throat. Pope's finger massaged a circle in the skin, over and over again, until the spot was red from rubbing. "Do you have a mirror?" he asked. His calm was clearly forced now, his expression grave.

"Here," Dr. Ashton said.

Pope tilted the mirror until the lump appeared, then

changed angles to see it from as many sides as possible. "A goiter," he said. "How do you know?"

"It's my business." Dr. Ashton forced a laugh.

"But what do I do? Once the influenza's broken, do I go about my work as usual or would you have me check into a hopital?"

"You watch it."

Pope read the man's fear through the layers of circumspection. "I don't want to live with this forever, Doctor."

"No one would want you to, Mr. Chance."

Laura gave Tom the news the following morning on the telephone and, within three quarters of an hour, he was at their house on Thirty-fourth Street. "Damn terrible thing, influenza," he began after a handshake and a minute's appraisal of Pope's condition.

"They're overdoing the whole thing." Pope smiled. "Laura wants to keep me home and the two of them are in it together."

"As far as I can see," Tom said, "you're probably right." He swallowed, thought for a minute. "Ashton's a good man, but he's not a specialist in this sort of thing. He's the first to admit that."

"I should have known that you'd talked to him."

"As soon as Laura hung up," Tom said kindly. "You're twenty-four years old. You'd have to be a damn fool not to have guessed that I would."

Pope looked at Tom carefully. "Thank you, Father," he said, his voice swelling to the breaking point.

Tom cleared his throat. "Don't let this throw you, Pope. Every family has its problems, and we've licked plenty of them. All we have to do is to be calm and do it one more time. Goiters are a thing I don't know much about, but after I talked to Ashton, I got hold of the chief surgeon at the New York Hospital and he seems to think they may know more about them in Boston. He gave me a name . . ."

"Who?" Pope asked.

Tom reached into the side pocket of his coat and withdrew a long strip of paper to which he lowered his glance. "John Collins Warren. At the Massachusetts General Hospital."

Pope smiled. "Class of sixty-three," he said. "Warren's an old Porcellian name."

"Figures," Tom said, his eyes flashing from paper to Pope. "It says here that his great-grandfather was Washington's surgeon, that he actually sent Paul Revere on the ride to Lexington. His grandfather planned the Harvard Medical School and served as its first professor of surgery. His father pioneered the development of ether and he, himself, recently published the *American Text Book of Surgery.*"

Laura shook her head from side to side. "No one else in the world could have found all that out so quickly."

"I hope not," Tom said.

"Father," Pope said, "I had quite a lot of work planned. The reports on Pulling and Trumbull. The new man at North Atlantic Port. And the plan for San Ambrosia . . ."

"Arthur and Phillip will no doubt be more than happy to carry your load for you until you're back on your feet. They won't do the job you would." Tom grinned. "But, they're hardworking boys and I'll be there to cover."

Moved to repay his father's generosity, Pope said: "I don't see any reason why I can't be back at the office in a few days. I can go to Boston week after next, once things have slowed down."

"One step at a time," Tom cautioned, "and you'll be back before you know it. Then we'll take a trip, you and I—through the Caribbean and over to Costa Rica. I'm going to show you every boat, every inch of track and cargo in the Chance lines."

Forty-eight hours after Pope's fever broke, Tom, his son, Elizabeth, and Laura traveled to Boston by train. Only the monotonous, dread-filled sound of the metal wheels against the track and the swaying of the car as it banked into sharp turns along the Connecticut coast disturbed the wordless, velvet-curtained atmosphere inside.

They were met by a carriage at South Station and conveyed, at a breakneck pace, to the Bullfinch building, which was the Massachusetts General's principal structure and centerpiece.

"The luggage goes on to our hotel," Tom told the driver, "in Copley Square. We'll meet you back here—exactly—after they've unloaded."

Boston that day was tropically hot, but the sky was pallid, and not until two thirty in the afternoon did the sun break out from the overcast clouds. When it did, shooting obliquely across the Charles River, it lit the huge granite blocks of the Bullfinch building to a gleaming ivory, brought up the ripe summery greens and blues of the marsh grass that rioted from the hospital's clustered buildings to the edge of the water, and bathed the long timber piers at which the boat ambulances were docked in a yellow, monochrome mist.

Together, they awaited Dr. Warren in a ground-floor anteroom, just outside whose door two slender, iron-railed staircases rose like the halves of a circle. And Tom knew that directly above them, in the natural light of the great, domed rotunda, the operating rooms were even then in use. They listened raptly to every footstep that fell on those stairs, to every transient conversation, until Warren entered.

He was a courtly man, wearing a green surgeon's gown. But, after returning with Pope from a nearby examining room, he brought bad news.

"Without question, it is a growth," he said.

"But we've all known people who've lived for years with goiters," Elizabeth interjected.

Dr. Warren smiled patiently. "That's certainly possible."

"Could it be more than a goiter?" Pope said.

"Yes."

"Could it spread?" Pope continued.

Dr. Warren hesitated. He looked at Elizabeth, at Laura, at Tom. "My opinion is that it already has."

"Oh, my God," Elizabeth cried. "What does that mean?"

Laura searched Dr. Warren's face.

"In feeling your lymphatic glands, in both sides of your neck, I find quite a bit of hard tissue."

"You've told us about the probable; now tell us about the possible," Tom demanded.

"Very little here," Warren said, glancing down. "I know you asked me to be candid."

"Why?"

"Oh, we have men who work in this field. But these things are specialties. Often one man knows more than any other. It would, therefore, be . . . ridiculous to expect you to have any but that one man attempt to deal with the problem."

"You are, as I understand you, telling me that there *is* such a man."

"Any doctor wishes he could satisfy distinguished men, Mr. Chance. I'm certain you're aware of that. Rich men build hospitals. And there are many specialties on which the work here is the most advanced in the world. But I'm afraid I must suggest that you take your son to Baltimore."

"Baltimore?"

"Dr. William Stewart Halsted, at the Johns Hopkins Hospital."

That night, before the journey, Chance left his hotel and walked in the warm starlit evening to the brown-earthed banks of the Charles River. He walked along the river for miles until, across the mud, the channel, and the swamp, he could see the weak, yellow lights of Memorial Tower. He had always dreamed—for himself at first, and then for Pope. And now he felt powerless and, what was harder for him to bear, mortal. He crossed the bridge, walked through the square, past Massachusetts Hall and into the Harvard Yard. The students, couples in one another's arms, ignored him. He walked past the Porcellian Club, remembering that, on one occasion, Pope had asked him there and he had been forced to wait in a damp bicycle room because only members were allowed upstairs. He recalled a pang of jealousy, but also a fierce pride, pride in his flesh and blood. And now Pope was dying.

Chance walked the pitch New England night alone, too broken to cry. Near him a quartet of wood and strings practiced a haunting theme from Anton Dvořák's new symphony. Then a troubadour sang to a small arc of young people in the pungent summer dark.

"I was a god in my time
It was very, very fine
I was a kind of god, in my time.
My women came callin'
My money was all in
The rarest and purest of gold.
I had young loves and luck
Like no man's ever known.
I believed I . . . would never grow old."

CHAPTER

31

EDMOND DE FONTAINVILLE, OWING TO HIS ACUTE NEAR-SIGHTEDness, strained his face into a squint as he dropped his monocle and looked up from his copy of *Le Monde* and across the drawing room of their Paris house to his wife.

Katharine, dressed in blue and seated against a backdrop of sixteenth-century arabesques, was holding up part of a leather harness. "Which do you prefer, Edmond, this or the one Monsieur Hermès showed us yesterday?"

Edmond bit his lip in thought. In another moment, he stood and, approaching Katharine, nodded courteously to Adolphe Hermès, the harness maker, seated opposite her. "No, no," he said, restraining the merchant in his chair. "No need for you to stand. I wouldn't either—except that I have to in order to see." He took the harness in his hand and examined it closely. "*Very* fine. Very fine work indeed."

"Very expensive," Katharine laughed.

"If it's what one wants," Edmond said, "no price is too much. If it isn't, any price is."

"We made many just like this for Czar Nicholas," Monsieur Hermès told him.

Edmond looked at Katharine. "Aren't Russians amusing? I'm certain they'd buy all of Paris, if they could, and transport it to Moscow." He paused. "We'll take six, then, Monsieur Hermès. Two each for my wife and myself. One each for our daughters' ponies."

A moment after Hermès departed, the downstairs maid

entered with a silver tray bearing a large kettle of water from which a light steam was still visible. Katharine thanked her, took the kettle in hand and, as Edmond returned to his reading, began to move about the room, pouring measured amounts of the tepid liquid into dozens of potted geraniums, delphiniums, anemones, tulips, and ferns.

She had been about this for no more than a quarter of an hour when her butler appeared. "A cable, Madame. Just arrived."

"Cable?" Edmond asked with automatic curiosity.

Katharine's fingers quickly tore at the thin envelope.

"Why so frantic, darling? Most probably nothing. Very likely from Guerlain telling you they're out of some perfume." He smiled to himself.

Katharine smiled too. "For me, an unexpected cable is like hearing a dog's howl in the middle of the night." Then, as she read the message, a terrible cry escaped her.

Halsted was a nervous man. Of average height, with receding hair parted in the center, he had pale skin, a remarkably straight nose, and a blond moustache which contained a sprinkling of gray. His gaze was intense and sometimes frenzied, a trait which others ascribed to his having once addicted himself, as a result of medical experiments, to narcotics. And he was a dandy. Curiously, it was the velvet-like roll of Dr. Halsted's lapels and his obviously Parisian shirts that first struck Tom.

Halsted offered little hope, but did operate. He injected Pope's nerves with cocaine in order to deaden the pain and, carving a long but razor-like incision into the lowest crease of the neck, removed a large cancer from the young man's throat.

Tom, having sought and been refused permission to attend the operation, sat with Laura and Elizabeth in a low, dustless waiting room for three hours, until Dr. Halsted emerged from the operating theater.

"We removed a tumor and a large section of your son's thyroid gland," he reported.

"Will he live?" Elizabeth and Laura asked at once.

"Perhaps. *If* he can survive on the small amount of the gland he has left. But, if we had not done the procedure, we can say with certainty that he would have died shortly."

Pope recovered consciousness in a few hours. He was plainly weak. His throat was sore, his voice rasping, but when Elizabeth asked him how he felt, he replied "Never better" and smiled.

Two days later, Pope's temperature began to climb, until it reached 102 degrees after nine hours. He developed a pain in his side and a cough. At first colorless, his expectoration slowly grew rusty and frothy. His urine decreased. His pulse and respiration quickened.

"Pulse to breathing less than two to one," Dr. Halsted muttered, his fingers clasped tightly at Pope's wrist.

"What is normal?" Laura asked, sensing that, with the doctor's count complete, the necessity for silence had passed.

"Three–or four–to one," Dr. Halsted answered.

Elizabeth gasped.

"Pneumonia," the doctor announced on the third day. "Acute lobar pneumonia." He glanced intently about the room. "It may be complicated by pleurisy. The pain under his ribs makes that more likely, but there's no way to be sure. There will be a crisis in three to five more days. If there is going to be a favorable outcome, his fever will fall dramatically."

"Meanwhile, what's the treatment?" Tom asked.

"Serums and vaccines made from the pneumococcus. But they are only experimental."

Tom regarded Laura and Elizabeth, then asked, "Is it contagious?"

"Not directly," Halsted answered. "It seems to move in waves."

At the end of the fifth day, Pope slipped into a coma and,

while Elizabeth wiped the perspiration from his forehead, he missed a breath and died.

They came out of Johns Hopkins through the reception hall, past the beckoning marble figure of Christ, and paused for a moment in front of the entrance. Elizabeth's body wove from shock as she moved. Laura was drawn. Her hand stretched out nervously before her, fisting the air at sudden intervals as though to summon succor from it. Tom's eyes gazed about the sky, vainly searching for a vanished star, but finding, again, that God was inscrutable. He put an arm around Elizabeth, a hand in Laura's, and let out a muffled, inarticulate sigh.

Before them, a graceful flight of cement steps wandered down the grassy embankment to Broadway, interrupted only by a circular slate promontory. Tearless because he was numb, Tom brought them to a momentary stop as he contemplated the view of Baltimore across a valley. Defined by the politely limited aspiration of its spires, the picturesque city raised no awe in Tom. And yet the sight of it, recalling the joys and torture of his youth, seemed to force his entire life into question now and, as the sun rose up behind him, warming his collar, he wondered if he, like Icarus, had flown up too close to its fire.

After a moment, Tom's eyes settled upon the old brass sundial, oxidized by age and exposure, that had been set out on a pedestal in order to remove it from any building's shadow. Arched above it in high relief, the words of a short rhyme seemed to pluck some deeply buried chord within him.

One hour alone is in thy hands,
The hour on which the shadow stands.

And, terror in his face, he gave in to deep and inconsolable tears.

* * *

Katharine's ship docked at South Street on the morning of her brother's funeral. Tom met her on the gangway and delivered the news in person.

"I know," she told him. "I've known it since our second night out of Southampton. Suddenly, it was as if something that had been going on in me all my life—like breathing—just stopped without warning and I . . . just *knew,* Daddy."

"But, now, *why*?" Tom responded softly. "None of us can ever know why. For fate to do what it's done, it's like . . . tearing the wings from a butterfly."

Edmond in tow, they proceeded, in Tom's coach, to the Pope family burial ground near Tarrytown, the ride through the Hudson Valley being nearly as furious as the two squalls they had encountered at sea.

That afternoon, with the preacher's final incantation "of the Grace of Our Lord Jesus Christ," the low, rumbling thunderheads that had threatened all day exploded and the almost mystical horror of wild lightning emblazoned the desolate Westchester sky. Rain, falling in sheer parallel planes, washed the young sod and topsoil from the burial ground so that the departing mourners implanted deep tracks in the earth.

Elizabeth stood, immobile, over Pope's grave as the diggers' shovels raced to refill it, her heels sinking farther into the earth as the water soaked her dress and veil and the new, brutal wind sent shivers of ice into her lungs.

"Come, Elizabeth," Tom pleaded. "Come out of the storm, for the sake of God." But he was no more able to uproot his wife than the dogwood beside her.

A week later, consumed with fluid and confined to her bedroom, Elizabeth's fever began to repeat the ascendance of her son's. She coughed in great, involuntary heaves of her weakened frame and was cared for by doctors at every hour of the day.

"I was told it was not contagious," Tom admonished the chief of these doctors.

"If I know Dr. Halsted, you were told that pneumonia travels in waves."

Tom shook his head. "A thing like pneumonia," he exclaimed, "that you see so much of. And there's not a cursed one of you can do a thing about it!"

In the middle of her fourth day of fever, as Tom remained beside her in the vaporous room, Elizabeth looked up at him. And, for an instant, catching a playful light in her wide eyes, he could see in her infirm and life-ravaged face the ghost of the girl she had been. When the doctor stepped into the hall, Tom, still trembling from his vision, knelt on the small prayer-rug beside her bed, took her hand and kissed it. "I'm sorry," he said in a soft, choked voice.

The playful light was gone, but Elizabeth smiled. "You were always stronger," she told him weakly.

Tom's desperate grip tightened about her. "Don't die, Elizabeth," he begged. "Don't die. If you die, there won't be enough of me left to go on."

"You always looked forward," Elizabeth said. "I always looked back. That was the difference between us. You shouldn't change now, Tom. It's too late."

"I've never forgotten the first day I saw you, when you came into the shop," Tom said. "That was the day I came alive."

For the last time, Tom felt life in Elizabeth's hand. Her smile was still there, but faint, as though the fever were about to erase its final lines. "At Goelette," she said. "And I never got my *ferronière*."

CHAPTER 32

The chair on which Eliot Chance, Pope and Laura's son, did his best to remain seated had been upholstered and fitted with embroidered covers. It was located directly in the center of his grandfather's splendid "Moorish" sitting room and was one of a set of amorphously shaped pieces that had been covered with identical material and gay, fringe skirtings. Directly beside it, on the otherwise empty, ebonized surface of a small table, his chocolate soldier, less than four inches tall, stood at parade rest. The child studied it carefully. His young hands reached for it time and again, moved it slightly to the right or left, then returned to his lap while he appraised the effect of his work. Behind him, by the light of the mantel fixture, his grandfather sat in his armchair, reading. And at intervals Eliot would check on the older man. When he did, his eye would rise up the intricately patterned walls, skip across the exquisite joinery, the ivory, and the mother-of-pearl, and return to his soldier with no appreciation of the expense that had gone into creating this atmosphere. Because his soldier was only a short distance from the fire in the hearth, and directly in the path of the heat as it escaped, it was becoming moist on its surface and its edges were beginning to blur. So the boy turned for help to the man in the chair.

"Grandfather," he asked politely.

"Yes," Thomas Chance answered.

"Are you nearly finished reading?"

"More than halfway."

"How much more, Grandfather?"

"Eliot, don't be a—difficulty for me."

"No, Grandfather. But my soldier—"

Thomas Chance spoke as he read. "What about your soldier?"

"He's gotten soft. All of a sudden."

"Then move him out from the heat. Take him farther away from the fire."

"He's not—really near the fire," the child replied. "And you *told* me to sit here."

"Quietly. I told you to sit there *quietly*."

"I'm sorry, Grandfather," Eliot said.

Tom put down the fold of papers in his hand and looked straight into Eliot's eye. "Sometimes, Eliot," he said, "if we split hairs, we don't get anything. Do you understand what I mean?"

"I don't know what split hairs are." The boy smiled. "I'm only six, Grandfather."

Tom returned his grin. It was 1903 and he was sixty-three. His hair was three quarters gray now, but his eyes had not aged and his skin looked forty. "Splitting hairs," he continued, "is an expression. It is called a 'figure of speech.' If I say that you should take your soldier away from the fire before it melts and you say that it is not near the fire, even though it is plainly near enough to be melting from the heat, that's splitting hairs. And no matter who is right and who is wrong, while we argue about it the soldier will melt."

"I didn't want to *argue* about it," Eliot said.

"No," Thomas Chance agreed, sensing that he had not made himself clear.

"May I move then?"

"Yes. Into the far corner. That's a fine place for your candy. Then come back and talk with me."

Eliot slid off the chair and did as he was told, but he had

no sooner returned to his grandfather's side than the familiar perpetuelle began to chime. "One-two-three," he counted out loud, "four-five-six. That's what I was afraid of. Six times. Cook will be here any minute and want to take me away. Oh, Grandfather!"

"I wouldn't let Cook see you with that face. She might very well let you go without your dinner."

"Or poison me."

"I hardly think so. Not Cook."

"Because she's afraid of *you.* Only because of that. Oh, Grandfather, I so wish there were other children in this house. I so wish I had a brother! Did you have a brother?"

"No," Tom answered gently, "I didn't."

"A sister?"

"No."

"Were you lonely?"

"Not always. But at times, I think, I was very lonely." He hesitated. "Loneliness is not entirely a bad thing, Eliot."

"I asked my mother for a brother once," the child said.

"Oh?"

"Did you ever ask your mother for a brother, Grandfather?"

"No. No, I didn't."

"Do you know what I want—more than anything in the world? I want to have dinner in the dining room with you and Aunty Frances and Mummy. I don't want to have dinner alone anymore, with Cook and all those wretched people in the kitchen."

Tom stared at Eliot severely. "*People* are not wretched," he said. "I don't know where you learned it, but 'wretched' is a word that makes a young boy very ugly when he says it. So ugly that no one will want to have anything to do with him. When you're old enough to know better than to use a word like that, we shall see about the dining room."

At this moment, a knock came at the door. Eliot pressed. "*Must* I go? *Why* must I go?"

Tom regarded his grandson kindly. "To build a habit," he explained. "All of life is habit, Eliot. So, if we want to amount to anything, it's essential that we get the right ones early."

When the door opened, it revealed Arthur Forrest and Phillip Grainger. Both men were thirty now. Forrest's hair had receded a few inches on his scalp and Grainger's forehead had begun to crease, but in no other respect did either appear ravaged by the eight years of seven-day weeks and fourteen-hour days they had put in at Chance and Company. English suits from Hawes and Curtis, the same tailors Tom used, flattered their figures. And though Chance and Company had but one partner, as Tom liked to say, the two young men had the distinct look of more than assistants. Compounding the sentimental advantage they knew they enjoyed as a result of having been Pope's friends with shrewdness and energy, both had fulfilled Tom's prediction, rising to positions just below his own—Grainger's responsibility still being roughly for figures, and Forrest's for words. "Excuse me, Mr. Chance," Forrest began at once. "Very sorry to interrupt, sir. And Eliot. But we've had word from Washington on the shipworkers' strike." His expression was unusually grave. Grainger appeared to be inhaling anger.

"Go to Cook, Eliot, right now," Tom said in a suddenly sharper voice. "You'll find her in the kitchen."

"It's the political problem," Forrest went on. "What we've been afraid of all along. Only worse."

"Roosevelt's released the results of his meeting with you and the other shipowners. He claims that the unions were willing to accept arbitration, but that the owners urged him to break the strike with the military."

Forrest added: "Here are *The Times* and the *World*. The other papers were either sold out or not yet available. To make a long story short—"

"—We've been *had*," Chance concluded.

"I could think of other words," Forrest said.

"Oh, do shut up," Tom snapped. "At your age I should hope you could." He stopped himself short, reached up to the back of his neck and stretched. ". . . I'm sorry. For heaven's sake, don't mind me."

"No, sir. I understand."

Grainger said, "The public is bound to be irate."

"Of course. The emotion will get them. The poor fools don't *understand* anything. They never have. Damned President did the same thing, exactly, to the anthracite people. I told those fools in our business, the very day we went to the White House, that we couldn't trust him."

"And you were right," Grainger agreed. "They'll see that now."

Tom's eyes grew fierce. "I've seen the public when it's angry. They took off after Gould like a pack of hounds on the trail of a fox. That's the danger of visible success. And I am visible, God knows.

"We'll be compelled to arbitrate now, to save our skins. And, that, of course, is exactly why he did it. Politicians are dangerous people; the farther they rise the more dangerous they become. With all the opportunities around them, I've never known one who could survive in this free-enterprise country of ours—what used to be a free-enterprise country—and make his way. And so, what do they do? They try to make their way politically, which means stealing, grafting, trying to cut down the very people who pay their salaries. That's what they do, because what they really want, pure and simple, is power over people."

"The whole of this country depends on ships for trade," Forrest said. "That's a large constituency when you bring it together. And that's what he's done."

"So it seems. When McKinley was shot, I knew it would happen. I could feel it in my bones."

"One wonders how he ever got so far," Forrest said. "Why he wasn't *stopped*. Even though one hears he's after Rockefeller, sir, and others, more than he is after us."

"I can tell you boys it makes me madder than hell that we're going to have to go to arbitration. But that's *not* the thing that worries me for the long run. What worries me is that Mr. Roosevelt seems to want to destroy the trusts. And if he does, he will destroy capitalism in this country . . . probably forever. With McKinley, we had Hanna in control of everything. And Hanna is Rockefeller's man, but that's in the past now."

"Hanna was a much more clever man," Grainger said.

"Yes. But the immediate danger is Congress—the House particularly. There are quite a few in there—Charles Phitts among them, I'm afraid—who will take this as a signal, one they've been waiting for for years. Not a week ago, the Attorney General entered suit against the Northern Securities Company, Morgan and Harriman and Hill, so they will know that it's more than a straw in the wind. With his right hand Roosevelt is hitting the rail and coal men in the groin and with his left he's trying to knock out the shipowners. But whatever we hear about his feud with Rockefeller, my advice is to treat it cautiously, because Rockefeller is a very big fish. Standard has a lot of agents, not just in Washington but all over the world; and there are a great many more government people on their payroll than there are on ours. There is always the possibility that we are just big enough to be seen and just small enough to be beaten. And we shouldn't forget that."

"I think you should stand pat, sir, if you don't mind my saying so," Forrest offered. "If the shipowners would all stand pat, what could he do really? The Antitrust Act's a dozen years old, but no one enforces it. It's toothless, in my opinion."

"It is possible," Grainger said, "that if the public is allowed to go without their usual imported luxuries they might very well end up clamoring to have them back at any price."

"It *is possible*."

"Even probable. I know–"

"No," Chance interrupted. "Never make the mistake of assuming that you are one of the people. Because you, most definitely, are not. Swans fly with swans, Grainger. Ducks fly with ducks."

Arthur Forrest interrupted with a smile. "What I believe Phillip means, sir, is that the real difference between us and them is simply that *we* understand how much more sensible it is, economically, to have resources concentrated in the hands of those who best know how to make use of them. That's not a popular opinion with the public right now. But if they had more information, the *right* information, it would be."

"There are twenty-seven enterprises," Grainger added cunningly, "that have assigned their stock to the Chance and Company Trust, sir. And I daresay not one of them would be half so well off were it still on its own. And every product produced by them would cost the public twice as much, at least, if it weren't for the trust."

Chance laughed ironically. "I've never heard that pack of lies delivered more convincingly. But, do me a favor and save them for the press. Don't use them on me. I wrote them." He sneezed suddenly, raised his handkerchief to his nose.

"Now, I will meet with the other owners about this strike matter and we will do what we have to. But I want you boys to make a careful study of what they are saying in Washington and I want you to have me prepared, with answers that no one will be able to contest, if suddenly attention should fall on us."

"As soon as the *Sun* is out, I'll see that you have it," Forrest said as he began to leave. "You're often treated rather better there. It will be interesting to see what they say."

"*McClure's* will no doubt give a banshee cry."

"Yes. Would that Cleveland were still President," Chance

added. "We'd have had the army in there in a day."

Grainger and Forrest nodded, turned, and walked out from the room as Chance returned, undisturbed, to the reading from which Eliot had distracted him. When they had reached Fifth Avenue, Forrest paused for a moment and looked skyward with very solemn eyes. "What's the problem?" Grainger asked. "Caught a stone in your boot?"

"I'm not in a mood to be humored," Forrest said. "I'm thirty years old, Phillip. And that egotistical old fart might as well be my father."

"It's the converse of that that I find tantalizing, Arthur: the fact that *we* might as well be his sons, and heirs."

"We might be on the street, too, one day. And not so young when we are, if he ever tires of us," Phillip said.

"High risk for high reward," Grainger said. "There's no getting around that fact."

CHAPTER

33

A FEW WEEKS LATER CONGRESSMAN CHARLES PHITTS, NOW thirty-seven years old, still freckled, and looking ever more Irish as his youth escaped him, stood in the corridor outside his office on Capitol Hill. He was talking with a young man of twenty-five who had come down to Washington from New York, where he was employed on Wall Street. "Thank you, Congressman," the young man said. He had a large kidney-shaped mole on his upper right cheek.

"On the contrary, thank *you*," Phitts replied. "For it is *you* who have performed the public service. And bravely, too." He touched the young man on his back.

"I didn't know what to do, what was right," the young man said. "I've never so much as repeated a secret before."

"It becomes a question of the greater good, doesn't it?" Charles Phitts said. "The value of keeping the confidences people have *thrown in our laps*, so to speak, has to be judged against the public good. These men we're talking about are robbers, really. And if they are not stopped in their tracks and routed, they are going to steal the very land out from underneath us. And, remember, you haven't passed their confidences on to just anyone. It isn't as if you had done that, or sold them to a competitor. No, you have passed them on to the Congress of the United States, to the sworn representatives of the people."

"Yes, I know," the young man said. "I could probably

get you more on some of the others, too. Perhaps on Harriman. And maybe Frick, if anything comes across my desk."

Phitts thrust his hands into his pockets and hesitated. "The feeling seems to be that these trusts differ in their quality, that while the worst of them are undeniably wicked, perhaps the best of them may not be."

"I don't understand, I'm afraid."

"At the moment, the White House seems to feel that the emphasis must remain upon Mr. Rockefeller." Phitts' eyes assured his visitor that he had been taken into the highest confidence.

The young man paused. "To my mind it's only a matter of time before *you'll be* in the White House. Five years, many people say. Nineteen aught eight."

Phitts smiled slightly but quickly. "Five years seems a long way off."

"I suppose I really should be going," the young man said after a minute. "I'll keep in touch, though."

"Thomas Chance?" Phitts asked suddenly. "You're certain you don't know anything more about him?"

"No. Everything that I knew I told you."

"You said that his assistant was unhappy. Your friend. What was his name?"

"Arthur Forrest. I wouldn't call him my friend, really."

"But you haven't heard anything more?"

"No."

"Chance is the man I'd like to get." There was a slow, fanatic tempo to Phitts' speech. "I'd like to pull him out from behind that mask of his. I'd like to put a torch to all that secrecy. But the problem is there are just so many goddamn layers to it. I've tried, but I've never been able to penetrate it far enough."

"I can't imagine Arthur Forrest would help you. He's nearly an adopted son of Thomas Chance."

"You never know until you try, do you?" Phitts said deliberately.

The young man paused. "Well," he began, "I'll make it a point to see him. But I wouldn't count on anything."

From the windows behind and beside his desk, Thomas Chance gazed out at the noontime drizzle, then turned his chair and began to stare. The calendar was already midway into the second week of December, but the air was still thick and warm, and the light, having been filtered through clouds, seemed somehow sultry as the gray buildings absorbed it. Pressing his face against a single prophylactic pane, Thomas Chance watched not only the lunchtime traffic of horses, humans, and an occasional motorcar as it moved past Twenty-one Wall Street, but the play of the rain on the glass: It seemed to rise as well as fall now, to spread out with all the patterned intricacy of a spider's web. He took a deep breath and thought of the thirty-six years that had passed since he had come to New York from Baltimore. New York's bold facade had grown ever more angular as one "skyscraper" after another claimed to be "the tallest building in the world." First the Tower; then the St. Paul; now the Park Row. He studied the sidewalk beyond the wall of his bank and remembered the long, bright morning in 1876 when he had stood there and watched as his lintel was chiseled. Every detail was still clear in his mind. Cleveland had been President. The trusts had been young, but ascendant, absorbing in their great reach a huge slice of America. They had been subject to scant attention then, and to no regulations, for they had been animated by the country's almost religious faith in the freedom of individuals to become as strong and as large as they might. Chance had been taught that faith, in school, at home, and mostly through experience. And as he watched the movement on Wall Street he recalled, longed, and feared for it, for he believed it was under attack. He paused and thought of Pope. At the time he had opened Chance and Company, Pope had been his heir presumptive. But that seemed long ago now, all but in another life. Then, suddenly, his eye fastened on a brand new Duryea as it hopped magically and noisily along the road and, for a moment, he smiled.

"Mrs. McCorquadale." Automatically, he spoke the name of his former secretary, although she had been dead for more than two decades.

There was no answer.

"Mrs. McCorquadale . . . Mrs.—" Finally he caught his mistake. "Mrs. Townsend," he said then.

"Yes, Mr. Chance," his secretary answered, appearing then within the frame of his office door.

"Would you ask Mr. Grainger to come in here, please?"

"Yes, Mr. Chance."

"And Mr. Forrest too, I suppose."

"Of course, Mr. Chance."

"Thank you," he said, turning his eye back to the rain.

When Phillip Grainger came into the office, Chance, without looking up, said: "Take a careful look at this, Phillip. If I were your age, this is precisely the thing I'd want to know about."

So Phillip, taking Chance's posture as a cue, approached and put his eye against the window. He looked. He waited. "Excuse me, sir. But *what*?" he said at last. "All I see is the rain, some people, a few carriages, and that Duryea that's parked across the street in front of Stillman's." He bent slightly now and regarded his employer's eyes. "That's what you mean, isn't it?" he ventured at last. "That Duryea?"

"It could just as well be an Olds," Chance said, "or a Winton."

"Automobiles are certainly the coming thing," Grainger said.

"Do you think so?"

"Well, to tell you the truth, I don't prefer them—for most purposes. I think there's no comparing their charm to that of a good coach. But, yes, sir, like any machine, I do think they have a future."

"You would invest in them, then?"

"If I were *you*?"

"If you were *you*."

"No."

"Because you are unsure of your judgment?"

"Because I don't understand machines. I am a banker—that is, I hope to be. So perhaps one day I shall have to learn about them, but right now I don't think I know enough to make a good decision."

"Sounds sensible. Tell me something, Phillip. And think carefully before you answer. When you look at that . . . contraption, what exactly is it that you see?"

Phillip squinted despite the weakness of the light. "Well," he stalled, "I see an automobile, of course. Steel. And a lot of it. I see Duryea, a man who may need money if he wants to grow. I see—"

"The internal combustion engine. That's the first thing you should see. That's the first thing that comes to *my* mind. I see an engine. You're right about the steel, of course, but because it's an engine it will need more than paint. It will need fuel: gasoline. And that means that the oil business is going to be better than it ever has been. And do you know what else? It means that, over time, and not too much of it, the whole real estate market of New York is going to be upset because there won't be any more need of stable streets. And the market for hay could drop. And the price of oats."

"Very clever, sir, the way you've thought the whole thing through."

"I haven't thought the whole thing through, Phillip. That's what I am trying to tell you. I've simply seen the same opportunities that are there for anyone to see." He paused, brought his chair back to his desk while Phillip returned to face him. "That and only that has been my talent, unless you count the discipline that was necessary to do something about it. I'm telling you this because you were one of my son's closest friends. And I want you to know what it is you're going to have to develop in yourself if you're going to meet your goal. Of course, in one way you are much farther along than I was at your age, but in others you aren't. You haven't been toughened in the same way. And you're facing a much more brutal world than I faced, even including the War Between the States. Because my timing was right, if nothing else. And I'm not sure yours is, if you mean to be in business, if you mean to build the factories and the companies that make this country what it is." His eyes sank. He picked up an outsize paper that had been lying face down on his desk pad and handed it to Phillip, whose face dropped as he read it.

"Why, this is a subpoena, sir," he exclaimed. "To appear before a committee of the United States House of Representatives."

"You look so distraught. Don't be. It hasn't got your name on it." Chance laughed.

"No, sir. It has yours."

"Phitts' committee. Needless to say."

"I suppose I never really thought it would happen. This is what you meant about my timing, is it not, Mr. Chance?"

The older man nodded. "I'm afraid that unless we begin to fight back, this new century may belong to men like Phitts," he said.

"They're damned Socialists, that's all."

"Yes. Well, some time ago, I asked you to gather the necessary information so that we would be ready for this day."

"I have it in my desk, sir. If you'll pardon me one moment, I shall go and fetch it."

"Fine. Do. Oh, and Phillip, where is Arthur? I thought I made it clear to Mrs. Townsend that I wanted him to join us."

Grainger looked up awkwardly. "Arthur went home early,

sir. I believe he took ill from something he'd eaten at lunch."

The hearings had been called for the sixth of February, 1904, at ten o'clock in the morning. But Chance, along with Grainger, Forrest, two secretaries, two bookkeepers, six lawyers, his valet and cook, took the train a day early. They debarked only a few minutes past dawn and, contained within his private car, Chance, his assistants, and his advisors spent most of the four and a half hours of their journey discussing strategy.

Over a plate of waffles, Chance asked the senior lawyer what limits there were to the principle of Congressional immunity.

"Well, Phitts cannot assault you physically." The attorney laughed. "But he *can* say anything he chooses. He *can* try to provoke you that way. And probably he will try. I understand that is his style."

"Exactly his style," Chance said.

"And so long as he is on the floor of the House, or one of its committees, he is not liable for his remarks. No matter what he says, you may not sue him."

"But the reverse is not true?"

"No," said the lawyer. "Show the slightest disrespect and he may cite you for contempt. You might win your point in a court at some later time, but my advice would be to comply as courteously as possible with the requests of any member of the committee."

Chance turned to Grainger. "You've let our friends in the House and Senate know where we will be? And that I'd like to see them?"

"I've been in contact with the representatives," Forrest interjected. "Reed, Cannon, Payne, all of them, just as you asked."

"Senator Aldrich promised he would be down to see you

at your convenience," Grainger said. "And we heard from Platt, Spooner, and Allison even before we tried to reach them."

"Fouraker?"

"He wants to see you for lunch."

"Ask him to our suite. I don't want to be seen dining with any of these men until the hearings are over."

"I could not agree more," the lawyer added.

"Our problem is not in the Senate," Chance said. "It's in the House and the House only. We can block any bill in the Senate, but we can't keep the House from drawing public attention to us. And Roosevelt, naturally. And, most dangerous of all, the newspapers. If I had it to do over again, I'd buy at least one newspaper in every major city."

Forrest smiled.

Chance looked back at the papers piled beside his plate. Moment by moment they seemed to absorb him more fully, as his body fell in with the rhythm of the train.

"Has it occurred to you, sir," Forrest said eventually, "that perhaps even Phitts might be brought around to our side? If there is anything preferable to having a powerful friend in one's pocket, surely it would be to have a powerful enemy." He grinned cleverly.

Chance removed his reading glasses carefully and glanced up. "Nothing has ever occurred to you, Arthur, which had not previously occurred to me. And long, long before. Remember that."

The lids on Forrest's eyes fluttered nervously for an instant, then lowered as he turned sideways to Phillip Grainger, who refused to meet his stare.

"I've known Charles Phitts since he was starting out," Chance continued, "and even then he had the same God-awful piousness he has now. Only the Lord himself could bring him around, I'm afraid. He's a man on a crusade. . . ."

There followed a long, thoughtful pause. During it, one of the lawyers muttered something about Constitutional protections, but without sparking a response. And so they rode in silence until, just out of the Baltimore tunnel, the brown fog of a winter fire suddenly bellowed up beside their windows. At first it seemed as if they had gone into a second tunnel, for the smoke was dark and opaque, but gradually, as the wind of the train dispersed it, they could see it spreading all the way back to the flat horizon, shimmering beneath the sun. The smoke licked about the edges of the windows and soon, through the crack the lawyer had made to allow the fumes of his pipe to escape, they could smell the burning tar and the roasted cedar, the evergreen, the pine, the mud and clay, and the wild stink of animal flesh. Cocooned in their car, but no longer inviolate, they watched with a kind of terrified curiosity as all the land around them burned; then, as the track turned sharply west, they could see the pyre of the city: a violent funnel of smoke where Baltimore should be . . . had been.

Grainger said: "I'm going to find out what in the world's going on." He got up from his seat and quickly disappeared through the door that led to the public cars of the train. No one spoke. When he returned he stood over his seat and, leaning on it, said: "There's been a terrible fire in Baltimore. It seems as if the whole city has been destroyed." His face and tone were appropriately solemn, but there was no emotion in his voice.

"Terrible!" replied the lawyer. "Who told you, the conductor?"

"Yes. He heard it on the platform in Philadelphia, he said, from one of the men going north."

"Awful," Forrest said. "A whole city. Think of what it will cost them to rebuild."

Chance was silent, transfixed, for the moment, by the sight of a pile of fallen bricks.

Grainger sat down again. A thought buried in his memory gnawed at him, but he could not retrieve it. He studied the long, level, ruined landscape, the smoldering corpses of buildings. Then, all at once as it occurred to him, he said: "You come from Baltimore, don't you, Mr. Chance? Oh, I'm sorry."

"No," Chance said. "Not for me, Phillip. I don't have anything left there."

CHAPTER

34

CHARLES PHITTS KICKED HIS CHAIR SIX INCHES BACK FROM THE committee table to make room for his legs. He filled his glass with water from the large pitcher beside it and began to sip slowly. He raised his eyes to the ceiling, glanced at his notes, then looked directly across the table and aisle at Thomas Chance.

"Mr. Chance," he said. "You have been brought here, asked to come here, as part of an investigation into certain business practices which have drawn considerable attention of late and which, in the view of many, pose a danger to the economic and political life of our country, not to mention to the lives of millions of men, women, and children, or to our Constitution. You understand that you are not alone in having been subpoenaed to appear before this committee?"

"Mr. Chance so understands," his counsel responded.

"And you are aware that this is a legislative committee and not a court of law."

"Yes."

"However, the Supreme Court, in the case of Gibbons versus Ogden of 1824, has affirmed the right of Congress to regulate commerce and, by the Interstate Commerce Act of 1887, certain practices have already been proscribed. I refer here to the practice commonly known as 'pooling' and to the charging of exorbitant or discriminatory rates by rail carriers."

Chance stared blankly ahead.

"The Sherman Antitrust Act of 1890 does, as you know, render unlawful any combination in restraint of trade," Phitts continued, "the principle having been extended and applied in the Supreme Court's recent decision against Messrs. Morgan, Hill, and Harriman in the Northern Securities Case."

"Mr. Chairman, Mr. Chairman," Representative Washburn interjected in a calm Ohioan voice. He was a plump man, seated at the extreme right of the committee table. "With all due respect, we are not here for a civics lesson, I don't believe. Our witness has come down to Washington from his home in New York, and has been forced to give up valuable time from his own business activities. I should think that, out of simple respect for that fact—"

"Thank you, Mr. Washburn. But you will be heard in due time—in your turn." Washburn tilted his head back. His mouth fell open. Phitts wiped his brow, then paused as he sneezed into his monogrammed handkerchief. "Mr. Chance, you were asked, *ordered* in the original summons issued by this committee, to supply us with certain documents. To the best of your knowledge, have you, or has any member of your staff, complied with that provision of the summons?"

"Mr. Chance has forwarded all such documents to this committee," his counsel said.

"For the record, may I say that the documents with which we have been provided, if those be the ones to which you refer, appear to me both inadequate and unsatisfactory. They have been consolidated from a number of Mr. Chance's businesses and it is very difficult for anyone to conclude anything specific from them."

"Mr. Chairman," Chance said. "Also for the record—may I point out that the documents which I have given this committee are identical to those which I use in the administration of my companies. If, as you suggest, you've found them obscure, I assure you that *we* have *not.*"

Phitts took another drink. "Goelette and Company," he said suddenly. "Is that a familiar name?"

"I was President of Goelette and Company."

"When was that?"

"From the spring of 1869 until, let me see, sometime in 1877."

"Eight years, then."

"Yes. Eight years, Mr. Chairman, or very close to it," Chance said.

"Goelette and Company was then a prominent retailer of fine jewelry in New York, is that correct?"

"That is correct."

"And it has since been absorbed by other interests? By the Katzenstine interests?"

"Yes."

"The catalogue house."

"Among other things."

"Yes. Now, Mr. Chance, would you explain to this committee how it was that you came to acquire Goelette and Company in the first place?"

"I purchased one hundred percent of the stock from Monsieur Laurence Goelette. That is a matter of public record."

"Is it?"

"It must be." Chance did not blink.

Phitts shuffled his papers until he found an old and wrinkled ledger sheet. "The fact of the sale *is* a matter of public record, Mr. Chance. But the details surrounding it, indeed precipitating it, are not."

"Then why exactly are you introducing them into this inquiry?"

"I believe you know the answer to that," Phitts said.

"I know the difference between fact and innuendo," Chance responded.

"That sort of remark could be misinterpreted."

"The most common innuendo in this case suggests that I

was party to some brand of swindle," Tom Chance declared. "But if that were true, why were no charges ever brought against me? And if they were brought, where is the record of them now? Surely, Mr. Chairman, every man who has been fortunate enough to meet with some success in his life has also met with such groundless accusations as I have. Surely, every member of this . . . august committee, in trying to pursue his duty, and the right as he sees it, has heard such baseless scandal aimed even at himself."

"That's quite enough, Mr. Chance. You're very touching."

"Not I. The truth is touching."

"Yes, and you send shivers up my spine just saying so."

"I don't know what you mean exactly. But if it's a compliment you intended, then thank you," Chance said. "I'm flattered."

"This is not a drawing room, Mr. Chance. Nor a comedy, either. This is a duly constituted committee of the United States House of Representatives."

Chance sat up. "I beg the chairman's pardon. I meant no disrespect. Indeed, I should like it noted that, although subpoenaed, I have come here of my own volition, without coercion."

"I'm certain we all agree that that is very noble of you," Phitts replied sarcastically. "But I'm afraid I must ask you to confine your remarks to answering those questions put to you by the members of this committee. Now, without abandoning the history of your early career in business, I would like to move on for the moment. You remained with Goelette and Company, you say, until 1877. But, before then, you had begun to become involved in other businesses?"

"Yes."

"And it was then that you acquired a principal interest in the Front Street Shipping Company?"

"Yes."

"How large an interest exactly?"

"A complete interest."

"For cash?"

"No. I inherited the stock in Front Street."

"From your father?"

"From a friend," Chance replied sternly.

"A friend by the name of Charlton C. Chamberlain?"

"That is correct."

"Would you be kind enough to reveal to this committee the value of that inheritance?"

"Then?" Chance asked. "Or now?" He glanced first at Grainger, then at a paper before him.

"At the time you received it," Phitts explained.

"Approximately one," Tom said.

"One what?" Phitts demanded.

The audience held its breath. "One million dollars," Chance answered flatly.

The audience breathed a great, collective sigh.

"And what has become of that asset?"

"It has . . . changed ownership."

"Who is the present owner?"

"It is owned by a trust."

"Would that be the Chance Trust?"

"Yes."

"Of whose board you are the chairman?"

"Yes."

"Now, then, to your knowledge, Mr. Chance, does this same trust hold any interests whatsoever in other companies engaged in similar enterprises?"

"That fact is no secret, despite the efforts of some to make it seem so now."

"In how many such companies does the Chance Trust hold such interests?"

"I am not sure I can say exactly."

"More than one? . . . More than two?"

"Many more than two. The Chance Trust holds interests in some twenty-seven enterprises altogether. I should say that roughly three quarters of these are involved in one phase or another of the transportation business."

"By 'transportation' I take it you mean both ships and railroads?"

"But we are very small fish in the railroad business. Virtually every prominent name associated with railroads commands many times more miles of track than we do."

"Perhaps. But then you would not describe yourself as 'small fish' in shipping, would you?"

"No. That would be inaccurate, I think."

"Nor in cocoa?"

"No."

"Nor sugar? Nor tropical fruits. Bananas?"

"No."

"Nor in banking?"

"No. Not in merchant banking."

"Nor in the real estate markets?"

Chance's eyes were cold now. "The eastern real estate markets," he elaborated.

"By which you mean New York and the other coastal states?"

"Principally New York. Also Maryland, Pennsylvania, and New Jersey. And, of course, in the Caribbean Islands and Central America."

"Nor do you represent an inconsiderable factor in the silver market, here and in London. And in the gold markets, too, from time to time."

"That could be because, as a very young boy, I was brought up on the Parable of the Talents," Chance said.

"And took your lesson literally?"

"Do you not take your Bible *literally,* Mr. Phitts?"

"That question is neither here nor there," Phitts replied testily. "Of course I take my Bible literally."

"Good," came Chance's response.

"But one can, of course, quote the Scriptures in support of just about anything."

"So they say." Chance ran his tongue across his upper lip. "So they say."

"For example, there is the well-known point about the rich man and the eye of the needle," Phitts countered.

"Which I don't quarrel with," Chance said.

"Oh?" Phitts showed surprise.

"I would be a fool to quarrel with that, for it seems to me self-evident that a man of great wealth might be in danger of losing touch with his humanity. But then that's the challenge, isn't it? It's not meant to be easy."

"No." Phitts shrugged. "Now, Mr. Chance, I'm still going to fill in various episodes of this history we've been discussing, but, for the moment, I would like to pursue the matter of the Chance Trust. I am interested, specifically, in the relationship among the various businesses whose stock your trust holds. Would you describe those relationships as 'cooperative'?"

"Naturally. I would hope so."

"So that if two of your companies were to supply the same product to the same customer they would not compete as to price?"

"That is your conclusion, not mine. And it is my impression, Mr. Chairman, that such a policy as you have outlined would contradict the present laws of the United States."

"Therefore, you are saying that they *would* compete?"

"Yes."

"Despite the fact that they are under the management of the same board."

"I would not want you to be confused on this point, Mr. Phitts. Each company, no matter how related to the trust, is independently managed and responsible for its own activities."

Phitts, his eyes uncomprehending, nevertheless pressed on. "And would the same principle hold true in the event that, say, the Chance Steam Engine Company were to supply an engine to one of Front Street's ships? Would they charge an amount equal to what they would charge a nonallied company?"

Chance crossed his legs and straightened the crease of his trousers. "I can't think why not."

"And, to complete the point, would you further claim that products manufactured or imported by a company whose shares the trust holds do not and have not received preferential transportation rates aboard those carriers whose shares the trustees also manage?"

"I would. In general. Of course, I cannot testify as to every shipment ever undertaken, as to what may have once happened—by accident."

"And yet, Mr. Chance, I believe it is plain to the majority of the members of this committee that there have been quite a few of these 'accidents' you mention over recent years. And that, from them, we can deduce the presence of something larger, of a conspiracy both to thwart competition and to restrain trade."

Chance allowed a long pause to fall upon the committee room. "*Deduce*," he said at last, "but not *prove*."

"*Res ipsa loquitur*," Phitts declared then, in stentorian voice.

"Pardon?" demanded Congressman Washburn.

"The thing speaks for itself," explained Phitts. "*Res ipsa loquitur*. It's a legal expression."

"I know full well," said Washburn. "But I don't agree."

Three rows back in the audience, Forrest broke his stare for the first time since the hearings had gone into session, glanced at Grainger, and shook his head.

"Then you would go on record, under oath, denying that such a conspiracy has existed?"

"The purpose of our business structure is and has been only one thing, Mr. Phitts; and that is—and has been—to utilize our resources in the most efficient ways possible in order to keep our costs as low as we possibly can. This, in turn, benefits the American consumer by providing him with goods for which, under any less carefully administered system of manufacture, he would have to pay considerably more. In the process we create a great many *secure* jobs and so, in that way, we also contribute, we feel, to the entire economy of this country."

"But surely it is not all altruism. Surely there is some self-interest. Surely you make a profit."

"Profit is the object of business."

"I can see that you are very well rehearsed, Mr. Chance."

"Simply logical. When one is logical—"

"Don't contradict me, *please, sir,*" Phitts interrupted. "And do not for a minute think that you will slide out from the scrutiny of this committee on the sleigh of your much-renowned glibness and charm. For it is not charm to me, sir; I know it too well and too long. You have responded to the subpoena of this committee with evasion, with grandstanding, and with a profusion of documents that render it all but impossible to assign responsibility for any given action. But lack of proof is not proof that proof is lacking. It exists somewhere. And we shall find it, sir, I give you my word. This committee is not finished with you. Not by a long shot. We have barely begun."

CHAPTER 35

EACH NIGHT FOR A WEEK, WHEN THE FINAL LAMP HAD BEEN extinguished, Tom would lie in the high goosedown bed of his hotel room, with two pillows beneath his neck, propping his head against the thick, mucous cough that a cold had given him, and watch the slow rotation of the shadows on the plaster frieze and ceiling. From his window, he could see, across Lafayette Park, the north face of the White House in the ivory moonlight, obscured a little by the barren limbs of dogwood and magnolia trees. He would study the lean Ionic columns of the portico and, above them, dropping from the smooth sandstone of the pediment like a finger pointing to earth, a long stalactite of frozen snow and rain. His eyes would scan the great mansion, run west along Jefferson's pavilion, its greenhouse dark, until at last they would settle upon the low new office wing that Roosevelt had just completed for his multiplying staff. Chance's gaze would remain there for a moment, in wonder and in fear of the conspiracy he believed it to contain. Anxious that his hearings should conclude, and with this anxiety fighting his fatigue, he would see in that new wing a symbol of the fresh assertiveness of government, a tombstone for the death of his old certainties.

Then, on the sunny Friday of the following week, Charles Phitts, giving no reason, abruptly adjourned his committee's hearings into a two-week recess. And Thomas Chance, without packing, returned at once to New York. He was tired, alarmed, and very largely mystified by Phitts' motives. He wanted to rest. He wanted to initiate some investigations of his own: "inquiries," he called them. He wanted to consider what favors were due him, and by whom. But just after porridge on Saturday, the whole matter was precipitately plucked from his mind by Katharine's unexpected arrival from Paris.

"*Bon jour, mon père,*" she said, trotting suddenly ahead of the butler, wearing a thin smile.

Chance stood up from the square Hepplewhite table. "By God," he exclaimed. "Kathy! I'm startled. How long has it been?"

"More than two years." The words fell from her tongue. "The longest time we've ever been apart." She gave him an amused look, but he knew that it masked some concern. "Oh, Daddy," she let go at last, running, jumping into his arms.

Staring into the space beyond her as she clutched him and cried against his shoulder, Tom knew instinctively what the matter was.

"I left the children in the library," she said. "I had to see you first. Alone."

"Of course." He said it softly.

"Anne-Marie and Giselle," she told him, regaining her composure. "They both came with me. They're nearly twelve now, you know, and, Daddy, I can't wait for you to see them–"

"Sit down," Tom said.

"Oh, Daddy. You really shouldn't have such intuition. You know everything, don't you?"

"No. Tell me."

"I've left Edmond."

"That much I guessed." He showed her a comforting smile.

"To hell with love," she replied with a distracting flash

of brightness. "How could any man make me happy, when I've had *you* for a father? Dear Daddy!"

"Kathy, would you care for something to—"

"Drink. No, it's too early. And too *French*."

Tom's smile broadened. "Too French? I see."

"Oh, Daddy, if he had been merely unfaithful, I might have been able to go on for the sake of the children. But he was so—so, *publicly* unfaithful."

"Publicly?"

"Everyone knew and—"

"But not the children."

"No. No, I don't think so."

"No. Certainly not. They're twelve, as you said."

"But in a certain set, in Paris and at Deauville and wherever we went on the weekends, everyone knew and took it for granted. Everyone smiled, accepted the fact. I daresay in New York they would not have been so brazen, but Paris is another matter in regard to, to, to—"

"Is that where you left him?"

"In Paris. Yes."

"And there's no chance that . . . things might be set right?"

"I don't see how."

"Still, if I were a genie and I could promise you that they could be, would you want them to be?"

Katharine thought. "I don't know, actually. I don't suppose that I truly could say at the moment."

"Have you stopped loving him?"

"Stopped? He has something, Edmond: a certain indefinable . . . *je ne sais quoi*."

"Oh, yes. You've always seen that in him."

"And so did you once, I might add."

"And I admit it, too," Tom laughed. "Do you want to let the lawyers handle it?"

"Edmond *is* Catholic."

"They've handled that before. You would be surprised

what a small sum of money in the right places, at—"

"What I would like to do would be to stay here for a while. To rest. And think. And then decide, Daddy, if that would be all right with you."

"Perfect," Tom replied.

"Thank you. Anne-Marie and Giselle, they resemble you."

"Do you mean that they are already gray and wrinkled?"

"No, silly. They're exquisite, that's all I meant."

"Will they remember me, do you think?"

"They've been looking forward to seeing you again ever so much."

"Two years is a long time at their age. When they were last here, I remember distinctly, McKinley was President."

"'McKinley was President'? Why, that's an odd way to put it."

Chance studied Peale's *Still Life with Fruit,* which hung on the opposite wall. "Less so in the circumstances," he said.

Katharine's face betrayed her puzzlement. "Circumstances?" she asked.

"I gather no one's told you."

"No."

"I'm under subpoena by the Congress. They're trying to break me, Katharine. They're trying to break the trusts."

"That's ludicrous!"

"Well, don't tell me. Tell your old friend, Phitts. He's the one behind it."

"Charles?"

"*Representative* Phitts now."

"I guess I did know that. But . . . Charles was never vindictive."

"Katharine, there are certain qualities about a man's character that only another man can discover. Do you understand me?"

"Look at me, Daddy." Katharine smiled. "I'm a woman."

"A very *clever* woman."

"Enough to know that nothing is insuperable. Nothing and no one. Not even Charles Phitts."

"Not even the black Irish?" Tom pressed.

"Not even the French nobility."

Tom laughed. "It's strange, isn't it, how the same names haunt one all one's life?"

The next week Katharine traveled to Washington. She told her father that she would be staying, on Sixteenth Street, with a classmate from her days at school in Virginia, the girl's husband, and her two-month-old child. But once arrived at Union Station in the afternoon, she made her way directly to the Willard Hotel, from which, before retiring for her nap, she dispatched an equerry to Capitol Hill with a short handwritten note for Congressman Phitts.

That evening, at the last moment of dusk, Charles Phitts presented himself at her room. "It's an extraordinary coincidence," he said, "your stopping here."

"At the Willard?"

"I live here, you know."

"You?"

"I thought, surely, you knew that."

"But you've married."

Phitts smiled. "Indeed," he laughed. "And my wife lives here with me."

"How unusual," Katharine said, "to live in an hotel."

"Instead of a house? It *is,* I imagine, but I don't know why it should be. I find that most of my life is work, and so living in a hotel is very convenient."

"Who knows?" Katharine said, having lost her original thought as she studied Phitts' face.

He smiled ironically. "Fifteen years," he said. "It's certain to have aged."

"Improved."

"Not at forty-two. They say that, after forty, you have the face you deserve."

"No, no. *You* have the face you were born with," Katharine said.

"You're not drunk, are you?" Phitts teased.

"Not for a minute. I'm never drunk, *never, ever.*"

"Good. Neither am I. Should we have dinner then?"

"You and I and your lovely wife. Who in the world did you marry, Charles?"

"Lucy Peterson. From Chambersburg. But she's in Pennsylvania this week."

"So it will be just the two of us? And we can get very drunk?"

"Yes," Charles smiled. "Let's."

Over dinner, which they took in an out-of-the-way cabaret, Katharine said: "You know, I didn't come here for romance. I came here to give you hell."

"On behalf of your father?"

"But without his knowledge."

"What stopped you?"

"*Delayed* me. What *delayed* me? Well, to be honest, I'd have to say it was . . . you."

"That sounds flattering," Charles replied.

"It was meant to be." Katharine raised, studied, and sipped the Clos des Mouches; then Charles refilled her glass. Her voice dropped a little. "I've always said there was something about you, some little sign of vulnerability that I couldn't resist. I don't think most women could."

"Sign?" He toasted. "Vulnerability? That's a large word. Where?"

"In your mouth, mostly, and a little bit around your eyes. I wouldn't call it weakness—more a kind of imperfection. But in a good way. I mean, no matter how angry I ever was with you, the moment I saw it, I couldn't stay mad. Does that make any sense to you? Any sense at all?"

Charles remained silent.

"Also in your freckles," Katharine added nervously. "As if they were the outward and visible sign of an inward and spiritual . . . *flint.*"

"You've certainly developed a very philosophical side since you've lived in Europe."

"Washington shows on you, too," Katharine replied. "You used to be a Socialist. Are you still?"

"You're much more beautiful when you are not talking politics."

"That remark's so smooth, Charles, that all it does is prove my point. Answer my question."

"Not really a Socialist," he said finally.

"Daddy says you are."

"The wine is very good, I think, don't you? Look, why don't—"

"Yes, I think it's very good. Much too good for a Socialist to be seen drinking. Almost embarrassingly good, I'd say—"

"I told you, I'm not really a Socialist."

"Have you read Marx?"

"Yes, Katharine. Have you?"

"Do you admire what you've read?"

"Parts."

"What are you then?"

"Who knows?" Phitts said. "Perhaps a Utopian."

"Do Utopians enjoy destroying other people's lives?"

"Have you ever been inside one of your father's factories?" Phitts asked her. "At one of his yards? Or roads? On one of his ships? It's the trusts and the holding companies that are wrecking people's lives."

"Those people are paid," Katharine ventured. "If it weren't for men like my father, where would they even find a job in the first place?"

"Yes," Phitts said. "They are paid. And do you know how much? Perhaps two dollars, for sixteen hours a day, six days a week—for an eight-year-old child."

Katharine's twins were already twelve; for a moment, the thought made her quiver. "I just can't bear this," she said eventually. "I just can't bear to see the two of you doing this to one another, the only two men I've loved in my life destroying one another. You filling him with fear. And my father filling you with hate."

Charles took her hand and pressed it, beneath the weight of his, against the hard surface of the table. "Only *two* men?" he asked.

"Don't pretend you haven't always known."

Charles looked at her intently, lost himself, for a moment, in those bright, green eyes whose ancestry he loathed. "I thought it once. I believed it. But you were only a girl. And when you went to France, I knew that I would never see you again."

"Your wife, how old is she?"

"Only a year younger than I am."

"Is she . . . very pretty?"

"She once was. I think she still is, in her way."

"So that she's *enough*?" Katharine pried.

Charles hesitated. "She has been," he said slowly, "until recently."

"I've left the Duke," Katharine told him suddenly.

Charles smiled, considered this news against the suggestion of her voice and words. "So," he said, tightening his squeeze of her hand. "It's happening at last."

"Yes," she answered, in the old beckoning voice of her girlhood. "I suppose that some things have to."

That night Charles remained with Katharine in her suite and they made love. The air was cold and drafty, the light like powder from a distant star. But, too long—and too long ago—rehearsed in mind, their passion assumed an instant and automatic quality, a mechanical rhythm that could not satisfy either one of them. In the morning, barely conscious, as if coming out from under ether, Charles moved his hands along her sides and stared down at the smooth but loosening skin that told her age. Young still—in its prime even—but skin from which the dew had vanished.

"I wish I'd never married," he forced himself to say at last. "Then, we'd be able—"

Katharine awakened in a smile, gradually leaned up and nibbled his lip.

"But we can't begin anything, Katharine," Charles continued. "It's simply too late."

She swallowed her stale and wine-soured saliva. "We're not *that* old," she said.

"I meant too *late* in my career. I'm running for the Senate, Katharine. You know that. And probably I'll win. There are rumors, just little ones, but I've made quite a name for myself and the Presidency will be up again in four years. We just can't begin now what we once could have."

Katharine smiled wryly. "I told you," she said. "I didn't come here for romance. I came here to give you hell."

Charles kissed her, paused. "Be a mother," he said. "Concentrate on that. You've been a daughter long enough."

"He's tough, Charles. And he's a good man, whether you believe it or not."

"Be a mother," he repeated.

Katharine boarded the early Baltimore and Ohio for New York, selecting a seat on the dark, western side of the car. She closed the curtains at once and brought a pillow up to her face. Then, more disappointed than hurt, she hid her eyes among the folds and shadows and wept for a time at the inevitable death of old fire.

She had nearly missed her train, hurrying from the Willard lobby in so confused a state that she had accidentally dropped a small bag on the foot of a young banker as he climbed the exterior stairs. She had smiled in reaction, told him that she was sorry, and begged his forgiveness. And he had smiled in return, flashing the large mole on his cheek, without recognizing her.

From there, the young man had gone directly to Charles Phitts' suite on the second floor, where the Congressman, apparently dressed in last evening's clothes, sat with the morning newspapers.

"Come in," Phitts had said. "I'm glad to see you."

"I wouldn't have disturbed you so early, sir, but I trained

down in the sleeper once I had this. And I knew you'd want it right away." From his bag he had then produced a large and full brown envelope.

Phitts had taken it from him at once, removed a handful of the long documents it contained, and appraised them individually. His smile had opened like a flower.

"From Arthur Forrest, sir," the young man had said. "And I never would have thought we'd have stood a chance of getting them."

"There's quite a bit here, it appears."

"Enough to force court action on a hundred counts, would be my guess. Arthur seems very disillusioned, very angry. Luckily for us, he's at one of those low moments when he feels he's getting nowhere. Thinks Chance is taking advantage of him. He had his thirtieth birthday last year and, ever since it, success has seemed more urgent to him. I assured him that, once you were in the Senate, you would find a position for him. And that, later, from the White House, you'd be able and only too glad to make it worth his while."

"That's fine. Just fine."

"The records detail all Chance's holdings," the young man had said. "But the most useful part, from your viewpoint, is that they reveal quite a few secret agreements, that sort of thing."

"Oh."

"*Unlawful* secret agreements. When the public gets a look at these—"

"Chance will be out of business."

"All sorts of things might happen," the young man had suggested.

Phitts' stare had frozen then; his pupils had grown large for a moment. "Yes," he had said. "I hope you're right."

That night, during the fourth blizzard in eight days, Katharine dined with her father, her sister-in-law, Laura, and Frances. The meal was served on trays in the larger drawing room and the moment it had been put in front of her, Katharine said: "What in the world is that?"

"A kind of meat cake," Laura said.

"It's called a hamburger," Tom said quietly. "It's named after the city, I think. And quite delicious. I first had one at the Great Exposition four years ago."

"How do you know what's in it? I've always thought that if something were chopped there must be a reason. In France, I'll grant you, there's a certain code of honor about those things, but in America?"

"Either one must trust his butcher and his cook," Chance said, "or else one must make the hamburger himself."

"Are you all right, Dad?" Laura asked Tom. At Laura's use of the word "Dad," Katharine felt and suppressed a shudder.

"What?" Chance asked in an absent tone.

"You seem so deep in thought."

"It's gone too far," Frances said, waving her short white hair back into its net. "Too much pressure. We're none of us as young as—"

"Sixty-four is not ancient. We're not dead yet," Chance interrupted. "I can still take these people on, still whip them."

"Of course you can," Katharine assured him.

"I'd better damn well be able to. For everyone's sake."

"Give me your hand," Katharine said. "Let me tell your future."

Frances smiled.

Chance stretched his hand across the open space between his chair and his daughter's. Katharine took it, raised it into the pool of lamplight, and began to read the clear nails of his fingers, one by one. "No new friends," she began, moving from the thumb. "No new foes. No new riches. No new beaux. And a long journey to go."

"Long journey?" Chance asked.

"Long life. Give me your other hand now. . . . No new

friends. No new foes. But, ah, new riches, Daddy. Definitely new riches. Look! Now, no new beaux." Katharine smiled at Frances from the corner of her eye. "But a *long* journey to go."

"Thank God for *you*, girl," Chance told her. "Thank God for *you*."

"Did you enjoy your trip, Katharine?" Frances asked after a long silence.

"You weren't gone long," Laura said. "One day."

"They'd taken cold, everyone in my old friend's family. So I didn't even stop there. I stopped at the Willard."

"You could have taken my hotel suite," Chance said.

"I didn't think of it."

"It's empty. I'm not due back there for a fortnight."

"Perhaps that monster Phitts will have heart failure by then," Frances said.

"I suspect he hasn't any heart *to* fail," Katharine responded.

"Oh," said Laura, "if only the people at the top had just seen what was coming, they could have avoided all of this. There were plenty of signs. You can't have huge trusts on the one hand and people starving on the other."

"Sermons are for half past ten on Sundays," Frances said. "And even then the audience is voluntary."

Laura smiled kindly. "But look at the history of things, Aunty Frances. The world is absolutely *riddled* with the corpses of people who refused to give up just a little bit in order to keep everything."

"The world works the way it works," Frances said. "I didn't know that once, but I learned it."

"Nor did I until recently," Katharine added.

"But Laura's right," Chance said.

Katharine looked astounded. "What!" she exclaimed.

"I thought you disagreed with me," Laura said. "You always have before."

Chance forked and finally chewed the last bite of his

hamburger. Katharine waited breathlessly for his reply.

"I still do," he said ultimately. "But you're right. For other reasons." He smiled. His eyes were gleaming now, and ageless.

"I think Dad has a secret," Laura said.

"Have a little more wine," Tom suggested. And then, when it had been poured into the last glass, raised his own and added: "Here's to happy days! The nights are always good."

Over the next two weeks public pressure for government action against the trusts continued to grow, recorded and magnified by the press. *McClure's* ran yet another feature article. *Collier*'s displayed two pages of angry letters in echo of its recently published editorials. The *Daily Advance*, in Baltimore, caricatured Chance, "a miser among misers, a disgrace even to his despicable class." He was shown, in one New York cartoon, dining on a feast of small children. In another, outfitted in the sleek black mask of a burglar, he attempted to pry a heavy White House up from its foundations. Phitts, from the floor of the full house, railed against the titans generally, and at Chance in particular, and his phrases were turned into headlines. Other representatives, especially those with large labor constituencies, followed his cue. Senators who had once accepted personal contributions from the men they now portrayed as villains, decried the ambiguous concept of "privilege." Teddy Roosevelt, to his own mind now above the fray, sermonized from a "bully pulpit."

When the hearings finally reconvened, the number of working reporters who arrived to cover them was just less than twice what it had been before the recess. For, accompanying the flood of news had been an insistent series of rumors that Charles Phitts was about to make a revelation of consequence. The hearings thus had been rescheduled into the largest of all committee rooms; and a special lounge, ordinarily at the disposal of the Supreme Court, had been assigned to the press.

Frances took a seat in the front row of the audience, between Katharine and Laura. On Katharine's left sat Phillip Grainger; on Laura's right, Arthur Forrest. Two rows behind them, a small, gray-bearded man with curious jet-colored eyes made his way to the center of the section without speaking. This was Felix Hardenstein, now the chief accountant of Katzenstine and Company, in New York. Two seats farther on, a balding, middle-aged Wardman Parton sat unself-consciously in overalls, rolling and smoking one cigarette after another, shifting his whole bulk at regular intervals in order to improve his view of Katharine. His father sat quietly next to him, but the old man, whose memory of the distant past was many times more vivid and pleasant than his recollection of the day before, harbored no envy of his boyhood friend. For him, the sight of Thomas Chance had always been a little awesome.

"Mr. Chance," Phitts said, looking directly into Katharine's eyes. "Two weeks ago we discussed the matter of certain relationships among the many businesses which are controlled by you, by the Chance Trust. And you made it clear to this committee at that time that, to the best of your knowledge, none of these relationships stands in violation of any antitrust legislation. Is that correct?"

"It is," Chance said.

"Louder. Please."

"It *is*."

"And you delivered documents in support of your position to us, did you not?"

"I did," Chance replied.

Phitts paused, twisting his neck as if to work an old stiffness out of a muscle. He spread a group of papers fan-like before him. "Attesting to these under oath?" he asked.

"Because they were true," Chance said.

"Brazen!" Phitts said under his breath. "I think not. I

think that they were *not* true. And that you know, and knew then, that they were not."

"I knew no such thing."

"Evidence has come to this committee which, when presented, will prove otherwise, I believe."

Chance made no reply. Phitts' eyes sought Arthur Forrest. Reporters dropped their pencils from their lips.

"Mr. Chance, remembering that you are under oath, will you inform this committee, please, whether you have ever owned any shares in a concern known as the Lodestone Steel Company?"

Chance looked right to his counsel, then flipped the pages of a ledger before him. After a moment, he repeated: "Lodestone Steel?"

"Yes."

"No. I haven't."

"Have you held shares, then, in the Masley Shipping Company, later Masley Shipbuilding and Dry Dock?"

Another pause. Another "No."

"The Ferquer Line?"

"I have never so much as heard of the Ferquer Line."

"Did you enter, in the spring of the year nineteen hundred, into a secret agreement whereby Lodestone Steel received highly preferential transport rates from a number of transport carriers, including the Ferquer Line, in return for shipping large bulks of raw materials to and finished metals from their mills in Pittsburgh?"

"I think I made it clear that I have never *heard* of the Ferquer Line, much less negotiated on its behalf."

"Very clear. Have you, at any time, owned or controlled stock in G. J. Fownes and Sons, Glassworks?"

"No, sir."

"Or in Hornpipe and Company?"

"The explosives house?"

"Exactly."

"No, I have never owned shares in that—or any—explosives house. For reasons of conscience, I disapprove of that type of business."

"I am sure that we all find that very touching in you," Phitts said.

Chance gave a demure nod.

"Or rather that we *would* find it touching were we to believe, for one minute, that it were true."

Tom's lawyer stared first at him and then at the floor. He knew that his eyes already betrayed his alarm, and he wanted to hide them.

Phitts waited before continuing. He folded his hands, stretched his fingers, cracked his knuckles. He looked at the ceiling thoughtfully, then, once more, at the array of papers before him. Sitting up, while forcing his voice to rise from even lower down in his chest than it had all morning, he slowly began his announcement. "Mr. Chance," he said, "the papers in front of me are signed documents. All thirteen of them bear *your* signature. But that is only the first thing they share in common. What concerns me is that all thirteen either refer to *or authorize* business arrangements which, under the present laws of the United States, are clearly criminal: business arrangements, moreover, involving those concerns of which you have just denied knowledge."

Chance's face reddened. He leaned toward his lawyer. "The son of a bitch," he whispered.

Phitts' eyes were bright now, his movements and speech increasingly rapid. "Consider this letter, written and signed by you on the second of September, 1903, last year, and sent to Mr. Marcus Brook, President of the Lodestone Steel Company in Pittsburgh, Pennsylvania. 'Dear Mr. Brook,'—and I quote: 'Enclosed you will find our draft for one hundred sixty-seven thousand dollars, representing dividends due you from our last period. This exceptional return has been possible, of course, because of the large measure of cooperation among our companies and our consequent ability to hold down our costs. With regard to this, I hope you will provide to Pulling and Trumbull the same discount we have customarily given the North Atlantis Port Company, plus an additional five percent. For we feel that it is important that they enter new markets with at least that advantage in price if they expect, eventually, to dominate them. The cash value of the discount, whatever it is, can easily be made up in your balance sheet by adding it to the price charged outside companies. I expect that there is no need to emphasize, in the present hysterical climate, the need for rigorous secrecy about such as this. Signed, Thomas Chance.' "

Chance was silent, the color and emotion gone from his face.

Frances looked at Katharine, Wardman at Peter, Hardenstein at the reporter beside him. "My God," the reporter said. "They've got him this time."

"Have you any comment, Mr. Chance?" Phitts demanded.

"No. None," his lawyer said.

"The next document is a tripartite agreement among the Habana Empire Company, the Lower Antilles Trade Company, and the Herbaceous Fruit Company of New York not to lower prices for cocoa or bananas in certain jointly shared markets. And the signatories to it, on behalf of the Herbaceous Fruit Company, include you, Mr. Chance."

Tom whispered something to his lawyer. "Congressman," his lawyer asked in reaction, "would you be kind enough to give us the exact date of that alleged agreement?"

Phitts studied it. "February twenty-ninth, 1900."

"Thank you."

"We also have here transportation receipts for the shipping of finished goods by the G. J. Fownes Glassworks to various of your shipyards, which prove that a considerable preference was granted them by the Cumberland Railroad of which, I believe, Chance and Company is the sole stockholder. Would you confirm that fact for me, Mr. Chance?"

"I would confirm that Chance and Company *is* the single stockholder of the Cumberland Railroad."

"That's all I was looking for. I believe that the receipts will confirm the rest."

"And the date of those receipts, please," said the lawyer.

"Also February 1900, and running through the following eighteen months. Definite records," Phitts elaborated. "And good reason to believe that the arrangements have existed long before the date of our first actual receipt."

By this time, the reporters had begun to race their pencils across the top sheets of their tablets, the soft hum of whispers had replaced the cautious silence of the audience, and the dozen members of the committee had been brought to the edges of their chairs by the zeal of Phitts' voice and accusations. Chance tapped the walnut table before him with his golden watch fob and gazed into space, as if in the process of self-hypnosis. The soft taps occurred at measured intervals, and, for a time, they seemed both sound and symbol. With his free hand, Chance wiped the perspiration from his brow and raised a glass of cold water to his lips, but never did he miss his metronomic tap. His eyes, having been turned inward, were motionless, oblivious to the commotion which surrounded him.

Phitts held two wide papers up over the committee table so that the audience could see them. "These," he announced, "are bona fide copies of your personal balance sheet, and of the balance sheet of the Chance and Company Trust. They detail precisely what your assets are in each instance and, upon examination, you will note the very considerable discrepancies between them and your answers to the questions asked here today. A copy of these statements is available to the gentlemen of the press, who will note its listing of shares in Lodestone Steel, in Masley Shipbuilding and Dry Dock, in the Ferquer Line, in G. J. Fownes, and in Hornpipe, all of which you earlier denied possessing."

Chance smiled politely. "If a copy is to be made available to the newspapers and magazines," he said, "I wonder if one might be made available to me and to my counsel as well."

"Certainly, Congressman," Chance's lawyer added, "if this were a trial, under the rules of evidence we would be entitled to peruse the original."

"You needn't beat a dead horse," Phitts interjected "This committee shall be happy to supply you with all pertinent documents forthwith. And a copy has been entered into the records of this committee." He glanced at his colleagues. They nodded. After a moment, the documents were passed to Chance's lawyer, who applied a pince-nez to his Roman nose before perusing them. Silence, like frost, sprung magically out of the atmosphere, chilling the nerves, quickening the pulses, unsettling the stomachs of those who waited. The lawyer passed the sheath of documents to Chance, who drew out five minutes to consider them, bringing his shoulders in as he did.

Phitts beamed contentedly. "Well?" he asked. "Have you anything to say?"

Chance hesitated, continued to tap.

"Really, Mr. Chance," Phitts insisted. "It is not, after all, as if you have never *seen* these documents before!"

Chance's eyes settled on Phitts in silence. His arms moved slowly back to his sides. Then his shoulder spread; and suddenly, snake-like, his entire body uncoiled. "Indeed it is," he snarled, *"since these documents are forgeries!"*

A great swell of conversation rose in the committee room. Phitts swallowed a huge breath which he seemed unable to release. Washburn, his chin and eyebrows stretched in astonishment, stared uncomprehendingly at Chance.

"I'll just . . . shit in my pants," Wardman exclaimed.

"Forgeries?" Phitts repeated. "That's impossible!"

"I know my own business," declared Chance. "And these *are not* genuine."

"A very skillful try, Mr. Chance," Phitts said.

Chance announced slowly, "I swear that these are not accurate, in any way. This is *not* my signature. The 'T' is different at the base and the 'a' is not made in the same way that I make it." He returned a single document to his lawyer. "I am sure that my counsel, who has witnessed my signature thousands of times, will support me in this conclusion."

The lawyer nodded.

"Nor," continued Chance, "have I ever been invested, or entered into agreements as these papers would suggest."

"Mr. Chance," came Representative Washburn's voice, "this committee, protected as it is by the principle of Congressional immunity, has made a great many accusations here today. But one thing we have not done—and that is to honor our country's long tradition of law and fairness by allowing you to confront your accuser."

"This is not a courtroom," Phitts interjected. "The rules of trial do not apply here."

"A man's character has been assassinated," Washburn responded belligerently.

"A man," explained Phitts, "to whom, Representative Washburn, you are well known to have especially close connections. . . . I had hoped it would not be necessary, but, in view of your apparent wish to serve as an apologist for Mr. Chance, I think it is only fair to bring to the public's attention the fact that your own law practice is now, and for many years has been, heavily dependent upon the patronage of companies which are in Mr. Chance's control."

The fire in Washburn's eyes slowly dwindled as a look of hurt took possession of his face. "My law firm is in Cleveland," he replied. "And I have no knowledge whatsoever of its day-to-day affairs. It is, of course, true that, from time to time, my partners and I have represented the interests of Mr. Chance. But, I hasten to point out, we have more often represented those of his largest competitors: men who would stand to gain considerably were any action to be taken against him. And for you to insinuate that, as an elected member of Congress, I would allow such personal considerations to influence the manner in which I discharge my duty–"

"Offends you?" Phitts asked with heavy sarcasm.

"Every bit as much as it would offend the chair were I to suggest that you have called Mr. Chance here in order to fulfill a particularly vicious brand of family vendetta."

Phitts shivered for a moment. "Mr. Washburn," he began, "as I passed your blotter, did I notice, in its sleeve, a letter that had come to you from Mr. Chance?"

"You did. But it was not a personal letter. I shall read it to you if you like." He paused as he lifted the small paper closer to his eyes. "'Dear Representative Washburn: This is to advise the committee that, subsequent to the death of my wife, Elizabeth, in March of 1897, the assets listed in her name on records made before that year have been inherited by my daughter, daughter-in-law, and grandchildren. Yours very kindly.'" Washburn smiled, then squinted again at the square of Chance's stationery. "But to tell you the truth, Mr. Phitts, there is one thing about this letter that suddenly strikes me as significant . . . the signature! It does *not* match the signature on the evidence you entered just a few moments ago. Mr. Chance, you did sign this letter, did you not?"

"I did."

"I must admit, Mr. Chairman," said Washburn, "that this *is* the signature with which I am familiar, and not that on the purported documents."

"I can attest to the fact that Mr. Chance signed the letter to Representative Washburn," declared Chance's lawyer, "for he signed it in my presence."

"I see," said Charles Phitts, erasing some, but not all, of the puzzlement from his face. "I . . . am begin-ning . . . to *see*."

"Mr. Chairman," Washburn pressed, "as a member of this committee, I once again *demand* to know from what source the disputed evidence was obtained."

Phitts' voice was proud and severe. "From Mr. Chance's own people. From people in his own employ, who cannot, in conscience, tolerate his practices."

"I am afraid I must insist on having a name."

Phitts hesitated. "Arthur Forrest," he said at last.

"That's a lie—a terrible lie," Forrest called out, as Chance whirled suddenly around to face him.

"You received them directly from Mr. Forrest?" Washburn interrogated.

"Not directly. We received them through the service of a friend."

At that moment, Grainger rushed to Chance's side, and, whispering, opened a folder on the table in front of him.

"And, without further checking, you accepted this evidence from a self-proclaimed friend of one of Mr. Chance's assistants and presented it here as gospel," Washburn asked, "despite the fact that it now appears to have been forged?"

"It seemed an impeccable source," Phitts said.

There was a long silence.

"Excuse me, Mr. Chairman," Chance's lawyer interrupted. "With your permission, my client would like to make a statement with regard to those companies about which you questioned him earlier."

Phitts studied Chance's momentarily emotionless face. "Does he wish to change his testimony?" he asked cautiously.

"He wishes only to make a *brief* statement."

Phitts thought. "All right," he said. "You may make your statement, Mr. Chance."

Thomas Chance nodded, carefully took up two papers from the folder which Grainger had brought to him. "Lodestone Steel," he began deliberately. "Masley Shipbuilding. The Ferquer Line. G. J. Fownes, Glassworks. Hornpipe Explosives. I reiterate my sworn declaration that I have never owned stock in any of these concerns. Nor have I ever been an owner or principal in the Herbaceous Fruit Company of New York.

"Yet, inasmuch as the documents which suggested that I did were forged—a fact that will no doubt be proven to everyone's satisfaction as soon as the appropriate examinations can be made—I became curious to know more about these companies. I wanted to know what, if anything, they had in common. Just twenty minutes ago, I asked my assistant, Phillip Grainger, to find this out for me. And the answer proved so obvious that it did not require much time for him to secure it.

"When I was subpoenaed to testify here, I suspected that there might be certain personal motives on the part of a few members of the committee. And, therefore, I made inquiries of my own about *them*—in order to assess the danger to which I might be unfairly subject.

"In brief, I discovered in the course of these investigations that the chairman of this committee owns only two stocks in his own name. They are both very large and well-known firms. One is Fairnswirth Industries; the other, American Factory Supply. All very harmless until it is discovered that Fairnswirth Industries owns both Masley Shipbuilding and the Lodestone Steel Company, while American Factory Supply owns G. J. Fownes, the Ferquer Line of steamships, and, yes, even the Herbaceous Fruit Company of New York."

"This is ridiculous," cried Phitts. "Whatever few shares I own, I bought on the stock exchange, like anyone else. I don't pay any attention to the management of those companies. I don't know what businesses they own."

"You take their dividends."

"This is a travesty! You said yourself that the papers were forged."

"Those with my signature are forged," Chance responded complacently. "But I don't know about all of the others. Some look real enough to me." He smiled, his eyes glowing. "I see a payroll here for Fownes showing clear violations of child-labor laws, and Ferquer would appear to have negotiated illegal transport rates, though not with one of my companies. . . . How ironic that evidence deliberately forged and rushed before this committee to incriminate me should, in fact, incriminate you."

"Can't you see how preposterous it is, Mr. Chance, to compare me with yourself? Even if what you say is true, *I* am not responsible. I do not have any say in how these firms are run. Like working people all over the country, I try to save and invest the little I can, but our shares of these giant companies are so small as to be invisible to men like you."

"Oh, you may not control these companies outright, but you set their tone by your passivity."

"I could cite you for contempt," Phitts said.

"I have been slandered with false evidence. I should hope that would be enough for one day."

Phitts' stare penetrated Arthur Forrest, but the young man returned it coldly. "You have made a circus of these hearings, Mr. Chance," Phitts proceeded. "You have deliberately misled us with the sleight of hand for which you are much renowned. I suspect that you have deliberately plotted out this whole affair, that you knew the evidence had been forged because *you* had it forged in the first place and then saw to it that it made its way to us."

"No, but you were very careless when you got it, weren't you?" Chance said. "Careless with *my* reputation. Careless with the integrity of your own committee. All that mattered to you was that I be vanquished. That was your end. And you gave precious little thought to the means by which you would reach it."

"Perhaps for the moment," Phitts said, "you may succeed in forestalling the action that this government ought to be taking against you—and that, for the people of this country, is indeed a tragedy."

Chance smiled. "Let me tell you something, Congressman," he said. "Means are what the age-old struggle over ends has always been about. You might bend them to your purposes. You might even trample them in your zeal to get after *me*—"

"Because you and men like you are a scourge," Phitts interrupted. "Like the most virulent malignancy, you would consume everything in your sight. Possess everything. Destroy everything."

"And," Chance said, his voice rising, "when you had brought the whole of this mighty government low, to the level of an ordinary criminal, by forging, by lying, what would *you* be, Congressman Phitts? A king? I promise you, sir, the world has had enough of them."

"All your conjurer's tricks," Phitts shouted, "will not obscure the fact that certain large industrialists and financiers —you among them, Mr. Thomas Chance—have, for the last quarter century, been involved in a calculated plot to steal the . . . 'cow from the common' as my Irish grandfather used to say."

"At the same time," Chance replied, "that certain political and rabble-rousing demagogues have been attempting to steal the common out from under the cow. Why, to quote Mr. Roosevelt, 'I could carve out of a banana a figure with more spine then my adversaries have shown today.' "

"Your facile tongue does not fool anyone, sir. And I warn you to hold it, or face the consequences of insulting this House. No words can ever mask your abrogation of public responsibility, or the fact that you have squandered princely sums on yourself and your family while offering no Christian succor to anyone else." He paused to give weight to his point.

"Christ, if memory serves me, was a quiet man," said Chance.

"You are intentionally confusing the issue."

"No, Congressman. You are. You see, I was brought up, not as a rich man, to believe that good works are better carried out in private. *Quietly*. But, for the sake of my family's name, you force me, sir—"

Chance went on in a solemn voice, hesitant: "My son contracted a glandular disease some years back and died. If you had cared to look, Mr. Phitts, you would have found that an entire hospital and research facility has been established in his name. Indeed, they are soon to rise along two blocks of Riverside Drive in New York, as a memorial to Pope from his family . . . and at a cost to us of some ten or more million dollars."

Peter Parton swallowed hard enough to induce the hiccups. Laura gasped. Phitts shook his head.

"And we mean this merely as a first effort," Chance said. "With others to follow. Pope loved his fellow man. And we want to follow his example and share our good fortune."

"I think," said Congressman Washburn, when the excitement of the audience had quieted, "that we have all put you to quite enough trouble, Mr. Chance. And I move that we adjourn."

"Seconded," came another voice.

"All in favor?" asked Phitts in a voice that was worn now. "All against? Then, it's unanimous."

Half of the partisan crowd swelled up around Chance as Phitts and his other enemies drifted back to its fringes. Among the fog of pipe and cigar smoke, the shouting and laughter, Chance found himself next to Arthur Forrest, and, in the faint light of the windowless room, noticed that the young man's face was sweaty. Neither man made a sign of recognition. Tom took his hand, pressed and shook it.

Keeping a distance between them, they walked on until they had come out of the yellow smoke into the long, stone, frescoed corridor that led to the rotunda; then, as the traffic parted around them, Arthur asked: "Was everything all right?"

"Fine. Fine," Tom replied. "And thank you very, very much. You did a hell of a job. You really had them fooled!"

CHAPTER

36

"MAY THE *fourth*?" FRANCES ASKED SUDDENLY. "IT CANNOT possibly be May the *fourth*."

Tom smiled. "Well, it is," he replied. "May fourth, nineteen hundred and ten."

"This is the third night we've come out looking for this blasted thing," Frances said. "And I know we didn't come out on the first, because of the rain, so, I suppose you *are* right."

They were arranged, like figures in a Glackens cityscape, on a green and private bank of the Hudson, just above One Hundredth Street, waiting, in the first minutes past sunset, as the funneling dusk grew purple, for Halley's Comet to appear.

"Tonight's the night it's been predicted," Laura said.

"Really?" said Arthur Forrest.

"That's what I heard."

"Not by Halley," said Tom. "He only gave the year."

"Who was Halley?" Eliot asked.

"Sir Edmund Halley," Tom told him. "He was an English astronomer two centuries ago. He was a friend of Sir Isaac Newton's and, on the basis of Newton's mathematics, he was the first man ever to predict the return of a comet."

"Also the first to catalogue all the stars in the Southern Hemisphere," added Arthur Forrest.

"When did he predict it would come?" Eliot inquired.

"Every seventy-six years or so," Tom answered. "He saw the comet in 1682 and realized that it had to be the same comet that had come in 1607 and, before that, in 1531, and—"

"Honestly, Dad, your memory," Laura exclaimed. "I never cease to marvel at it."

"Especially when it comes to numbers," Frances said. "He's seventy years old and I know, for a fact, that he can remember the price of . . . well, a theater ticket on the night we last saw a comet."

Tom glowed as the last wisp of cotton candy spread across the sky. "Twenty cents," he said. "At the Old Drury in Baltimore."

Frances's hand covered his and pressed it into the grass. "That was 1861," she reminisced. "What lives we've lived since then! So many people have come and gone and we're still here. Every night I get down on my knees and thank the good Lord for that. Charles Phitts rose, lost an election, and fell. Roosevelt's come and gone. They all seemed so important in their time, but they weren't really."

"I won't say I miss Phitts, or T.R.," Chance replied. "But there *are* people who have gone who are important to me still."

Frances's face, so white and proudly lined beneath its layers of powder, was arranged into an expression of extraordinary tenderness. "I didn't mean Pope," it said silently. "Nor Elizabeth either."

"One thing I'm glad of," Chance said, "is that Katharine's happy now. And Anne-Marie and Giselle. I suppose they'll probably marry soon, have children of their own, and I'll be, what, a great-grandfather! When I can still remember the price of a ticket in Baltimore and a good deal before that!" He smiled.

"You see how time goes," Laura said. "It's been five years since she went back to Edmond."

"*Five* years since he came back here for her?" Frances asked, astounded.

"A few months more than that," Laura told her.

Chance's eye wandered up the sky dome, as if, for a transitory moment, it had been compelled there by a star. "The fabulous thing about this comet," he remarked, "is that Kathy can see it in Paris, Roosevelt in Oyster Bay; we can see it here. And perhaps they can even see it in heaven." He smiled cunningly. "Maybe a little piece of it could even fall on Phitts."

Eliot laughed politely. Being fourteen, he found himself at once absorbed and bewildered by the soft and erotic senses of the night: the spermatozoic aroma of the fresh-mown grass, the warm and dew-drenched air, the breeze. He stared beyond the dim reflections of the river at the long, thin horizon of western light. Embarrassed by his true thoughts, he asked: "What is a comet, really?"

"Mostly gases," Tom said.

"Yes," Frances added. "That's all. A comet is not an omen of anything terrible, despite what they say."

"Next year," Tom said, "when you're up at Groton with Dr. Peabody, you'll be able to learn a good deal about comets —about all the planets and stars."

"I hope so."

"Astronomy is a very important part of one's education, Eliot."

"Did they teach it when you went to school, Grandfather?"

Tom smiled. "They did."

"To be honest about it, what I most want to learn about is banking."

"That will come afterward."

"At college."

"Even after that. When you have finished at Princeton, and during your summers, of course—"

"Grandfather"—Eliot spoke into the older man's pause—

"my father went to Harvard, didn't he? And Uncle Arthur and Uncle Phillip. Why can't I go there?" For a moment, he studied Grainger and Forrest as if to discern from their outward appearances the answer to his question.

"Harvard has changed, Eliot," Tom said. "Men like Roosevelt have changed it."

Eliot nodded his acceptance, at least temporarily, of this truth. "I was talking to Uncle Phillip, Grandfather," he announced after a pause, "about the early banks. About Alexander Hamilton and—"

Tom stared at him suddenly, the power of his eyes undiminished by the dark. "When you want to know anything about banks, Eliot, in the future you are to come to me. Do you understand?"

"Yes, sir."

"Oh, my God," Frances called out loudly. "There it is! Look, all of you! Look, Tom! Look at its . . . e-nor-mous tail. I wonder where it's come from. I wonder where a comet goes . . . between its visits here."

CHAPTER

37

ELIOT COULD NOT ARTICULATE WHY, BUT, DURING HIS SECOND year at Groton, Harvard, as an idea, began to cool in his breast. Perhaps proximity had been the cause, or his grandfather's strictures against it. He had, like almost every boy in his form, made as many forays into Cambridge as had been permitted, lingering for hours over one of Bailey's fruit and chocolate sundaes, or standing by the ornate subway kiosk in the square, studying the legs of town and college girls as they hurried down to, or up from, the trains. At the sight of a Porcellian tie, or a plush gray Varsity letter, something invisible still raced in his blood, for he was at a time in his life when gods came down to earth disguised as upperclassmen. But, the more he considered the matter, the less drawn he felt to Harvard's iron New England soul. Although it was his father's alma mater, it seemed to him too large, serious, urban, and exigent—too much of the world. And what little he knew of Yale (largely bits of doggerel about its secret societies and Midas touch; more than half of it from the older brother of a roommate) impressed him similarly. They were slick tracks, designed to carry those with definite ambitions to professional success in the great Eastern cities; and, only partly because he had seen that glittering prize firsthand, he was not sure he wanted it.

Eliot was a sensitive boy with his father's fair hair, fine

brow, and brilliant smile; by the age of sixteen, he had begun to come into his own. To his clean looks, a sudden animal quality had been added, as if, at the last moment, nature had decided to bestow upon him yet another present. Over a single summer, his height shot up to an inch over six feet, his biceps doubled their size, his legs acquired a new and frightening speed, and, most startling of all, he grew into his eyes. Those moist, green symbols of his curiosity, no less penetrating or compelling than they had always been, became a little more hidden as he moved toward manhood, deeper in color, less rambunctious, more introspective.

Women—of his own age and considerably more—responded at once to this ripening, but Eliot invariably stepped back from their advances, no matter how slight. He surprised himself by doing so, for he liked and wanted them as much, he suspected, as any man could. Sometimes tame, occasionally wild, always lithe and naked, they romped through his fantasies, day and night. But that was the only part of his life to which he dared admit them; he could not deal with them in the flesh.

He understood that he possessed virtually every gift that more average men believed would make them happy. But he was not content to bask in the sun of youth, beauty, charm, or fortune. For, at heart, he had become a melancholy boy, prone to dwell not on the beauty of a thing or season, but upon its essential impermanence. Without ever having known his father, he had nonetheless felt Pope's presence and, by it, the imminence of death. Thus, when he looked toward the future that schoolmasters forever insisted was bright, he saw, as often as not, a sudden end to his very being, and reordered his values accordingly.

Thus, when the day came to enroll at Princeton, he was glad of the long pastures, the bright azaleas, the scent of subterranean springs; he was especially pleased about the distance which separated the gothic spires of this bucolic township from the life of New York, New Haven, and Boston.

Tom had told him, "Princeton is an altogether different thing from Harvard or Yale. The prevailing wind is from the south."

"I've been told that," Eliot had replied. "And yet I know at least a dozen boys from Groton who are headed there with me. And another two from Hotchkiss . . ."

"Moses Pyne's a friend of mine," Tom had interrupted. "And I've known quite a number of the men who built that place: Moses is the big fish, though."

"I thought I might go on a little way in mathematics, Grandfather."

"By all means do," Tom had said automatically. "Charles McKim, that's who I was trying to think of. He designed a number of their buildings. He also designed my house in New York. I guess you knew that."

"I think I did," Eliot had said. "It's not that I have a great desire to be a mathematician, but there's something about the solitude you have when you're working out a problem that I enjoy. I must confess, I'm looking forward to the quiet of being out there in the country."

"It's a gentleman's place," Tom had said. "I remember when they became a university, it must be fifteen years ago now, professors came from all over the world and lectured there. Pyne, himself, will be damned if he doesn't turn it into another Oxford. And he's made a good start with his architecture. He told me himself that he is positive that it all starts with the buildings, and if you get those right—"

Eliot had smiled.

"I'll give you some advice, Eliot: 'You'll be fine in this world if you travel with just three things: a clever mind, a sound discipline, and a good English wardrobe.' You'll probably want to play football and join the Ivy Club."

Eliot's eyes rolled up toward the ceiling. "By the way," he had offered, "the suits arrived from London. Thank you."

"Within limits," Tom had said, "I think you should get used to the idea of being a Chance. Too many young people grow up without any idea of who they really are. Then, when it all comes upon them suddenly, they're unprepared."

Eliot shared rooms at Number 16 University Place with a Grotonian from Philadelphia and two Baltimore men. One of the Baltimore men had "prepped" at Lawrenceville, the other at Gilman and, among every class, both had a wide circle of friends. The Lawrenceville boy, who had chipped a corner from his front tooth on the first day of tryouts for the freshman team, bore the name of Philander Ober. He had an even nature that Eliot admired. Extremely bookish and terribly farsighted, Philander had an attractiveness that transcended an otherwise banal appearance. He was an accomplished dancer and a legend at lacrosse, and because no arena seemed too imposing for his confidence, Eliot decided to be like him.

One afternoon the two of them were standing in the shadow of the great Tower, dressed, as all freshmen were required to be, in black shoes, black ties, corduroy trousers without cuffs, and "dinks." Philander had a book under his arm. He smiled, turned a full three hundred and sixty degrees and, spotting no one, removed the "dink" from his head and gave his hair a light wave of his hand. "It's getting too cold for anyone to stay out of doors," he said. "Look. Do sit down. I've got to read you something."

"Not until you put your 'dink' back on," Eliot said. "You know the rules as well as I do. We'll be 'beaten up individually and collectively by the entire sophomore class.' "

"Too timid for words," Philander said. "But, if you insist, I will. Although only because this *thing* I'm about to read you is as good as it is."

"What is it, for heaven's sake?"

"You've heard of Rupert Brooke?"

"Never," Eliot replied.

"He's a young English poet. A good deal older than we are, of course. Ten years at the least."

"So?"

"So, he's wonderful. Listen, Eliot:

'But there's wisdom in women, of more
than they have known,
And thoughts go blowing through them,
are wiser than their own.'

"It's marvelous, isn't it?" Philander said. "Let me read you one more thing:

'Breathless, we flung us on the windy
hill
Laughed in the sun, and kissed the
lovely grass.' "

"Well, it's very good," Eliot said. "But it has a kind of sadness to it, doesn't it, being in the past tense?"

"I never really thought about it that way," Philander said.

"Well, don't start, because it won't make you very happy."

"That's the best part of being our age, Eliot. All the wonderful things are in the future. All the terrible things too, but so far away that it doesn't really matter."

"Do you know who Sally Hammond is?" Eliot asked suddenly.

Philander smiled broadly. "*Every*one knows who Sally Hammond is," he said.

"But have you met her?" Eliot pressed.

"I'd like to," Philander said.

"Then you can go in my place."

"Go where?" Philander asked.

"McAuliffe and some of his friends have 'invited her over,' " Eliot told him.

"Gilman friends?" Philander asked.

"A few. And one St. Marker," Eliot replied.

"If I didn't know better, I'd say she frightened you a little," Philander remarked shrewdly.

"You don't know better. And she does." Eliot hesitated. "Phil—" he began.

"I won't put you on, the answer is no. Have you?" Philander asked.

"I've had the chance a few times."

"I knew that the moment I saw you," Philander said.

"But I'm . . . waiting, as they say."

"Aren't we all! McAuliffe, of course, would lay anything in a skirt."

"Or say he had," Eliot said.

"No. I'll have to admit that he's not a liar when it comes to that. Last Friday, when you had gone into New York, he had two in the same night. He has a very creaky box spring, so you can imagine the effect the whole thing had on me. But he doesn't think a thing about it."

"Where'd they come from?" Eliot asked. "Were they hideous?"

"One was quite pretty in an ordinary sort of way," Philander said.

"Were you jealous?" Eliot asked.

"Too much of what I learned in Chapel rubbed off on me for that," Philander replied. "Well, a little jealous, naturally. But not enough to bother me. Were you thinking about taking a crack at Sally Hammond?"

"In a weaker moment."

"Don't. You can do better than that by far. She's all right for McAuliffe. But, then, he's a totally amoral character and you're not."

"No, but I am a male, aged eighteen and—"

"As you said," Philander interrupted, "you've had the chance a few times. Look, I'll make you a deal—if you don't decide to stick around for the party with Sally, come out with the group of us. My friend Fitzgerald that I told you about, and some men from the *Lit* and the Clio Society."

Eliot smiled.

They dined that night at the Kenilworth, filling their stomachs with cheap, fatty tips of beef served beneath a thick and nearly congealed gravy, then retired to the juniors' rooms in Holder. Two bottles of Kentucky bourbon appeared at once from the bottom drawer of one of the university's desks, and an urgent search for six glasses was begun. The older among them appropriated the various couches and overstuffed, velveteen chairs, while the freshmen arranged themselves on the worn Oriental carpet. In fifteen minutes, the last of them felt a slight "buzz" descend upon him. Within half an hour, they were drunk.

A blond freshman with an exquisitely patrician profile sat between Eliot and the fireplace. This was Scott Fitzgerald. "I've written a story for the Nassau *Lit*," Fitzgerald told him. "I'm also writing songs for the Triangle. What relation are you to Thomas Chance?"

"My grandfather," Eliot said.

"Isn't that something," Fitzgerald said. "Do you want to be a financial man too?"

"I guess this is a room of writers," Eliot said.

". . . without their ladies," Fitzgerald added.

Eliot paused, reclined thoughtfully against the side panel of a bookcase. "I don't know what I want to do with my life," he told Fitzgerald. "But I want to be more than just another young gentleman in a bank."

"You already are," said Philander.

"Say," said Fitzgerald, "did you go to Lucy Paine's party in Westbury? It was just before school started, in early September."

"Yes," said Eliot. "It was swell. Were you there?"

"No," replied Fitzgerald. "But that's what I heard."

"Math-ematics!" a sophomore from the *Lit* exclaimed suddenly. "Chance, is that *true*? How can you pos-sibly keep your soul in math-ematics?"

Eliot blushed. "It was just a passing fancy," he said. "I don't imagine that I could."

"I think you may be an artist at heart," Philander told him.

Eliot's face rose into a smile. "I read *Endymion* after you gave it to me," he said. "And all the time I was thinking: I'd like to be immortal like that."

Scott Fitzgerald laughed pleasantly. "You may have too much money," he said.

CHAPTER

38

Spring 1917.

Eliot awoke in a stupor, stale of breath, and still in his evening clothes. Outside the leaded windows of his bedroom in Blair, dawn hid behind a nearby ridge and battlement. It was bitterly cold and, as he became conscious, Eliot realized that there was no blanket covering his chest. Currents of wind leaked through the broken panes and casements, sliding along the surface of his shirt and jacket on their way to escaping out the open door and flue. Almost reflexively, he reached toward the blanket and sheet that were bundled just below his waist and began to tug them toward his neck.

Then, with the side of his wrist, he suddenly touched something he had not expected. It felt to be a large object and, after a moment, he drew himself up and saw that it was a young woman. She, too, was dressed for a party, in a subdued pink gown whose straps had come down from her shoulders. He studied her carefully, smiled. Only then did he realize that his right arm was asleep, pinioned beneath her head. With care not to wake her, he proceeded to free himself, then bring the cover up around them both; and he had gotten it as far as their breasts when, all at once, he hesitated. He looked at her eyes. Their lids were closed into a tight squint. Her breathing was slow and even and, impulsively, Eliot kissed her on the cheek.

Then he gazed out the window and around the room. But he soon brought his hands back to the woman, kissed her lips, her neck, caressed her sides, trying to decide whether or not he should undress her. Blair Hall was quiet in the early morning hours: no sound of footsteps in the stairwell outside his apartment; no purr of conversation; no outbursts of laughter. He heard only the drip of a bathroom faucet and, behind it, the slow, murmurous rippling of water. He ran his hand along his own collar, removing the small brass button that had begun to choke him. Then he lay his head back on his pillow, gazed at the now-bright ceiling, and considered what he should do. The girl slept soundlessly; occasionally, he thought from the cold, she would twitch faintly and cuddle closer against his side. He waved the long reddish hair away from her eyes and unfastened the top hook at the back of her gown. There were three more catches below it and he had undone them all and begun on her corset when a great splashing sound came from his bathroom. "Holy shit!" Robin McAuliffe exclaimed.

Eliot brought the covers quickly up to their chins, but the woman had drunk too much to be easily awakened.

"Jesus Christ!" McAuliffe said. Eliot could hear the water as it rose and fell over the smooth porcelain side of the tub, could visualize the puddles it would make. McAuliffe stormed immediately into Eliot's room, still dripping, completely naked, with a partially soaked copy of *The New York Times* in the grip of both hands. He paused momentarily at the sight of the woman. "She asleep?" he asked.

"Yes," Eliot said.

"Good. Look at this—"

Eliot yawned. "Read it to me," he said. "I still have sand in my eyes."

"I don't think I've ever had a redhead," Robin said parenthetically. "And maybe I won't ever have one. Listen, Eliot, there's going to be a war. I'm more sure of it than I've ever been. They've found this thing called the 'Zimmerman

Note.' It's a dispatch from the German Foreign Minister, named Zimmerman, of course, to President Carranza, or something like that, of Mexico. And the fucking Kraut has the gall to offer them Arizona, New Mexico, and Texas if they'll ally with the Central Powers in a war against us. We ought to go in and kill the bastards and get the whole thing over with once and for all."

"I'm afraid you're right," Eliot said.

"I am right. We'll be at war by Easter."

"Will you volunteer?"

"In a minute," McAuliffe said. "There's nothing I'd like better than to get a shot at a few of them. Ever since they sank the *Lusitania*, I've felt that way. And how long can it take once we get into the picture? Couple of months, that's all."

"If you're so eager and confident," Eliot said, "why didn't you go with the British two years ago, like Philander did?"

"Philander's dead," Robin said.

Eliot paused, stared at him coldly. "If you're right, we shall all be dead—probably."

"Then you *won't* volunteer?" Robin asked.

"Of course, I will. I'm already drilling in Professor Root's unit. It's just that I don't relish war, Robin, the way you do."

"Who's the girl, anyway?" Robin asked. "I always knew that, sooner or later, you—"

"Her brother's in Cottage. I met her last night at the winter dance. We had a little too much champagne and . . . I didn't even know she'd come back here with me until this morning."

"I was going to say, it's not your style."

Eliot grinned. "Does that mean that you would like me to get up and invite you to hop in the sack?"

Robin thought for a moment. "No," he said. "In times like these one must think of his fellow man. And you need her more than I do. I'll see you at Ivy at lunch—but, for God's sake, Eliot, get her name."

Eliot slipped out of bed a few moments after Robin had left. He made his way to the bath, where he first relieved himself of the liquid consumed the previous night, then brushed his teeth. The floor was covered with a thin surface of sudsy water and he spread a small towel in front of the sink where he stood. He undressed completely, smiled into the mirror, and took his boar-bristle brush to his hair. Carrying the pile of suit, shirt, stockings and underwear, he crept back into his bedroom; but the girl was awake when he got there.

Her head was back. She was wiping her eyes. "Good Lord!" she said when her world returned to focus. "What's going on?"

"I've been awake for half an hour," Eliot said. "I rather thought—"

"Did I fall asleep in your room?" she asked. "Was I here *all* night?"

"Apparently you *were*."

She paused as she felt the looseness of her gown. For a moment her face was utterly without expression, then it grew more severe, then less, until the whole of it was consumed by the humor of the moment. "Why, Eliot Chance," she said. "Were you going to seduce me? Is that why you are naked as a jaybird and I'm—apparently—about to be?" She raised one strap of her gown back onto her shoulder. "And you were going on just last night about how you had no interest in purely physical affairs. All that poetry about perfect love." She laughed. "But, poor Eliot, *not* in the morning, dear. That's not romantic at all. I loved you last night, of course, but that was different. Right now, my mouth is parched from the wine. And I'm a . . . mess . . . and I'd better get out of here, hadn't I, before I'm caught and you're expelled."

A week before the April fourth declaration of war on the German Empire, Eliot lunched with his grandfather in the great egg-shaped dining room of the Ritz-Carlton Hotel.

"I've had a letter from Hawes and Curtis," Tom said, "informing me that you have asked them to cut you an American officer's uniform." He breathed heavily, brought the painted chair nearer the table, away from the potted fern. "Of all the damned fool things!"

"I've applied to take the examination for a commission, Grandfather."

"I suppose you're hell-bent for the mosquito fleet."

"I don't know. I know I don't believe that it's simply a question of rivalry among kings, or even one of economics. I don't believe that the war is being fought over colonies, either. I'm afraid, Grandfather, that I believe the 'Hun is at the gate,' as Mr. Kipling said."

"It's out of the question," Tom replied. "War in poetry is one thing. War in fact is quite another."

"I appreciate that."

"Impossible," the elder said, gesturing to the luxury surrounding him. "You've grown up with this all your life."

The waiter fluttered by, obsequious to the famous older man who, though wrinkled, was still lean, still flat in the stomach.

"Please don't make it sound as if I were glad there's a war going on over there. I'm sure that some people may be, but, believe me, I'm not one of them."

"I should hope that my own grandson would have more sense than that. But life is very precious, Eliot. I know that belief barely has meaning anymore, but it's just as true as ever. And there are times in life when you have to be . . . well, *practical,* if you are going to survive. Do you understand me?"

"I think so."

The two sets of eyes, exquisitely matched, stared into one another. The older man's were darker, more passionate; the younger's finer, more feminine—even, despite their age, less energetic.

"Each man," Tom continued, "has two identities, I've always thought. The first is as his father's son, the second as his son's father. And one of the times when we are most susceptible to problems, Eliot, is when we are between those two. You, of all people, have so much to look forward to. You haven't known what it is to fall in love yet, to find a woman. You haven't known what it is to build something up with your hands and brain and see it grow along the course that you set for it."

"No," Eliot answered abstractedly. "But perhaps I've known a different sort of love. I'm really not at all sure that what, or whom, one loves is important as long as one feels love within himself."

"Wrong," declared Tom. "Maybe while you're young enough to go around like a male animal, that kind of thinking will do. But after that, it's the other person. Which just proves how much of life you've yet to go through and what a tragedy it would be if—"

Eliot studied his grandfather as the old man twisted his body on the velvet cushion and began to spoon his soup.

"In war, Eliot," Tom explained, "people's limbs are torn from them. You will meet a fellow. He will become your *best* friend. And then, suddenly, his blood will gush out of him: like this." He turned the handle of his spoon so that the clear turtle broth poured noisily back into the half-full bowl.

Eliot paused. "I'm sorry," he said at last. "Truly, Grandfather."

"Grainger and Forrest are snakes," Chance announced out of the blue. "But I'm old now, on borrowed time; my reflexes are going. I won't be able to protect you too much longer."

"Then fire them," Eliot said.

"It's not as simple as that," Chance said. "It's not so easy to train someone to know the way you think, to know your business."

"The war won't last forever. God willing, I'll be home by Christmas."

A mist came to Tom's eyes. "Promise me," he begged. "Promise God."

Immediately after Eliot had submitted his final examination paper, without awaiting the ceremonial conferring of degrees, he stored his furniture and wardrobe in the attic of his grandfather's New York house and headed to Fort Leavenworth, Kansas, for officer's training. There, briefly, he encountered an old acquaintance from Ivy.

"It's a funny thing," the young man told him. "You get into one group in your life and the same people keep popping up all through it."

"Don't they?" Eliot said.

"Do you know, Chance, I'm afraid it may not be for that much longer. It's a ghastly time to be alive."

"I know what you mean." Eliot smiled. "We should have been born in the British upper classes, been too young to serve in the Crimean War, and died in our sleep the night before the Archduke was assassinated."

The young man thought for a moment. "Exactly!" he said.

Eliot sailed for Europe in October, ten days after an Austro-German drive had broken through the Italian lines at Caporetto. The Italians had retreated. The French had failed to retake the offensive. The English had seen more than a hundred thousand men massacred at Ypres. At that moment, when Eliot landed at Cherbourg, the whole of Europe seemed to depend for its survival upon the American forces of which he was a part. His brigade was dispatched to relieve the exhausted Englishmen of Haig's army at La Fere, and when Field Marshal Ludendorff opened an attack in March, he retreated with them back to Armentières. The spring sun, exposed by the clouds, settled on them as they walked, raised their sweat through their pores, brought the aroma of new grass toward them in wonderful, fleeting whiffs.

They carried their wounded on stretchers, or supported

between the shoulders of exhausted men. Whenever they were available, ambulances were used to withdraw the badly hurt to Paris, but, as the Germans advanced, this became all but impossible. Disease was everywhere: in the trenches, on the marches, in their camps. The Central Powers were the enemy, but no less so were influenza and typhoid, dysentery and gangrene. Staphylococci multiplied in the crowded, improvised operating and recovery rooms, and in the wards. Streptococci grew in the throats and nasal canals of soldiers on both sides of battle. And there were no antibiotics.

Eliot, marching beside a thin and black-haired Scotsman as their company passed an undisturbed field of April flowers, heard the man ask: "What's that?"

"The flower or the smell?" Eliot asked.

"Aren't they one and the same?"

"Hyacinth," Eliot said.

"My grandmother used to have it in her garden," the man said. It was plain from his tone that he was getting to something.

"*My* grandfather too," Eliot added.

"They're moving closer and closer to Paris. Every day they take a little more ground. I had a long leave in Paris last year. I hate to see them take it."

"It's the Russians' fault," Eliot said. "Ever since they signed the treaty with the Kaiser, he's been free to concentrate his men and guns on the western front."

"He's a damn fool, too," the Scotsman said. "He'll have three divisions at the Channel ports and they'll strike him right in the heart. So much for the treaty of Brest-Litovsk!"

"I'm not so sure," Eliot told him. "I wouldn't be surprised if the Germans had encouraged the revolution in the first place."

"But the Kaiser's no Marxist. And there's no love lost between the Germans and the Bear."

"I hear we may be going south," Eliot said.

"It won't make any difference if we don't get more troops. Look around you!"

"When we first got here," Eliot went on, "everyone was saying that this was a new kind of war. No more trenches. No more fixed positions and 'going over the top.' The Frenchmen taught us *la guerre de la manoeuvre,* and it was common knowledge that Ludendorff must have been mad not to keep his men sitting because, once they were up on the ground, we could take them out with a few men. I believed that then, but now I'm not so sure."

"That's what they told us," the Scotsman agreed. "Did you hear where in the south, Leftenant?"

"All the way to Cantigny, I heard. But it may have been a rumor."

"No," the Scotsman said. "Not since the bloody Germans' Big Bertha shelled that Paris church Good Friday."

"Do all the men know about that?"

"Your whole platoon. You can't keep secrets in a war, Leftenant."

"Shit. They haven't even *lived* yet and–"

"You Yanks were such a jolly bunch once. All your songs. 'Mademoiselle from Armentières' . . ."

"Yes." Eliot reflected. "Once we were like a children's crusade."

The Scotsman said, "The nearer they push us to Paris, the nearer we get to some of the best women in the world. If I'm going to die, I'd like to have one more night in a good woman's bed. I'd like to have just one night and do everything right."

Eliot turned and looked into the faces of the men who marched in double formation behind him. "I'll bet you half of these kids are virgins," he whispered.

"Why do you call them 'kids,' Leftenant, when you're only a kid yourself? How old are you?"

"Twenty-one."

"That's what I would have guessed."

"And you?"

"Three years older."

"Have you had a lot of women?"

"Yes. I can't lie." The Scotsman smiled.

"That's good." Eliot hesitated.

"You are a fine-looking man, Leftenant. I'm sure that you have had your share."

"No," Eliot said abstractedly. "Until recently, I always believed in the future."

Eliot escaped from the fighting at Chateau-Thierry in May with only the red mark of a powder burn above his waist. Then, during the long rest of the German forces, he waited with the First Division, poised for the Seine River, recuperating from the defeats of the spring. The sun was high over France by that time. Daylight lasted until nearly nine o'clock; dusk for forty-five minutes after that. The stench of disinfectant rose from the stations where men relieved themselves of waste. When there was no disinfectant, and no time to bury the dead, the smell was enough to make even a strong man hold his breath for as long as it took him to finish his business.

On July fifteenth, 1918, Reinhardt's shock troops attacked on either side of Rheims and, for two days, it seemed that nothing would stand in the way of their drive to the Seine. Their mortar exploding a hundred yards ahead of them, renting the still, summery air as their grenades broke upon scant resistance, the Germans seized their objectives a full day ahead of their own battle plan.

On the eighteenth, the American First, with French and Scottish troops, launched a counterattack at Soissons. Eliot's brigade was assigned to the right flank and his platoon was given the mission of destroying a German machine-gun position that fired onto the attack road from behind a hill. The "hill" was actually no more than a gentle mound when approached from the road, but, in back, it sloped acutely down to the bed of a stream. The long days of hot weather had parched the stream, dried and cracked the mud of its bank and, between it and the guns, there was the natural camouflage of a grove of birch trees.

Eliot, in the dark, using short, silent hand signals that were only visible to his men because of the moonlight, directed three soldiers to the point at the base of the mound nearest the Allies. To the Germans, he reasoned, this would seem the most probable route of assault; once fire had commenced, they would be inclined to fire back with everything they had. The terrified doughboys, waiting anxiously to open their rounds, wondering whether the Germans' eyes were already bearing down on them through the sights of their guns, lay in the high grass of a pasture, chewing reed after reed, until they heard the sudden high call of a great auk. That was their signal, given by the blond corporal from California who could "do" any bird and who had decided upon the great auk for "reasons of safety"—because it was extinct.

The men fired two rounds, charging against the German guns, which immediately turned on them. A weak searchlight shone from the German position; it rotated slowly, so that the path of its beam could be predicted. The doughboys scurried to avoid it, always firing, until they came to the wide coils of barbed wire. Lying prone, one soldier fired and another reloaded, while the third worked the wire cutters.

On the other side, Eliot led twelve men in two groups of six in a forked assault. The declining moon exaggerated their shadows, throwing their long, spiky shapes toward the machine-gun position. They moved in stealth until they were no more than thirty yards from the Germans. Then, one at a time, silently, they began to crawl. The land, though dry, felt cold against their stomachs and shins as they maneuvered over it. Among the blades of grass, pebbles and larger rocks, shells and shrapnel—remnants of earlier battles—tore at their fatigues and skin. The men bit their lips to contain the pain.

Eliot glanced at the half dozen men beside and behind

him, then at Jon Katt, a private from North Dakota. Jon's square jaw was growling. Eliot signaled the boy with a quick flag of his arm and Katt, who had pitched for his high school only three months before, pulled the pin on his grenade, stood, and hurled it toward the Germans.

Now, together, the dozen opened fire.

"Charge!" cried Eliot.

"Murder the goddamn bastards," Katt cried.

"Kill!" called a soldier from the other flank.

"*Kill*!" came the chorus.

The German sergeant turned two guns on his rear, spraying the land from the close-in areas out. The remaining guns stayed on the three who had cut through the barbed wire, but the searchlight rotated a complete three hundred sixty degrees on its turret. When the light fell onto Eliot and the Californian, they dug their faces into the earth, swallowed, and counted to five. By that time it had come round to the three in front, and found the youngest. Sensing the touch of the light on the back of his neck, as if by some mysterious antennae, the boy looked up and gasped before the bullets pumped into his neck and chest.

Of the men, including Eliot, who were closing in on the enemy, three were dead, two were wounded, and one, shot in the groin, was howling as he died. Katt's throwing arm hung limp, all but amputated by the rounds that had perforated it at the socket.

Eliot was coming over the guns now. Teeth clenched, feet spaced, his upper torso balanced on his knees, he held his own carbine breast-high in front of him, emptying its barrel. Four of his men appeared from the other flank, fanned out so that, with the two survivors of the original attack, they had the enemy caught in a circle.

But even surrounded, the Germans fought. There had been five of them, Eliot could see, but only two had lasted. They spun their guns as they fired. They were young men, cotton-haired, one tall, one short.

For a moment he shot simply to wound, but the Germans shot to kill, and soon he did the same. The skirmish blazed for five minutes. Finally, the Californian hit the shorter German in the abdomen, but as the soldier fell he triggered a grenade and bowled it down the slope. At first, his action had gone unnoticed by the Americans, but when Katt saw the black sphere coming toward him he cried out and the men rushed to either side. Eliot, pulling Katt by his good arm, missed the central force of the explosion by several lengths, but shrapnel flew and an arrow-like piece of it impacted his skull, tore an inch of hair root and flesh from above his right ear, fractured his mastoid, and knocked him unconscious, only thirty seconds before the final German surrendered.

CHAPTER 39

AT SEVENTY-EIGHT, THOMAS CHANCE WAS STILL SPRY, BUT, against his will, he was being forced to relinquish his hold on life. His sight was as fine as it had been when he was a boy. His gait was slower, yet untroubled by such a limp as most of his contemporaries possessed. His hearing was acute, even across distances which seemed to dim sounds for younger men. But his heart was weak. Often he could hear it. Always he could feel it, the rhythmic thuds recalling for him the mighty fall of a ship upon the sea.

In succession, he had begun to put the varied houses of his life in order. And even as death, like a delicate presence, hung in the atmosphere, he thought out the future of each of his enterprises, possessions, and heirs. It was as if he had returned through a long-forgotten gate of his childhood, for the act of making these plans required him to imagine the world in which Eliot would live.

He arranged for his house to become the centerpiece of a new museum; for his farm to become a school. He poured two hundred carats of rubies and three hundred of diamonds into each of two velvet bags, marked them "Anne-Marie" and "Giselle," and placed them into Katharine's hands for safekeeping. Paintings suddenly came down from damasked walls, revealing squares of deep unfaded fabric. Lawrence's *François Napoleon* was crated and prepared for future shipment to the de Fontainville chateau in Brie. Rembrandt's pen-and-bistre view of Bruges made its way into storage and waited there for Eliot's return. A much-petticoated Gainsborough lady replaced the second mirror in Frances's dressing room. Horses were sold or given to Miss Houghton's Academy. Carriages were donated to The New York Coaching Club for preservation in Westchester County. The books were catalogued, oiled at their spines; a prized few, including an early *David Copperfield* and a marble-backed script of *The Tempest* from Tom's days as an actor, were boxed, sealed, and wrapped for his grandson.

So, too, were his corporations gathered in, their once deliberately labyrinthine structures reconstructed into shapes more comprehensible to those outside. The Clayton Antitrust Act of 1914 and the United States government's successful suit against Standard Oil had, some time ago, suggested to Tom the advisability of establishing a public market for most of the shares he owned. Rockefeller, he recalled, had been forced by the courts into just such a step, with the ironic result that the bull market's appetite for Standard stock had more than doubled its value within a week. With extreme furtiveness, Tom therefore merged most of his smaller firms into one combine.

"My idea," he explained to Phillip Grainger—ironically, for it was the very day the shrapnel tore into Eliot—is that all of the shipping, shipbuilding, and drydocking companies, including the tropical railroads, will be merged. No more separate names. Everything, from here on, will be known as Chance Maritime. We will keep approximately sixty percent of the stock and offer the balance on the Exchange. Eliot, on my death, will inherit all of that sixty percent. That way, he will enjoy the luxury of not having to run the company if he doesn't want to."

"Very well," Grainger said.

Chance looked up. "It's not an equitable division, but it *is* a sensible one." He studied Phillip's reaction. "After me, Eliot will be the only living Chance, and this is the sort of thing that was always done in his grandmother's family. Katharine has already received a good deal of cash, and I'm going to leave her some very fine real estate as well. Then I have two small railroads that I want to give to Anne-Marie and Giselle."

"You want to take them out of the trust?" Phillip asked.

"Exactly. The Blue Range and the Cumberland."

"So you are removing all of the maritime interests, both of the railroads, and a parcel of real estate from the trust. That leaves three trading companies, your bank, and assorted real estate."

"Are you trying to do the mathematics, Phillip?" Chance smiled.

"I thought I'd grown less . . . *obvious* with age." Grainger blushed.

"Somewhere in the neighborhood of sixty million dollars," Chance said. "You're forty-five years old, are you not? Pope would have been forty-five."

"Yes," Grainger answered.

Tom's gaze had wandered out to Fifth Avenue and settled with the splashy summer light upon the dry concrete. He turned his head suddenly.

"Once we have made a market for the big companies and established each branch of the family on its own, I want to put the rest into a holding company. That's why I asked you and Arthur to assemble all the charters and statements. There's no mistaking it: Those income taxes are small enough now, they're just beginning, but they're not going to stop here, and I want to have all these smaller things inside a corporation that experienced people can watch. My various heirs will have shares in that company, but you and Forrest will administer it. You will run the bank, trade the gold and silver, see that the properties return the kind of income they should—and a better one, if possible—and you will know how to reinvest the profits in all the clever ways you've learned since you've been watching me." Tom smiled.

"I thought that was what you had in mind," Grainger said.

"I want my family to be linked in some way. Not too many American families are, but the great families in Europe . . . that's a different story."

Grainger swallowed, diverted his eyes, then returned them to Chance. "Running this company you propose," he began. "It's quite a responsibility. Why, running the bank alone–"

"Too big?"

"Not at all."

Chance felt the percussion of his heart against his chest wall. "You were going to make a point," he said. "Finish!"

"It's a point that doesn't come easily, Mr. Chance." Grainger clasped his hands, squeezed his fingers as tightly as he could. "Arthur would like to join me, I think," he added suddenly.

Chance's eyes betrayed only a trace of the frigidity within him. "Then get him," he said.

The two men returned almost at once. "May we sit down?" Grainger inquired.

"Of course," Tom said.

The men took comfortable chairs, Grainger leaning forward from the edge of his cushion while Arthur reclined. "Mr. Chance," Arthur began, "it has occurred both to Phillip and to me that, for the past several years, we have been acting . . . well, as *regents* on behalf of Eliot."

Chance lowered his eyelids for a long moment while he considered the remark. "What you say is true."

"And, of course, we like the boy," Grainger interjected.

"I rather like him myself," Tom replied.

But Forrest was too intense to be derailed. "The problem is," he said, "that we are not young men anymore and yet that is how you seem to think of us. We find, Mr. Chance, that we are doing all of the work for none of the profit."

"I see," Tom declared. "Although Eliot is in the war. You gentlemen have no objection to such service, I trust."

"It wouldn't matter if we did," Grainger said.

"Nearly all of our work is done," Forrest said. "All of the agreements you asked us to review, the charters and financial records. We can have everything prepared for your next step in twenty-four hours, if . . ."

Tom seemed bewildered. "You can't mean what I think you're saying! You don't want to leave Chance and Company."

Forrest's eyes darted to Grainger. He scratched his wrist. "Not unless we have to."

"More pay then."

Forrest shook his head.

"I'm weakening," Tom told them. "You know that, and that's why you're doing this, isn't it? You know that I need you to put this last thing together. I suppose I was a fool all along."

Tom shook his head incredulously. Grainger's jaw grew limp.

"I thought I'd emphasized to both of you the urgency of this matter," Tom continued. "Surely you must have guessed that some expression of my appreciation would accompany it—without your having to resort to extortion."

The two men studied Chance's face. They had expected hostility, but now he surprised them by starting to smile. After a moment, he was beaming. "I may be weakening," he repeated, "but once I was just like you! Eager. Abrasive even. That's at least half of what I saw in you, why I hired you, why I kept you on."

Grainger hesitated, turned to see if Forrest mirrored his disbelief.

"Oh, I expected this," Tom declared calmly. "I expected you to make your move for power when I was . . . when you thought you could. That was always when I struck."

Grainger's voice struggled to hide his astonishment. "You are very understanding," he said.

"Then that's settled," Tom said. "And—"

"No," Arthur Forrest announced.

"Aren't we finished?" Tom asked. "I told you that there would be a good bonus for—"

"A larger *piece* of the action," Forrest demanded. "If you will pardon our timing, sir, we felt we deserved more."

Silently, Chance lifted his long, varicose hands to his face and paused. Finally spreading his fingers, he asked, "How could it be much larger than *one third* of the new holding company?"

Grainger whispered rapidly into Forrest's ear. But before either spoke, Chance slid open the wide center drawer of his desk and removed a long, typed document that had been backed with stiff gray paper. He pressed its two folds out on his blotter and pushed it toward Phillip Grainger, who spread it at once on his lap. Forrest came quickly around to a new seat on the armrest of Phillip's chair.

"Why, this is your last will and testament," Phillip said.

Tom seemed amused. "Page five," he said.

Arthur reached out and flipped the pages impatiently.

"Farther down," Tom commanded.

Arthur brought his finger to rest at the top of the next-to-last paragraph. ". . . Said holding company to have one hundred shares," he muttered, "to be divided: twenty to Eliot Chance; and sixteen each to Katharine de Fontainville, of Paris, France, her heirs and legatees; Laura Chance; Frances Alexander; *Phillip Grainger;* and *Arthur Forrest,* all of New York City."

Instantly, both men grew numb. "Don't . . . don't think another word about what we were saying," Phillip Grainger broke the silence with a stutter. He had a sudden fear that Chance might be about to change his mind.

Tom appeared faintly amazed. "No, no. But I admire you for it," he assured them.

"You're more than generous," Arthur Forrest promised, stealing a final glance at the will.

"Then I take it that our talk is *not . . . to be continued.*"

Phillip rose into a slant of afternoon sunlight, removed his watch from his waistcoat pocket and considered the hour. "By this time tomorrow," he declared, "I am quite sure that everything can be in order."

"Marvelous," said Tom, extending, with his wobbling hand, the most visible symptom of his decline.

Arthur lifted his cheeks into a smile that mixed deference with triumph; his shoulders hinted at a bow. Wordlessly, he began to turn. But, for a moment, his eyes lingered upon Tom's hands and watched their nervous shaking.

CHAPTER 40

AWAKENING UNDER THE VAULTED CEILINGS OF A CONVERTED church basement, Eliot strained right and left to orient himself. On either side, for as far as he could determine, cots were arranged in a perfect row. All of the beds were occupied by men who lay on their backs and stared at the plaster as he did, yet, despite its crowding, the room was almost without noise. Far away from him and to the left, he noticed that a woman and a man stood, huddled in consultation. The woman was dressed in a smock. At the back of his skull, a spear of pain seemed to be thrusting forward to his temple, and only when he felt for it did he realize that his head was bandaged. Touching the gauze and tape with one hand, Eliot struggled to raise his other immediately, but found that it had been strapped to the wooden frame of the cot. He rose gradually. A nerve at the base of his spine began to tingle with his first motion, and by the time he had bent up far enough to make out the needle in his arm, a line of pain had shot from his waist through the center of his neck. He took a short breath and collapsed. "Help," he cried, then fell unconscious.

He did not awaken again for seven hours; when he did, there were faces over him, not more than a yard away. They were unfamiliar, and he studied them uncertainly. His vision was blurred. Even the faint light forced him to squint, and it was necessary to blink for a long while before he could perceive the depth of the ward. He closed his eyes and opened them a final time. His head fell limp on the shallow pillow. He raised his free hand to remove the sleep, but, lacking strength, it fell automatically back to his side. He smiled at the woman.

The woman leaned over and pressed a clean moist swab of cotton against his eyelid; the feel of it soothed and restored him. He took a heavy breath.

His first thought about the faces, once he could distinguish them clearly, was that they were plainly civilian. Having decided this, he felt relieved. The doctor bent toward him and examined his eyes through the round, holed mirror that was banded to his head, and Eliot was suddenly certain that the doctor was French. His nose and forehead were formed into a kind of wedge that Eliot had identified among his fellow soldiers as a national characteristic. And Eliot had never been so partial to it as he now found himself. "You're French?" he asked as the doctor seemed to drift backward.

"Yes."

"Then I'm in France?"

"Paris."

"Good. How long?"

"A long time," the doctor replied in a heavy accent. "I cannot say exactly."

"Only a week," the woman interrupted. She had fine high bones with lovely pink cheeks—and beautiful English diction.

Eliot supposed the woman was twenty-five. He paused. "My head?" he complained at last.

"Précisément." The doctor smiled. "You have fractured it."

"Oh, God," Eliot said mildly.

"But that's all," the woman added.

"Of course you have some surface injuries. And the surgeon stitched you thirty times," the doctor explained.

"But am I going to—"

"Live? Yes, you will live, Lieutenant."

Eliot smiled. "You said *lieu*tenant, not *lef*tenant. From your voice I thought you were English."

"I lived in England for many years."

"You must have been a child. A person can't learn to speak another language like that unless he learns it very young."

"Don't strain yourself. You're very weak still."

"What's your name?" Eliot struggled to give his voice a fuller timbre.

"Nicole." The women pointed to the man beside her. "This is Dr. Perigola. Now, you must rest."

Eliot swiveled his head. "This doesn't look like a hospital," he said.

"Perhaps because it is not," the doctor said pleasantly. "This happens to be the Cathedral of Saint Stephen."

A new feeling of lightness came over Eliot. He felt as if he were rising through water. "The Germans," he said finally. "How far away are the Germans?"

"In retreat," Dr. Perigola told him.

"In *retreat*?" he repeated in a voice of quiet astonishment.

"After the Marne," the woman said.

"There was a hill," Eliot said. "We were going after a hill."

"You took it," the woman assured him. "The medic told us your men captured it only a minute after you were hit. Now rest, Lieutenant, until you have your strength back."

The ward was damp. Eliot lay on a narrow cot. The cot was several inches shorter than his body and, from his ankles down, his legs and feet hung over its edge so that, every few hours, they felt as though they had been pricked with a thousand needles. The doctor visited after dawn and before dinner. For a long period in the middle of each day, there was only Nicole to attend what appeared no fewer than a hundred men.

"Why does the doctor stay away from here so long?" he asked her on his eleventh day. "Is he conducting a private practice, too?"

"This is not the only ward, Mr. Chance."

"But it's a very big one."

"And *you* are in it. Isn't that what you are trying to say?"

"Not by any means."

"You sound as if you feel you're entitled to better."

"I don't feel any such thing. Look, you've been very kind to me—that is, you *were* very kind to me and then all of a sudden. . . . What have I done? Why do you try to read some larger meaning into everything I say?"

"A message was received about you," she began, then momentarily broke off. "From General Pershing's office."

"Pershing's office, no less." Eliot quickly thought better of this light-hearted approach.

"No one above the rank of captain has ever so much as asked us if we needed more alcohol and then, quite out of the blue, General Pershing's aide-de-camp orders Dr. Perigola to find you a bed in a proper hospital."

"I don't expect you to believe me, but I have never met General Pershing *or* his aide-de-camp."

"I wouldn't care if you were his grandson. I wouldn't care if your father were Field Marshal Foch!"

"Now, just a minute!"

"Apparently it means something to be *Lieutenant Eliot Chance,* but there are men here who might be able to live if they had a bed in a real hospital and we can't get them within a mile of one, so when something like this comes along—"

"Then, for God's sake," Eliot interrupted, "take it out on General Pershing, not on me. I'm not going to move to any hospital."

"Indeed you are not. Dr. Perigola told Pershing's man it was out of the question."

"Good for Dr. Perigola. Anyway, I'm feeling much too well even to stay here for very much longer."

"You seem to want to decide everything for the doctor. I suppose next you'll move to the Ritz," Nicole added flippantly.

"I didn't know it was still open."

"I'm sure it is. Luxuries of that sort are usually the last things to go."

"Really? I would have thought they were the first."

Nicole appraised him carefully. "That's a schoolboy's answer," she ridiculed him. "Did the army draft you out of school, Lieutenant?"

"No," Eliot said. "I enlisted from college. Have you always been this cynical?"

"College? You look younger." She was silent for a few seconds, then began to turn away. "I'm sorry if that's how you find me, Lieutenant."

Eliot sighed inwardly. "It makes me feel like a spoiled child," he said, gradually dropping his voice to a whisper. "And I'm not."

"Aren't you?"

"No. And that's only half of how I find you." Eliot's words were now so soft that Nicole was forced to lean closer to his mouth. "In addition to being an overworked nurse, you're also a very beautiful woman." His voice raced with his thought. "In fact, you've gotten to be all I think about."

Nicole remained silent, but did not move away.

"I can tell you've heard that before," Eliot said after a minute.

"Plus variations on it."

"The first time I saw you I didn't think it was going to happen. It took about three or four days."

"That long?" she laughed.

"I think that's always the way with beautiful women. The flashy ones make an impression in the beginning and it fades.

But you have to look at a beautiful woman more than once, because there is never enough time for it all to register."

"You're very flattering."

"On the fourth day, you had let your hair down and you looked like a little girl and I thought, Jesus, I'm a lucky man to be in this ward, of all wards, and have that lovely girl to look at."

Nicole smiled. "I remember that day," she told him softly. "I had to come down right away. One of the Scottish soldiers had developed pneumonia and I hadn't time to put my hair up."

Eliot fixed his eyes upon her and, for a second, she lost herself in them. "When I'm out," he said, "if I have a day in Paris—"

She placed her finger on his lip, paused, then nodded. "Yes," she promised.

But, rather than a day, Eliot had two months of recuperative leave in the city and, after beginning their courtship with one *citron pressé* and a half hour's walk through the Tuileries, he soon insisted that they dine together every night. When time allowed, they would rendezvous at Nicole's apartment, a modest single room in the Third Arrondissement, whose genteel, though fraying interior struck a complete contrast with its working-class environs. And occasionally they would dine there, at a table that had been fastidiously set with heirlooms: old bone china from which the pattern had been washed to half its former brilliance; silver flatware of three distinct patterns; a Venetian lace cloth whose tears had been repaired with spool cotton by an amateur hand. Both of Nicole's parents were dead, she told him—her mother from a stroke, her father in the war—and she was an only child. All that her family had left her—all that she owned—was contained within this room.

More often, however, their meal would take place under the most unpropitious conditions: in a small cafe, among a wartime crowd, with too much noise and smoke, beneath the constant, unspoken pressure of time. But, it was not long before he came to depend on it.

"Dear Eliot," Nicole told him after a week. "What an awful thing for you, with all the women in Paris, to want to spend your time with someone who can't give you very much of her own."

"You've given me time," Eliot said.

"Perhaps when the war is over."

"They say it will be very soon."

Nicole glanced at his hair. "Your wounds are healing so fast," she said. "I hope that the fighting will be over before they are finished."

"They must be ugly to look at," Eliot said. "I avoid mirrors now, whenever I can."

"No, no," Nicole told him. "You have a fine face."

"But too Egyptian at the moment. Like a mummy."

"I don't see that at all."

"Don't you? What do you see?"

"I told you. I see a fine face—and I'm afraid when I see it."

Eliot felt a shock go through him. "For the same reason *I'm* afraid when I look at you?"

"I hope so."

"I think we should be glad, not afraid," Eliot said. "In fact, I want to say it right now. I love you, Nicole, more than I have ever loved anyone in my life."

"And I too, my dear, sweet boy."

Eliot blushed. "Stop calling me a boy," he laughed.

"But you are," she said. "You're four years younger than I am."

"Four years isn't anything. Do you want to go to a better place than this?"

"The place doesn't matter," Nicole told him.

"Then let's have champagne here."

"No, silly. I can't, because I have to work tonight. And you can't, because there's a prohibition against serving alcohol to Allied officers on leave. Have you forgotten that?"

"I did." Eliot smiled. "Do you want to go to my room then? I have a bottle there."

"At midnight, if you want to."

"You'll be able to sleep it off by morning without any trouble."

"Yes. But in my own bed." She smiled.

"You're going to make me propose, aren't you?" Eliot teased, touching her chin, lifting it, bringing their eyes into solemn contact.

For a long moment, she gave no answer.

"Well, that's fine enough with me," he continued. "Nicole, will you?"

"As soon as possible," she said.

CHAPTER

41

THE LEAVES TURNED AND THE WINDS CAME EARLY IN SEPTEMBER, and by the official arrival of autumn they funneled along Fifth Avenue and in the cross streets, rapping with a light, almost musical touch at the windows of houses and stores and schoolrooms, imparting, to the great, enigmatic city, a lonely, howling, orange-hued beauty. Fires, stoked a month before schedule, smoldered in hearths, and the clean, dry fragrance of wood pierced the chill.

Tom and Frances, in the pair of matched embroidery chairs, flanked the pinewood fire that blazed in his sitting room. Between them, set back on the ebony table, a single vase of roses stood before the mantel. Tom was silent, nodding. "Can you get me Eliot?" he called out suddenly to his valet.

"Your secretaries are trying, Mr. Chance."

"There's a cable, for God's sake."

"But it's after midnight over there," Frances said. "And there's a war on."

Tom reared back against the mesmerizing effect of the flames. "I know there's a war on every bit as well as you do." And then a smile spread out from the corners of his eyes, as though the young boy in the old man's body found such cantankerous behavior amusing.

Frances beheld him gently. "You fought a good fight," she told him.

"In the beginning," he said.

"And even now."

He paused. "Yes," he said. "And that turned out to be the prize."

"We'll meet again."

"For lunch?" he teased.

"No." She smiled. "No lunches for me. Not in the next life. It will be dinner and a show. And a good dinner, too."

"Delmonico's," Tom said weakly. "Do you remember the first time we went there, so long ago?"

"Not *long ago,*" Frances said. "The past doesn't die out like some winter's fire."

"No," Tom whispered. "Not for us."

"For us, it's always alive," Frances said.

Outside the window, the light fell across Central Park. Tom looked up. "Damnit," he called again to his valet, "will you tell them who it is? Will you tell them that *it's Thomas Chance*?" Then, in one long, forward movement, he leaned out from his chair and died.

"We're rich," Forrest told Grainger when they heard the news.

"One third of sixty million between us," Grainger exclaimed. "Indeed, we are!"

And after the funeral at Trinity, after the discreet interval, in the gray light of the lawyer's office, they gathered for the reading of the will: Phillip Grainger and Arthur Forrest, Laura and Katharine, Frances and the closer servants.

The presiding attorney, a giraffe-like man named Rohrbach who had a prominent Adam's apple, seemed to enjoy his duty, for he smiled, between twitches, as he delivered every word of the brief holograph.

> I, Thomas Chance, being of sound mind, do hereby bequeath the following:
>
> One hundred percent of my interest in The Chance Maritime Company to my grandson, Eliot Chance.

One hundred percent of my interest in The Belvedere Hill and Holliday Street Real Estate Companies to my daughter, Katharine de Fontainville.

One hundred percent of my interest in The Blue Range Railroad Company to my granddaughter, Anne-Marie de Fontainville.

One hundred percent of my interest in The Cumberland Railroad Company to my granddaughter, Giselle de Fontainville.

To Frances Alexander, the sum of fifty thousand dollars to be maintained by the administrators of this instrument as a balance in her banking account, at all times and no matter how much above it she spends.

And of my interest in my holding company, Chance and Company:

Thirty-three and one third percent each to Eliot Chance, Katharine de Fontainville, and Laura Chance.

Arthur's cheeks grew limp. Phillip slid forward on his chair.

Finally, to Phillip Grainger and Arthur Forrest: the sum of one dollar each.

Mr. Rohrbach made a small bark of a laugh, returned the will to his mahogany desk, lifted his pipe, and tapped it against a rectangular frosted crystal box which bore his initials.

The words, as powerfully as poisoned arrows, numbed Chance's assistants, paralyzed their bodies and minds equally. For a short second, they stared at one another like two wax figures.

It was Forrest who spoke first. "But we *saw* the old man's will," he cried. "Saw it! Ourselves. We were meant to have inherited a third . . ."

"We?" Rohrbach's voice carried a patrician accent. He gargled briefly.

"Phillip Grainger and Arthur Forrest," Grainger clarified the pronoun anxiously.

Rohrbach smiled. "Treachery," he declared. "It was treachery that did you in."

Frances, Katharine, and Laura searched the lawyer's beaming face for meaning.

"This won't go uncontested," Forrest said stridently.

"There's nothing to contest," Rohrbach replied. "This is the last will of Thomas Chance. The absolutely *last* one." He paused, nodding to the ladies, as he lit fire in the bowl of his Dunhill. "Now, I know that you were mentioned once, for a considerable sum. But that will was only in force for . . . what, a matter of hours."

CHAPTER

42

Eliot and Nicole were married in Paris a month before Armistice Day. In New York, a month afterward, Laura gave them a large reception in the ballroom of Tom's house.

The orchestra played the old songs of war to new dancing tempos, but sometime after "Alouette," Eliot took Nicole off to the tortoiseshell library and presented her with a box.

"Do you want me to guess what it is before I open it?" Nicole asked.

"That would never work," Eliot said.

"I don't know why not."

"Open it!"

"All right . . . *mon Dieu* . . . I can scarcely believe this pearl."

"It's a family pearl," Eliot said. "The Pearl of Macao."

"The Pearl of Macao," Nicole repeated.

"Mother inherited it too."

Nicole paused. "I love it," she said. "But it's much too fine for me."

"Nothing is," Eliot said.

Nicole laughed. Then a thought occurred to her. "Do you know," she said, "I've always loved beautiful things. Of course, I've never had many, certainly never anything like this. But, in a way, I don't feel silly with it at all. I don't know if I ever told you this," she continued. "But my mother's family—it was a long time ago—used to have one of the finest jewelry stores in America. Of course, they lost it somewhere along the way. I don't know how."

"No. You never told me. What was it called?"

"I think . . . Goelette and Company," Nicole said. "That was my grandfather's name."

Eliot smiled. "I'm sorry," he said. "I've never heard of it."